Duets™

Two brand-new stories in every volume...
twice a month!

Duets Vol. #95

A return to Morning Glory Ranch! Charming author Molly O'Keefe serves up not one but two deliciously funny stories starring the Cook family. Once again, those Cooks are embroiled in the sweetest shenanigans in *Cooking Up Trouble* and *Kiss the Cook*. Don't miss out on this tasty treat! Be sure to check out this superb Double Duets volume.

Duets Vol. #96

Two talented authors make their debut this month. Hannah Bernard, who hails from Denmark, learned how to write romance by checking out the eHarlequin.com Web site! Her hard work resulted in *Catch and Keep*. Tanya Michaels's first Duets novel will keep every bride-to-be on her toes! *The Maid of Dishonor* will have you hanging on to your husband and rolling down the aisle!

Be sure to pick up both Duets volumes today!

Cooking Up Trouble

Mark wasn't buying Dirk's Hollywood idol garbage.

"Let me see if I have everyone straight here," Dirk said, ignoring Mark's hostile stare. "Ethan is the oldest, then there's Mark, head horse trainer. And Billy is the baby of the Cook family."

Everyone around the kitchen table nodded and smiled adoringly at the handsome movie star. Mark rolled his eyes.

"Which just leaves the beautiful mystery woman with the pretty green eyes I met earlier."

Mark felt the blood pound in his ears. Did Dirk Mason, the actor who once dated Julia Roberts, just say he thought Alyssa—*his* Alyssa—was beautiful?

"Lis has been the cook here at the ranch for about six summers," Mark's mother explained. "She's as much a part of the family as my children."

"So," Dirk said casually, looking at Mark. "You two aren't an item, then?" he asked suggestively.

"An item?" Mark asked, surprised. He was about to laugh when Alyssa walked in wearing a new skirt. A *short* skirt. And suddenly Mark felt as if he'd been punched in the chest. *Where did those miles of knockout legs come from?*

For more, turn to page 9

Kiss the Cook

"One more step and I'll blow your brains out."

Behind him, Billy heard the unmistakable sound of the old shotgun being awkwardly and improperly cocked. He could be sure of only one thing—there was a woman in his family's cabin.

He turned slowly and faced the inept gun holder. *"Kate?"* he gasped, dumbfounded by the sight of the familiar, stunning blonde in front of him. "Kate Jenkins? What are you doing here?"

The agonizing heartbreak and humiliation he felt whenever he remembered Kate raced through him. That had been a perfect summer with Kate thirteen years ago, one Billy had occasionally considered describing to *Penthouse Forum.* On the edge of his thirtieth birthday, he had never felt that strongly about a woman since.

He shook the memories away and tried to focus on the fact that Kate was standing in front of him pointing a gun at his head. But she wasn't too steady on her feet, and as Billy watched she groaned and fell backward against the cabin wall, dropping the gun and putting her hands to her belly.

Her big, pregnant belly.

"Damn," Billy swore, and fell to the floor in a dead faint.

For more, turn to page 197

HARLEQUIN DUETS

ISBN 0-373-44161-4

This edition published by arrangement with Harlequin Books S.A.

Visit us at www.eHarlequin.com

Printed in U.S.A.

Cooking Up Trouble

Molly O'Keefe

TORONTO • NEW YORK • LONDON
AMSTERDAM • PARIS • SYDNEY • HAMBURG
STOCKHOLM • ATHENS • TOKYO • MILAN • MADRID
PRAGUE • WARSAW • BUDAPEST • AUCKLAND

Dear Reader,

Welcome back to the Morning Glory Ranch! My amazing editor at Harlequin, Susan Pezzack, thought maybe we just hadn't heard enough about the Cook family from *Too Many Cooks,* so the family saga continues....

While the course of true love never runs smoothly, I think that the Cook family might just be jinxed. Mark, the middle brother, has been the object of Alyssa Halloway's affection all her life. She has been his best friend and companion since she was five and he has never looked twice at her. Of course, anybody who has carried a childhood crush into adulthood knows that it's not an easy thing. If only we all had a conniving movie star and a meddlesome mom to help us out!

Happy reading!

Molly O'Keefe

Books by Molly O'Keefe

HARLEQUIN DUETS
62—TOO MANY COOKS

For Andy Gensler and Allycia Marie…
I just keep counting my lucky stars

1

OUT OF THE CORNER of her eye Alyssa Halloway caught her best friend, Mark Cook, heading for the front door.

"Gotcha," she murmured as she threw her dish towel onto the counter and ran after him. He had been avoiding her for the better part of a week, and had been acting like a jerk for most of the month, and Alyssa was going to get to the bottom of it.

Mark opened the screened door and walked out onto the large front porch of the Morning Glory Ranch, his family's home. Alyssa slipped through behind him before it slammed shut.

"Go away," he said over his shoulder.

"You can't run forever, Mark."

Mark grabbed the ladder that had been left propped against the side of the house and walked down the steps to the yard.

"Come on, Mark, you've been acting like a baby all day," she shouted, and followed him down.

"Have not." He reverted to his usual infuriating calmness and Alyssa felt the old familiar urge to grab him and shake him until words with more than one syllable fell out.

Mark kicked open the ladder and looked at it in relation to the peak of the porch roof. Alyssa crossed her arms, waiting impatiently for him to look at her. She watched and continued to wait while Mark made minute adjustments to the ladder and effectively ignored her.

Stupid infuriating cowboy! Alyssa thought.

Mark reached for the sign he had left on the porch, the sign Alyssa had spent most of the night making, but she beat him to it and quickly put the sign behind her back.

"If you want this sign, you're going to have to talk to me," she said, arching an eyebrow at him.

"I don't really want the sign," he said reasonably. "*You're* the one who wants it put up."

Alyssa gnashed her teeth but didn't give him the sign. For the moment, at least, she had his attention. "You're right, I do want this sign up. What I can't figure out is what has crawled up your butt."

"Nice, Lis." Mark shook his head at her.

"Well?" She ignored his censure. "You've been walking around like the Grinch for weeks while the rest of us have gone nuts getting the place ready. What's wrong with you?"

"Nothing is wrong with me. I just have better things to do than hang signs and move furniture and spit shine every piece of tack we own." Alyssa watched with satisfaction as the skin under Mark's collar turned red. She couldn't help but smile; it was so rare that Mark got this upset.

Mark must have taken offense to the smile because he reached around her and grabbed the sign before she could stop him. He turned and started up the ladder.

Alyssa blew one of her long curls out of her face and went after him.

"It's not good for you to hold all of this in," Alyssa told him. "You should talk about this stuff. You know...*vent.*"

"Hold the ladder, would you?" Mark asked without even looking. Alyssa grabbed the rickety ladder as he climbed. He got to the top and heaved the sign into place.

Well, she thought as she looked up at Mark and felt the

old warm sizzle of attraction in her stomach, *I might as well enjoy the view.* His muscles bunched and flexed under the worn work shirt he was wearing. He wasn't a big man, like his brothers. His muscles were lean and he was not much taller than Alyssa, but there was something about him that captured Alyssa's attention and imagination. He had attracted plenty of attention over the years from the girls in town, because he was truly one of the nice guys. Athletic and handsome like his brothers, but unlike Ethan and Billy, Mark was respectful and considerate.

And sure Alyssa liked that he was a good guy, but it was so much more for her.

It's his eyes, she thought as she watched him pull nails out of the pocket of his shirt. They were pale blue and they always made Alyssa feel as though he could see right through her. He had a way of watching people, of measuring them up and seeing their worth, that made those eyes something special. They could be eerie and haunting...

And you have no business standing here, thinking about Mark Cook's eyes, let's move on. Alyssa's practical better sense jabbed her into action.

"I don't know what the big deal is, Mark," Alyssa said, watching him place the sign. "Over a little to the left," she advised, and Mark shifted the sign over a few inches. "Your other left," she clarified, and Mark shifted the sign back a few more inches. "This is going to be good for the ranch," Alyssa told him.

"Good?" Mark asked. "How in the world could this possibly be considered 'good'? We're going to have a movie star traipsing around here..."

"Not just any movie star...Dirk Mason!" Alyssa felt obligated, on behalf of her absolute favorite movie star, to keep Mark from maligning him.

Mark looked down at Alyssa and batted his eyelashes in

mockery of a starstuck teenager. Alyssa tried very very hard not to indulge Mark's little fit by laughing, but she couldn't help it.

"Don't you think you're overreacting?" Alyssa asked. She waited for Mark to answer but he remained silent on the top of the ladder. "Dirk Mason is an international star." Again she felt duty-bound to remind Mark who exactly they were going to be dealing with.

"International? What does that mean?" Mark muttered under his breath, clearly unimpressed.

"He's huge in Thailand," Alyssa said defensively.

"They don't even speak English in Thailand. He's not an international star, his butt is," Mark said, referring to Dirk Mason's gratuitous flashes of nudity in his pictures. Gratuitous flashes of nudity that were one of the real small pleasures in Alyssa's life.

"Don't I know it," she said, and smiled cheekily at Mark when he looked down at her with a scowl.

Poor Mark, he's really not taking this well, she thought, surprised.

"Okay, okay, Mark. Seriously, what's wrong with Dirk Mason?" Alyssa persisted, hoping that maybe if she didn't goad him he would tell her what was really eating at him. "Everyone knows he's your favorite actor, too."

"Nothing is wrong with Dirk Mason," Mark answered, and looked back up at the sign. "What's wrong is having him here disrupting everything."

"Mark, what is he disrupting?" Alyssa exclaimed.

"Look at all the stuff that's not getting done because you and I are hanging this stupid sign." Said sign slipped and Mark grabbed it and slapped it back against the roof. "Work around here has ground to a halt and we're just getting ready for him. My family has gone crazy about this whole thing. Mom redecorated the living room," he said as if it had been some crime against the family to replace the BarcaLounger.

''Well, it needed it,'' Alyssa said reasonably. ''We can't live in the fifties forever.''

''Dad bought a new car,'' Mark added, having gotten himself onto a roll. ''What in the world do we need a new car for?''

''Well, I don't think he wants to drive a movie star around in a pickup that smells like manure.''

''Billy's done nothing but practice his rodeo skills.''

''There's nothing different about that. He barely works anyway.''

''And you've been walking around like a lovesick teenager. Last week you burned dinner and we all had to eat scrambled eggs.''

''Everyone likes eggs,'' she said defensively. She would have been embarrassed if she had been the only one distracted by the prospect of Dirk Mason's arrival. But Mark was right, the whole family had become consumed with the movie star's visit. Work had certainly slowed down, but the Morning Glory would survive. Alyssa didn't know if Mark would, though.

''And that's just *getting ready* for him,'' Mark continued. ''I can't imagine what it will be like when he's actually here!''

''Mmm-hmm,'' Alyssa hummed, unable to resist.

It's just so much fun teasing the poor guy, she mused silently, forgetting her resolve to try to take Mark's issues with Dirk Mason seriously. She had spent the majority of her life at the mercy of Mark's teasing, and the urge for revenge was too powerful to resist.

''Imagine Dirk Mason sitting down at my kitchen table.'' She stared off into the distance and dropped her voice to what she hoped was some kind of purr. ''Dirk Mason's mouth drinking coffee out of my mugs, laughing over something funny I might have said. Or maybe—'' Alyssa managed a gasp and put her hand to her chest ''—riding one of the horses. After a hard day checking fences—''

''Checking fences isn't that hard,'' Mark interrupted peevishly.

''He'll be all sweaty.'' Alyssa bit her lip to keep from laughing.

''It's May. He'll probably be covered in snow…''

''He'll take off his shirt…slowly…''

''Oh, come on, Lis, don't even try to pretend you have those kinds of fantasies.''

''He'll be unable to resist my allure, my charm, my…''

''Meat loaf?'' Mark snapped, and turned back to the sign. ''Earth to Lis, you're a ranch hand.''

''Ouch,'' Alyssa whispered, and quickly looked down so Mark couldn't see the blush that was creeping up her neck.

Because they had been friends for so long Alyssa knew exactly what Mark meant so she couldn't even get mad at him. He just meant that she was too practical to imagine sexy movie stars without shirts, too levelheaded to have fantasies of a man with dimples flashing them at her. Movie stars didn't fall in lust with the ranch cook.

I wonder what you think I fantasize about? she thought, nudging the ladder with her toe. Since she was the Morning Glory's cook, he probably believed she had a head full of recipes for chicken and dumplings and chili. *New and innovative uses for the kidney bean?* She smiled ruefully.

Maybe, since she just received her degree in veterinary science in December, he thought she was consumed with thoughts of pink eye treatments and barbed-wire infections.

After twenty-one years of friendship with Mark, Lis figured she should get the hang of his double-edged compliments. After twenty-one years she should be used to being treated just like one of the guys or another kid sister.

And she was. She was used to it and, more than that, she was okay with it. Most of the time. Well, not really at all, although it is better than it was, she reminded herself.

She had spent several of her formative years pining for Mark Cook, and his brotherly treatment had been torturous.

Alyssa watched Mark mutter to himself under his breath. He reached up an arm and wiped it across his forehead. Alyssa's heart beat just a little bit faster. Just a little. Just as it always did. Since the day she'd met him he had been doing funny things to her heart.

On the day when they first met, Alyssa had run away from her house and her father's temper and was walking alongside the barbed-wire fence that separated the Cook and Halloway lands. Alyssa and her family lived on the land next to the Morning Glory. Alyssa's father, Wes Halloway, was not nearly as successful a rancher as Mac Cook, a fact that ate away at Wes until it made him angry and bitter.

At first she'd thought the animal caught in the wire was a small cow but when she got closer she realized it was just one fat dog. Alyssa'd almost had the dog untangled when a blond boy showed up, and despite her grip on the dog's tail and the remaining barbs in its fur, the dog charged toward him.

Unprepared, Alyssa had held on and was yanked through the fence until she'd been as caught as the dog had been. Stuck between the wires, with barbs caught in her skin, she'd watched the dog jump up and lick the boy's face as if *he* had saved its miserable fat hide. She'd immediately started to cry.

She'd cried as the blond boy walked up and she saw his pale blue eyes. She'd cried as he murmured comforting things to her, and she'd cried as he carefully and patiently untangled her from the wire.

It was as if she had always known Mark Cook was going to break her heart.

Her sobs had turned to sniffles when her rescuer pulled a few pieces of candy out of his jacket pocket and handed one piece to Alyssa and kept one for himself. He'd introduced her to the dog, Queenie, and they'd sucked on the candy and watched the dog lick his wounds.

''Why's your dog so fat?'' Alyssa had asked around the candy.

''He likes Popsicles.''

''You shouldn't feed a dog Popsicles,'' she'd chastised, her candy falling out of her mouth and landing in the dirt. She'd picked it up, studied it for a second, blown off a leaf that had stuck to it and popped it back into her mouth.

''I don't. My mom does,'' he'd explained, his tone calm and quiet. For a girl who was used to angry silences and shouting, his voice was like a Band-Aid.

''You should put your dog on a diet.''

''Yep.''

Alyssa had watched as Mark unwrapped another piece of candy and, when Queenie looked up at him, tossed the candy to the dog. Queenie had snagged it out of the air with his mouth and given Mark a woof of thanks.

''You shouldn't feed your dog candy.'' Alyssa had been outraged on behalf of the poor overfed dog.

''He wanted a piece.''

''Why's your dog named Queenie if it's a boy?''

''Our dogs are always named Queenie. My dad says it makes things less confusing,'' he'd explained.

Alyssa had thought about it, crunching her candy.

''You're bleeding.'' The boy had leaned over her to look at a cut on her back through her torn shirt. She'd turned to look, too, her T-shirt hiking up to reveal a large bruise, yellow and purple with age but ugly and angry all the same.

"What happened?" he'd asked in his careful way.

Alyssa, who hadn't yet been to school and hadn't had much reason to leave the ranch wasn't used to those types of questions. When she lied, she did it badly.

"I fell down," she'd said belligerently, her eyes skittering away from his level gaze.

Mark had looked at her silently for such a long time that Alyssa had grown uncomfortable and finally realized he didn't believe her.

"Please don't tell," she'd whispered, her brown eyes filling with more tears.

Perhaps Mark had just wanted the crying to stop, or maybe he hadn't really understood what he was promising, but he'd nodded and sworn he would never tell.

Soon the two were inseparable.

Mark's mother, Missy, had taken Alyssa in practically as her own child. Alyssa's mother, glad her daughter was being cared for somewhere, had allowed it. Alyssa ate dinner at the ranch, spent many nights in a room that everyone came to think of hers. She even did chores.

When Mark could drive, he'd driven them around in his pickup: to school, from school, into town, and home from different practices. Sometimes he'd just taken her driving and, in the small cab of that truck, feelings that Alyssa couldn't stop began to grow.

During high school, when all of her friends were experimenting with boyfriends, Alyssa had waited for the breathless moment when Mark would lean over to her and press his mouth to hers. She'd waited and waited, and before she knew it, it seemed as though her entire life had passed by. She'd thought the feelings she had for Mark would fade. After all, that girlish crush she had had on TV actor Kirk

Cameron had gone away. But what she'd felt for Mark turned over and over in her heart until the edges became sharp and the feelings painful.

She'd gone to college in Billings—far away from Mark and his blue eyes. But, because the Morning Glory was home and Mark was there and no other man made her heart race and ache with the same feelings, she'd returned every summer to be the cook at the ranch.

That was then. This is now. Alyssa shook her head to clear her thoughts as she watched Mark hang the sign. And she was *over* Mark Cook. Come September she was heading back to Billings. She and her college roommate had an apartment lined up and she had a line on a couple of jobs at different vet clinics. There was even a handsome guy in her apartment building that she was looking forward to getting to know better.

It was time to leave girlhood crushes behind, to act like an adult and to find a man who saw past the little kid with bruises and a big mouth.

Perhaps a different set of dimples, a Dirk Mason set of dimples, will put an end to this, she told herself with a smile.

"Mark, you're supposed to hang the sign, not rip it to shreds." Billy Cook, the youngest of the Cook boys, sauntered up in his usual in-no-hurry way and winked at Alyssa.

Mark said nothing and Alyssa rolled her eyes. Billy just grinned.

"You've been spending too much time with Ethan, Mark. It's making you surly," Billy said, referring to their oldest brother who, until a few years ago when Cecelia Grady had rolled onto the ranch, was probably the orneriest, grumpiest man in the state.

Cecelia's flashing eyes and temper had changed all that. Their newborn daughter finished the job and now, according to his two brothers, Ethan was the biggest soft touch west of the Mississippi.

Alyssa watched the back of Mark's neck and knew that fireworks were about to start. She had lit the match for Mark's slow-burning temper and Billy was going to light the fuse.

"You upset about something, Mark?" he asked.

When Mark stopped hammering on the sign, Alyssa hid her smile behind her hand.

Mark turned and dropped the free corner of the sign, which swung down drunkenly in the doorway. "Do you have any idea how much...*trouble* this guy is going to be?"

"He's an actor, Mark. Not a government agent, or a police officer, or a lawyer, or a..." Billy trailed off and looked to Alyssa for help. "What was Dirk Mason in his last movie?"

"An alien bounty hunter."

"That's it." Billy turned back to his scowling brother and grinned. "He's not even an alien bounty hunter..."

"He just plays one on the big screen," Alyssa chimed in.

"I can see you guys still aren't taking this seriously," Mark growled as he grabbed for the sign, which repeatedly swung out of his reach. He started swearing and Alyssa laughed and then covered it up with a cough. Billy looked over at Alyssa, clearly unsure of how to take Mark's attitude. Alyssa only shrugged.

"For crying out loud, Mark, it's a done deal. Like it or not, Dirk Mason is coming to the Morning Glory Ranch for three weeks to learn how to be a cowboy in his next movie," Billy said.

Alyssa clapped her hands and did a girlish jig; it was something she did every time "Dirk Mason" and "cowboy'' were mentioned in the same sentence. Dirk Mason's dimples, horses riding into sunsets and tight jeans: it was all of her fantasies rolled into one.

''Why here?'' Mark asked. ''Why now? I'm up to my ears in horses I'm supposed to be training. Ethan's got the baby, which makes him worthless for a hard day's work, and—'' he looked pointedly at his brother ''—you are almost always worthless.''

Billy ignored the insult and pressed on, much to Alyssa's delight.

''Mom and Dad are doing a favor for some hot-shot friend of Samantha's,'' Billy answered, referring to the last and final Cook. Their sister, Samantha, was a social worker in Los Angeles. Alyssa didn't know much more about the movie star's visit than that, or how Sam was involved.

Three months ago, Mac and Missy Cook had called a family meeting. They told everyone that after a series of begging and pleading phone calls from Samantha, Mac and Missy had decided to play host to Dirk Mason to help him learn how to be a cowboy for his next movie.

''Mark,'' Billy said, approaching the ladder, ''he's probably just going to watch things around here. You know, 'observe.' He'll sit on the porch and lean over the corral and wear a hat and think he's a cowboy. Piece of cake.''

Mark grunted, took the hammer out of his pocket and began to pound a nail into the sign. Billy winked at Alyssa and leaped onto the wide porch railing in front of Mark. He squinted out of one eye and put his hands on his hips.

''You ignoring me, son?'' he said in his best imitation of New York policeman Joe Edge, a part made famous by their soon-to-arrive houseguest. ''Because if you're ignoring me, I've got something to show you.'' Billy pretended to pull a gun out of the back of his pants, then pretended to cock it and aim it at his brother. Alyssa could tell Mark was trying not to be amused. It was hard. Mark loved that movie, and this speech was something Billy recited all the time.

"You still ignoring me?" Billy asked incredulously. "Hey, that's okay. You need more convincing. I've got it right here." Billy pulled another "gun" out of his pants and cocked his thumb back and pretended to spit out of the corner of his mouth.

Mark was smiling and shaking his head, and Alyssa knew that they had him.

"Maybe you want to pay attention before I blow your brains out." Billy finished and turned to saunter as best he could down the railing.

Alyssa got in on the game and leaped up in his place, squinted her eye and started her own favorite speech from Dirk Mason's courtroom drama, *Above the Law.*

"Lady," she growled, "I think I've got what you're looking for, but you need to look a little higher."

Mark was shaking his head and smiling while his grip on the loose corner of the sign was slipping.

"I'm no hero," Billy said, continuing the game. "I'm just putting aliens where they belong…"

"Six light-years under," Billy and Alyssa finished the line together. It was from Dirk Mason's summer blockbuster *Galactic Supercops.*

Alyssa fluttered her eyelashes and clasped her hands together like the female lead from *Love on the Last Train to Manhattan,* Dirk's only romantic comedy and Alyssa's all-time favorite movie.

"Where are we going?" she asked in a husky purr.

"Anywhere you want, sugar. Anywhere you want," Billy answered. Carefully he swaggered across the railing to the ladder and leaned against it, pushing his hat up in what was a very Dirk Mason kind of way.

Billy's weight was just enough to jostle Mark and to make him lose the corner of the sign. It swung down and clobbered Billy, sending him sprawling to the hard wooden floor of the porch. Alyssa, trying to avoid the swinging sign, made a wild kung fu leap off the railing and rolled gracefully onto the grass, coming to a jarring stop against the ladder. Mark, who was leaning over, trying to catch the cardboard sign as it swung back toward him, went flying through the air when Alyssa crashed into the ladder. He was able to catch the sign and succeeded in tearing it off the awning. When he landed, flat on his back in a cloud of dust, the Welcome To The Morning Glory Ranch sign floated down like a feather to cover his face.

Alyssa rolled over onto her stomach and slowly opened her eyes. Right in front of her was a pair of boots. She tilted her head back and followed the boots up past the well-cut, tailored black pants and fancy suit jacket. The sun was hitting the man on the back of the head and Alyssa squinted against the glare. The man smiled and Alyssa felt her whole body go numb.

''Oh, my God,'' she whispered.

''Don't worry, Lis. I'm fine,'' Mark assured her. She darted a pained look over at Mark and watched him pull the sign off his face.

''Oh, my God,'' she said again, on a slightly more hysterical note.

These things really do happen, was the only thing she could think.

''Really, Lis, I'm fine.'' Mark sat up, facing the house, and waved the dust away from his face. Alyssa watched him squint and knew exactly what he was going to say next.

''Don't do it,'' she croaked, mortified and disbelieving.

But Mark was going to do it, anyway. Mark selected a line from his favorite Dirk Mason movie, *Front Line Com-*

mando, and delivered it in what she knew was his best soldier-caught-behind-enemy-lines-captured-and tortured-for-three-hours voice.

"I've had dates that hurt more than that," he said, turned his head and, just like Dirk Mason in the movie, spit.

"Hey," said the painfully familiar masculine voice that belonged to the painfully familiar masculine smile. "That's my line."

2

OH, SHIT, Mark thought.

Mark slowly turned on his side and caught sight of Billy rolling around on the porch, laughing so hard he was crying. Mark turned a little further and saw Alyssa stammering and blushing at the person standing behind him.

He had a very bad feeling about this.

Mark stood and completed the turn to come face-to-face with screen idol Dirk Mason.

Oh, shit, Mark thought again. The movie star looked… like a movie star. His expensive black suit was being covered in dust as he stood on the front lawn. He wore a blue shirt and a tie in the exact same color and a pair of sunglasses that he pushed up to his forehead. Sun glinted off the silver toe of his obviously brand-spankin'-new cowboy boots. Mark hadn't seen so much hammered silver and Spanish tooling on a pair of boots since last year's senate election.

Mark immediately sized Dirk Mason up as a smooth operator and wasn't going to trust the man as far as he could throw him.

"I'm Dirk Mason," the movie star said, and held out his hand to Mark. In the settling dust and embarrassment of the last few minutes, Mark said the first thing that came to mind.

"You're much shorter than I thought."

Did I say that out loud? he immediately wondered.

''Oh, my God, Mark,'' Alyssa shrieked, stepping between the two men.

I guess I did. Mark mentally knocked himself upside his own head.

''Don't listen to him, Mr. Mason,'' Alyssa was saying. ''Mark's just a cowboy, you're...perfect,'' she finished on a breath.

''Please, call me Dirk...''

''What do you mean 'just a cowboy'?'' Mark asked, feeling foolish and tongue-tied. He started smacking the dust off his clothes to hide his complete and total discomfort.

''It is such an honor to have you here, Dirk,'' Alyssa gushed, ignoring Mark. She grabbed Dirk's hand and began shaking it vigorously between both of hers. His longish black hair shimmied with the force of her handshake.

''This is my assistant, Guy.'' Dirk extricated himself from Alyssa's handshake and gestured to the man at his elbow.

Mark stopped dusting himself off to stare in wonder at Guy. The man looked as if he was preparing for some kind of African safari or military invasion. He wore one of those vests with a million pockets, a safari hat and commando-style boots. Around his neck on a sturdy cord was a whistle, flashlight and asthma inhaler. The pockets on his vest were filled with cell phones and tissues.

''Nice to meet you,'' Guy said, and held his hand out to Mark, who was able to stop acting like an idiot and shake his hand. Alyssa however, Mark noted, was still being an idiot and was too busy staring at Dirk to notice Guy. Billy was only just getting to his feet having busted a lung at Mark's expense.

Two of Guy's pockets began ringing and he turned away to answer his phones.

"I'm Billy." Billy stepped off the porch and introduced himself with an easy grace that made Mark's introduction to the movie star look that much worse.

"You'll have to excuse us," Billy was saying, "it's not everyday we embarrass ourselves in front of famous people."

"It's not everyday I see such skilled actors at work," replied Dirk, obviously joking. "Did you choreograph that last part?"

"Improv, pure improv." The two men shook hands, and before anything else could be said the rest of Mark's family came flooding out of the house.

Mark's mouth fell open in shock. His mother was wearing a dress and what appeared to be lipstick. And his father, Mac, who had to be pried out of his favorite flannel shirt to go to church, was wearing a sport coat.

This is what was making him crazy. His family bending themselves in two to impress some movie star. During the past month Mark couldn't even have a conversation with anyone without having to talk about how great Dirk Mason was, or how handsome or talented he was, or, if he happened to be talking to Alyssa, what a great butt the man had.

His family were kind, decent, hardworking people and it chafed Mark that they felt the need to dress themselves up for Dirk Mason. And Alyssa—reasonable, practical Alyssa—was the worst.

"Well, if it isn't Dirk Mason," Mac said as if the movie star had just stopped by after church.

Brother, Mark thought, rolling his eyes. The rest of the family talked over each other and shoved each other out of the way to greet the movie star, who took it all in with a practiced and gracious air.

"It's wonderful to have you here," Missy said. Throwing caution to the wind, she wrapped Dirk—who did seem shorter in real life—in a big hug.

"Mr. and Mrs. Cook," Dirk said graciously, "it's a real pleasure to meet you."

Mark's sister-in-law, Cecelia, approached, carrying her daughter Sarah. Even the baby was "dressed to impress" in a new outfit. As Cecelia shook hands with Dirk, Mark watched as Sarah drooled all over herself and for good measure took the hand she had been shoving into her mouth and planted it on her mother's new blouse.

Sarah generally ignored Dirk and smiled at Mark—a great toothless smile—and blew a spit bubble.

Loyalty like that is hard to come by these days, Mark mused.

"Let's go inside," Missy said. "Are you hungry, Dirk? Guy?"

"Not really..." Guy said.

"Well, we'll fix you right up." Mark had to smile. He knew in Missy's estimation no one was ever really not hungry for very long.

Just then, Queenie, eager to get in on whatever action there was, came barreling at full dog gallop from the back of the house. At the sight of the giant dog, Guy shrieked and ran for the car. Looking over his shoulder as if Queenie was Cujo, he fumbled for the door handle.

"What is that thing?" he squawked. Queenie, with that ironic canine sense, ran right for Guy. The poor man was whimpering and moments before he was about to be tackled by the dog, he opened the car door, threw himself inside and locked the door behind him. Queenie leaped up on her back feet, planted her front paws on the window and licked the glass that separated her from Guy.

The Cooks looked on in silence.

"Guy has very bad allergies," Dirk explained. From inside the car, Guy was shouting something like, "Call off the monster—very, very bad allergies."

Mark, taking pity on the allergic, safari-garbed assistant, whistled to Queenie and led her off to the barn where she wouldn't bother anybody.

"I'LL BE RIGHT IN," Dirk said with a smile to the gathered group of Cooks. "I need to have a few words with Guy."

"Is he okay?" asked Mac, who looked to Dirk like a body double for John Wayne.

Dirk and everybody else looked back at the car where Guy had his forehead pressed to the window while he sucked on his inhaler.

Not your best moment, old buddy, Dirk thought, and inwardly cringed.

"I'm sure he's fine, if not a little embarrassed." Dirk put on his best sheepish look that usually got him off the hook with women.

"Let's give the poor man some privacy," Missy said, and started to round up her considerable family. Dirk smiled and nodded at each of them as they slowly made their way back into the house. When the last one was out of sight, his smile vanished and he quickly ran over to the car where Guy was lying in the back seat with his inhaler in a death grip.

"Poor Guy," he mumbled, and unlocked the door. "You okay?" he asked his assistant.

"This has got to be some kind of joke," Guy said, sitting up, his face pinched in a way Dirk knew meant trouble.

"You're the one who thought this was a good idea," Dirk reminded him, hoping to cut this little bitching session short. "I wanted to rent a couple of Westerns and call it research."

"How was I to know they would be so..." Guy trailed off.

"Perfect?" Dirk supplied with an arched eyebrow. "Come on, Guy, they look like extras for a modern *Bonanza.* This couldn't be any better."

"It could certainly be less dusty," Guy said, his nose scrunched up with distaste.

"Well—" Dirk gave Guy a hand, pulling him out of the car "—then it wouldn't be authentic, would it?"

"I suppose not," Guy conceded, and Dirk had to smile. While Guy may be a little fastidious, he had the instincts of a shark. Months ago when Guy had suggested that Dirk do real research, such as go to a ranch and actually learn how to ride a horse, Dirk had hated the idea. But looking at these people and these mountains and even that gigantic dog was making Dirk think that maybe a little authentic research might be the difference between being nominated for an Academy Award and actually winning it.

"I don't have to eat their food, do I?" Guy asked when they started making their way back to the house. "If I have to so much as look at Velveeta or that disgusting green bean casserole with those fried onions on top, you can kiss your assistant goodbye."

"Come on, Guy," Dirk said, and slapped Guy on the back. "It can't be that bad."

WHEN MARK RETURNED from the barn his mother had ushered everyone inside the house where there was coffee brewing and an assortment of food set up, the likes of which Mark hadn't seen since Ethan and Cecelia were married three years ago. Mark was pleased to see that his favorite green bean casserole with the fried onions on top was a part of the spread.

Guy was breathing heavily through his inhaler while

Missy grabbed Kleenex for him. Mark heard Alyssa mumble something about getting cleaned up as she ran to her room.

Mark listened with half an ear as his mother prattled on about the nonstop thrill it was to have Dirk at the Morning Glory. Mark grabbed a cup of coffee and a turkey sandwich before his mother started practically force-feeding Dirk. He noticed the movie star grabbed the only things not covered in mayo or butter, a couple of pieces of turkey and some carrots. Guy, still looking squeamish, had a glass of water and a slice of apple.

''Do you want some ranch dressing with that?'' Missy asked the pair. Missy Cook's cooking motto was that without the proper condiment, usually ranch dressing, food might dissolve.

''No, no thanks.'' Dirk said graciously.

''Guy?'' Missy asked.

''Good God, no,'' the man said. Dirk coughed and Guy smiled weakly. ''I'm allergic.''

Finally, as if to officially start the proceedings, Mac leaned back in his chair and gave his guest a thorough once-over.

''So, Dirk. You want to be a cowboy?'' Mac hooked his thumbs into the waistband of his pants as though he was the living, breathing authority on cowboys. Which he could have been, but it was a little much in Mark's estimation.

''Yes, sir,'' Dirk answered, taking a cup of coffee from Missy and smiling. Missy had to hold on to the back of a chair for support. ''I'm starring in a Western in a few months and I thought it best to get some experience before filming starts.''

''Well, son, you've come to the right place,'' Mac said with a laugh. Billy rolled his eyes at Mark and Mark shrugged. There was nothing anyone could do when Mac got in a bragging mood, except hold on and hope he didn't bring up the "native blood."

"My family has been ranching this land for a hundred years," he continued. "Missy's family has been here since her people walked down here from the Arctic." He leaned in close as if he was sharing a secret. "She's got native blood."

Everyone at the table groaned, except for Dirk, who looked at Missy quizzically.

"Lemon square?" She offered a plate of the gooey bars as a diversionary tactic. Dirk reached up to grab one.

"Dirk," Guy interrupted. "Yellow goo and butter crusts aren't part of your diet." Dirk looked, it seemed to Mark, a little pleadingly at Guy who only smiled apologetically. Dirk put his hand down and passed on the lemon squares.

"Go on, Mac," Dirk urged, returning to the subject at hand. "You were talking about native blood."

"It explains why our boys turned out the way they did," Mac said.

Dirk's amused gaze turned to the boys. Billy pretended to shoot an arrow while Mark and Ethan only shook their heads. Missy put her hand on her husband's shoulder and applied direct pressure.

"Dirk Mason does not want to hear about this, honey," Missy said with a pained laugh.

"Sure I do!" Dirk disagreed adamantly.

"See, honey." Mac beamed. "You see, Ethan's about the best damn breeder in these parts and I'm not talking about my granddaughter. People bring their horses from all over the country to be trained by Mark, and Billy is..."

"Dad," Billy pleaded, "please don't."

"The Wild Man Rodeo Grand Champion for the fifth year running."

Billy's head fell into his hands in defeat.

"Want to see the buckles?" Mac asked brightly.

"No, he doesn't!" Billy's head came right back up. Dirk opened his mouth to disagree but Billy shot him a level look.

"Trust me on this one," he advised.

"I'll pass on the buckles."

"What's the name of the movie you're in," Cecelia asked, effectively changing the subject.

"*Spurs.*" The Cooks responded with blank faces. "It's an ensemble piece," he explained.

"Well, it sure is a real pleasure to have you here," Missy said. "We hardly see anyone famous up here."

"Never," Billy amended. "You never see anyone famous around here, unless you count Miss Montana 1972. She lives on the next mountain over. Occasionally you catch a glimpse of her riding a horse with her tiara on, but mostly she's normal."

"If anyone around here can be considered 'normal,'" Cecelia said with a laugh.

"Let me see if I have everyone straight here," Dirk said. "Ethan is the oldest, married to Cecelia, with one brand-new baby girl." Dirk tickled the baby under her drooly chin. "Then there's Mark, head horse trainer and resident sign hanger." Dirk flashed a smile at Mark and Mark grudgingly raised his mug in acknowledgment. "Samantha is the younger sister and only daughter, and Billy, the rodeo champ, is the baby."

Everyone around the table nodded.

"Which just leaves the beautiful mystery woman I met earlier with the pretty green eyes."

The kitchen fell into astonished silence. Mark felt the blood pulsing in his ears. Did Dirk Mason, the man who dated Sharon Stone, just say that Alyssa—*his* Alyssa—was beautiful and had pretty green eyes?

"Alyssa?" Mark asked for clarification. Dirk did it all so coolly, as only a movie star among starstruck ranchers could. Had it been anyone else expressing that kind of interest in Alyssa, Mark would have gotten his guard up, but this was Dirk Mason.

Dirk Mason didn't just walk into the Morning Glory Ranch and come on to Alyssa...did he? Sure, Alyssa was pretty, but she was *Alyssa.* And Alyssa wasn't...well, a movie star.

"How does she fit in?" Dirk asked into the slack-jawed quiet.

"Lis has been the cook here for about six summers," Missy explained. "She's about as much a part of the family as any of my children."

"So," Dirk said casually, looking at Mark, "you two aren't...?" He trailed off suggestively.

"Aren't what?" Mark asked stupidly. He felt a hot, itchy tide of blood warm his face. *Oh, my God, I'm blushing.*

"An item," Dirk explained.

"An item?" Mark asked, shocked. It was all he could say. He was about to laugh but Alyssa walked in at that moment dressed in a skirt, something Mark hadn't seen since they'd gone to her senior homecoming dance together. But this wasn't just any skirt; it was a short skirt. He could see Alyssa's knees. Mark felt for a moment that he had been punched in the chest.

Alyssa had knockout legs.

Alyssa scooted along the wall trying not to call any attention to herself. She leaned against the counter beside Mark and grabbed a cup of coffee off the counter.

"Now, how do you know our daughter Samantha?" Missy asked, trying to steer everyone's eyes from Alyssa.

With everyone's attention diverted by Missy's question,

Mark shifted closer to Alyssa and turned his back to everyone else. He took his time getting a glass of water.

"What are you wearing?" Mark asked Alyssa out of the corner of his mouth. He was absolutely unable to remove his eyes from the long, lean expanse of leg visible beneath the denim hem of her skirt.

"A skirt, Mark," she quipped. "Stop staring! You're making me nervous."

"Well, I don't actually know your daughter," Dirk was saying, answering Missy's question. "But I believe you know the woman who wrote the screenplay. She was a college friend of Samantha's. Kate Jenkins? Perhaps you remember her, she speaks very fondly of you all."

"Kate Jenkins?" Billy asked, his lip curling. "She wrote a movie?"

"You should change!" Mark snapped at Alyssa as he turned around to face the room. She shot him a quelling look and continued her study of Dirk Mason's mouth.

"Yep, she wrote a good script." Dirk answered Billy's incredulous question.

"Well, that's wonderful!" Missy exclaimed, and Dirk smiled at her.

"Kate Jenkins?" Billy asked again. "She came here for a summer a couple of years ago. She had so many screws loose I'm amazed she found her way to L.A."

"Come on, Billy," Ethan said, his eyes alight with trouble. He clapped a hand on Billy's back. "Surely, you remember *something* else about your summer with Kate."

Billy, the charming playboy, started a long, slow blush.

"Knock it off, Ethan," he mumbled.

"Billy—" Ethan turned to Dirk with no intention of knocking it off "—was in love with Kate Jenkins."

"I said knock it off!" Billy said tersely.

"Ethan, leave your brother alone," Missy said in the

voice of a woman who had been handling these fights for years.

Mark, barely aware of his brother's fight, finally tore his eyes away from Alyssa's legs only to see Dirk's gaze slowly make its way from Alyssa's slim ankles to the bottom of her skirt.

Mark felt a surge of protectiveness, like when he'd pick her up after cheerleading practice in high school and the football team would whistle at her as she climbed into the cab of his truck. Mark had wanted to punch the quarterback out then for looking at Alyssa the way Dirk Mason was looking at her now.

Mark felt his hands clench. He poked Alyssa in the side and she poked him back.

"Be quiet, Mark!" she demanded from between her teeth.

Mark crept closer and as subtly as possible picked up a dishcloth. Casually he put it in the hand closest to Alyssa and let it drape across the exposed part of her thigh.

Ha! he thought triumphantly. *Try checking her out through my mom's terry cloth.*

Alyssa's hand slid up and jerked the towel away.

"Well, Kate made it to Hollywood and she's taking it by storm," Dirk said, dragging Mark's attention back to the conversation. "Clint Eastwood is costarring with me and Julia Roberts is my love interest."

"Lucky you," Billy murmured.

"Tell me about it," Dirk murmured, and the two men grinned at each other.

"I always liked Kate," Alyssa said, sipping coffee. "She was just always kind of...reckless."

All eyes turned to Billy, whose ears were getting red.

"Am I the only one here who's had an ex-girlfriend?" Billy asked defensively.

"No, but you're the only one who had a girlfriend who walked down main street naked," Ethan remarked, leaning back against the counter and crossing his arms over his chest.

"She was in her underwear and it was a dare!" Billy pointed out.

"She told a good story," Mark cut in, trying to snake his arm around Alyssa to grab the towel again. Alyssa pushed it into the sink with her elbow.

"Remember those campfires we had that summer?" Alyssa asked, turning to Mark. "She had all of us so spooked by her ghost stories. Billy slept with his knife under his pillow!"

Billy looked up at Alyssa and when he saw her in a skirt, his breath came in a soft whistle.

"Alyssa? Are those your legs?" Billy asked.

I can't believe it, my own brother!

"Shove it, Billy," Alyssa said.

Mark looked at the remains of his sandwich on the plate he held in his hand, which included a piece of iceberg lettuce covered in a small heap of mayonnaise. Without a second thought he used his thumb and forefinger to flick the lettuce at Alyssa. More specifically at what little bit of skirt she was wearing.

The lettuce landed on her skirt and skidded down the denim, leaving a greasy trail of mayo and landed on her big toe, the nail of which was painted a rosy pink.

"What," Alyssa demanded under her breath, without looking at him, "are you trying to do?"

"You should change," Mark said from behind his coffee cup, unable to look away from her rosy-pink toenail.

"You should mind your own business," she said, leaning down to pick up the piece of lettuce. She threw it back on his plate and grabbed a towel to wipe off her skirt.

"You should—" Mark looked directly at his friend and gasped. "What's on your face?" He couldn't believe she was actually wearing makeup!

"What does it look like, Mark?" she retorted angrily. She didn't seem to mind that they were no longer whispering.

"Gunk! You look..."

"Wonderful," the movie star butted in.

Mark turned astonished eyes on Dirk. The look in the movie star's dark brown eyes was warm and very appreciative.

He is *hitting on her.* Mark was appalled.

"I need to use your bathroom," Dirk said calmly into the thrumming silence.

"Show him to the outhouse," Mac said, jerking his thumb toward the front door.

Dirk's jaw dropped in horror and Guy made some kind of gasping-choking noise. Missy slugged her laughing husband's arm and looked apologetically at Dirk and Guy.

"He thinks that's hilarious," she explained. "I'll show you to the bathroom with running water."

"I'd appreciate that."

Missy left the room with Dirk following and everyone swiveled in their seats to look at Alyssa.

"If Dirk Mason had said I looked wonderful, I would have died—just died. And the way he looked at you..." Cecelia said.

"If he'd looked at *you* like that, I would have killed him," Ethan added.

Suddenly they all remembered Guy and they turned slowly to look at him. Guy shrugged elegantly, for a man dressed in safari gear, and smiled.

"He looks at all the women that way," he told them.

"It definitely seems as if something has caught his eye,"

Mac said. "It's about time you stopped hiding your light under a bushel, Alyssa Halloway. You're a lovely girl."

"I'm glad someone around here thinks so!" she said, and turned a killing look toward Mark.

"What?" He put his hands up and faced his family, shocked that she would see his efforts to protect her from a man that is clearly up to no good as a bad thing.

Ethan cringed and sucked air through his teeth. "You blew it, Mark."

Which Mark took as his cue that his presence was not needed; he left the kitchen without a backward glance.

I have much more important things to do than sit around listening to some idiot talk about how pretty Alyssa is, he told himself on his way to the barn. *Since no one else is going to be working around here for…*

Halfway across the lawn he stopped and hung his head.

I'm a jerk.

He had gone out of his way to make Alyssa, no doubt already self-conscious, even more embarrassed. He was normally more sensitive to certain things, but it seemed these days that when it came to Alyssa he was losing his head. He wished he could blame it on the sight of her in a skirt.

Talk about hiding a light under a bushel… He continued walking to the barn.

She had legs for miles, legs any woman would kill for and any man would be happy to look at. And with that gunk on her face, making her eyelashes darker against the green of her eyes and that color on her lips making her smiles sweeter…well, Mark had been taken by surprise.

When did that little girl with the bruises and nonstop mouth grow up?

When you weren't looking, something in him answered,

and Mark had to agree. Alyssa was beautiful and he wondered how he could have not noticed.

He looked over his shoulder at the house and saw that everyone was filing out onto the porch. No doubt Mac was pointing out the different buildings on the ranch along with their complete history.

Mark opened the gate to the paddock where his horse, Bojangles, was chewing on hay. Mark whistled and brought his hand to his chest and the horse reared up and came running. When the horse was at the right distance, Mark grabbed onto its mane and in one fluid motion heaved himself up onto the animal's back. He leaned low over Bojangles's neck and almost as if they were one body, they barreled out of the open gate and headed across the meadow.

I'VE GOT THE OSCAR in the bag, Dirk thought as he watched Mark's all-in-all impressive manly horseback riding trick. And if the little gasp he heard from Guy was any indication, his assistant thought so, too.

Dirk turned to everyone standing behind him on the porch; he was calm and serious but he felt lit up with a fiery excitement.

"Mark will teach me how to be a cowboy," he declared.

"Well, there's something we should talk about," Billy said, lifting his hand to his lips and then out in the direction that Mark had gone. "You see, Mark's not exactly—"

"Guy?" Dirk interrupted. Dirk looked at his assistant who with a casual flourish pulled a small envelope from one of his hundred pockets.

"Dirk and I have learned a few things the hard way," Guy said in his calm voice. Dirk took one step back and tried not to smile. Hollywood was as cutthroat as any town in the Old West and the only thing that kept the outlaws and cheats away were contracts. Legally binding, signed contracts. And, of course, better than any kind of tin sheriff star was having a man on staff who could get anybody to sign the contract.

They won't know what's going to hit them, Dirk mused, and watched Guy work his magic.

It was as if in front of everyone's eyes the man who seemed so wholly helpless and out of place turned into a man in control. His patrician features that had seemed weak now took on a kind of nobility. His blond hair glinted in the evening light and his eyes were sharp and knowing. Even his thin body, which had been swallowed up in his safari gear, took on another dimension.

A wolf in sheep's clothing, Dirk thought.

"We have an agreement we'd like you to look over, nothing...*serious,*" he said, taking in the mixed emotions on the Cooks' faces. "But we want it understood that Dirk is here to learn and do a job. A job he takes very seriously. He's not going to be content leaning against a fence wearing a cowboy hat and learning how to spit."

The Cooks turned en masse to look at Dirk, who shook his head.

"Damn," Billy said under his breath.

"Dirk is here to learn in a few weeks what it has taken your family years to learn." Guy continued, "He is serious about this role and he's going to need your help. Everyone's help, especially Mark's. We are asking for that help."

The Cooks looked at each other and Dirk waited, knowing even before Mac nodded and Missy smiled that somehow Mark Cook would be teaching him how to be a cowboy.

3

MARK DIDN'T LOOK UP at the sound of the barn door closing, despite the fact that it was predawn and there was a movie star and his asthmatic assistant roaming around loose. His attention was focused on the dog in front of him.

Besides, he knew without having to look who was going to walk in behind him. Alyssa had been meeting him at the barn after she put the coffee on and before she started breakfast for four years. She would check the animals and help with the births, deaths, and everything in between. As she'd studied to get her degree in veterinary science, the Morning Glory had given her good practical experience.

She was a good vet and, even more, she was a good companion on these predawn rounds.

Although, perhaps not this morning. After his behavior yesterday he fully expected Alyssa's version of the silent treatment, which could be very chilly indeed.

Somewhere in the darkness behind him there was a thud and a muffled curse as Alyssa ran into the open stall door.

She's probably still asleep, he thought with a smile.

Finally she walked in and crouched beside him while rubbing the spot on her shoulder that had connected with the door.

"How is she?" Alyssa asked, referring to Queenie, who was restlessly lying on her side whimpering. When the dog smelled Alyssa, she tried to rotate her bursting body closer to the woman. Alyssa stopped her by sitting near the dog's head, knowing what the dog sought.

Female companionship.

"She's doing fine," Mark answered, running his palms over the dog's belly. "She's a little nervous. This is her first litter, isn't it?"

"I think so," Alyssa answered, unsure. "All of these Queenies kind of run together." Alyssa crooned and murmured. Without looking at him, she held one hand out toward Mark.

Mark took one hand off the dog's belly, reached into his pocket, and pulled out a piece of candy, which he dropped into Alyssa's palm.

Lemon, her favorite.

For a moment Mark was somehow surprised by this gesture, even though it was something he did every day. In the morning he grabbed a handful of candy off his dresser, on the way to the barn, making sure he had at least one lemon for Alyssa. He dumped all of his candy into his right pocket, but he put hers in his left pocket, so he wouldn't accidentally eat it.

When she walked into the barn, usually rubbing some part of her body she had bumped into a door or wall or table, she would hold out her hand and he would give her the candy.

Years of this little ritual and he'd never thought twice. Today, the hair on the back of his neck prickled. This candy ritual somehow seemed more intimate today.

"I'll stay with her. You can go check on the horses," Alyssa said, the candy clacking against her teeth.

He rose from his crouch and looked down at his best friend and his dog. Alyssa was wearing a pullover to ward off the dawn chill. Her hair was pulled back in an efficient, no-nonsense braid that somehow made Mark want to tug on it, just to hear her yelp.

When he didn't move, Alyssa looked up at him. Her freckled brow was wrinkled in what Mark knew was irritation.

She *was* mad at him. *Damn.*

The hair on the back of his neck raised again an awareness of the inherent intimacy of knowing someone the way he knew Alyssa. His understanding of his childhood friend was something he took for granted and it was as natural as breathing.

Mark blinked and shook his head once. *Relax,* he told himself, *seeing her in a skirt's got you all screwed up.*

"I'm sorry," he said. Apologies were easy for him when they were deserved and this one certainly was. "I was rude to you yesterday," he continued. "I treated you like you were my freshman sister and I had to protect you from some senior football player."

"You did that in high school," she reminded him peevishly.

"Yep, and yesterday I guess I had a flashback."

"I don't need protecting, Mark."

Mark looked at her. He took in the steel in her voice and in her eyes, but something in him still howled with disagreement when he said, "You're right, I'm sorry."

She nodded once.

He nodded back and turned to walk out.

"You did look nice," he said from the shadows past the stall door, "and you do have pretty green eyes." He walked on, his boots soundless on the ground.

MARK JOINED THE FAMILY later for a hastily thrown together breakfast and the news that Queenie had had her babies.

"Just what we need, more dogs named Queenie," Ethan said, biting into his eggs.

"I think Sarah could use a dog," Cecelia suggested.

"Great idea," Ethan agreed easily, "we'll name it King." He leaned over and kissed his wife and Mark felt an odd pang inside of him. Marriage and family was not something he thought a whole lot about. He thought about horses and the ranch and work, but looking at his brother cup the back of his daughter's head made something inside him squirm.

"You okay, Mark?" Ethan asked.

Mark snapped out of his thoughts. "Fine," he said, and walked over to the coffeepot. He was tired. Doing everybody's work while they got ready for Dirk was making him tired and that's why he was thinking weird thoughts about family and intimacy and candy and his best friend's legs. *Just tired,* he assured himself.

"Where are our houseguests?" Cecelia asked.

"Guy, the poor man, is suffering from an allergy attack and is in bed," Missy answered. "I just took him some tea, you've never seen a more pathetic creature."

"Where's Dirk?" Billy asked.

"Probably still sleeping," Mark answered caustically, pouring himself some coffee.

"He's in the corral," Alyssa announced. Slowly, all eyes turned to her as if she had said, "I left him in my bed."

"I saw him when I came in," she said defensively.

"Is he with a horse?" Mark demanded, feeling unreasonable.

"No, he's exercising or something."

"In the corral?"

"He said something about the view." Alyssa shrugged and replaced the empty coffeepot in the middle of the table with a full one.

Mark stood, convinced Dirk was in the corral up to no good, and headed out onto the porch to find him. Curiosity got the better of everyone else and they followed.

The sun was barely up and in the hazy light of dawn the movie star looked as though he was attempting to break his own legs.

Balancing on one foot with one arm out, Dirk grabbed the heel of his other foot, and without bending his leg, attempted to pull that leg straight out to the side and then up toward his head.

"What the..." Billy murmured. He tilted his head to the side, hoping the new angle might help the scene in front of him make sense.

Carefully, Dirk brought his leg down and tucked his foot into the crease between his opposite leg and the trunk of his body. Slowly, maintaining his seemingly precarious balance, he brought his hands together in front of him as if he were praying.

"Is this some kind of religious thing?" Missy asked in a whisper even though Dirk was well out of hearing.

"I don't want a cult follower on my land," Mac said firmly.

Dirk put his foot down and his arms at his sides and in one slow, sure movement bent over backward until his hands touched the ground behind him.

"Can you do that?" Billy asked Mark under his breath.

"Why would I want to?" Mark answered. "He's standing in horse crap."

"We shouldn't stare," Cecelia admonished them all, hitching Sarah up higher on her hip and heading back into the kitchen. Everyone followed except for Mark and Alyssa.

Mark looked at Alyssa, who was watching Dirk contort himself, while standing in a dirty corral, as if he was saving the world. Mark began to feel a little irrationally jealous and, remembering where that had got him last night, he curbed it and tried to look at the movie star through Alyssa's eyes.

But no matter what eyes he used, all he saw was an admittedly very flexible man in a tank top and tight pants standing in horse crap.

If it had been him out there—not that it ever would be—Mark considered, Alyssa would be laughing, not worshiping. Mark's head snapped back toward Alyssa. *Not that it matters what Alyssa thinks of me. We're just friends, she can laugh all she wants.*

Mark took the steps off the porch in one leap and made his way to the corral.

"What are you doing?" Mark asked Dirk without preamble.

Dirk, still in his back bend, turned his head, saw Mark, and kicked his legs over his head until he was standing again.

Mark, despite his intentions, was impressed.

"Hello, Mark." Dirk greeted the cowboy with a smile. He was alarmingly red in the face but seemed none the worse for wear. "Quite a dawn you've got here. These mountains are incredible."

"Any reason you're trying to break your back in my corral?"

Dirk laughed so good-naturedly at what had been a small dig that Mark felt about three feet smaller.

"It's yoga," Dirk explained. "It helps me stay strong."

Mark didn't quite believe that, but he nodded in understanding and, with his questions answered, turned and began walking toward the barn.

"So, Mark, how does your day start around here?" Dirk asked, matching Mark's long strides.

"Not with headstands," Mark answered cryptically.

Dirk chuckled as if the joke wasn't at his expense. "I'm serious, Mark. Give me a feeling for what you do."

"A feeling?"

"Yeah, a sense of your life."

Mark didn't quite know how to answer that, so he didn't. He started walking a little faster hoping Dirk would get a "sense" of the fact that Mark had better things to do than talk about "feelings."

"You start off your day with a run?" Dirk asked, keeping pace. They reached the barn almost at a trot. Mark grabbed the barn doors, yanked them open and ducked inside, making every effort to discourage him.

No such luck, the guy was quick and slid into the cool darkness of the barn with him.

This guy just won't take a hint, Mark thought, making his way toward the tack room.

"Mark?" Dirk prompted, not about to be shaken off like some bothersome kid.

"I get up real early," Mark finally answered.

"What do you do?" Dirk asked after the silence had stretched for a while.

"Check on the animals." Mark grabbed his saddle and bridle from the tack room and headed toward the stall and Bojangles.

"What are you going to do now?"

"Ride my horse."

"Where?"

Mark stopped and looked at Dirk. His eyes were lit with the same excitement, curiosity and determination that Billy's had been when he was a kid following Mark around.

"I'm not teaching you," Mark said bluntly. "Go bother someone else."

The movie star didn't budge.

"Dirk, there are a dozen people on this ranch who are real excited to have you here and just about everyone would be happy to give you cowboy lessons. Except me." The determination in Dirk's eyes did not dim one bit and Mark began to feel a little nervous, being the focus of all that…focus.

"Mark, you do know about the agreement, don't you?" Dirk said carefully.

"What agreement?" Mark asked.

"The one your family signed last night."

Mark suddenly felt as if he was in quicksand.

"What did it say?" he asked, knowing—just knowing—his family had somehow rigged it that he would be forced to work with Dirk or look like a total schmuck.

"It said that you and your family would teach me in stages the things you all know."

"Stages?"

"Billy would teach me the basics and you would take over when you thought I had mastered them." Dirk was looking at Mark with the smug satisfaction of a man who had crossed every t and dotted every i.

"Well, then go bother Billy and learn the basics," Mark finally said.

"Well, I'm hoping you—"

"Sorry, Dirk," Mark interrupted. "I'm about to do some intermediate to advanced cowboy stuff…I'd hate to break that agreement." Mark didn't even pretend to be shame-faced. After the way Dirk had ogled Alyssa's legs last night, Mark was happy to stick it to the cocky movie star. Mark smiled and lifted his hands as if to say they were tied.

"Well done," Dirk said gracefully, and some of Mark's triumph deflated.

The guy didn't have to be so nice about it, he rumbled to himself.

"I'll see you when I've mastered the basics," Dirk said. "I'm gonna get some breakfast. I'll talk to you later." Dirk turned and left Mark feeling like the worst was still to come.

IN THE KITCHEN Dirk found the mood much more to his liking. Guy finally came down, dressed in his silk pajamas.

"You look miserable," Dirk said, taking in Guy's drippy red nose and swollen eyes. Guy only answered with a combination cough/sneeze and Dirk didn't have it in him to make him talk to people. "Go back to bed," Dirk told him.

Guy turned around and shuffled back up the stairs.

Dirk's stomach growled and with a glance over his shoulder to make sure Guy was gone, he looked around the table for breakfast meats.

Diet schmiet, bring on the bacon.

"What kind of allergies does he have?" Missy asked, lingering over her coffee.

"Who?" Dirk asked, momentarily distracted by a platter of leftover French toast. "Oh, Guy...fur and dust," Dirk answered.

Billy laughed a little bit in astonishment. "Those are bad allergies to take to a ranch."

"Guy's a determined man," Dirk answered.

As if somehow able to read his mind, Alyssa put down a full platter of sizzling bacon. The smell nearly scent Dirk into orbit. It had been years since he had eaten bacon. He had bacon-flavored turkey and bacon-flavored tofu, but real, honest-to-God, five-million-grams-of-fat-per-slice, real pig fat had been banned from his diet for years.

If I really brush my teeth, Guy'll never know, Dirk told himself and, like a starving man, he grabbed his first piece, ate it in one bite and closed his eyes in bliss.

"Dirk?" Missy asked.

Dirk opened his eyes, realizing Missy, Alyssa, Cecelia and Billy were all watching him.

"I love bacon," Dirk said, and grinned. Everyone seemed to accept that kind of answer and Dirk set about eating as much bacon as he could.

Dirk chatted over lots of coffee, and because Guy and his fat counting were in bed, he splurged on buttermilk biscuits that were so far removed from his diet that he had three. He sent a smile in Alyssa's direction, which caused her to drop a platter of eggs. In an effort to endear himself to this family, he held Sarah and let her drool all over his arm.

And made plans for a trail ride with Billy the Kid.

Finally, some cowboy action, he thought and surreptitiously wiped baby spit onto his pants.

HOURS LATER Mark hauled Lucky's saddle into the tack room and stopped short.

What the—

He stood openmouthed as Dirk swung his fist and connected with Billy's chin, snapping his head back. Billy retaliated with a gut punch and Dirk doubled over with a groan. He lunged at Billy, but before he could get close enough to damage Mark's baby brother, Mark had the movie star in a headlock.

"What the hell is going on here?" Mark shouted. *First you hit on my best friend and now you're punching my brother?* Mark fumed silently, and gave Dirk's head an extra squeeze.

"It's really not what you think!" Billy said, trying to pry Mark's arms from around Dirk's throat. But Mark pushed his brother back with a scowl, thinking Billy was trying to get in a few more swings.

"You're not standing in the tack room, knocking the snot

out of each other?'' Mark asked dryly, dodging Billy's attempts to get to Dirk.

Dirk gurgled something and Mark gave him an extra squeeze.

''Mark, he was teaching me stage combat,'' Billy said with a helpless laugh, ''but I think you are strangling him for real.''

Mark let Dirk go and the movie star fell to his knees and immediately began sucking in deep breaths.

''Stage combat?'' Mark asked incredulously.

''Fake fighting,'' Dirk explained as his color returned to normal. ''I pretend to hit him and he pretends to be hit. Some people in my profession call it an art form.''

''Why in the world were you fake fighting with Dirk Mason?'' Mark turned to his brother, who was hiding his grin behind his hand.

''He offered,'' Billy said with a shrug. ''He wanted to thank me for teaching him how to ride today.''

''By pretending to hit each other?''

''It's fun, Mark. You should try it.''

Mark snorted through his nose and went back to the saddle he had dropped in his effort to stop the fake bloodshed.

''You should come out to the corral, Mark,'' Dirk said, seemingly not holding any kind of grudge against the man who had closed off his windpipe. ''Billy and I are going to show everyone what I learned today.''

He was so damn nice and accepting, it made Mark want to tear out his hair.

''Fake horseback riding?'' Mark muttered under his breath.

''Everybody is out there. Go stand with them,'' Billy said. ''We'll be out in a second. You're going to want to see this.''

Mark put his stuff away and grudgingly wandered over

to the corral to join Alyssa and the rest of his family who were gathered there. Guy came out of the ranch and started picking his way across the front lawn like a man avoiding land mines. While he was no longer dressed for safari, the slim, elegant little man with his hundred-dollar haircut and pressed blue jeans still looked wildly out of place.

Of course, the surgical mask tied across his face didn't help. Neither did the two inhalers he had clenched in his fists like six-shooters.

"Hello, Guy." Alyssa greeted the man warmly.

The surgical mask lifted and his thin cheeks twitched, so Mark guessed he smiled back. Guy stepped gingerly to the fence and eyed the old wood. He lifted off a potential splinter, brushed away a few dead leaves, and blew at a dead spider that hung on to the wood before resting his arm on the fence.

"Ready for the big show?" Mac asked. He slapped Guy on the back and Guy's chest slammed into the fence and bounced back.

"I certainly am," Guy replied, his voice muffled by the mask.

"How much can someone learn in a day?" Mark asked skeptically.

"I think you'll be surprised. He's picked it up awfully fast," Mac answered.

"He's very determined," added Guy.

"I watched for a while from the porch," Alyssa chimed in, leaning away from the fence to look at Mark over Mac's back. "I'm telling you, Mark, I think he's the real thing."

You would, Mark thought childishly.

As if cued, Billy and Dirk came riding out of the barn into the corral. He was bent over the horse's neck and balancing his weight evenly over the horse, and Mark did have to admit that Dirk Mason looked pretty good. A cloud of dust was kicked up and Guy, even with his mask and inhalers, began a wicked coughing fit. Dirk took two wide loops past his fans and onlookers and finally came to a halt in front of where everyone was standing.

"Guy?" he asked, concerned, "you sure you should be out here?"

"Wouldn't miss it," he said, gasping. His cheeks twitched again in what had to have been a smile and he lifted his hands and waved them at Dirk. "Go on, give us a show."

Taking the reins in one hand and tilting his hat up with the other, Dirk leaned low over the saddle and Mark had to blink his eyes. Right in front of them from one second to the next, Dirk turned into somebody different. Mark didn't know if it was a trick of light or something Dirk was doing with his eyebrows, but even Dirk's face looked different. A slow smile spread over his face and he nodded at Alyssa and Missy Cook.

"Howdy, ladies."

Alyssa giggled nervously.

"I'd be obliged," Dirk said in a sliding Western drawl that didn't have its origins anywhere except in the movies, "if you could give me a small token of your regard for good luck."

He was so persuasive, his eyes so confident, Mark felt as if he was watching The Duke himself charm the pants right off Alyssa and his mother. For a second, Mark had this wild image of Alyssa and his mother tossing Dirk their underwear.

Alyssa might have had the same thought because she blushed furiously and looked everywhere but into the grinning eyes of her favorite movie star.

Missy had no such hesitations and with a girlish squeal

she reached up, tugged on Dirk's shirt until he was halfway off his horse and planted a big kiss on his grinning lips.

"That'll bring you luck for sure!" Mac laughed. He threw an arm around his wife and when he thought no one would notice, gave her a little squeeze.

"Remember," Mark heard him mutter into his wife's ear, "dance with the one that brung you."

Dirk nudged his horse forward a step and leaned down until Alyssa had no choice but to look up at him.

"Ma'am," he said, reminding her that he was waiting for that favor.

Mark watched her hesitate and half expected her to hold out her hand for a handshake, which was certainly more like the Alyssa he knew. He smiled and crossed his arms over his chest. Alyssa wasn't about to get sucked in by this little act.

Before he could even finish the thought Alyssa scrunched her eyes closed and grabbed Dirk's face and smashed her lips in the general proximity of his mouth. But with her eyes closed, her kiss ended up on the side of his nose.

Nonplussed by the nose kiss, Dirk reached a hand up and tugged loose the piece of green ribbon that was holding her ponytail.

"If you don't mind..." He let the sentence trail off hopefully, holding the ribbon dangling between his fingers.

Mark's mouth fell open in shock, his arms slid to his sides.

Alyssa put her hand to the hair that was falling down around her shoulders and smiled shyly. She looked up at Dirk from beneath her lashes and Mark had to stop himself from leaping over the fence and grabbing back that hair ribbon.

"Go ahead, Dirk." Alyssa hesitated shyly over the

movie star's name, and Mark felt his heartbeat in his temples. "For luck," she said.

Dirk nodded, tipped his hat, and shot off into the center of the corral before Mark could lunge at him.

Dirk took several turns around the corral at a trot, then a canter and finally at a full gallop. Everyone watched Dirk show off his lassoing skills as he threw a rope around a pole. When he asked for a volunteer, Missy put her hand up and Dirk threw a rope around her.

Everyone clapped and exclaimed as if they had never seen such a feat, while Mark felt more and more as though he was a part of some joke.

"Mom, you've seen this a thousand times," Mark said. She ignored her son, who had once spent three hours showing his mother the many ways he could lasso his younger brother, and continued to holler.

Dirk rode back toward his audience and swung off his horse as if he had been doing it all his life.

"Well, I'll tell you what," Mac said, laughing delightedly. "That was some show. I haven't seen anybody rope my wife in a long time."

"You know, Dirk," Billy said, beaming at his prize student like a proud teacher, "the Wild Man Rodeo is coming up in a couple of weeks. You should think about entering."

"Oh, I don't know about that," Dirk said modestly, although a sparkle was ignited in his eyes. "I'm hardly a wild man…"

"Neither are most of the other riders, that's why I keep winning. I'm the only one under forty-five and sober."

"I'll think about it," Dirk agreed. But Mark could see by the look in his eyes that the decision was already made. Dirk was feeling like a wild man.

"Well, Mark, what do you think?" Dirk turned laughing eyes to Mark. "Am I ready for intermediate lessons?"

"I'll say," Alyssa proclaimed, looking at Dirk with stars in her eyes.

Suddenly it all became very clear to Mark what had to be done in this situation. And what was better, he was the only one who could do it.

The only way to stop Dirk Masonmania was to keep the movie star too busy and too tired to hit on Alyssa or start fake fights with his family. In fact, as Mark thought about it, the only way he was going to feel better about having this movie star on the land was if he was personally keeping an eye on him.

Perfect, Mark thought, feeling some of the tension seep from his body. It's the perfect plan.

"I'd be pleased to teach you a few things," Mark said with a smile while he silently plotted. But the family, who had never really seen Mark act devious, breathed a sigh of relief.

"So," Dirk said, looking around at the Cooks, "what's next on the agenda?"

Everyone looked at each other blankly.

Agenda? Mark mocked, taking a break from his devious plot. *Who says things like that?*

"Dinner's coming up in a half hour..." Alyssa offered.

"Excellent, then what?"

Again, blank looks all around.

"Well, I, uh, usually do some reading or watch TV," Billy offered.

"No thanks," Dirk said quickly.

"I look over some of the books and the farm reports..." Mac said.

"Tempting, but no. What do you do, Lis?"

Ahh-ha! You old dog. Mark's eyes narrowed.

"Dishes," she answered, not catching on to Dirk's line.

"Then what?"

"I take a walk."

"Excellent. I'll join you. Now, Billy," he said, casually changing subjects, "what do I do with my horse?"

And just like that, Alyssa had a date with Dirk Mason.

4

SOMEHOW AFTER DINNER it was Mark and Ethan standing at the sink up to their elbows in soapy water. Alyssa had pushed a towel into Mark's hand and run up to her room.

No doubt to put on a short skirt, Mark quietly brooded.

"Hey, Mark," Ethan said, interrupting Mark's short-skirt thoughts, "I think that plate is plenty dry."

Mark smiled uneasily and put the plate he had been drying for the past minute in the cupboard. The last thing he needed was for his brother to think he was upset about Alyssa and Dirk taking a walk. Because he wasn't.

Nope. Not upset. He tried to assure himself.

"Dirk did all right on that horse today, don't you think?" Ethan asked.

"Yep," Mark answered, and felt a muscle in his jaw twitch. Everyone wanted to talk about Dirk all the time, wasn't there anything else for them to talk about?

Such as how Alyssa is going to be alone with that operator?

"Real fast learner, that Dirk," Ethan said casually. Ethan held up a wet pan for Mark to dry. Mark snatched the pan, wiped it with a towel and threw it into the appropriate cupboard.

"Yep," Mark answered brusquely.

Am I really the only one who thinks Alyssa going on a walk with Dirk is a bad idea?

"Moves pretty fast, too," Ethan said with a very masculine chuckle. There was no mistaking that the moves he was talking about were the ones on Alyssa.

Mark stacked two coffee cups too vigorously and the bottom one cracked. He threw them onto the shelf with the others and the cups crumbled in a heap.

"You agitated about something, Mark?"

"Nope!" A handful of dripping wet silverware clattered into the drawer.

"You *seem* a little agitated."

"Well, I'm not."

"Okay," Ethan agreed quickly, throwing his sudsy hands in the air. "You're not agitated."

For a while the silence was broken only by the increasingly violent stacking of the dried dishes.

"'Cause you seem upset, that's all," Ethan finally said. "I was just wondering if something was on your mind."

Mark turned and looked at his brother, ready to throw the wooden spoon in his hand at him. He wanted to fight for no good reason, like they used to. But he was smart enough to know that a couple of lumps wouldn't make him feel better. The only thing that would would be Alyssa coming down in a pair of sweatpants and a ski mask for her walk with Dirk.

"I'm worried about Alyssa," he finally said. "Not *upset,* just worried."

"Why?" Ethan asked.

"Because fast-moving Dirk is going to try to make some kind of move on her tonight."

"So, she's a big girl," Ethan reasoned. "She's dealt with guys making moves on her before. Remember her senior prom? She punched that guy out cold."

"But this is different than Chris Thompson grabbing her butt on the dance floor," Mark protested.

"How?"

"I don't think she'll punch Dirk Mason!" Mark said.

"So?"

There was a silence. A deep, dark, breathless silence while Mark searched for the answer.

"He'll take advantage of the fact that she is starstruck," Mark finally answered.

Ethan's eyes narrowed. "Don't sell Alyssa short, Mark. She's still the same girl."

"No she's not!" Mark replied hotly. "She wears skirts and makeup and kisses strangers. That's not the Alyssa I know."

"Hmm." Ethan went back to his sink of dishes.

"If you have something to say, you'd better say it!" Mark threatened, his pale blue eyes flashing with the heat of his frustration.

"All I'm saying is that that girl has been following you around for years, and maybe you've forgotten that the Alyssa you know is not all there is to the girl."

"I know Alyssa better than anybody!" Mark said hotly.

"Maybe that's not enough for her anymore, Mark."

"What the hell are you talking about, Ethan? What's not enough?"

"Oh, forget it, Mark." Ethan shot Mark an exasperated look that Mark shot right back at him. Nothing, absolutely nothing, was making sense to him. "Are you going to get your head out of your ass and help me with these dishes? Or do I have to go get Mom?"

Mark didn't answer. Instead he was lost in thought about what Ethan had said.

Not enough for her?

Mark absently grabbed the pan Ethan handed him and bent to put it away. Ethan took the opportunity to twirl a towel and snap him in the butt.

"Hey!" Mark hollered, spinning and grabbing his stinging cheek. Armed with his own dish towel he went after his brother until Missy and Cecelia both came in to deal with the brothers.

ALYSSA STOOD in front of the mirror in her bedroom and sucked in her belly. Holding her breath, she turned to the side and wished she could stop baking brownies. She exhaled, pulled the shirt she was wearing over her head, and threw it on the bed with the rest of her discarded clothes. She was reaching deep into her closet for something to wear on this walk and was coming up empty.

How many denim shirts does one woman need? she thought furiously. Didn't she have any other clothes? Turtlenecks, long underwear shirts and flannel seemed to be the sum total of her wardrobe. She pulled her favorite turtleneck from the bottom of the pile and tried it on again in hopes that it had magically changed in the past twenty minutes.

A knock on the door saved her from a pure female whimper of fashion meltdown.

Cecelia stood in the doorway with a small stack of clothes over her arm.

"Thought you might need a change of pace," Cecelia said with a knowing twinkle in her eyes.

"I love you," Alyssa said seriously. "Like you were my flesh and blood, I love you." Alyssa pulled her in, shut the door behind her, and pounced on the clothes over Cecelia's arm.

Alyssa looked at herself in the mirror skeptically.

"I don't think I can wear this." Alyssa pulled the neck of the forest-green shirt up to her chin.

"Why not?" Cecelia asked, yanking Alyssa's death grip off the V-neck.

"It's awfully...low-cut."

"Lis, it shows your collarbones, which are lovely. It brings out your eyes and makes your hair look red, and I'll tell you, I've never seen your boobs look perkier."

"Perky?"

"Absolutely."

Alyssa continued to look at her reflection. The shirt was beautiful and did do wonders for the parts of her body she spent a long time trying not to call attention to, but still…

"It's just not…me."

"You're absolutely right. That's why you're going to wear it!"

Alyssa stood still while all the possibilities of that idea came crashing in on her.

It wasn't her and that was the best part. This was the kind of thing women who walked with movie stars wore. Women with perky breasts.

Alyssa decided she was going to wear some lipstick.

MARK WASN'T GOING to think of it as lurking, just like he wasn't going to think of it as spying. He was simply sitting on the porch enjoying the night air and enjoying a couple of beers. And just because he was going to sit in the shadows and not move until Alyssa walked up those steps was not going to turn his innocent actions into spying or lurking. But he was going to wait.

He waited for a long time and with nothing better to do than drink beers and rock back and forth on the porch swing, it wasn't long before Mark had a couple more than his nightly beer.

This walk could be considered a night hike, he thought grumpily. It had occurred to Mark in the hour since he'd watched Dirk and Alyssa leave from where he had been standing behind the pine tree in the corner of the yard, that perhaps his friendship with Alyssa was not what he thought. He had felt for years that in a way, she was his. That no one knew her better or could know her better. He thought about her family and the way she talked about her dad, and wondered if she was telling Dirk Mason all those secrets. The thought made him sad and angry. She would cheapen their friendship if she turned around and spilled her guts to a man she didn't know just because he was Dirk Mason.

But maybe they weren't the friends he thought they were.

Finally, on the edge of his vision, Mark saw Dirk and Alyssa emerge from the woods on the path that circled up and behind the house to a small clearing. The small clearing that all the Cook boys had taken young girls to on so-called night hikes, because the sky was clear and the ground soft and every other Cook was far, far away.

Mark's teeth clenched with the idea that Alyssa had taken the movie star up there for the same reason he had taken Jennifer Kaminski up there in high school. But Alyssa and Dirk walked side by side without touching. Alyssa's head was bent and tilted a bit to the side, a sure sign she was listening attentively.

They reached the steps and Mark settled deeper into the shadows and strained to hear their conversation. He watched as Alyssa went up the first one, but Dirk stopped her with a hand on her arm. She turned and because of the step she was eye to eye with Dirk Mason.

"Thank you, Alyssa," Dirk was saying, his voice low and deep. "It was a wonderful walk."

"It was. Thanks, Dirk," she said politely, and turned to lead the way up to the front door. He stopped her again.

"Aren't you coming in?" Alyssa asked, because Dirk was sleeping in one of the best rooms in the house.

"No, I've decided to sleep in the bunkhouse with the rest of the guys."

"Oh, well…then, sleep well." Alyssa smiled at him and turned to go into the house. Mark felt little firecrackers of relief and satisfaction. Alyssa—good old Alyssa—was leaving the movie star on the porch. Kissless. Dirk, however, stopped her by putting both his hands on her shoulders and turning her himself.

"It's customary for at least a handshake, isn't it?" he asked, laughter in his eyes.

"Of course." Alyssa put out her hand and Dirk took it. They shook hands and Dirk pulled her hand to his mouth and pressed a kiss to her palm.

Mark, a little drunk and plenty mad, stood in the shadows, ready to break up the little scene, but Alyssa gave a little giggle and Mark ducked again. He could take the movie star, but a furious Alyssa wasn't something he wanted on his hands.

"Good night, Alyssa." Dirk turned and left, making his way to the bunkhouse.

Alyssa stood on the steps and watched him walk away with that dreamy look in her eyes that was beginning to give Mark heartburn.

When Dirk was long gone, he took one step out of the shadows under the eaves and when Alyssa turned to go back inside she ran right into him.

"Mark," she gasped, startled. "What are you doing here?"

"Nothing," he said quickly. Perhaps too quickly, because Alyssa's eyes turned flinty in the moonlight.

"Mark, you were spying!"

"Nope!"

"Yes, you were. You were lurking…"

"I was *not* lurking!"

"Then what do you call it?" Alyssa put her hands on

her hips and stuck her chin out, forcing him to call a spade a spade.

"Waiting," he answered sheepishly.

"Mark, I thought we had that talk already about how I don't need protecting."

"We did. I wasn't waiting here to beat him up or to spy on you or to check on you. I just wanted to talk."

"Mark?" Alyssa took a deep sniff of his breath and leaned back with a laughing smile on her face, "have you been drinking?"

"I had three beers while I was not waiting for you."

"Okay, let's talk." Alyssa turned to go inside and when Mark put a hand on her arm to stop her she threw her hands up in frustration.

"What do the men around here have against going inside?" She tilted her head back as if God might answer.

"Let's…stay outside." He knew what would happen if they went inside. She would start doing things; making lists, coffee, menus for the week. She would hide in the little whirlwind of activity that always surrounded her and she would be able to dodge his questions.

And he needed answers.

"Okay, Mark." She took a few steps back and leaned against the railing. "Whatever's on your mind had better be good."

Mark's breath suddenly caught in his throat. She leaned against that railing with the moon behind her and she looked somehow different than the girl he knew. Her hair was… Mark shook his head to clear it.

Too many beers, he thought, and gathered his thoughts back to where they should be.

"I want to know what happened tonight," Mark demanded.

"That's too bad, Mark, because I'm not going to tell

you.'' She had that wide-eyed, you-can't-make-me look and Mark felt his blood heat up.

''Did you go up to the bluff, the old turnout?'' he asked.

''That's a spying question and I'm not answering it. It would serve you right if Dirk and I made out on this porch right in front of you.''

''Did he kiss you?'' Mark asked, rising to her bait.

''Spy question,'' she chirped, and looked at her fingernails in the moonlight.

''Did you kiss him?''

''Definitely spy question.'' She picked a piece of lint off the shoulder of her sweater and looked down her nose at him.

''Oh! For crying out loud what isn't a spy question?''

Alyssa pretended to think it over for a second and then turned back to him with a prissy little smile that just sent him over the edge. ''Nothing.''

''Oh, come on, Lis,'' he said, as if she should know better, and her temper snapped.

''No, Mark, you come on.'' She advanced, with her finger jabbing, and Mark took a few protective steps back. ''I am twenty-six years old and, in case you didn't notice, I'm a grown-up, as in adult. As in, I can kiss whomever I want. I can walk with whomever I want and I don't need your permission or blessing. And I certainly don't need you hovering over me!''

''I know, Lis.'' Mark ran his fingers through his thick white-blond hair, making it stand on end. He felt that things were somehow spinning out of control and a series of different questions sprang to his lips.

What's not enough for you anymore? What is happening to you? To us? Why are we fighting? He caught the words before they came out of his mouth, realizing, as he looked at the set of her chin that that just might be a road best not taken at the moment.

"I just want you to be…careful," he finally said, although it was only the very tip of the iceberg of what he wanted.

"Mark," she said to him as if he were a very smart dog, "butt out."

"Okay, okay I'll…butt out," he told Alyssa, and she smiled and patted him on the shoulder as she headed into the house.

When hell freezes over or that movie star is off my land and not one minute before, he silently vowed as he followed her in.

5

WHEN ALYSSA MET MARK at dawn, he was armed with another barrage of questions about her walk with Dirk. She ignored him and when he finally stormed away, fed up with her silence, she felt pretty smug and satisfied.

Serves him right, she thought stubbornly, and bent back down to her work. But something was not quite right. As sweet as it was watching Mark make an ass of himself over her time spent with Dirk, it was not *exactly* how she imagined it.

At sixteen years old, Alyssa had been heartsick and sleepless over Mark. And night after night she lay in her bed and dreamed of making Mark suffer the way she suffered. In the fantasy she had perfected over those sleepless nights, she would be kissing Chris Thompson on the porch and Mark would see them and leap out of the shadows insane with jealousy.

Dirk Mason is soo-oo much better than Chris Thompson, she thought, smiling with a certain amount of vicious female pleasure. She wasn't about to tell Mark that for most of their walk, Dirk had been on his cell phone. Or how Dirk had screamed in fear when the coyotes started crying in the distance.

Of course, at sixteen, her fantasy had ended with Mark punching Chris Thompson and then taking her in his arms. He declared his undying love and then, of course, he would kiss her, kiss her as she had never been kissed and they would live happily ever after.

"Stupid," Alyssa muttered to herself, breaking off her thoughts. If Mark wanted to run around spying on her and putting his nose where it didn't belong, maybe it really was time to make the man suffer. She thought of him spying on her and how he had embarrassed her when she had put on the skirt.

Perhaps this is not the best way to go about forgetting him, her better sense started to butt in, but Alyssa ignored it.

That vicious smile curled her lips and she began to formulate a plan.

ALYSSA WASN'T ENTIRELY sure how she was going to get her plan started. It was one thing to have a gorgeous Hollywood star ask to join her on her nightly walk in the woods. It was another thing entirely for her to ask him out, preferably in front of Mark and being somehow sure that Dirk would say yes.

This may be the stupidest idea you've ever had, Alyssa admonished herself, making her way back to the ranch to start breakfast.

When she walked into the kitchen, Mark was already there putting on coffee. Before either of them could say anything, Dirk and Guy came down the steps with a bunch of suitcases.

"What's wrong?" Alyssa asked, catching sight of the packed bags.

"Guy's allergies," Dirk said, and put a reassuring hand on Alyssa's shoulder. Despite the cell phone incident, she felt a nice little thrill that got better when she saw Mark frown out of the corner of her eye.

"Bad place for a man with dust and fur allergies," Mark

said, and Alyssa and Mark both looked at Guy who looked absolutely wretched.

"'Ell me abou ih," Guy managed to say with a wry, swollen, drippy smile.

"I'm going to drive him to the airport," Dirk said. He looked at Guy and smiled. "I can become a cowboy without him here dying."

"'Hanks," Guy said. "'Et's go."

"I'll be back this afternoon, Mark. For our lessons."

"I'll be waiting," Mark said, and lifted his coffee cup.

He's a little too agreeable, Alyssa thought suspiciously. *For a guy who wanted nothing to do with this whole thing, he's being awfully cooperative.*

"Lis?" Dirk said at the door.

"Yeah?" Alyssa tucked a curl behind her ear and smiled brightly at the movie star for Mark's benefit.

"It's a long, lonely drive back. Want to come with us?"

Am I really this lucky? Alyssa wondered gleefully. Unable to help herself, she looked at Mark for one long second and imagined him storming out of the shadows of the porch. Mark just looked at her and frowned.

"I'd love to," she said, still looking at Mark.

She grabbed a jacket and a purse, left a note for Missy about food in the freezer in case they should be late and skipped out the door with Dirk and Guy.

Score one for the good girls, she thought, loving the look on Mark's face when she waved goodbye to him.

A COUPLE OF HOURS LATER Ethan found Mark in the corral.

"What in the hell are you doing?" Ethan asked explosively. "The stalls are filled with horse manure!"

"I'm getting ready for Dirk's cowboy lessons," Mark answered. He slid his shovel under another pile of manure and heaved it into the half-filled wheelbarrow.

It's a long, lonely drive back, he mocked silently, thinking of Dirk and Alyssa alone together for hours in a car where, as he remembered, two determined people could do just about anything.

Ethan stared at his brother for a second. "So you've been hauling crap from all over the ranch."

"Yep." Mark found a particularly large pile and smiled wickedly.

I'd love to, handsome, hot-shot movie star, he thought, mimicking Alyssa with her bright smile and devious eyes.

"You figuring on asking an international movie star to shovel crap?"

"Yep."

"Mark—"

"You know," Mark interrupted, "that whole international thing is a bunch of hooey." Ethan's mouth fell open. "And," Mark continued, "if I am going to teach him, I'm going to teach him like Dad taught us."

"Dad never filled stalls with extra manure," Ethan pointed out.

"Yeah, well, maybe he should have!"

"Mark." Ethan was clearly concerned and there was nothing Mark could do about it. He was on a mission. "You know you're not making much sense."

"Of course I know!" Mark answered, throwing the shovel in the wheelbarrow and picking up the wheelbarrow handles. "Now get out of my way." Ethan took a step out of the way of the wheelbarrow and Mark walked past him to the barn.

IN THE TIME IT TAKES Dirk to get out of the car, walk around it and open my door, I could be in the house, in my bed and asleep. Alyssa stifled her millionth yawn. As a rule Alyssa was asleep by ten and awake at five. It was now past eleven-thirty and Alyssa had no idea how they had spent the whole day going to the airport and having dinner, but they had and Alyssa was just glad to be home. And away from Dirk and his cell phone.

The man just doesn't know the meaning of quiet, she thought. Dirk opened her door and put out a hand to help her out of the low sports car. He kept her hand and curled it around his forearm as they made their way across the lawn.

"Home again," he said with a smile. He was so handsome in the moonlight that Alyssa forgot to be tired.

They approached the front porch and Alyssa spied Mark making quick dash from his lookout at the window to the seat around the kitchen table. He lifted his cup of tea to his mouth and idly turned the page in his book, pretending to be focused on whatever nonsense was in front of him.

That rat! she thought furiously. *Waiting up for me like I'm a kid.*

"Hello, Mark," Dirk said cheerfully as he and Alyssa walked into the warm kitchen.

"Mark, what are you doing in here?" Alyssa asked suspiciously.

"Drinking tea and reading," Mark answered with a smile. He lifted the book as if to illustrate, and cringed when he looked down at the cover. A woman with ridiculously long hair and giant breasts leaned against a bare-chested man while he ripped open the front of her dress.

"*Love's Brazen Splendor*?" Alyssa put her hands on her hips and cocked an eyebrow at him. *I'm on to you, Mark. I'm on to you and I'm showing you no mercy!*

"It's all I could find," he said defensively. "Where the hell have you two been? You were supposed be back this afternoon for cowboy lessons." Mark looked at Dirk, shifting his eyes from Alyssa's accusing glare.

"I am sorry, Mark." Dirk apologized gracefully. "It took a little longer to get Guy off at the airport so Alyssa and I had dinner in Billings."

"Sushi," Alyssa said succinctly, thinking Mark would be impressed.

Dirk looked over at her and smiled. "Lis had never had sushi before so we found the best sushi restaurant—"

"The only sushi restaurant," Alyssa interrupted, gazing at Dirk with what she hoped Mark would interpret as an adoring look.

"True, true," Dirk chuckled. "In any case, Alyssa had her first sushi."

"What are you talking about?" Mark asked.

"Raw fish," Alyssa said to him without any of the warmth she seemed to now reserve for Dirk.

"You're six hours late because you've been eating raw fish?" Mark looked at Alyssa. "You don't even like *cooked* fish."

"Well..." A slow blush made progress up her face. *Damn him!* There was no way that Alyssa was going to let Mark know that sushi was the most disgusting thing on the planet. "I love it raw!" she lied, and linked her arm through Dirk's.

Nice recovery, she congratulated herself.

Mark turned to Dirk. "Dirk, if you want to be a cowboy, if you want me to teach you how to be a cowboy, you're going to have to take this seriously, or I'm out. Agreement or not. Understand?"

The smile faded from Dirk's face and he looked as serious as Mark.

"Absolutely," he answered, and as if he could read Mark's mind, his hand slid from around Alyssa's shoulder.

Alyssa narrowed her eyes at Mark, just about fed up with the man.

"Dawn in the stalls."

Mark's triumphant smile made Alyssa rash. It must have been his smile, because it certainly wasn't in her plan to press herself up against Dirk and say, as seductively as she could considering she had murder on her mind, "Well, I guess we had better say good night now." She leaned up and kissed Dirk hard on the lips, then turned and left both men standing openmouthed in wonder.

Take that, Mark!

"YOU'VE GOT TO BE KIDDING," Dirk said, eyeing the mountain of manure waiting for him in the stalls.

"Nope," Mark said. He slapped a shovel in Dirk's hand. "I'll see you at lunch." Mark turned and walked away.

"Mark, I came here to be a cowboy," Dirk said, taking a few steps after him.

"This is where it starts. Take it or leave it." The two men stared each other down and Mark hoped Dirk would throw in the towel and find some other ranch to learn at, some other guy's best friend to charm and seduce and…

"All right, Mark," Dirk said. "I'll see you at lunch." Dirk turned and headed back to the impossible job Mark had given him. Mark watched him bury his shovel in the manure and lift it into the wheelbarrow that Mark had used to put it there in the first place and some of the satisfaction he felt in the victory left him.

Why can't the movie star just act like a movie star? Not that Mark particularly knew how that would be, but he certainly didn't think he would take to mucking stalls without complaint.

If I had to face the amount of crap I put in those stalls I would have walked right out of there. Mark began to feel a little respect for Dirk's determination.

Not so fast, remember that kiss? he reminded himself, and turned to seek out Alyssa for a little talking to.

HE FOUND ALYSSA in the small garden on the north side of the house. She was kneeling in the soil with dirt on her face and her hair being blown into some kind of cyclone. He watched as she tucked the majority of her curly hair into the collar of her shirt, trying to keep it out of her eyes. He watched as she pulled weeds and picked the ripe vegetables. He watched and thought about the first time he had gone to visit Alyssa in college.

He had visited her out of the blue; the first in what would become a small tradition. For three years he would sometimes surprise her on Sunday mornings with bagels and coffee. They would sit at her tiny table and laugh and read the newspaper. He would tell her everything about the ranch and she would tell him the things she was learning and the things she was doing, and Mark felt as though things would never change.

He wondered now, watching her body, strong and sure as she went about her business, why there had never been someone with her on those Sunday mornings. Dozens of visits, all surprises, and not once did he interrupt her with some guy. He knew she had boyfriends, although none of them lasted very long; he never ever met one of them.

He pushed himself away from the side of the house where he had been watching her and made his way to where she was kneeling in a small bed of tomato plants.

"Hey," he said. She looked up and shielded her eyes from the sun.

"I'm not speaking to you," she told him and went back to her tomatoes.

"Then let me talk," he replied, and crouched in front of her.

"I think you've done enough talking," she said, not looking at him.

"Your tomatoes look good," he said, ignoring her, to which she responded with silence. "Must have been the extra manure we put on before the first freeze." She continued to pick tomatoes without looking at him.

"Dirk's shovelling manure, just like I had to."

Alyssa looked up and scowled at him; that feeling of things spinning away came back to him.

Not enough anymore.

"Remember when I came to visit you when you were in college? Sunday mornings? Remember?" he asked before he thought twice.

"Of course I remember. You were there almost every Sunday." She practically spat the words out.

"We had fun, didn't we? Doing the crossword?"

"Mark, please tell me that you aren't squatting in my tomato plants just to reminisce about coffee and bagels and the Sunday *Times*!"

"Where were all your boyfriends?" he asked bluntly.

Alyssa looked up at him as if he had spoken Swahili. "What?" she demanded.

"All those Sundays I brought you bagels and we spent the day together. There was never any boyfriend over," Mark said, balancing his weight on his toes, his hands hanging between his knees. "Why?"

"Mark? Have you lost your mind?"

"No..." *Yes, clearly I have. Help me out here, Lis.*

"It's none of your business where my boyfriends were or when they stayed over." She sat back on her heels.

"I know, but, Lis, you're my best friend and I'm just wondering why your boyfriends didn't spend the night Saturday nights."

"You're my best friend, too, but this is none of your damn business."

"I'm just wondering why you didn't spend Sundays with your boyfriend?"

Alyssa was silent, so silent and so angry that Mark suddenly felt bad. He couldn't understand why it was so important to him, but it was and he wasn't going to back down now. Change was in the air and Mark didn't like it.

"Mark, you say you should butt out and you say that you'll try, but it's impossible for you, isn't it?" she asked bitingly.

"No," he answered indignantly.

"Yes," she countered, her voice rising. "It's become so easy for you to just step right in and boss me around."

"I'm not bossing you around, I'm just wondering where your boyfriends were in college?"

Alyssa cocked her head at him and looked at him as if he were a cat with its tail stuck in a bridle.

"Is this about Dirk?" she asked.

"No!" he denied quickly.

"Well, time moves on, Mark. I wasn't going to be your Sunday morning bagel partner forever. I'm leaving in September," she reminded him. "I'm leaving and I'm going to have my own life, Mark. One you can't get in the middle of."

"I know," he said quickly, making it known to both of them that he didn't really. Or didn't really understand until right now, with Alyssa looking at him sadly and the smell of ripe tomatoes between them.

She had gone to Billings for school, she had left and come back a dozen times.

This time, he realized in a panic, *she isn't coming back. Ever.* Mark felt everything he knew tip a little bit and go out of focus.

"I think," she said slowly, "if you want to come over for bagels on Sunday mornings in the future, you should call first."

Alyssa stood, grabbed her basket of tomatoes and turned to walk back to the house. Mark, dazed and shocked, sat back heavily on a tomato plant.

This isn't right, he thought. *None of this is right.* There was a feeling in his chest, a great yawning ache. He brought his hand up to scratch the skin over his heart and realized he was beginning to feel lonely.

ALYSSA STOOD at the kitchen sink and wondered why her hands were shaking. She wondered why her face was so hot it felt as though it was going to explode. She turned on the cold water tap and cupped her palms under the stream. Hurriedly and repeatedly, she filled her hands and splashed water on her face.

It hurt. Something in her chest hurt and ached, and she felt her heart beat fast and hard against her chest.

All those Sundays, twice a month usually, while she was at school. Her boyfriends, few and far between, never stayed over Saturday nights on the off chance that Mark would be there in the morning. She hadn't even realized it; it was just one more of the million things she had done to keep Mark in her life.

Never let him know, she had always thought, never let things be different. Keep him comfortable so he'll come back so that maybe twice a month you can sit in the warmth of his company and pretend.

Years and years of pretending that Mark loved her. It had become second nature, as routine as breathing. Her life was set up around him and the feelings she had never quite gotten over.

Foolish, she thought, *foolish and stupid.*

She put her face in her hands and fought back tears.

LUNCH WAS A supremely uncomfortable meal. Dirk took his lunch outside because he smelled so bad, and the entire family opted to eat outside with him. Mark thought about joining them, but when he walked out onto the porch with his sandwich Alyssa had nearly killed him with her look.

He looked down at his family and the ranch hands who were all gathered around Dirk despite the fact that he was caked in horse manure. Even from several feet away, Mark could smell him.

If everyone wants to make fools of themselves over a smelly movie star, fine. Mark took his sandwich to the barn. But after five minutes of trying to rationalize his behavior he realized he was acting like an idiot. Nobody, not even Dirk Mason, could make him eat in the barn as if he were a scared, sulky kid. So he took his sandwich back to the house. He walked past everyone gathered on the steps, looking especially for Alyssa, but she wasn't there so he made his way to the kitchen where he had been eating his lunch for years.

That's where lunches are supposed to be eaten. In fact, Mark thought, *I think...*

Whatever else Mark thought vanished as he turned the corner into the kitchen and caught sight of Alyssa.

She stood at the sink, the kitchen window in front of her open and the screen lifted so the wind blew in, fluttering the curtains and cooling her face. Her eyes were shut and as Mark watched, she lifted her chin and tilted her head so the breeze blew across her neck and into the collar of her shirt. Her lips fell open and she took a deep breath, her back arched and her breasts pushed against the soft cotton of her T-shirt, and she sighed happily.

The sound of his heartbeat was in his ears and Mark was

suddenly filled head-to-toe with desire. It had hit him hard and low in the chest and spread out in his blood. He felt his knees weaken and had to put a hand on the wall.

I—I shouldn't be here, he told himself, feeling as if he was intruding on a private moment. Part of him felt ashamed for looking at her and feeling this way, but the rest of him couldn't look away. She was the most beautiful thing he had ever seen and it was impossible for him to move. He knew she might turn, might see him standing there staring with lust in his eyes, but he was powerless.

She was so gorgeous, her hair falling down her back in soft curls, her neck long and smooth. Without warning he was hard with need. He took one step toward her, unsure of what he was going to do only knowing that he had—absolutely had—to touch her.

"Alyssa?" For a moment Mark thought he had said it, but when Alyssa started and moved away from the window, he realized Dirk was standing in the yard at the window.

"Sorry, Dirk. I didn't see you there," she said with an embarrassed half laugh. Mark panicked and took a step back into the shadow of the hallway.

What am I doing? he wondered, shocked at his behavior. *What would I have done if Dirk hadn't been there? Touched her? Kissed her?* He brought a hand up to his forehead and shut his eyes tight.

"I brought you these," Dirk said.

Mark opened his eyes.

"Thank you. They're beautiful." Alyssa buried her nose in a small bouquet of wildflowers as if she had never smelled Columbine before.

"So are you," Dirk said. Instead of sounding creepy or cheesy, he made it sound like the most matter-of-fact compliment.

Alyssa blushed charmingly with her nose buried in the blooms.

Mark walked soundlessly back into the hallway and leaned against the wall. He wanted Alyssa. Blood-pumping, hands-sweating, *wanted* her. And he didn't know what to do about it.

THROUGH THE COURSE of the week the situation deteriorated. The more Dirk courted Alyssa, the more angry Mark got. So, Mark found even worse jobs for Dirk. Dirk had to curry and comb every horse, every day. He fed the dogs and the chickens. Every disgusting job there was to do, Dirk did it. And Mark couldn't figure out what made him more angry, that Dirk did it without ever complaining or the reason Mark was making him do it.

On Tuesday, Mark had Dirk fix the broken fence along the north pasture, the very same fence he had spent most of the night breaking. While Dirk was doing it, his shirt off and stupid it's-okay-Mark-I-can-take-whatever-you-give-me smile on his face, Alyssa brought him a thermos of lemonade and a bag of cookies. She passed Mark on her way back to the house and stuck her tongue out at him. Mark had to do deep-breathing exercises to keep himself from flying off to chase after her and her tongue.

And since he couldn't chase her down and show her what he wanted her to do with that tongue, he took his frustration out on Dirk.

"Mark, are you really serious about this?" Dirk asked. He was standing with Mark in the barn trying, mostly in vain, to round up all of the cats.

"You want to be a cowboy don't you?" Mark asked, feeling stupid chasing the old one-eyed mouser.

"Nowhere have I ever heard that cowboys give cats

heartworm pills.'' Dirk looked down at the little pill in his hand and Mark felt a stab of guilt.

''Well, they do at the Morning Glory,'' Mark said anyway.

Dirk finally shrugged and grabbed the cat closest to him and put the pill in his mouth. ''The Academy better appreciate this,'' Mark heard him mutter.

In his more sane moments Mark tried to tell himself that Alyssa was a grown woman, fully able to take care of herself and that Dirk had been nothing but polite and respectful. These moments were giving him heartburn. Of course as soon as he thought these rational thoughts he would catch sight of Alyssa giggling and batting her eyelashes and brushing up against Dirk and he turned into the barnyard bully again.

All of this was bad enough, but Mark could not shake the feeling he got when he walked in on Alyssa in the kitchen. Everyone on the ranch at one time or another had caught him staring into space with what his father called ''that dopey look.'' He couldn't tell anyone that he was thinking of Alyssa. Of her long, lean body and the way sunlight hit her hair and the curve of her throat and dip of her upper lip.

Mark dreamed about it at night in dreams so erotic that he couldn't look his best friend in the eye the next day.

I'm not getting any sleep, Mark conceded Thursday morning. *I'm not getting any work done and watching Alyssa and Dirk is killing me.* He was standing on the porch, watching Alyssa and Dirk walk out to the barn. As Mark watched, Dirk put his arm around Alyssa's waist. Alyssa turned around and when she saw Mark she waved, and the great yawning hole in his chest opened up again.

Something's got to give.

''WHAT IS THIS?'' Mark asked at dinner that night. He looked down at this bowl full of indistinguishable food and looked up at Alyssa with a snarl on his face.

"Tofu," she returned, as if it were commonplace. As if she hadn't had to drive all over western Montana to find the stuff.

"Wonderful," Dirk said with enthusiasm. "You remembered I told you how much I loved it."

"Of course I did." Alyssa smiled and put her hand on Dirk's shoulder, checking out of the corner of her eye that Mark saw her do it. She had to bite back a grin when Mark pushed back in his chair. "I always listen to what you say, Dirk."

"I worked all day, Lis. Hard work. The last thing I want is health food garbage," Mark complained.

"You've worked hard? That's a laugh, Mark. Dirk's been working harder than anybody else around here, thanks to you!" she countered.

"I, for one, think a little change is good for us!" said Missy brightly, into what was becoming a full-blown fight. She smiled at the table in her best "do as I do" manner and picked up her fork. She took a big bite of the tofu and chewed. She eyed her husband, who did the same and after a long incredulous moment, so did Billy.

Alyssa knew Billy was breathing out of his nose and chewing quickly. His throat moved once in a gag reflex, but in a supreme force of will he hadn't had to exhibit since Alyssa made liver, he closed his eyes, rubbed his throat gently and swallowed the mouthful.

"It's great," Mac said, chewing and swallowing quickly. He brought his hand up to his nose to pinch it so as not to taste the tofu, but Missy kicked him under the table. "I love it!"

Look at them, Alyssa thought, shamed to the bottom of her feet that she had let this situation go this far. She was doing everything she could think of to make Mark think she and Dirk were falling in love. This new cooking experiment was becoming a nightmare. She had no idea what she was supposed to do with tofu. She put sun-dried tomatoes in the tuna salad and wheat germ in Mark's favorite chocolate-chip cookies. She was so busy giggling and flirting and making sure Mark saw her do it that she wasn't sure if she was coming or going.

But I'm not giving up! she told herself firmly, watching the Cook family, who had been nothing but good to her, choke down tofu. *Mark needs to learn a lesson about his nose and other people's business. He knows he can't boss me around or take me for granted. Not anymore. No sir.*

"Do you see what's happened here?" Mark said to Alyssa, gesturing to his family. "You've made my family into a bunch of liars."

"They're only lying to shut you up!" Alyssa snapped back.

Mark leaned over his plate. "They wouldn't have to lie if you served real food."

Alyssa planted her hands on the table and leaned forward, all but shoving Dirk and his bowl of tofu surprise off the table. "You've got a lot of nerve coming into this kitchen and bossing me around! Maybe if you had an open mind and a sense of adventure..."

"Are you saying I'm close-minded?" Mark asked.

"If the shoe fits."

"Oh-hh..." Mark's eyes were all squinted up and Alyssa's jaw was set in stone.

"Why's your eye twitching?" Alyssa asked.

"Because you and your Marilyn Monroe eyelashes are making me crazy!"

"My...?" Alyssa gasped, outraged. "You..." Before

she could consider her actions, she grabbed Billy's plate of tofu surprise and dumped it over Mark's head.

"Yow!" Mark yelled. Before Alyssa could even back up out of firing range, he had Mac's plate of tofu surprise over her head.

"You jerk!" As Alyssa reached for Missy's plate, Mac stood, grabbed Alyssa around the waist and carried her to the front porch.

"Don't go away, you lousy..." Alyssa yelled at Mark over Mac's shoulder as he made his way down the hallway.

"What the hell has gotten into you, girl?" he asked after he dumped her onto her feet. "I've never seen you act this way." He knocked a few stubborn pieces of tofu off her shoulders and out of her hair.

"Why don't you ask Mark? He's the one acting like he owns the place!" Alyssa jerked her thumb back toward the house. *What nerve he had to boss her around, to complain about all the things she did when he never ever used to even notice. Well, he can choke on his tofu surprise!*

Mac only looked at her with a sad kind of sympathy. "I'm the closest thing you've got to a dad and you're breaking my heart here, sweetie. There's a lot of unrest in my home."

"It's not from me," Alyssa said stubbornly, although the rational part of herself that she had buried under all of her flirting and running around with organic lemonade knew better.

"We've been watching you make eyes at Dirk and then turn around to make sure Mark is watching. You're dressing up and making fancy dinners and all but spitting fire at my son so he'll watch you do it."

"I am not," Alyssa said hotly. Mac lifted his eyebrow. "Well, I just want him to get the message."

"What's the message?" Mac asked, his brow furrowed.

''That I'm all grown up!'' *That I'm attractive to other men, other movie star men,* she thought but didn't say out loud.

''You've always been real stubborn when it came to my boy,'' Mac said. ''And it seems to me growing up and becoming a woman hasn't changed that.''

''I'm not a little girl anymore,'' she told him, as if it made a difference. ''I don't have a crush on him, Mac.''

''Then what are you doing, trying to make him crazy?''

''His being crazy is just a reaction to my relationship with Dirk. I'm not trying to do anything!'' she said, but she didn't believe it. She had been taking a lot of satisfaction in Mark's irrational jealous behavior. She was about to say some more about how she wasn't trying to make Mark crazy, but Mac's eyes were soft and understanding and Alyssa knew they saw right through her.

Mac chuckled and pulled the girl he considered a daughter into his arms. ''I love you, sweetheart,'' he whispered. ''But I gotta tell you I hate tofu.''

Pressed into his worn flannel shirt and the smell of old spice and leather and pipe smoke, Alyssa grinned. ''I don't care for it much, either,'' she admitted.

6

MARK FLIPPED OVER onto his back, looked at his clock and groaned.

Two in the morning. Why can't I fall asleep?

He had washed out all the tofu smell in his hair. He had even taken Bojangles for a long ride so he should be exhausted. *He* was exhausted, he just wasn't asleep. Instead he was staring at the ceiling thinking about how bad things had gotten. His great plan had crashed and burned.

Dirk gives the cats heartworm pills without complaint, while I throw tofu at Alyssa. All in all, not a good day.

What was worse, all the bullying and scheming wasn't keeping Dirk away from Alyssa. It had done just the opposite.

And if she wants to waste her time with a good-looking, rich, famous, nice movie star then that was her business.

There was a blinding, stabbing pain behind his eye and it made his face twitch. Last night he'd woken up and looked at himself in the bathroom mirror. Sure enough his eyelid was twitching all over the place. He'd looked like a crazy man. Mark never got headaches or heartburn or crazy-man facial tics and, even though he really wanted to blame Dirk Mason for this pain, he couldn't; he couldn't even blame Alyssa. This headache was all his.

I'll apologize. I'll be the better man and put this whole stupid thing to an end. That'll show her. He wasn't sure what it would show her but it let him get to sleep before dawn.

ALYSSA AND MARK AVOIDED each other at the barn, and while she made breakfast Alyssa tried to come up with an apology.

I'm sorry I dumped tofu over your head, even though you deserved it, she thought, getting eggs out of the fridge. *Ah...not so good.*

I am sorry I have been giving you heartburn and tics... Alyssa smiled, cracking eggs into a bowl. *I'm really not that sorry.*

She heard Mark walk in behind her and she waited a moment, letting him sweat before turning to face him. She was ready for whatever irrational thing he might want to say, but suddenly when she turned and looked at him she found herself fighting for breath. Mark was looking at her, watching her and his light blue eyes were hot. Alyssa was no dummy and she knew what a look like that meant. Well, she knew what it meant from other men, not from Mark.

He wants me, flittered through her mind. *That look...he wants me?* But as soon as it came she discarded it. There was one constant in her life and that was Mark Cook did not want her.

He looked down quickly, and seemed uncomfortable, and Alyssa shook her head to clear it. He wore a deep red shirt, worn and soft, which clung to his back and shoulders. He rolled up the sleeves and his forearms flexed as he wiped the hat off his head, leaving his white-blond hair standing on end.

Alyssa had no control over the heartbreakingly familiar feeling that flooded her. Since she was five she'd had no control over what she felt or how she thought about Mark. He looked up at her and smiled, his face breaking into all of the lines and dimples that she loved. And because no matter how tough she wanted to pretend she was, she was weak and in love and she wondered for the millionth time: *why can't Mark feel just a little of what I feel for him?*

"Hey, Lis..." Mark said, breaking the quiet spell around them.

That was then, this is now, frantically she repeated her motto, her practical instincts kicking in. *Don't be weak. Don't let this hatless cowboy with his dimples and blue eyes trick you. He thinks you're a kid sister. He dumped tofu over your head.*

Mark took a step toward her. His look was so unguarded that she knew he was going to do something that would make her forget how mad she was at him, so she took drastic measures.

"Dirk is taking me to the Rose Steakhouse tonight," she blurted, effectively stopping Mark in his tracks. She put her hands on her hips and met Mark's light blue eyes head-on.

After a silent moment during which Alyssa would have given her arm to know what was going on behind Mark's eyes, he nodded and put his hat back on. "I'm going to take a shower," he said, and turned to go upstairs. When he left, Alyssa ran out the door to find Dirk to tell him he was taking her to the Rose Steakhouse.

ALYSSA PUT THE CASSEROLE in the fridge for Missy to warm up later for dinner and went upstairs to get ready for her date with Dirk. After what seemed like an appropriate amount of time for her to be decent, Mark followed.

He had had a stern talk with himself in his cold shower this morning. He was going to tell Alyssa that he was sorry, that he was glad she and Dirk got along so well and that he hoped they had a good time.

Even if it kills me.

"Lis?" Mark knocked once on the door of her room.

"What?" she called through the door.

"Are you decent?" he asked, feeling foolish.

After several moments Alyssa opened the door to her room and stood in the doorway in her green terry-cloth robe and a cloud of sweet feminine scent. The green matched her eyes, but Mark did what he could to ignore it and the shadow of skin left visible by the gaping neckline of the robe. He tried, he really did, but there was just no way he could go back to looking at her or thinking about her as just a friend.

"You, uh, going out for dinner?" Mark stated the obvious and looked down at his feet.

"Yep," she said, and turned to her mirror above her dresser and fumbled around with the bottles and compacts she had there. Mark stood silently for a moment, caught on the edge of her room. He felt the pull of time and he was all too aware that as soon as he gave up this fight things would never be the same. It was all too clear that he was the only person fighting to keep things the way they were and he couldn't hold back time anymore. It was just too damn hard.

"What do you want, Mark?" she said, looking at him in her mirror.

Mark forced himself to meet her eyes and to say what needed to be said.

I want you. I have no idea where this came from but it's killing me imagining you under that robe. It's killing me to watch Dirk touch you when I know I can't. It's so hard to ignore this and I don't know what to do with it or myself or you. I need to know what's not enough for you? Me? The Morning Glory?

She lifted her hair and piled it on top of her head with

a rubber band. Mark wanted nothing more than to kiss the long elegant line of her neck. *God, I want you.*

"I, uh, I'm sorry." He finally pushed it out. He looked at her eyes in the mirror and felt like he was drowning. "You're a grown-up and I've been acting like a four-year-old." Alyssa's mouth fell open and Mark smiled ruefully. "And I..." The words were sticking, reluctant to come out. *That's enough,* he thought, desperate to get out of here and away from her eyes and the smell of her.

"Have a good time, Lis," Mark said softly, and left Alyssa's room with a general sense of defeat.

DIRK MASON was the King of Chitchat, the Master of Small Talk. After six moonlit walks, a sushi dinner, the drive from Billings and countless not-quite-chance encounters on the ranch, Alyssa knew almost nothing about the man. She knew he had a dog when he was a kid, he loved sausage and lemon squares, he was a Democrat and he'd grown up in a small town in Missouri.

That was it. It was like going on a date with a sound bite.

They talked about a hundred different things without really talking about anything and his ability to seem as if he was listening when she really didn't think he was made her nervous.

I don't even think he knows my last name, she realized.

But he was one handsome man and Alyssa guessed she could handle a little nervousness. And while she didn't really want to spend her date with a movie star thinking about Mark, Alyssa was also feeling a little sick to her stomach. Ever since Mark had stood in her doorway, his hat in his hands and his eyes on everything but her, she had felt queasy, as if she was standing at a guardrail at the Grand Canyon and leaning too far over.

It was his acceptance, his hoping she had a good time, that hurt so much more than all of his opposition.

This is good for you, her better sense told her for the fourth time since Mark had left her bedroom. *That pain means it's working. You're getting over him...soon you won't even feel queasy.*

But she didn't entirely trust her better sense on this one.

"Do you go to this steakhouse often?" Dirk asked as they made their way to town. He looked over at her with his grin and Alyssa felt her heart stop and then try to catch up.

"We go a couple times a year, for special occasions," she answered.

"Well, this is certainly a special occasion." Again with the grin and the heart stopping and starting.

"I guess so," Alyssa answered brightly. For some reason Alyssa was feeling panicked. She took a couple of deep breaths and tried to think of relaxing things, but she couldn't think of any. All she could think about was the Grand Canyon and Dirk's expert small talk skills and Mark's face as he'd told her to have a good time.

"Dirk, you've never told me why you started acting." Alyssa was suddenly bound and determined to feel some kind of connection to the man besides heart palpitations.

"It was something I always felt I should do. Like a calling, you know?" he answered, and Alyssa thought that sounded familiar and then remembered his *Barbara Walters Special.*

"What did your parents think?" she asked.

"My mom was very supportive, my dad wanted me to go into business with him, but he came around." He smiled at her, a disarming smile, and abruptly Alyssa realized that that smile was a diversionary tactic. She was supposed to be so dumbstruck by that smile that she would stop asking questions. She had seen it work on a million interview shows with him and she had been suckered in by it a dozen times since he got to the ranch.

"What kind of business was your father in?" she pushed, hardening her heart against his smile.

"Which way do I go here?" he asked instead of answering, even though the sign for the steakhouse could be seen just down the block.

"You can park behind the building," she answered. "What does your father do?"

"I'm starving, aren't you?" Dirk turned the corner into the parking lot and made a big show of looking for a space in the nearly empty lot.

"Come on, Dirk." Alyssa was beginning to feel like a reporter. "You can tell me."

"Sweetheart," he said, and turned the wattage up on the charm, but Alyssa quickly looked down at her purse avoiding the dumbstruck feeling. "We're having a good time..."

"I'm not going in unless you tell me," she said. She was absolutely unsure of why she needed to know, she just knew that she couldn't sit across from him and talk about the fat content of steaks and childhood pets. She would go crazy. Maybe she already was.

"All right," he said, his smile vanishing. "But if you tell anyone I will sic Guy on you like killer bees. He's got the entire world believing my dad was in advertising."

"Okay," Alyssa said, feeling breathless, like Dorothy about to see the real Wizard of Oz. "I won't say a word to anyone."

Dirk looked around and then hunched close to Alyssa.

"Septic tanks," he whispered.

"Septic tanks?" Alyssa repeated loudly.

"Yes, sh-hh." Dirk pulled her down so their faces were

beneath the line of the dashboard. "My father empties and fixes septic tanks."

"Really?" Alyssa squealed.

"Yes," Dirk said. He blew out a big breath and smiled at her. "Can we go eat now?"

Dirk chose the table in the middle of the restaurant. He pulled out her chair and Alyssa sat, feeling as if she was in a fishbowl. She looked around and saw everyone staring at them. The usually loud kitchen was silent and every cook was peering over the edge of the counter, shoving aside orders of baked potatoes and prime rib trying to get a look at Dirk Mason.

"You sure you want to sit here?" Alyssa asked, very uncomfortable with all of the attention they were getting.

"Your chair isn't comfortable?' Dirk asked.

"No it's fine, but..."

"Wonderful, I'm starved." Dirk pulled out his own chair, sat and beamed up at the nervous sixteen-year-old-girl who was supposed to take their order but could really only stare and drop her pencil.

The night went horribly downhill.

News traveled fast through Lincoln, Montana. Apparently it traveled just as fast through the whole tri-county area. As Alyssa and Dirk ordered steaks and got up to go to the salad bar, it seemed as if the entire state of Montana had descended upon the Rose Steakhouse, ordered coffee and stared.

"Excuse me," Dirk said politely, edging past the crowd of people standing around their table. Every table and booth was filled and the line at the counter stretched out the door, so people milled around with cups of decaf in their hands.

"You Dirk Mason?" Alyssa heard a barrel-chested man with car grease on his face ask Dirk.

"I am," Dirk said, and put out his hand for a shake. "And you are...?"

"Jim Manning." The man laughed nervously and elbowed his wife before putting his big hand into Dirk's. "I own Manning Motors down on Third Street. Yes, sir, Mr. Mason, if you have any kind of vehicular needs while you're here, you know where to come." The man continued to grin and pump Dirk's hand. "That's Manning Motors on Third." There were a few more seconds of pumping and grinning until his wife intervened and dragged him back to the counter.

Just like that, the floodgates opened and people gushed forward, eager to talk to the movie star. Dirk smiled and laughed and charmed the socks right off the folks that approached them. He shook hands and kissed cheeks and signed a variety of napkins and matchbooks and things dug out of purses and pockets.

"Hi, Carrie," Alyssa said to a woman who approached their table. Carrie was one of Alyssa's old friends from high school and Alyssa, who was tired of being ignored and having her napkin taken away for autographs, was happy to see her.

"What are you doing with Dirk Mason?" Carrie asked. She didn't even look at Alyssa but instead stared at Dirk as he kissed someone's baby.

"Trying to eat," Alyssa answered wryly.

"Oh, my God, he's gorgeous," Carrie breathed. Alyssa looked over at the object of Carrie's fascination and felt only tired.

"Yep," she answered honestly, but with no real emotion. "He sure is. You want me to introduce you?"

Carrie nearly passed out at the prospect, so Alyssa introduced her and watched Dirk Mason smile and charm and just about blind the regular folks of Lincoln, Montana, with all his star power.

Alyssa ate her salad and nodded at some of her other old high school friends.

"Lis?" Dirk asked her after the steaks had arrived and he had not even stopped to see if his was done correctly. "I need a pen."

"What?" Alyssa asked, startled from her thoughts about the fat content of steaks.

"A pen," Dirk said urgently. "Do you have one in your purse?"

"Of course." Alyssa pulled up her purse from the floor and started digging through it. "Why?"

"Autographs, sweetheart." He smiled at Mr. Anderson, the high school track coach. "Autographs."

And in that one moment, Alyssa went from date to assistant. She even helped the editor of the paper, Bob Green, put together a few photos for the paper.

She ate her steak without really tasting it, and watched Dirk's grow cold. She ate all the broccoli off his plate and ordered a doggie bag thinking that Mark would probably be up for a midnight steak snack.

Four cups of coffee and a dish of Jell-O later, Alyssa realized sadly that the worst date of her life was with a Hollywood star.

Punishment, her conscience told her. *You are being punished for treating two good men like fools.* Alyssa sighed and handed over her ninth crumpled napkin so Dirk could sign it for Mrs. Simon, Alyssa's fourth-grade teacher.

"THIS IS THE LAST PLACE I thought I would find you," a voice from the back of the crowd shouted over the din and Dirk felt his heart kick.

Relax, you didn't actually eat any steak, he told himself.

Slowly, the crowd parted and Guy, smiling and suave, stepped up to their table.

Dirk smiled with real pleasure at his assistant. Gone was the man on safari and in his place was some kind of haute couture cowboy. He was wearing a red flannel shirt with black velvet piping. His jeans were pressed, creased, and made out of some kind of dark glittery material, with gold stitches. His pants were held up with a snakeskin belt complete with gold buckle.

Oh, Guy, you've topped yourself this time.

He was a Hollywood cowboy angel and, like magic, the crowd took a few steps back. Maybe it was the way he so studiously ignored them, or that he was so ridiculous that he was unnerving. Whatever it was, Dirk was delighted to see him.

Guy put his hand up on the back of an empty chair at the table and people scattered like birds.

"I suppose you've been eating steak," Guy said accusingly.

"Nope," Dirk said honestly. "I have, however, been enjoying a variety of breakfast meats thanks to the Morning Glory," he admitted with a grin.

For a second it looked as though Guy was going to scold him, remind him of fat grams and cholesterol, but instead he sat and clapped a hand on Dirk's back.

"What's a few sausages?" Guy said, and they both smiled. "This place looks like a movie set," Guy added, taking in the log walls and the hanging chandeliers that were made out of steer horns.

The crowd had taken several steps away from the table but nobody had left, and as Guy glared at what was almost the entire population of Lincoln, Montana, they all looked away.

Guy had that kind of effect on people.

''Are these people for real?'' Guy whispered, his face a strange mixture of delight and apprehension. ''You couldn't find extras any better than this.''

''I know,'' Dirk leaned in and whispered back, happy to have someone around who realized just how weird all of this stuff was. ''Our waitress's name is Darlene and her father is a retired rodeo clown.''

''Get *out,*'' Guy breathed.

''No lie and...''

''Guy,'' Alyssa asked impatiently, ''what are you doing here?''

Ooops, Dirk thought. *That's right, I'm on a date.*

''Well,'' Guy said, wiping the table with a napkin before putting his arms on it. ''There are a few business concerns that have come up and I needed to go over them with Dirk. He needed to sign some contracts and okay a few deals.''

''Oh,'' Alyssa said lamely. ''Why don't we all go home and you can discuss it there?'' She grabbed her jacket and began to push back her chair.

''I'm not staying at the Morning Glory,'' Guy said, shooting a glittering look at Dirk, who tried not to smile. ''Too much dust and fur.''

''Where are you staying?'' Dirk asked.

Guy swallowed as if there was something unpleasant in his mouth. ''The Bit and Bridle Motor Lodge on the outside of town.''

Dirk began to laugh, slapping his hand against the table.

''This is not funny, Dirk,'' Guy said, turning, if possible, even starchier. ''I have one queen-size bed and a fold-out couch! A couch! Not to mention shag carpeting, which has been outlawed in all the other forty-nine states. My view is of a junkyard, where there lives a very loud and unhappy dog. My in-room shampoo controls *dandruff.*'' Guy's nose turned up and Dirk knew that just mentioning the word made him a little queasy. "And the whole room smells of wet mud. And please, do not even get me started on the sheets, which might as well be made of burlap!"

"Poor Guy," Dirk gasped.

"Right, well laugh all you want. I'm going to get a disease or lice or some kind of rash..."

"Oh, stop," Alyssa finally said, clearly tired of the whole night.

Belatedly, Dirk felt bad. "Lis, you must be tired. Why don't you take my car," Dirk said, fishing in his pocket for the keys to his sports car. "Guy can drive me back to the ranch when we're done."

"No!" Alyssa said abruptly and put her hand on Dirk's arm, stalling his efforts. "No way am I driving that car. I'll call Mark and he'll come and get me."

"Here." Guy reached into the breast pocket of his funny shirt and pulled out a tiny cell phone. He flipped it open, pushed some buttons and handed it to her.

Alyssa talked to Mark on the phone while under the table Guy put his hand on Dirk's knee and squeezed. Dirk was suddenly very eager to see the Bit and Bridle Motor Lodge.

MARK REMEMBERED that as a kid he would read long past his bedtime and perfected the ability to look as though he was sound asleep in a split second. He was so good at this that his parents believed he fell asleep with his lamp on almost every night.

He was counting on this skill as he sat up waiting for Alyssa in the den. He figured he couldn't be accused of spying or lurking if he was sound asleep with a book across his chest. He practiced a few times when the wind rose and rattled the screened door on its hinges, startling him into thinking Alyssa was back.

However the night wore on and he was almost truly asleep when the phone beside him rang.

"Hello?" Startled and sleepy, he barked into the phone.

"Mark?" He could barely hear Alyssa over the static.

"Lis? Where are you?" he asked, and checked his watch. Ten-thirty.

"I'm at the Rose Steakhouse!" she shouted. "I hate to bug you, but could you come get me?"

"Are you okay? What happened?" he asked, wide-awake. Sleep disappeared under the sharp edge of worry.

"Yeah, I'm fine. I'll explain it when you get here." Alyssa hung up and two minutes later Mark was on his way.

He tortured himself during the twenty-minute drive to town with visions of Alyssa and Dirk, eating steak off each other's forks and necking at the salad bar. He imagined those big dark booths and all of the things he had gotten away with on dates in those booths.

I should have stopped this whole mess from the beginning, he thought, *headache or no.* By the time he squealed to a stop in front of the restaurant his eye was twitching and he was ready to teach Dirk how to artificially inseminate cows, right after he punched him in the nose.

Alyssa was waiting for him outside.

The truck was barely stopped before he hurtled out the door and took Alyssa's shoulders in his hands. "What's going on here?"

"Nothing, Mark. Relax." She put her hands on his and squeezed them before pushing them away. "Why is your face twitching?"

"Because I spent the last twenty minutes thinking you were—" *making love to Dirk in a restaurant* "—hurt."

"And that made your eye twitch?" Alyssa looked at him in confusion.

"Gave me heartburn, too, so what's going on?"

Alyssa smiled and started toward the truck with her jacket over her shoulders and a doggie bag in her hand. "Guy came back to talk business, so I left."

"Where are they?" Mark asked.

"They're gone."

"Gone?" That took some of the wind out of his sails. "He's gone?"

"Guy's staying at the Bit and Bridle, apparently he's in the penthouse," she told him.

"The penthouse?" Mark took slow steps back toward the truck. "You mean, the room with the couch?"

"That's the one."

Mark looked at her over the windshield. "They've got a lot of money to throw around."

"You're telling me," Alyssa said. They opened their doors and slid onto the truck's bench seat. Mark started up the engine, backed out of the place he had squealed into and headed back up the mountain.

Alyssa turned on the heat in the truck against the cool night air and pointed the vents toward her. Within a few minutes, Mark reached over and turned the heat down. It was a routine they performed every time they got in the truck together and Mark got that disarming feeling with the hair on the back of his neck.

"How was dinner?" he asked after all temperature concerns had been dealt with.

Alyssa smiled and spent the next few minutes describing her unusual evening with Dirk.

"His pants were shiny?" Mark asked. When Alyssa nodded, he laughed. He laughed and slapped the steering wheel, and when Alyssa giggled, too, he felt pretty good about things between them.

Maybe getting back to the way things were isn't going

to be an issue after all. Now if I can just stop thinking about her naked…

"I brought you his steak," Alyssa said, lifting the doggie bag and putting it between them.

"Thanks," he said, and turned to look at her for a second. Their eyes met and warmed and they both took a deep breath.

"I'm so sorry, Mark," she said. "I can't believe how horrible I've been."

"Forget it, Lis. Really, I was so out of line."

"Yes, you were," she agreed with a smile that took the sting out of her words. "But it doesn't make it okay for me to be horrible."

"You did throw tofu first," Mark conceded, happy that they were joking together. Happy just that she was in the truck with him smiling as she always was. Happy that things might just go back to normal.

"Well, you threw it right back," she said, and shoved his shoulder. Even that small contact lit Mark up like a Christmas tree.

Jeez, that's not normal! he thought, and quickly unrolled his window. He was quickly coming to understand the need to have things they way they were and the need he was feeling to *have* Alyssa were not going to work out side by side.

They drove in silence for a few moments. As they turned past the long winding driveway that led to Alyssa's family's ranch, Mark looked over to watch her turn to watch it go by.

"Have you heard from your folks?" Mark asked, and noticed that Alyssa's mouth tightened.

"I'm heading up there in a few days," she answered. Alyssa went up to her parents' land twice a month to check on her folks and to get her dose of guilt and resentment from her father. She didn't have to go, but out of love for her mother she went, although her visits went mostly unnoticed.

Mark knew, however, that Alyssa, despite knowing better, constantly held out hope that things might be different. Mark watched her out of the corner of his eye, waiting for the telltale sign that she was overwhelmed or nervous about something. Sure enough within seconds she brought her thumb to her mouth and started to chew on the corner of her nail.

The lights from the dash lit her face and Mark found it difficult to look away from her. There was an ugly mess of feelings inside of him that was hard to figure out.

He tried not to think about the sharp jab of lust he had felt the other day when he'd watched Alyssa at the kitchen window, he tried not to think of the million jabs of lust that had followed. None of it made sense and in the silence of the cab and her companionable warmth only an arm's length away, his feelings got messier.

If she was any other woman he could just pull her close and let nature take its course and he could be rid of this sudden lust. But she was Alyssa and he didn't know what to do.

"You know Lis, I've been thinking..." He stopped.

What are you doing? he wondered, shocked at himself.

"Always trouble," she quipped. When he didn't respond she put her hand on his arm. "Before we started acting like idiots you would have known that was a joke."

Mark found it hard to concentrate past the touch of her arm on his skin. He wanted to grab her hand and press his mouth to it.

"You want to go up to the lookout?" Alyssa asked, rolling her head against the window and smiling at him. "We haven't been up there in a long time."

"Sure," he said, and felt a bead of sweat trickle down his back. "Sounds great." Alyssa, stars, and no one around for miles.

Sounds like torture.

He pulled past his driveway and headed up the mountain where the road dead-ended at a lookout that was private and dark and a place that they went to often.

"Remember the night I drank too many screwdrivers at that party and you had to come and pick me up?" she asked, looking at him from her side of the truck.

"I taught you how to twirl my hat and spit," Mark said, remembering the night well.

"I threw up all over your truck," Alyssa said, wrinkling her nose.

"You cleaned it up the next day," he said in her defense.

"Yeah," Alyssa sputtered, "you made me clean it in front of everybody."

"Hey, it's not my doing that everyone just happened to be on the porch," he protested lightly.

The conversation faded into another comfortable silence and Mark turned into the lookout and parked the truck. They each jumped out of the cab to go sit side by side on the hood of the truck, their backs against the windshield, their faces tilted up to the sky.

"How many times do you think we've done this?" he asked, and Alyssa looked at him, surprised.

"You have been really nostalgic lately, Mark," she commented.

"Nostalgic?" he asked, shifting his weight so that her arm touched his. It was the kind of torture he used to sit through on first dates in high school and it was still as thrilling now as it was then.

"Yeah." Alyssa pushed her hair behind her ears and turned on her side, propped up against the windshield. The sky was lit behind her with a million stars and Mark took in the picture she made with an ache deep in his body. "Wanting to talk about the past, visiting me in college and now this...that's not like you."

"Well..." Mark paused. "It's been a weird week."

"You can say that again." Alyssa rolled her eyes and flopped onto her back. "I ate sushi. Ugg-hhh." She shuddered dramatically.

"Well, you ate it with Dirk Mason," he said, easing into the subject that was eating at him. From the way she talked about what happened at the Rose, the romance between them was over. But he didn't know for sure.

"Very true, but Dirk didn't make it any more edible. I'll take cooked meat and potatoes any day of the week."

"Yeah, but what about Dirk?" Mark asked, desperate to keep her on track.

"What do you mean?" she asked. Mark was about to pull his hair out when she looked at him with joking eyes. He smirked at her and gave her a shove.

"Whoa..." She laughed and would have slid off the hood if Mark hadn't reached out and grabbed her, both of them sliding a little bit on the hood of the truck.

"Careful..."

"Ouch..."

"Very funny..."

"Lis, just sit still..." Alyssa was trying to sit up and Mark, with his hands on her hips and her smiling face inches from his, found he didn't want her to sit up. He didn't want to move, to change the perfection of this instant.

For some reason Mark remembered lying on his back with Alyssa by the river that ran through the southwest corner of the property. They used to go there after church to catch things that they could put in jars and take home to Missy. This particular time they were lying on their backs, their full jars beside them on the grass. Alyssa's hands were beneath her head and her hair was spread across the grass like a carpet of curls. Mark had lifted a curl and laid it over his upper lip like a mustache and she had said nothing. It was something he did often.

"What are you looking at?" he had asked as she squinted and turned her head in the grass as she'd peered up at the clouds.

"I think..." She'd shifted her head to the side and shut one eye and then nodded definitively. "Yep, I'm looking at a cow."

Mark had put his head in the same position with Alyssa's curl over his lip and closed one eye but hadn't seen anything but a cloud.

"I don't see it." He'd picked up the curl and run it down the bridge of his nose. It was soft and smooth and smelled like sunshine.

"You know something," Alyssa had said, exasperated as only a kid could be exasperated, "if you don't start using your imagination here, you're going to miss out on a lot of things!"

He had been eleven.

Now, lying against Alyssa on the hood of his truck, Mark reached out a hand to touch one of the curls that fell over her shoulder. His intent was to press it to his face to see if somehow it was still the same after all these years. To see if somehow he could go back in time and see the cow in the clouds and see the girl lying beside him in the grass for what she really was.

"What are you doing?" she whispered as Mark brushed her hair away from her face. Mark couldn't think of any kind of answer, not a single thing except that right now he wanted Alyssa against his body, in his arms, more than he wanted things to go back to the way they were.

Mark looked at her eyes and when her mouth opened on a gasp he knew she was seeing everything he felt and he didn't care.

"Lis," he whispered and bent down, and carefully, almost as though he was in a dream, pressed his lips to hers.

7

ALYSSA WASN'T SURE if this was real. If Mark's lips weren't just another dream that she would wake up from. She kept her eyes open wide and held her breath as Mark pressed his closed mouth against hers. His lips were chapped and firm and as they first touched hers, every girlhood and womanhood dream she had ever had about kissing Mark Cook went up in smoke. He was here, this was real and it was better than any daydream.

She could feel his breath against her cheek, the soft fluttering of his eyelashes. She brought her hand up to his neck and put her fingers against the skin there. There was an erotic stillness between them. A hesitation that made her dizzy with want. She could feel his breathing and every beat of his heart in every part of her body.

Oh... was all she could think. *Oh, yes.*

His tongue was soft and gentle and smooth when it touched her lips. Alyssa closed her eyes and opened her mouth in blissful happy surrender. She wrapped her hands around his neck, spread her body out beneath him, and melted into him. Her mouth was warm and wet, her body warm and soft. She was like a cloud; a slow warm rain. It was like lying in sunlight. It was like she ran through his fingers.

His hands slid back into her hair as she crept her hands up to touch the strength of his neck, the warmth of his cheek, the silky curve of his ear.

Oh, she thought as the quivering in her belly began, *I know you.*

She felt the tightness in him, of strength and desire reserved, and the slow warm drip of desire turned into waves. For years her eyes had lovingly traced the curve of his back, the line of his arm and now her fingers feverishly did the same. She had wondered if the skin at his neck would be soft, if the hollow of his back as it curved into his jeans would be smooth. A million questions were answered as her fingers skated across his skin only to return to test the strength of the muscles she had watched grow. The hunger she had for this man was alive in her.

She paid attention to every detail of sensation, every rushing nuance of feeling. This was Mark in her hands, filling her arms, kissing her mouth—and she could not get enough.

Years of longing roared through her body and before sense could grab hold Alyssa put her hands to Mark's head and kissed him for all she was worth. They fell back against the truck together. Their bodies fused and fire ignited in the soft and hard places that met in the tumble.

His hand slid up her body, dragging the sweater with it. She could feel his fingers on her bare skin and she could feel it all through her body. Just that. Just the touch of his hand on her stomach. Slowly, with grace and care, he put his hand over her breast, traced his finger around the edge of her nipple and Alyssa arched her head back and stifled a moan. He eased one thigh between her legs and she gasped against his mouth, arching her back to press her body against his leg.

Grabbing her hips he pulled her toward him and because the world was spinning out of control she dug her fingers into the muscles of his back. Her head fell back as her hips jerked forward, seeking more of the same.

Mark bent his head and put his teeth to the delicate skin at her throat and eased his hands back up to her breasts, taking their weight in his palms. His hands began to slide buttons from their holes and Alyssa blissfully let him. She felt her shirt fall from her shoulders and heard the soft breath he pulled in. Roughly, his hands covered her bra and she realized that Mark was beginning to lose control and nothing, nothing ever in the world, had turned her on as much. She arched her breasts into his hands, pushed her fingers into the waistband of his jeans. She pushed up his shirt and felt the heat and sweat that was beginning to rise off of him and began to undo Mark's belt.

Out of the deep outer reaches of her practical and prideful soul her better sense piped up, *You are on top of a truck. Your fantasies never included screwing Mark on the hood of a truck.*

Shut up! the hot, hungry woman that was undoing Mark's pants shouted back. Alyssa concentrated on shutting out the voices and tried to focus on the hard flesh that was pulsing in her hand.

She had never felt this way. This hungry and lush, this erotically charged. The silence between them was so heated and she kept her eyes shut against the reality that this was Mark and that they were no doubt making a mistake. He knocked her hands away and began to work on her pants. Alyssa felt giddy with feminine pleasure; Mark was barely holding on.

You don't have any condoms, her better sense chimed in just as Mark's hand slid past her jeans and his fingers began pushing against the practical cotton of her underwear. *Honey, I don't want to be the one to remind you but this is Mark. Mark Cook, your best friend, and you are going to have to see him for the rest of your life after this. You'll probably get invited to his wedding, you'll probably be the godmother to his children. Do you really want to do this?*

Oh my god, the wildly turned-on woman who wanted nothing more than to have sex on the hood of a truck butted in, *this is the moment you have been waiting your whole life for, Mark is about to—*

And then he did, one long finger slipped inside the very center of her body.

Alyssa bit her lip against the need to cry out in fear that any sound would break the spell between them. This was a dream and she had to keep it a dream, if they acknowledged what was happening it would fall apart.

"Lis, oh, sweetheart," he groaned into her ear, and her body went utterly still.

No, no no no, don't ruin this. Just enjoy this. People call people sweetheart every day, don't make this into a big deal. Who cares what he calls you when you're getting naked on a truck? This is Mark, this is what you've wanted for so long. You'll be gone in September and he'll never be the wiser.

"Mark?" Her voice came out on a breath but was like a shotgun blast in the heated silence between them. She regrouped and tried again. "Mark."

"Lis?" he whispered into her skin where her shoulder met her neck and she felt the tremors all through her body. But the moment was already gone. The stillness in his body reflected hers. He was wary and almost imperceptibly he began to lift his body away from her. And she knew it was over.

Great! Great! Now look what you've done!

"Ah...what are we doing?" she whispered over the clamoring voices in her head. She wanted to keep going and if it had been anybody else she would have kept going, but it was Mark and this was not something casual. This was not something that she could ignore when she met him over the breakfast table.

She loved him. She always had and if she did this and tried to pretend it wasn't something she had wanted forever it would be a big wound in her heart probably for the rest of her life.

She felt Mark smile against her neck and before he pushed himself off of her he kissed her neck one last time. Alyssa felt tears burn behind her eyelids. She had refused her entire life to cry over Mark Cook and she never had. She was tough, she had handled these feelings all her life, but at some point even tough girls fall apart.

Mark sat up against the windshield. He bent his legs, put his elbows on his knees and rested his head in his hands. He sat that way for a long time, breathing hard while Alyssa buttoned up her clothes and tried to figure out how to handle what happened.

Mark was offering nothing. He tilted his head back and rubbed his hands over his face and remained silent.

"Phew," she breathed, finally deciding that she was just going to have to laugh her way through this. Mark looked up at her, but didn't say anything, and Alyssa couldn't come close to meeting his eyes. Part of her reached out hungry hands toward hope that he might say something to make this right, that he might say that his feelings matched hers.

"Alyssa." His voice was quiet and her body clamored, *Come back!* "I'm so sorry."

Please don't be sorry. I'm not sorry. I love you and I'm not sorry. No, be anything but sorry!

"Nothing to be sorry about, Mark," she said, and felt her heart break into a million pieces. Alyssa closed her eyes and turned her back to Mark as she slid off the hood of the truck. She could feel his eyes on her back and so she turned with a smile that she hoped was believable and forced herself to look him in the eyes.

"I didn't mean to do this," he said, and his regret was horrible to see. Alyssa felt as though a knife was turning in her stomach.

"Well, me, neither," she said, and the laugh that escaped sounded hysterical so she cut it off.

"This doesn't change things," Mark said, clearly worried that she expected more. He hopped off the truck and stood next to Alyssa. So close that she wanted to put her head against his shoulder and cry. "We're still friends, right?"

"Of course, Mark," she told him even though she knew it was a lie.

"I don't..."

Love me, want me, need me to stay?

He reached out a hand and for a moment Alyssa thought that he was going to touch her and for a hysterical moment she didn't know what she would do if he did. She was barely keeping it together.

"I don't want things to change, Alyssa, between me and you."

"Of course not, Mark." She laughed again and she didn't care how it sounded. Here he was making real every nightmare she ever had. *Friend, just a friend. That's all you are, all you've ever been. Jeez, do you have to be hit in the head with a brick to get it?* she berated herself.

"Maybe it's best if we just forget it," she said, managing what she hoped was a nonchalant shrug.

Mark looked at her for a long time and finally nodded. "Let's just forget everything."

ALYSSA RESTED her forehead against the tiles of the shower. She had been in there since she and Mark returned from the lookout. She had managed to say good-night with a smile and had walked past all the Cooks who were sitting in the den and in the kitchen. She was even able to talk to them, telling Mac and Missy where Dirk was and that Guy had come back. She was able to joke with Billy about Guy's shiny pants. She had made it to the bathroom, gotten all of her clothes off and the shower on before the tears came.

Years of tears. More tears than she thought she would ever shed over Mark Cook. She felt sick. Sick of her own skin, her own life and excuses. Everything in her life had led up to this exact moment and she had no one to blame but herself.

Looking back on it without rose-colored glasses she figured there was a certain amount of inevitability to something sexual happening between them. They were two young healthy people, who because of her stupidity spent far too much time together.

Well, that's the first thing that will be changing, she told herself sternly, even as she cried more and more bitter tears. *No more meeting him at dawn for starters. He doesn't even need me there, I only go to spend time with him.*

But she knew that the dawn rounds were only the tip of what needed to be done.

And as she cried she tried to muster up some kind of energy for the rest of it.

I've got to get out of here, she told herself. She tilted her face up to the shower spray and washed away the unending tears. She had delayed this for too long. What was she thinking, wasting all of this time? *Did I really believe he was going to fall in love with me? That he was going to turn to me in August and say "don't go?"* Was she that naive and stupid?

Obviously.

"Well, no more," she said, and turned off the shower.

She had a professor at the university who had always told her that if she needed anything all she had to do was call, and Alyssa had never taken her up on it. Thinking about it now, she realized all the ways she had been ignoring her future, choosing in a million different ways to stay in the past.

It was time to make that call.

MARK RESTED HIS HEAD against Bojangles's side and swore.

"I am an ass," he whispered, and Bojangles turned his head and blew a giant raspberry in his ear as his two cents. "I know, I know." Mark rolled his head against his horse and wished more than anything that he could redo the past few hours of his life.

He had told her that he didn't want things to change between them, that he didn't want her to be mad at him for what he did. He didn't want her to think badly of him for losing control like that, but he could tell the second they got in the truck that already things were different. There was a coolness and distance where there hadn't been before.

What had he been thinking?

Well, obviously I wasn't. Or my brain wasn't. He had let himself react on the very last thing he should have been reacting to. Not only was Alyssa his very best friend, but she was like a part of his family. She trusted him and he had betrayed that by taking her clothes off on top of a truck.

She was right there with you, buddy. Don't blame yourself for everything, that little voice in his head noted pointedly.

Up until the moment she said his name with all of that doubt in her voice he was sure that everything was mutual.

That she had been as excited as he was. But then she had leaped off the truck and laughed and suggested that they forget everything.

How? How was that supposed to happen? Mark lifted his head and got back to combing and currying Bojangles. *Am I supposed to meet her at dawn in the barn and pretend nothing happened? Am I supposed to watch her flirt with Dirk and not remember the way her skin felt and the way her hair smelled?*

Mark wondered why she stopped. For whatever reason it wasn't because she didn't want him. The warmth and wetness of her body as he had slid his finger inside her haunted him. So she'd stopped for other reasons.

Mark was sorry, he truly was but as he thought about it, he didn't really know what he was sorry for. He had kissed her, sure, but she had undone his pants first and the way she had urged him on, pushing against his hips and arching into his mouth. *For crying out loud, she undid my pants first!* What was a guy supposed to think when a woman does that and then says forget it. Talk about mixed signals.

Alyssa wanted him as much as he wanted her. That much he knew. It was not a mistake, it was not an accident. At some point between Dirk's arrival at the ranch and last night, being friends with Alyssa was no longer enough for him and the last week had been building to just that moment on top of the truck. Mark was smart enough to know that. Maybe it had been longer, maybe this unrest had been building for years. Whatever the case, he knew being friends was no longer enough for him anymore, and he was beginning to wonder if maybe it wasn't enough for her, either, and maybe she just needed some help realizing it.

8

THE NEXT MORNING Alyssa didn't join Mark at dawn. He was surprised and very disappointed. He had spent all night practicing a speech. A rational, logical speech that talked about how they were friends and that they would always be friends, but that obviously, there was now something else between them.

Depending on how Alyssa took that part of the speech, he had another speech planned, pointing out all the numerous and spectacular reasons why they should be having sex.

Considering her absence at the barn, he filed the second speech for much later use.

He thought he would catch her in the kitchen before everyone came down for breakfast, but when he walked in he ran into his brothers and father staring at three boxes of cereal on the kitchen table.

"She didn't even make coffee," Billy was mumbling.

"What's going on?" Mark asked, concerned by his brother's behavior. "Is something wrong with Lis?"

"She left a note," Mac answered. "Says if we want breakfast we're going to have to pour cereal into a bowl and put some milk on it." Mac lifted baffled eyes to his middle son. "What does this mean?"

"Where is she?" Mark asked, slipping the note off the box of Wheaties.

"She went to Billings," Mac answered, picking up the box of raisin bran as if it might blow up.

"What?" Mark asked, suddenly panicked.

"She said something about job interviews," Mac elaborated.

"Uh-oh, Mark," Ethan said. "What did you do last night?"

"You?" Billy turned on his brother with sincere menace. "You're the reason there is no coffee?"

"Make it yourself," Mark said over his shoulder as he made his way back out to the barn with a burning in his gut. *You knew she was leaving,* that voice reminded him, *you've talked about it. Of course, she had job interviews. That makes sense, Mark.*

But it didn't, in fact it created havoc in him.

ALYSSA GOT BACK from Billings late that night. The interviews had gone well, considering that they were fairly last minute and informal. She had called one of her favorite professors who had set up the interviews as a favor.

Two of the clinics said that they were not currently hiring, but come fall they might need someone. A couple of the other clinics said that they would like to see her résumé and the animal hospital said that they would love to see her résumé and set up a second interview, whenever she was ready.

Ready? she thought, parking the truck and hopping out. *Am I ever.* She should have done this years ago, instead of getting lulled into being complacent with what was a ridiculous situation with Mark. Alyssa shook her head and opened the front door.

It was after midnight and most everyone was asleep, but she could hear someone moving around in the kitchen. She knew it was Mark. She knew because her heart was beating fast and her skin was warm and her stomach was in knots.

Get over it! she told herself furiously, and turned the

corner into the kitchen. Mark was standing at the sink, filling a teapot. Alyssa did not allow herself even the moment to look at him, to see him and appreciate the breadth of his shoulders and the strength of his legs.

"Hi, Mark," she said from the doorway, hoping to keep this conversation as short as possible.

"Lis," he said as he turned. He smiled at her and Alyssa hardened her heart further. "How was Billings?"

"Good." She leaned against the door frame and tried to do what she had known would be impossible. She tried to act casual, as though nothing had happened. As though she had never touched him, or kissed him. As though he hadn't taken her shirt off and kissed her breasts in the moonlight...

You're supposed to be forgetting, she admonished herself.

"The animal hospital has an opening right away." She looked down at her khaki pants, pretending to wipe something off them.

"I thought you weren't leaving until September?" Mark asked, his voice sharper than she expected.

"Don't worry, Mark, I won't leave without giving you guys plenty of notice," she said and smiled. "I told your mom that I would train whoever was going to replace me 'round here." She stood up straight and sighed. "Well, I'm beat. I won't be at the barn tomorrow morning, I'm exhausted." She waved at him and turned to go upstairs, thinking that that had gone better than expected.

IF MARK THOUGHT that he had had it bad before, it was nothing compared to what was killing him now. Not only did Alyssa not come to the barn, but for two days she had been going into town on one errand or another and not getting back until suppertime. If he walked into a room it always seemed as if she was walking out of it. The only time he ever saw her was at the dinner table with everybody else.

"Alyssa!" Mark shouted, catching her at the open door of her truck.

"Hi, Mark!" She turned and faced him, putting her hand to her forehead to shield her eyes from the setting sun. He could see her smile and felt his heart kick.

"You going into town? 'Cause I could use a ride."

"Oh, no, Mark. I'm just getting back. Dirk and I went to the grocery store." She jerked a thumb at the movie star, who Mark had not seen standing on the passenger side of the truck. "I should have asked if you needed something," she said, and Mark felt a well of frustration open up.

"That's all right, Lis."

She walked past him with another bright smile and Mark had nothing to do but watch Dirk and Alyssa grab bags and laugh as they made their way into the kitchen.

The night on top of the truck seemingly hadn't done anything to kill Alyssa's relationship with Dirk, and Mark was beginning to think that maybe the reason Alyssa stopped was because she had real feelings for Dirk. He wished he could get her alone a minute to talk to her, but the only person who got to spend any time with her alone was Dirk.

The jealousy burned bright in Mark, keeping him up nights imagining Alyssa allowing Dirk all the things she had denied him. And because he couldn't get Alyssa alone, Dirk was still cleaning tack and shoveling crap and Mark was still having heartburn.

ALYSSA WAS RUNNING OUT of excuses to avoid being at the ranch. People were beginning to catch on.

"How many résumés do you need to fax?" Missy asked

one morning when she had told everybody at the breakfast table that she was going back into town.

"Just one more," she said with a smile that she didn't feel. "The animal hospital wants to set up a second interview on Saturday."

"Alyssa." Missy looked up at her with wide eyes. "That's the Wild Man Rodeo."

"Well—" Alyssa shrugged "—I guess I'll have to miss it this year."

"But, Lis..." Billy looked at her with narrowed eyes. "You love the Wild Man Rodeo."

Alyssa swallowed hard and forced another smile. "It's time for me to move on. I can't stay here forever." She tried to make it sound as if it was what she wanted, what she needed, but she could tell by the concerned looks of everyone around the table that she wasn't doing as good a job as she thought. "I would think you guys would be a little happier to be rid of me." It was a lame attempt at a joke that did not go over well at all. Silently, Ethan and Cecelia looked into their mugs and shook their head while Billy made a face at her. Only Mark, standing by the counter, did not react.

"Never, sweetheart," Missy said firmly. Alyssa knew that the look of pain on her face was real. Mac and Missy would keep her here forever if they could, and it was surprising how much it hurt to be reminded of it right now, with Mark's silent presence behind her.

"Don't think it for a minute," Mac told her. "I still don't understand why you can't just stay here and open up a practice in Lincoln."

"Because I don't have any money to open up a practice." She gave them all a surprised look and crossed over to Mac and put her arms around his neck. "Besides, I don't even know if I could do it, that's a lot of work. Now stop acting like I'm killing you guys."

"I'll loan you the money," Mark said quietly. Alyssa looked up sharply and Mark was staring into his coffee cup. "I believe you could do it." He met her eyes and Alyssa had to ignore every pull in her body and heart.

"Mark, don't be silly," she said, and shook her head at him, feeling the strain of the act she was playing.

"I didn't think I was," he said as he put his mug in the sink and stood up straight. He walked out the door, taking Alyssa's heart with him.

WHY NOT? Why couldn't she just stay and work in Lincoln? We can get rid of Dirk, she can open up a practice in Lincoln and she and I can figure out this mess between us. It makes perfect sense, Mark thought furiously as he walked toward the barn. Listening to her talk about dates and times and leaving and moving on made his whole body feel as if it was being pulled apart. Nothing was as it should be and there was nothing he could do to fix it except stand around and watch it happen. Pointless, frustrated anger filled him.

"Good morning, Mark," Dirk said cheerily as Mark walked into the dim interior of the barn. "I thought I might go with you to check those fences or whatever it is you're going to do this morning."

"No," Mark said as he walked by him, flexing his hands against the urge he had to hit something, anything.

"Look—" Dirk took off behind him "—I've been real patient with you and I've cleaned every damn thing there is to clean around here..."

"You're not coming with me," Mark barked.

"Your family signed an agreement."

"If you're so tired of cleaning go back to basics with

Billy,'' Mark flung over his shoulder as he headed into the tack room.

''Is this about Alyssa?'' Dirk asked. Things inside Mark burst open and he whirled around and stomped back to where Dirk was standing.

''Is what about Alyssa?'' he asked dangerously.

''I think you're in a bad mood because of Alyssa.''

''I'm not in a bad mood,'' Mark snarled. He could feel an angry poison boiling up inside of him.

''Could have fooled me,'' Dirk challenged.

He got in close to the movie star and put his finger in his face. ''Butt out.''

''It's not my fault she's interested in me, and it's not my fault that you're jealous. So why don't you stop taking this shit out on me.'' Dirk put his hands up like an innocent man and since nothing could be less true Mark happily gave in to his anger and just hit him, square in the face.

''What the hell are you doing?'' Dirk shouted, holding a hand up to his face.

''I'm not jealous!'' Mark yelled, knowing he was lying.

''You are, too.'' With both hands, Dirk shoved Mark as hard as he could.

''Am not!'' Mark shoved him back while something in him shouted, *Yes, this is exactly what I want to do!*

Dirk took one second and then punched Mark in the nose.

ETHAN AND BILLY walked into the stables to find Mark and Dirk trading punches.

Ethan took a step to stop it, but Billy stopped him.

''They're pretending,'' Billy explained.

''Pretending to fight?''

''Yeah, it's called stage combat. Dirk taught me last week.'' Ethan and Billy watched for a moment while Mark charged at Dirk, butted him in the stomach, and got on top of him in the muck on the ground.

"Wow, Mark's really good," Billy commented.

Dirk threw a punch that connected and Mark began to bleed from the corner of his mouth.

"They're not pretending, you idiot!" Ethan ran over to the two men and pulled them apart.

"Knock it off!" Ethan said calmly, knocking Dirk back in the dirt while holding his brother down. "Stop acting like you're in high school."

"He started it!" Dirk scowled.

"Does this have anything to do with why there is no coffee around here?" Billy asked, still deeply wounded by Alyssa's breakfast betrayal two days ago.

"No," Dirk answered, using the back of his hand to wipe the blood from his lip. "It's about Alyssa."

"Man, Mark," Billy said, sympathetically. "You need to let this protective big-brother thing go. She's what, twenty-six now? Stop punching out her dates!"

"It's not like that," Mark said, tentatively touching the battered skin around his eye.

"Then why were you hitting me?" Dirk asked.

Mark looked at the faces of the men around him and it was Ethan's slightly pitying look that seemed to speak the loudest.

"I hit him because *she* likes *him,* not the other way around."

"Oh, brother." Billy turned and left the barn in disgust.

"If I leave, are you going to keep knocking each other around?" Ethan asked, eyeing the two bloody men. Mark and Dirk looked at each other and shook their heads. Ethan gave Mark one brotherly, conciliatory pat on the back and followed Billy, leaving Dirk and Mark to themselves.

"She doesn't, you know," Dirk said, pushing himself to

his feet with a grunt of pain. "Alyssa's plenty attracted to me but she doesn't *like me* like me. I think she thinks I'm ridiculous."

"Yeah?" Mark asked in the tone of one who wants details.

"Yeah," he agreed. Dirk reached a hand over to the man who was earlier trying to beat the snot out of him and helped him to his feet. "I think it was my cell phone."

Mark smiled and swore again as the cut on his lip split. "She's not real fond of those."

The two men made their way outside to a bench against the side of the barn. With grimaces and shared gasps of pain they sat to further probe their injuries.

"So," Dirk asked, "you in love with her?"

"Love?" Mark looked up at Dirk with all the panic he felt at being asked that question. "Let's go one step at a time here. I just know friendship isn't enough anymore," he answered truthfully.

"Is she going into town today?"

"She's faxing résumés," Mark answered, feeling his heart sink into his shoes. Behind them a truck started up and Alyssa was soon turning down the driveway toward town.

"Well," Dirk said, slapping his hand on Mark's shoulder. They both cringed. "You better figure this out."

"I've really blown it," Mark said, mostly to himself.

"Yeah?" Dirk asked.

"Yeah," Mark nodded. Mark was sliding into a deep silence that was a part of his deep confusion and soon to be a part of his deep depression.

"I can help you," Dirk said.

"How? By kissing her hand and taking her hair ribbons and taking her on dates?" Mark asked petulantly.

"Mark, I know a thing or two about women. I was voted

the sexiest man alive by three different women's magazines. Women send me pictures, their underwear, their hair. They get my name tattooed on parts of their body that have no business being tattooed."

"So?" Mark asked, completely unimpressed.

Dirk laid down his trump card. "And I have five sisters."

"Why do you want to help me with Alyssa?" Mark asked, suspicious.

"Mark," he said dryly, "I want to stop cleaning tack and get to the good stuff."

"This is blackmail," Mark said reasonably.

"Technically, it's extortion," Dirk corrected.

"I could hit you again," Mark said with no real heat.

Funny how it takes a few punches to really warm up to the guy, Mark thought.

"I could hit you back," Dirk replied with a similar lack of anger.

Mark just wanted a chance to find out where they were and if they could go someplace new. He wanted that chance with Alyssa.

"Okay, I'll teach you the good stuff and you can help me…" Mark didn't know how to finish that sentence.

"Seduce your best friend?" Dirk suggested.

"It's not like that," Mark protested.

"It's always like that," Dirk said, and put out his hand. Mark eyed the movie star warily and then took his hand in a firm grip and they shook on it. Mark had to reassess Dirk and guessed he was a pretty stand-up guy.

"Here's what we're going to do…" Dirk said, and leaned in conspiratorially.

THAT NIGHT Mark walked into the kitchen like a general taking the field.

Uh-oh, Dirk thought, and looked around at the family.

Obviously nobody else saw young General Patton walk in the door. *This is going to be good.* Dirk wished that Guy were there to see the fireworks.

He and Mark had worked on a plan but from the bulldog expression on the cowboy's face Dirk realized that all of the subtleties were going to go right out the window.

The man just doesn't understand nuance. Dirk shook his head sadly.

"Well, that date of yours is news all over town." Dirk realized that Cecelia was talking about him and he looked up to catch Alyssa looking at Mark out of the corner of her eye. "I went to the grocery store today and all anyone could talk about was how Alyssa had snagged a movie star."

"Well, it was a real nice date," Dirk said congenially, and when Alyssa turned and bent to put something in the refrigerator he saw Mark look with hot eyes at Alyssa's backside.

"Mrs. Meyers found out that Dirk Mason is in town," Ethan added. "She's your number-one fan."

Dirk snapped back into the conversation. "Number-one fan?" Dirk asked, suddenly terrified. That was a phrase to strike fear into the heart of any superstar—*number-one fan.* It insinuated any number of mental problems, restraining orders and made-for-TV movies.

"I think she has plans for you," Cecelia said, smiling, and Dirk felt his blood cool. "She wants you to judge the baked goods competition at the rodeo."

Dirk breathed a sigh of relief and looked around for something to eat.

Baked goods, these people are so damn quaint.

"Since when do rodeos have baked good competitions?" Dirk asked, putting some salad on his plate and covering it with ranch dressing. All of the hard work around the ranch had made him hungry. Although, Dirk was happy to admit that he had been hungry since the early nineties when he'd first met Guy.

Low-fat diets, he thought with a smirk, and put a little extra butter on his bread.

"Well, the rodeo has turned into a fair of sorts," Missy explained. "Quilting contests, livestock competitions, war reenactments. Three whole counties get involved. It's turned into quite a social event."

Sounds like death, Dirk thought, but smiled brightly at the Cooks who no doubt loved the fair. "How does one go about judging a baked goods competition?" Dirk asked.

"You sample all of the food and pick a winner," Mac explained eagerly. "It's a breeze."

"I can't judge cakes," Dirk said, helping himself to a wedge of lasagna the size of a small book. "I'm on a diet." *Guy will kill me.*

"Sure you can, boy," Mac assured him. He slapped his hand on Dirk's back. Dirk couldn't help but shoot the old cowboy a dubious look. "It's a real honor to be asked."

"Then you do it," Dirk said, pointing his fork at Mac.

"I have, son, I've been judging that thing for fifteen years." And he didn't look too happy about it, either.

Dirk shrugged and dug into his lasagna. He would do whatever these people required him to do. He had made that agreement with Guy, Mark and the devil. Whatever it took to get the Oscar he would do and if that meant judging angel food cake and brownies, then so be it.

There was a lull in the conversation and with a sixth sense for potential dramatics Dirk looked up just in time to see Mark address Alyssa.

Relax, partner, or you're going to blow it. This family could be uncanny at times when it came to matchmaking and if they sensed a scheme they'd be all over it in a minute.

"Alyssa," Mark said, "Queenie's puppies need to be looked at."

"Really?" Billy asked, looking at his brother before Alyssa could even respond. "They all look pretty good to me."

"Well, they're not," Mark said quickly, and gave his brother "the eye."

Dirk barely managed to suppress a groan. *Who gives "the eye" anymore?*

"Ethan?" Billy asked. Billy like the good snoop he was ignored "the eye" and turned to bring in the rest of the family, thereby giving Mark no place to hide. This family could smell a desperate young man in lust a million miles away. "Those puppies look good to you?"

Nice job, I couldn't have done that better myself, Dirk silently applauded.

"Yep," Ethan said. "Sleep in, Lis. Those puppies are all going to be kings."

"No!" Mark said loudly. Dirk subtlely coughed into his napkin and Mark regrouped. "I need her in the barn to look at the runt."

"Runt?" Billy asked.

"Yes, runt," Mark answered. "Lis?"

Dirk had carefully watched Alyssa's reaction while the brothers had argued among themselves and when she put on a smile and said, "Of course, Mark," he knew she didn't mean it.

Dirk rolled his eyes at his lasagna. *Baked goods, rodeos, star-crossed lovers, somebody should be making a movie out of this little drama,* he thought, and dug into his dinner.

9

THE NEXT MORNING, well before the time Alyssa would be joining him in the barn, Mark was trying to light a small wick on what Dirk had called a tea light. Mark wanted to call it a big fat waste of time.

"This is a big fat waste of time!" Mark told his ally, who was lighting a tea light of his own.

"Just wait, my friend," Dirk said, putting the tea light down on the dirt path that led from the house to the barn. There were a dozen lit candles behind them and a dozen more that led into the barn. Beside each candle was a lemon candy. "I don't expect a cowpoke like you to understand the finer points of romance, but this is a sure bet."

Mark had to admit that in the darkness the trail of tiny lights did look pretty cool coming down the front steps and across the lawn into the barn and he supposed that Alyssa would think the same. He hoped so.

"Now, remember," Dirk was saying as he bent to put down a light and pick up another. "All of this is wasted if you try to talk to her too much."

"I remember, I am supposed to 'interest her.'"

"Right. Step one to any good seduction is to leave her wondering and wanting a little more, so be aloof."

Considering Mark's usual demeanor was somewhere between reserved and distant he didn't think aloof would be much of a challenge.

"Gotcha," he agreed. "Now scram, before she comes out here."

Dirk turned to his friend, held out his hand for a firm serious shake, and wished Mark luck.

IF IT WEREN'T FOR the dogs Alyssa would have pulled the covers over her head and let the morning slide by. But there was breakfast to make and runts to look at and no time like the present to continue pretending that all was well with Alyssa Halloway.

What a mess, she thought glumly. Never in her life did she think that for her own self-preservation she would have to ignore Mark. For years she had been hiding her feelings so she could spend time with him and she had seriously believed that nothing could hurt more than keeping silent all the words in her heart. But she had been wrong.

This hurt so much more.

By the time she got up and dressed she had smacked her hip against the closet door and nailed her funny bone against the bedside table. Rubbing her sore elbow she finally stumbled over to her door and opened it. The predawn darkness of the hallway was broken by the glow of a dozen tiny candles that lit the path from her room, across the hallway and down the stairs. Taking a closer, amazed look, she saw that beside each candle was a lemon candy. The kind Mark handed her every morning before…when they were friends.

She gasped with surprise and pleasure and took an eager step out to see how far the magical path went. In between steps she leaned down to pick up the candies. By the time she got to the front door her hands were full, so she kicked open the front screened door and almost dropped her prizes.

The candles went down the steps and stretched across

the lawn in a curving line of flickering light. The candles stopped at the opened front door of the barn.

Mark.

In the dim trail of candlelight Alyssa's strong heart started to tremble.

Mark did this.

She took the steps down to the lawn and followed the glowing path her friend had laid out, shoving the candy in her pockets as she went.

The barn door was open and an electric lantern sat on the shelf above where Queenie was lying with her puppies in a soft heap of breathing fur.

Alyssa looked into the shadows for Mark but couldn't find him and that strong heart beating in her chest was disappointed. She looked back out at the candles and tried to find her anger and resolve. She was glad after a moment that he wasn't there, that he wasn't watching her with his stillness and quiet, his knowing blue eyes, because despite her resolved mind, her heart still trembled. She shoved the rest of her candies into the pockets of her pullover and ignored the ones that fell on the ground.

She turned back to the dogs and watched as the puppies one by one slowly woke and turned to find Queenie's nipples under the other sleeping dogs. There was some yelping and sleepy wrestling, but soon six of the dogs were sucking hungrily at their mother's belly. One puppy, which Queenie was trying to nose into waking, continued to sleep.

It seemed the runt of the litter was a bit lazy. He probably slept through mealtimes and by the time he got around to eating, Queenie was almost out of milk.

No wonder he wasn't growing.

Alyssa checked on the pups and Queenie and decided they all looked good, with the exception of the runt, whom she picked up when he started making soft mewling sounds.

She picked up the electric lantern with her other hand and turned to go back to the house and make breakfast.

Standing in the gently swaying shadows was Mark.

Startled, Alyssa yelped and dropped the lantern. Behind her there was a chorus of small chirps and half growls from the dogs.

"Sorry," Mark said. "I didn't mean to startle you."

"It's okay." She smiled nervously. "I didn't think you were here."

"I was here."

"Mark, did you do that—" she gestured toward the candle path "—with the candles?"

"Yep." He tucked a hand into his jean pocket and his denim jacket opened to reveal a dark blue flannel shirt. He tipped his hat back and his eyes gleamed silver in the light. His gaze was steady and sure, all the things Mark was and all the things she loved about him. She was warm and breathless, losing her way in all the weighted silence.

"Why?" she whispered past the lump in her throat.

"Didn't want you to get lost," he replied. He reached down, grabbed the lantern and handed it to her. With a gliding step backward he faded into the shadows and left her alone with her runt puppy and trembling heart.

"EXCELLENT!" Dirk said triumphantly after Mark had reported the details of their morning work. "She's hooked for sure."

"I don't know if I'd say hooked, but at least she was there," Mark hedged. He dumped the armful of burned out candles into the garbage bin in the tack room where they were meeting.

"What was she like when you were talking to her?" Dirk asked.

"Nervous..." Mark considered and the corner of his

mouth kicked up in a grin. "I don't know. Kind of sweet, I guess."

"In a word...hooked!" Dirk poked his finger at Mark's chest and smiled. In the face of all that confident enthusiasm Mark could only nod. As he had said, she was there and that was an improvement.

"So," Mark asked, "what's next?"

Dirk turned on his heel and began pacing the short distance between the workbench and the saddle post. "If step one is to interest her, then step two would have to be to attract her..." he said, pausing dramatically.

"What do you mean?" Mark asked, rising to the bait.

"Not so fast. You owe me one cowboy lesson."

Mark chuckled and clapped a friendly hand on his partner's back.

"You're right. A lesson for a lesson. Let's get you a horse."

"Excellent," Dirk said, thrilled to be let in on some real cowboy secrets. And Mark was surprised by how happy he was to be the one teaching him.

ALYSSA WAS CROUCHED on the floor of the kitchen with the runt, urging him silently to realize that he had to lap the milk in the bowl rather than try to suck, or sit in it, when Missy walked in.

"Is there some reason why my son was trying to burn down the barn with all of my tea lights?" she asked. "Are we landing planes in the front yard?"

"You'll have to ask him," Alyssa answered quickly. Frankly, she wanted to ask him herself. It was obvious that he had enlisted Dirk's help in this effort, but to what end?

Alyssa replayed every minute of the conversation she and Mark had after their near-sexual encounter the other night and she had his motives narrowed down to two, both of which were horrible.

Either he was making the most elaborate apology possible, which would be quite like Mark who didn't like to offend or hurt anybody's feelings, and perhaps enlisting the overly dramatic Dirk had changed the apology from a bouquet of flowers to the thing with the candles.

Because there was no way Mark had come up with that on his own.

The other option was that Mark wanted to have sex with her.

Duh.

But by saying that he didn't want anything to change between them, he was probably trying to clear the way for some kind of friends-with-benefits situation. They could fool around for a few months and then walk away friends.

And no matter how badly her hormones clamored for her to run outside, find Mark and jump him, she couldn't do it. She couldn't imagine doing it.

That's a lie.

Well, what she couldn't imagine was going on with her life afterward as if they were just friends. So, Alyssa spent the past hour deciding she was just going to have to stay the course. She was going to talk to him as little as possible, try very, very hard not to think of him or the events of the other night and she was going to get away from the Morning Glory as quick as possible.

It was the only way.

Missy stepped around Alyssa and the puppy that kept lifting a tentative paw to tap at the milk in the dish in front of him. His new nose could smell food, but he couldn't figure out how to get at it.

"Use your tongue," Alyssa told the dog. She pantomimed licking the milk. The dog watched impassively then lifted his milk-soaked paw and patted her cheek.

"Another runt?" Missy asked, pouring herself a cup of coffee leftover from breakfast.

"Yep. Do we still have that baby bottle around here?" Alyssa asked.

"You'll have to ask Mark. He used it for that runt goat last year."

Alyssa nodded and went back to the breakfast dishes she was finishing, all the while avoiding Missy's eyes.

"Look, sweetheart, we've been real patient with all of the nonsense going on around here, but I need some answers. Now, I've been able to read the writing on the wall for a long time and if you love Mark, why are you leaving?" Missy asked.

Alyssa nudged the runt with her toe and rinsed a few dishes before answering. "Because he doesn't love me," she finally said quietly into her sink of bubbles.

"What about Dirk?" Missy asked.

Alyssa looked up, confused. "What about him?"

"Well, honey, don't you think he should know. About you and Mark?" Missy waved a hand toward the window and the land outside. "He's been following you around here like a puppy, you should tell him how you feel."

Ouch. Alyssa in all of her planning and scheming had not once thought about the movie star's feelings. "You're right," she said, and felt just awful.

"Look, sweetheart..." Missy walked over and put an arm around Alyssa's shoulders and Alyssa gave in to the comfort that Missy provided. She turned and wrapped her arms around her thick waist and rested her chin on Missy's shoulder. "Something was bound to happen sooner or later between you and Mark," Missy said soothingly. "You've been growing those feelings for a long time. My boy may be slow but he's not dumb."

"Yes, he is," Alyssa mumbled childishly. "Oh, watch it, dog!" Too late, Alyssa reached down to pull the dog from out of the bowl, patted him dry with the towel over her shoulder and let the pup try it again.

Alyssa turned to Missy, ready to put an end to the conversation, but the understanding in the older woman's eyes stopped her.

"When I was little you used to tell me that what was going on in my family wasn't my fault. Remember?" Alyssa asked, and Missy nodded. Alyssa had countless memories of Missy trying to drive home that message when Alyssa seemed to falter under the weight and pain her family put on her thin shoulders.

"Remember the night my dad locked me out?"

Again, Missy nodded. It was before Alyssa had started spending the night at the Morning Glory. She'd been twelve and Mark must have been fifteen. Until that night Mark had walked Alyssa home just as it was starting to get dark after dinner. The two friends had walked along the property line between the two ranches, talking about animals and falling stars and why brown pop tasted better than clear pop. Mark had never treated her as if she was younger. Maybe it was because she'd seemed so much more mature than other girls her age, but they'd always seemed to be able to talk about things as equals. It was just another thing that her heart weaved into the ongoing infatuation she had with Mark.

They'd say good-night and Alyssa would walk up the porch steps to her house while Mark stood in the shadows waiting to make sure she got in okay. But that night the door was locked. Alyssa knocked and rang the doorbell and kicked at the door, but no one came. Unable to stand it,

Mark had climbed the steps, put his arm around his hysterical friend, and led her back to his house.

Missy and Mac had been sitting at the kitchen table when a worried Mark and hollow-eyed Alyssa reappeared. Alyssa had taken one look at Missy, who was more of a mother to her than her own scared mother could ever be, and flung herself into her open arms.

"You are loved here," Missy had said reassuringly over and over into the little girl's ear. "You deserve to be loved and you are loved here."

Now, standing in the same kitchen Alyssa repeated the words.

"I deserve to be loved," she said, and Missy nodded in firm agreement.

"Yes, you do."

SEVERAL HOURS LATER Alyssa found Dirk in the stalls, combing a horse.

"Hi, Dirk," she said softly, stepping from the shadows into the pool of light from the low-wattage light bulb above their heads.

"Hi, Lis." Dirk smiled at her and then looked back at his horse.

"Look…uh, Dirk?" Alyssa simply had no idea how to dump a movie star. But after that talk with Missy she couldn't keep leading him on the way she had, but it didn't make breaking up with Dirk Mason any easier.

"What, Lis?" Dirk looked concerned and Alyssa realized she was strangling a rope that was slung over the stall door. "What's wrong, sweetheart?"

The endearment galvanized her. "Dirk, I'm so sorry, this just isn't going to work out," she said in a rush.

"What's not going to work out?" Dirk asked, and Alyssa cursed the obtuse movie star.

"This—" she waved a hand between them "—you and me, it just won't work out."

To her surprise Dirk tilted his head back and howled with laughter.

"I don't think this is very funny," she said after several frankly baffling moments while Dirk slapped his knees and cackled.

"I know," he finally said, wiping his eyes.

"You know?" Alyssa wasn't hurt, but she was getting the creepy suspicion that something was going on that she didn't know about.

"Lis..." Dirk took the three steps between them and dropped his voice to a whisper. "I'm gay."

"Gay?" she squealed, and Dirk covered her mouth with his hand.

"People still get stoned for that around here, don't they?" he asked, peering into the shadows.

"You're gay?" she whispered again.

"As a bird." Dirk watched her absorb his news and waited for her to put two and two together.

"Guy?" she whispered fiercely as everything suddenly clicked into focus. She put her hand to her face when she realized that Dirk didn't sleep on the fold-out couch in the penthouse at the Bit and Bridle Motor Lodge. And here she had been worrying that he would be uncomfortable.

"We've been together ten years," Dirk said softly. He tilted his head and for the first time in all the time they had spent together she got the feeling that she was seeing Dirk Mason for who he was. "You'll keep that secret, won't you?"

"Of course," Alyssa said quickly. "But, what if I had been in love with you? Were you just playing a game..."

Dirk took her shoulders in his hands and gave her one quick shake. "Honey, I knew the score between you and

Mark the second I drove up the driveway..." Alyssa started to deny it, but Dirk gave her another shake. "I don't think you're ever going to love another man," he said, and Alyssa's mouth tightened to a thin line.

"You're wrong," Alyssa said firmly. "Look, as long as I'm keeping this a secret would you mind if we kept pretending to...well, be interested in each other?"

Dirk looked at her carefully and then smiled mischievously. "I wish Guy were here to see this," he said. "Of course, of course I'll continue to be the most charming movie star in the area, and you continue fawning over me and we'll drive Mark crazy."

He slung his arm over her shoulder, flipped off the light, and together they walked out of the stall.

"I was not fawning," Alyssa denied primly.

"Oh, honey, I've seen a lot of fawning but I've never had a woman make tofu for me in Montana. You are the new Queen of Fawning," he said it in such a pleasant, friendly, exaggerated way that Alyssa couldn't be upset.

"You did your own share of fawning, mister." She jabbed his side with an elbow. "My hand has never been kissed so many times!"

They walked toward the house laughing and whispering, and Mark, who was coming around the house, saw them and, indeed, felt as though he was going a little crazy.

10

"DIRK, THIS ISN'T GOING to work," Mark said out of the corner of his mouth. Dirk was limping beside him, holding an ice pack to his butt.

"Mark, my ass hurts. I'm in no mood to argue." Dirk was covered in filth from his advanced riding lesson with Mark and was pushing, pulling and kicking the wood chopping block from where it usually sat at the back of the house to the front of the house. He shoved it into a strategic location right in front of the kitchen window.

Right smack-dab in Alyssa's view should she look up.

"We don't need wood chopped," Mark argued. He was slowly beginning to realize what Dirk was attempting to do here. "Everyone's going to know this was planned."

Dirk stopped and looked at Mark and in a tone that brooked no argument, told him, "I don't care!"

Mark dropped the wheelbarrow, stood straight and decided that if Dirk was about to try to force him to be a laughingstock he was going to get to the bottom of what was really bothering him. "I thought you were going to back off her."

"What are you talking about?" Dirk asked, adjusting the ice pack to his other cheek.

"Last night you and Alyssa sure looked cozy. Maybe I don't need your help with this. You seem to be more trouble than you're worth." Mark crossed his arms over his chest and glared at the movie star who was supposed to be helping him.

''Right, and that whole candle thing was your idea?'' Dirk returned sarcastically.

''No, but...''

''Mark, we both know that if left to your own devices she'll never talk to you.''

''Well, if you're so smart, how am I supposed to attract her if everyone is laughing at me?''

''Mark, I have no doubt that you are a great cowboy,'' Dirk reasoned. ''You're probably the best around. But I am the heartthrob. In fact I would bet a million dollars that I am the best heartthrob around.'' He stopped to give Mark a chance to argue, but Mark had nothing to say. ''If there is one thing I have learned in my career as a heartthrob it is that attraction is fifty percent surprise and fifty percent lighting, and both of those things are in the front yard!''

The afternoon sunlight was mellowing and everything from the mountains to Mark was soon going to look as if it was gilded. Dirk had already explained to great lengths that in his first movie, *Hideaway,* he was filmed chopping wood in light just like this and he was sure that scene set him on the path to becoming a heartthrob.

''Now...'' Dirk adjusted the stump and took a quick glance up to the kitchen window. Sure enough, Alyssa was busy at the sink. He measured the sun for a moment, clapped his hands together, and finally looked at Mark. ''Take off your shirt.''

''Forget it.'' Mark threw up his hands. A man had to draw the line somewhere and partial nudity while chopping wood was where his line was being drawn. No matter what they did in movies chopping wood without a shirt would only end in splinters. Mark had his limits and this was it. ''I'll chop wood, but I'm not taking off my shirt.''

Dirk looked at Mark and then shrugged as if to say, *Have it your way,* and walked away.

Happy with his surprising victory Mark took a furtive glance around, hoping Billy and Ethan were far, far away. He picked up the first log from the wheelbarrow, tugged on the gloves from his back pocket, and picked up the ax. He suddenly realized Dirk never said he was going to back off from Alyssa.

He brought the ax down in the center of the wood and it split cleanly in two. He put up another log.

He wasn't about to compete with a movie star for Alyssa's time or affection.

He swung the ax and split the wood and repeated the process. As soon as Dirk came back he was going to make him promise to lay off the whole I'm-a-handsome-movie-star seduction routine.

Cutting wood was hard, but he liked it. Always had. The stretch and pull of his muscles, the cling and give of the wood under the ax; soon he had established his rhythm.

Mark's head whipped around at the sound of approaching footsteps.

Oh, God, he thought. *Not them, not now.*

He looked around for a place to hide, but there was nowhere to go.

"Hey, Mark," Billy shouted when he and Ethan got a little closer, "whatcha doing?"

Mark closed his eyes and swore. Maybe if he ignored them, they would ignore him right back. So, Mark went back to chopping wood as if his brothers weren't right behind him laughing.

"He must be sick," Mark heard Ethan say to Billy.

"Sick in the head," Billy muttered. "Mark!" he shouted, and Mark swung his ax a little harder. "What are you doing?'' he called, enunciating every word as if Mark might not understand English.

''What does it look like, Billy?'' he said from between clenched teeth.

''It looks like you're chopping wood, but something's weird about this, isn't it, Eth?'' Billy asked, pretending to be confused. Although Mark kept his back to them, he could just see them scratching their heads and looking baffled. For the millionth time in his life Mark wished he had been born an only child.

''Well, I know there's plenty of wood under the back porch...'' Ethan answered.

''That's right, Ethan. And don't we chop wood in the backyard?''

''As long as I've been chopping wood around here we have.''

''Yep, I guess that's why this situation is a little weird,'' Billy concluded.

Mark turned to glare at his siblings and they gave him angelic grins.

''Could you please leave?'' he asked. Alyssa was looking out the window and the sun was setting and for the first and probably only time in his life, Mark was very worried about chopping wood in the right light.

''No way, Mark,'' Billy answered gravely. ''You're acting strange. I think we should keep an eye on you. For support.''

''You might want to bring all the cows to the front yard or something,'' Ethan added.

Mark turned his back to the brothers he was determined to ignore.

''Where's Alyssa?'' Billy asked in false innocence.

''I'm right here.'' Alyssa leaned over the railing of the

porch to look down on the collection of Cook brothers. "What's going on out here?"

Mark looked up and felt as if he had been punched in the gut. He sucked in his breath. It was that damn light. Alyssa looked…amazing. Everything about her was golden and sunny, her green eyes sparkled and flashed in a way he had never seen before. He had never noticed the red buried deep in her hair, but as it fell over her shoulder and the sun touched it, he could see a million shades of auburn when he had always thought it was just plain brown. She would hate it if she knew, but in the light all of her freckles stood out on her face and Mark loved every single one of them.

Her skin was smooth and the light made it look like silk. For a moment Mark wanted to forget his brothers and run his fingers over that skin.

"I don't know what's going on," Billy answered. "You'll have to ask Mark."

"I'm chopping wood!" Mark answered tersely, shaking off his wonder over Alyssa's skin.

"Don't we have plenty?" Alyssa asked.

"Yes. Yes, we do, Alyssa," Ethan answered. "Which brings us back to the question, what is going on?"

"Well, you'll have to figure it out on your own. I have better things to do," she said with a prissy kind of tilt to her nose, which only made Mark want to tackle her to the ground and kiss it right off her face. Before he completely forgot his reason and threw down his ax to do just that, she went inside.

Mark swung the ax back; picturing his brother's faces on the log in front of him when something soft and wet hit him right between the shoulder blades. He whirled to see Dirk with an evil look in his eyes and his gloved hands filled with steaming horse manure.

"Take off your shirt!" Dirk hissed.

"Are you crazy?" Mark asked incredulously, and Dirk let fly with another handful of crap, hitting Mark square in the chest.

"I mucked crap for a week!" Dirk growled. "I did every stupid, petty disgusting thing you said, now a lesson for a damn lesson—lose the shirt!"

"I'm not taking off my shirt," Mark growled back.

Dirk hurled the last of his missiles. This time Mark's collar and neck were splattered.

Billy and Ethan doubled over with laughter. Mark made no move to remove his shirt and Dirk, a desperate and angry movie star, put up his fists.

"What is going on out here?" Missy shouted as she came around the side of the porch where she had been working in the garden. "Mark! What in heaven's name is all over your shirt?"

"Dirk's been throwing stuff at him." Ethan tattled, laughing so hard tears streamed down his face.

"Well, that's just great. My son and a movie star throwing punches in the front yard. We might as well bring all the cows into the kitchen." Missy marched up to her middle son, who was usually so reasonable. "Give me your shirt! You're filthy!"

Mark's eyes widened in disbelief. He and his brothers walked around filthy every day of their lives and she had never demanded their clothes.

"But, Mom..."

"Mark!" she said sharply. Mark began to unbutton his shirt. Over his mother's shoulder, Dirk smirked triumphantly.

"And you!" Missy turned on Dirk and his smirk vanished. "Is that what they teach you in Hollywood, to throw things?"

"No, ma'am," Dirk said quickly.

Missy sent Dirk a knowing smile as she took Mark's soiled shirt, and Mark caught the sly, conspiratorial wink they shared as Alyssa skipped down the porch steps. He'd been had.

ALYSSA TURNED TO THE BOYS with a mighty effort to appear casual but at the sight of Mark without his shirt, the smile on her face froze.

While Billy and Ethan were throwing their shirts off at every opportunity, Mark never walked around the ranch without a shirt and Alyssa could safely say that she had not seen the man's bare chest since he was about twelve.

Oh, the difference the years had made.

Every muscle was lean and firm and visible beneath the pale smoothness of his skin. From his broad chest to the ropy muscles across his shoulders and down his arm to the thin muscles standing out in ridges across his stomach, Mark had no hair to hide or distract from the perfection of his body. She blinked and the light seemed to change to a strange perfect glow that turned his skin to gold.

Alyssa had wasted all that time thinking about Dirk Mason's body, when this, *this* was underneath Mark's worn work shirts. She had felt it the other night, caught glimpses of it in the moonlight and in the shadows beneath the shirt she had partially ripped off of him, but this...this was something else.

His skin was smooth and the light made it look like silk. For a moment she wanted to forget the crowd and her resolve and run her fingers over that skin.

"Where's your shirt?" she asked; the breathless quality was something she could not control and it made her mad. So much was happening lately that she could not control and the sweet familiar sight of her best friend's face was becoming painful. Her bright, partially artificial good mood was being threatened, so she put her chin up, cleared her throat, and pretended the sight of Mark's chest didn't make the mysterious coils of affection and desire buried deep in her body turn a notch tighter.

"Never mind. Dirk, want to go for a walk?" She smiled at him and she heard Mark suck in a breath.

"I'd love to, let me get cleaned up," he said.

"I'll meet you in the kitchen in ten minutes," she said, and headed back in the house.

Mark whirled on his heel and headed for the barn. His brothers followed at a safe distance, leaving Dirk and Missy in the front yard.

"Well, Dirk," Missy said, "I don't approve of your methods, but you were right about that light." Dirk's jaw dropped and Missy put Mark's dirty shirt in his hands and began to lead him toward the house. "Now, I'll give you a little lesson on using the washing machine."

ALYSSA AMBUSHED Dirk when he came in to meet her for their walk.

"Jerk!" she shouted and threw a biscuit at him. Despite being light and fluffy and filled with weightless fat grams, Alyssa hoped it hurt a little bit when it hit Dirk in the ear.

"Hey, Lis," Dirk said, putting up his arms in defense. But she was crafty and was able to get three more solid lands against his nose and eye. "Come on, knock it off."

"You two-timer!" she stormed, and Dirk looked up in amused astonishment. She took that opportunity to pelt him with a wet washcloth.

"What are you talking about?" he asked. He tried to duck the wet cloth but it smacked him on the top of the head.

Alyssa looked around for something else to throw at him. "You're supposed to be helping *me,* not him!"

"Honey..." He raised his hands in supplication and took a step toward her but she lifted her spatula high and he stopped.

"Don't think for a minute that I think Mark came up with the candles and chopping-wood-in-the-front-yard bits by himself." Alyssa was spitting in her anger. Mark was bad enough, but he had somehow enlisted the help of Dirk and her will was not strong enough to withstand the cowboy she loved and a Hollywood heartthrob.

I'm not made of stone, for crying out loud.

"You aren't helping me, you're setting me up!"

"I *am* helping. I just don't think you really understand what you want help with."

"Of course I do!" she exclaimed and lifted her spatula again. "I wanted you to help me keep Mark at a distance."

For a second Dirk only looked at her as if he was mulling something over.

"Is there something in the air up here that makes everyone so blind?" he asked sincerely. "The water makes you all stupid?"

"Who are you calling stupid?" Alyssa demanded.

"You and Mark, two of the stupidest smart people I know." He put one hand on her shoulder, pulled the spatula out of her hand and looked at her sadly. "I'm out," he said.

"What?" Alyssa gasped. They had an agreement, he couldn't be out. She needed him!

"I'm done. You're going to have to keep him away on your own. I'm in over my head with the two of you. I'm supposed to be learning how to be cowboy and getting ready for some kind of rodeo, not playing Dear Abby."

"But, Dirk," she protested weakly, feeling all her

strength and resolve vanish. How was she possibly going to keep Mark away without Dirk?

"Sorry, sweetheart," he said. He pressed a kiss to her forehead, grabbed some sausage on the platter by her hip and walked back out to the barn.

Alyssa slumped against the sink, realizing she had just been dumped.

She had been dumped when she needed support most. She was weakening. Every glance Mark sent her way, heated and knowing, made her remember and want and need. She shouldn't be remembering, wanting and needing. She should be planning and leaving and forgetting.

Most of all she shouldn't be missing him. And she was, she was missing him so much her heart hurt. She felt a little lost and incomplete without Mark's friendship. She wanted to forget the whole sordid mess and go back to silently, secretly loving him.

It would just be easier that way than feeling like fool. She could so easily be a part of this seduction, but as her better sense warned her, he didn't mean this the way she did and she didn't have what it would take to pick up the pieces after they were done. She only had so much pride and it had to last her whole life. Swallowing it now wouldn't do her any good down the road.

If nothing else, she had her pride, which is how she was beginning to feel.

11

TWO DAYS LATER Alyssa was working at the kitchen sink watching Dirk say goodbye to Ruth Meyers—his number-one fan. Ruth had been up to the ranch five times in the past two days and each time Dirk agreed to be just a little more involved in the rodeo. She had already roped him into being grand marshal of the parade, livestock judge and he agreed to sign autographs after the rodeo at the women's auxiliary tent. Dirk had declined the kissing booth idea but he was going to show up to Ruth's grandson's sixth birthday party. Ruth drove away and Alyssa wondered what Dirk had been roped into now.

Not that Alyssa had much time to worry about it. The rodeo was two days away and she was busy putting together some things for the junior high bake sale, the junior women's league raffle and, the thorn in Alyssa's side, the Wild Man box lunch.

"What are you up to, Lis?" Cecelia asked as she walked in the door to the kitchen.

"Box lunch," Alyssa said glumly and Cecelia laughed.

"I thought you were having that interview and wouldn't be at the rodeo."

"I do." Alyssa looked up at Cecelia. "I thought I had figured out a foolproof plan so that I didn't have to be involved, but Missy suckered me into it again. I'm making the lunch and whoever buys it is going to have to enjoy it by themselves."

"Barbaric custom," Cecelia said, and patted Alyssa on the shoulder as she helped herself to one of the cookies she was making.

"You're telling me," Alyssa said. "Be glad you're married and exempt from it."

"At least you won't have to eat with the Groames boy again," Cecelia said. The Matt Groames situation had become a joke with everyone at the ranch.

For two years straight the oldest Groames boy had bid on her lunch and while exclaiming over her ham sandwiches had tried to kiss her. He was nineteen and nearly blinded by hormones and Alyssa was glad there wouldn't be a repeat this year.

"If you were married you could kiss the Groames boy goodbye," Cecelia said, turning and resting against the counter so she could look Alyssa in the face.

"That might be a bit drastic." Alyssa laughed.

"I don't know." Cecelia shrugged. "You've got two men around here running circles for your attention."

Alyssa looked up startled.

"Come on, you think we wouldn't notice?" Cecelia's eyebrow went up.

"I didn't think I was that obvious," Alyssa said quietly, and bent back to the cookies she was bagging up.

"It's not you as much as it is Mark. The guy is acting like a man possessed. Didn't he bring you those?" Cecelia pointed to the small bouquet of Indian paintbrush Mark had brought her this morning and Alyssa felt the strong bite of tears. Alyssa hoped Cecelia might get the hint if she just stayed silent. But Cecelia was a social worker, silence was not an issue. "So, what are you going to do about it?"

"About Mark?" Alyssa looked up. "Nothing," she said firmly, far more firmly than she felt. "I'm leaving."

"Really?" Cecelia looked surprised and somehow that made things hurt a little more.

"Of course, really. It's been my plan forever." Alyssa was bagging cookies with increasing violence.

"But you've loved him for so long," Cecelia said quietly, and Alyssa felt so crushed she couldn't say anything. "He's a man, Alyssa. You've got to give him time." Cecelia put her arm around Alyssa and again Alyssa was rocked by sadness.

"I don't have any more time to give him, Cecelia. And I can't handle a casual relationship with him. It would kill me." Alyssa shook her head, if he didn't love her now after twenty years why in the world would he love her later?

"Sweetheart, I wish I had an answer for you..."

"I've got my own and I'm going to have this second interview and that will be the end of it," she said resolutely.

After several silent moments Cecelia finally got the hint and left.

THE NEXT DAY Dirk smacked his forehead on a fence post and Mark had to go into the kitchen in the middle of the day to get some first-aid equipment. Alyssa was there, packing food into large Tupperware containers and sliding it into a duffel bag where there were already some basic vet supplies. He had seen her do this a million times in the past. She was packing up food and supplies for her family.

"You're going to visit your parents?" Mark asked from behind her.

Alyssa jumped half out of her skin. "Yes, jeez, Mark don't sneak up on a person like that!"

"Were you going to tell me?" Mark asked, wounded more by her failure to tell him about visiting her parents than all of her silence.

"No, Mark. I figured you'd be busy with Dirk."

''I don't know how you can think that,'' Mark said, hurt. ''I'll take you after dinner.''

''I don't...'' Mark's light blue eyes blazed and Alyssa suddenly fell silent.

''You know I hate it when you go up there alone,'' he said plaintively, willing her to remember, through all the recent problems, who he was. Or who he thought he was, anyway.

''I know,'' she finally said, and Mark felt relieved. ''After dinner,'' she agreed, and Mark nodded.

''What the hell does a man have to do around here to get a Band-Aid!'' Dirk stood outside the kitchen window with blood trickling out of a gash in his forehead. ''I'm bleeding to death!''

''Coming!'' Mark shouted, grabbed the first-aid kit and ran out the door with Alyssa on his heels.

''AN EVENING under the stars and you're taking something called Goo Goo Clusters?'' Dirk asked Mark as he was loading up his truck. He was prepared to pull out all the stops with Alyssa tonight. Something in him said it might be his last shot.

''Well, it just so happens Alyssa loves Goo Goo Clusters. The Goo Goo Clusters are a sure thing,'' Mark said, trying to feel confident.

''Well, at least you remembered the wine,'' Dirk said snidely.

''I still think it seems sneaky,'' Mark said, stowing the white zinfandel he filched from the back of the fridge in the cooler in the back seat.

''Of course it's sneaky. But it works every time.'' Dirk crossed his arms over his chest and leaned against the truck. ''Wine and seduction go hand in hand.''

Mark chafed at Dirk's words. He made it seem so much

less than it was, as though Alyssa was just a girl he was trying to pick up. Something had changed about this whole plan over the last few days. It became less and less about getting Alyssa to sleep with him and more about missing his friend. Somehow what he wanted out of this had changed. He didn't care so much anymore about making love to Alyssa, what he cared about was having her back by his side and the affection back in her eyes.

He missed her.

"Mark." Dirk put his hand on Mark's arm and Mark looked up, surprised by the compassion he saw there. "Maybe you should just tell her how you feel?" Dirk arched an eyebrow at Mark and then turned and left when Alyssa came down the porch steps toward them.

"You ready, Mark?" she asked, tilting her head to the side.

"I'm ready," he answered. *Ready as I'll ever be.*

ALYSSA TRIED not to look at Mark out of the corner of her eye. She tried for a little while to pretend he wasn't there, but it was impossible. The tension between them filled the truck and weighted the silence until Alyssa thought she might scream.

Mark always took Alyssa to her parents' house. He never went in with her or got involved in any way, which is the way she wanted it.

It's just enough to know he's there, she thought, staring at the window as the sun set behind the mountains, pink and orange.

"Pretty sunset," Mark said, his deep voice soothing her entire body, and she shut her eyes for a second against the pleasure.

"Yep," she agreed and kept her eyes glued to the sky.

Countless times Mark would sit in the truck and wait for

her to check on her dad's animals to make sure that they had enough food and that her mom was taking her medicine. When she came back to the truck feeling miserable, he would drive up to the clearing at the top of the mountain and let her talk it out or not say anything at all.

Whatever she needed.

Tonight, Alyssa had thought that Mark's familiar presence would be comforting, but it wasn't. It was tearing her heart apart. She had relied on him for so many things, even this. She felt weakened by him, by this need and longing she felt for him, rather than made stronger. And when it came to her family she didn't need to feel any weaker.

Mark stopped in the small driveway in front of their humble two-story house and Alyssa started to get out, taking the small duffel bag of medicine and food for her parents and their animals.

Mark grabbed her hand and squeezed it before she went in. Alyssa didn't want to look up, she wanted to steel herself against the understanding she would see in his eyes. The friendship. But in the end she couldn't help it and what she saw in his eyes made her breathless with longing and grief.

''I'll be right here,'' he said softly.

Alyssa nodded, for whatever reason unable to speak. She slung the duffel bag over her shoulder and took the long walk from his truck to the front door.

The door to her parents' house was unlocked. Alyssa knocked once and then walked in, calling softly for her parents.

''Alyssa? Is that you?'' Her mother's soft voice with the drawl she never lost seemed to come from the kitchen so Alyssa followed it to the back of the house. She looked around, amazed. The house was clean. Spotless. Everything that could shine did. Everything that could be pressed was.

Which was strange. Normally the house was covered in an inch of dust and three feet of clutter. She would swear that her parents never cleaned up and that Alyssa did it all for them on her monthly visits. Alyssa started getting a strange feeling at the back of her neck. *Something's happened.* She knew it. Things that never changed were suddenly different. She walked a bit faster into the kitchen and again stopped in her tracks in surprise.

Alyssa's mother, Liza, was finishing up the dinner dishes at the sink. When Alyssa walked in, Liza looked up with a wan smile on her face. Her mother's wan smile was the same, the tired look in her eyes and the rounded curve of her shoulders, but that she was actually up. She was and had been doing things around the house. Alyssa couldn't guess what this meant.

"Hi, sweetie," she said, going back to her sink of sudsy water. "I don't know where your dad is."

"That's okay, Mom." Alyssa slowly bent and kissed the fragile paper skin stretched across Liza's cheekbones. "How are you feeling?"

"Wonderful." Liza smiled again. "I'm feeling much better these days, sweetie."

"Really?" Alyssa asked, surprised. It had been years since Liza had said she was "wonderful."

"Really. It's this new medication. Doesn't make me tired like the other stuff."

"Have you eaten?" Alyssa put her bags on the table and dug out some of the food she brought. A Tupperware container filled with roasted chicken, a tin of cookies, and a loaf of bread she had baked that morning. Looking at the kitchen and what was left of their dinner she realized that her family didn't need what she had brought. "I guess so," she mumbled and put the food in the fridge.

Things were different, and it was making Alyssa nervous.

''What's going on here, Mom?'' Alyssa asked, picking up a towel to dry the dishes that were propped up in the drying rack.

''Nothing, Alyssa. I'm just on new blood pressure medicine. It's making a world of difference, that's all.'' Liza turned from her sink and propped her hip on the counter. ''What's going on with you?''

Alyssa was taken aback. She felt as though she had wandered into the wrong house, or someone had replaced her normally fragile and meek mother with some kind of alien. She looked at her mother quizzically.

''Nothing,'' Alyssa answered carefully.

''That's not what I've heard.'' Alyssa couldn't be sure as it hadn't happened in years but she thought that her mother was teasing her.

''Mom, you don't ever hear anything,'' Alyssa said, smiling.

''I went to church this weekend and all anyone could talk about was how you were dating a movie star.'' Alyssa looked at her mother with a blank face. ''That's not nothing. But I thought you were carrying a torch for that middle Cook boy?''

''Where is my real mother?'' Alyssa asked, absolutely amazed at her mother's transformation. ''Where did Liza Halloway go, because you aren't her.''

''Hello, Alyssa.'' Her father walked in the back door and Alyssa whirled to face him.

''Hi, Dad,'' she said, her voice careful. The bright fluorescent light of the kitchen put deep creases in his face, pockets of age and indicators of his weariness. Alyssa shared his strong chin and green eyes.

He walked to the sink to wash his hands and both she

and her mother got out of the way, but not until Liza smiled at her husband and put a hand to his shoulder. He smiled back weakly and turned toward the sink.

Alyssa sat heavily in one of the kitchen chairs.

What is going on? Alyssa thought as she watched her dad at the sink. His shoulders were bent and rounded under his worn work shirt. Alyssa realized what a small man he was, short and wiry. He was barely taller than Alyssa.

"How are the new calves?" she asked, watching her father's back.

"Healthy," he answered, drying his hands on a pressed tea towel and leaving dirt behind.

"The horses?"

"The mare has a hurt foot," he said.

"I'll go have a look." She put down the towel and grabbed her bag. She was happy to get out of the house, away from the confusion of this new mother and old memories. She walked out the back door and wondered if her father would follow. And what he would do if he did. She knew her father, proud and resentful, had a hard time asking for and taking help, particularly from his daughter. But his mind was thrifty, his pockets nearly empty and Alyssa was free. She mostly just looked over the animals. If he had any real problems he called the vet in town.

He had his pride.

We share that, too, she thought. She stopped, still caught in moonlight and self-realization. She could see Mark in the truck and she had a scorching, helpless instant of seeing herself for what she really was.

Scared. Just like my dad. Proud. Just like my dad.

Slowly she continued toward the barn. Caught as she was in her thoughts, it took her a few moments to notice the changes that had occurred over the past month. The buildings all had a fresh coat of paint and had been repaired.

The yard was cleaned up and there were even a few impatiens planted around some of the buildings. She stopped again, this time in surprise. There was a tractor she had never seen in the open door of the barn and two of the three horses her father owned were eating fresh hay.

The place looked better than it had in years.

"I see you still got your watchdog," her father mumbled behind her. She turned and saw him throw a hand out toward Mark in the truck.

"He gave me a ride," she said, and braced herself for the unexpected. Her father didn't yell anymore, hadn't put a hand on her, rough or otherwise, since she was ten, but those early instincts were hard to squelch.

"That family's been good to you," he said, and kept walking toward the barn. Alyssa's mouth fell open. Her father pointed her in the general direction of the lame horse and walked away. Her mind abuzz with the changes in the farm, she silently and with great care set about treating the horse.

Over the next hour she managed to forget her father was even in the barn. However, when she turned to go back to the house she nearly collided with him. The tension that had eased in her shoulders while she worked with the horse came back and she laughed uneasily.

"Dad, you startled me." She put a hand to her chest and felt the hard beating of her heart.

"You always spooked easy," he said. His gaze touched hers and then dropped as he made his way to the house.

Alyssa walked behind him, commenting on all the changes on their land.

"Makes your mother feel better," he rumbled.

"Dad?" she finally said, unable to keep her mouth shut. "What's going on here?"

"What are you talking about?" he asked. He stopped

but he didn't turn and Alyssa stared at the collar of his old blue work shirt and the gray hair the fell over its edge.

"There are flowers on your land," she said, as if that could sum up the radical differences.

He only grunted and shrugged and Alyssa realized he had said all he was going to say. She continued to walk behind him, attempting to give him instructions for the horse's medicine.

"I'd let her rest for another two weeks and you've got to...Dad?" Alyssa was nearly running trying to keep up with her dad.

"Yep," he said over his shoulder and didn't slow down.

"You've got to rub the ointment on five times a day, never let it...Dad?"

Wes didn't answer and Alyssa felt the giant well of frustration and pain inside of herself that should have been love for her father and she didn't think she could handle it anymore.

"Dad?" She finally stopped walking. "Please listen."

"I am," he called back over his shoulder.

"No you're not!" She had to yell to cover the distance between them. She wanted her dad to turn around, look her in the eye, and listen to her. "You're not listening, and if you don't take care of that horse, it could die!"

"I know how to take care of my animals."

"Just like you know how to take care of Mom?" she taunted heedlessly. She just wanted a reaction, that's all. Everything was changed around here and she needed a reaction.

He finally stopped, paused for a second, turned and took slow steps toward her. Alyssa took great strength in the fact that Mark was barely a hundred feet away, no doubt nearly out of the truck, ready to leap to her rescue.

But she was still scared. It took a tremendous show of will to keep her gaze steady and her chin up.

"Your mother is no worry to you," he said, his deep voice rough.

"She's sick, Dad. You can't pretend like..."

"You think I don't realize that?" he said quietly. "It may be too late to be a good father and I'll always be sorry for that, but I'll just have to live with my mistakes. But I still got some time to be a good husband."

"Dad?" It was all Alyssa could say through her astonishment.

"Thank you for what you do around here," he said. His eyes darted up to hers and then away. "It means a lot to your mother that you come around. And me."

"I'm glad to do it," she whispered.

Wes brought his hand up and old instincts kicked in and when his hand came toward her she flinched. He gripped her shoulder in his old gnarled hand and squeezed.

He walked past her back to the barn and Alyssa was left behind, breathless with surprise.

MARK FOLDED UP his newspaper and put it under his seat when Alyssa came out of the house toward the truck. By the time she was in and buckled up he was pulling out of the driveway, as eager to be away from that house as he knew she must be.

"How did it go?" he asked.

"There are flowers on the property," Alyssa said in a daze. "Dad..." She stopped, stared at her parents' home for a few moments and then shook her head as if she didn't believe what she saw. "Dad planted flowers for my mom." She turned to Mark with a half smile on her face and Mark couldn't help but smile back. It seemed all that hope she held out had come to some good and he couldn't be happier for her.

"That's great, Lis," he said. He gripped her hand where it rested on the seat and she laughed.

"Well, let's not get too excited, it is my dad after all," Alyssa said. Mark could tell she was trying to be reasonable but was thrilled by what had happened at her parents'. She looked out the window with a smile on her face.

"Last time I went there, I said that was the last time, remember?" She turned and looked at him. He wondered if she realized her hand still rested in his.

"I remember," he answered.

"I wonder why I couldn't just leave well enough alone and stay away? Millions of people every year grow up and lose touch with their parents, and their parents are good ones." She looked back out the window. "I guess it just goes to show."

"Show what?" Mark asked.

Alyssa didn't answer right away; instead she looked down at their hands and finally up at him.

"There are things more important than pride," she finally said, and squeezed his hand.

He wasn't blind, he knew what that look Alyssa just gave him meant. He read the invitation and it made him buzz with awareness and a sudden deep anticipation.

"You, uh, want to go up to the lookout?" he asked. His voice cracked and his breath left his body in a rush.

"Yes, I do," Alyssa answered softly and Mark thought that his chest might just explode. There was no way she couldn't know what he was asking. There was no way she could be immune to the currents between them. He was dizzy and sick to his stomach and overwhelmingly hopeful.

Mark turned off the main driveway onto the gravel road that led up to the lookout. Mark put the truck in Park.

Withdrawing his hand he reached behind his seat and grabbed the blanket, his whittling knife and the Goo Goo Clusters, but left behind the bottle of wine.

It just didn't seem right, it felt cheesy. Dirk may be a brother to five sisters and the most handsome man on the planet, but Mark knew Alyssa, and she deserved better than that.

"Let's go," he told her, and hopped out of the truck. He walked into the grass in front of the truck and when he found a good spot, laid the blanket out and looked around for a big stick to whittle.

ALYSSA REACHED BEHIND her seat and grabbed her fleece jacket and saw the cooler Mark had left behind.

Curious, she opened it.

Wine. Perfect.

Pride had nearly robbed her father's life of all possible joy. She wasn't ready to resign herself to the same. By the same token she, unlike her mother, wasn't going to wait her whole life for a man to love her as she should be loved. She had to move on, but before she did she was going to take what Mark offered and she was going to wrap it up carefully so she could pull it out and remember in the years ahead.

Seeing her father had made her sad and happy and nostalgic. She had made up her mind to swallow her pride and to grab what she wanted more than anything else. And tonight she wanted Mark.

Booze and sex, just what she needed. She grabbed the cooler and glasses and went out to join Mark.

"You forgot something," she said, holding up the wine bottle and glasses.

Mark shook his head. "I didn't forget it, I just don't think it a real smart idea."

''How about what I think?'' Alyssa asked, filled with nerves, swallowed pride and the low burning pain of unrequited love. ''I'm a big girl, Mark.''

''Yep,'' he agreed a little too easily, and Alyssa realized he was just as wary as she was.

Well, good, she thought. *I shouldn't be the only freaked-out one.*

''If I want a drink, I'm going to have it,'' she said firmly.

''Okay,'' he said, holding up his hands in surrender.

Alyssa sat and got to work opening the bottle. She offered Mark a glass and he took it. She stretched out her legs in front of her, leaned her head back and let the air, stars and wine do their trick. For several minutes they drank in silence. One glass. Alyssa refilled her own, but Mark declined.

''You want to slow down on that wine?'' Mark asked.

''No.'' She didn't really want more wine but she finished pouring her glass to show Mark that she made her own decisions.

''What's your mom's new medicine?'' Mark asked.

''For her high blood pressure,'' Alyssa answered. ''She said the other stuff made her sleepy so she stopped taking it. The doctors are going to try this one for a while.''

''What's your dad say?''

''Not much.'' Talking about her dad reminded her of her own pride and the things she was letting slip away. ''It's sad, Mark,'' she said softly, watching the wine in her glass tremble with her breath and with her heartbeat. ''It's sad to watch them be so careless with each other. Dad wasted so much time. They're married. They're supposed to be kind and thoughtful.'' She stopped abruptly, swirled the wine in her glass, and drank it. ''They are supposed to take care of each other.''

''Yes, they are,'' he said quietly, his voice rough and

deep. Their gazes locked and for the millionth time in her life she got a little lost in the blue of his eyes. The air seemed thick and heated, each breath seemed to fan the pull and desire she felt for him. She remembered what he had said the last time and she didn't want this to be another reason to be sorry, but she didn't think that was going to stop her. She remembered the feeling of looking over the guardrail at the Grand Canyon and realized it wasn't just love, it was fear, too. She took a deep breath and in her mind jumped right over the edge.

"Take care of me, Mark," she said suddenly, feeling airborne. "I need you to take care of me." She reached out and her hand tenderly stroked the side of his face. "I want to take care of you, too."

Slowly, because she had to, because things far stronger than her pride were making her move. Love was making her lean forward, and tuck her legs under herself so she was on her knees. She put her wineglass down and then her hands on the blanket and slowly crawled the three feet between them. He watched her do it, his eyes burning. And Alyssa hoped, just a little bit, that love was going to make him do some things tonight, too.

12

PERHAPS MARK ADDED shades of meaning, or perhaps the words just seemed profound, but at that moment Mark had never heard anything so alluring. He brought his own hand up to her face, beautiful in the moonlight, and stroked her just as tenderly.

Their kiss was seamless and their bodies seemed to lose definition. He rolled her onto her back and for long minutes it was only their mouths that touched in the most gentle kiss. His breath fanned her cheeks and he brushed his lips against hers over and over. He slid his tongue over them, nibbled on the bottom one and took it slowly into his mouth.

Suddenly she pushed him away and sat up. Mark felt the stab of fear that she had changed her mind, but her eyes were heavy-lidded and filled with want. In their heated silence, anticipation grew; he felt edgy and needful. Watching her watch him and knowing that by the end of the night he would make love to her was heady and exciting and when Alyssa sat back on her elbows and touched her tongue to her lips, Mark thought he might not make it through the night.

"Take off your shirt," she said.

"Pardon?"

"The shirt, cowboy, off with it."

Mark measured her for a second. *She wants a striptease?* For a moment he thought about refusing, uncomfortable with the idea, but he didn't want to mar this lovemaking and so he began to unbutton his shirt.

''Slower,'' she said, a corner of her mouth hitched up in a smile.

Mark ducked his head and then looked back up at her with an answering smile.

''Something going on here I should know about?'' he teased, easing a button from its hole. *Why the hell not?* he finally decided.

''It think it's time I was in charge of the decision-making process.'' Alyssa's bravado was paying off. Mark's shirt hung open in the moonlight. With an easy shrug, the shirt fell off his shoulders.

His pants clung loosely to his hips, the muscles of his stomach rising above his jeans in ridges. He rose up on his knees and hooked his thumbs in the front of his pants. He cocked his head as if to say, *What next?*

''Unbutton your pants,'' she whispered, her eyes wide and encouraging.

Mark's hands fell to his belt and his eyes were riveted to Alyssa's face. Slowly he opened his belt and after a provocative pause he unbuttoned his jeans and lowered the zipper. Every single thought and emotion Alyssa was experiencing was flashing across her face and he could see how much she wanted him and how much she liked what he was doing, and he realized that he had never been a part of something so erotic.

He flattened his palm against his chest and slid it down into the open vee of his pants. He slipped his hand under the fabric of his briefs and slowly measured the length of his erection. Once. Twice.

Alyssa moaned and closed her eyes.

Mark braced himself above Alyssa's body but he stopped just short of touching her; teasing her with the heat between them. Alyssa arched into him, a wave of sensation from his hips to his chest. He lowered his head and licked her lips. She opened them on a gasp, but he didn't accept the invitation.

"Take off your shirt," he told her. The command whispered into the night air was electrifying. Alyssa pulled off her sweater and the T-shirt she wore under it. The air was cool and Mark bent his head again, this time he licked her nipples, hard beneath her cotton bra and returned to take each one between his teeth.

"Mark..." Alyssa gasped, clutching at his arms.

"Take off your pants, Alyssa."

The fire inside her had been stoked well and she quickly undressed. She toed off her shoes and pushed her pants down to her knees, using her feet to pull them off the rest of the way.

Oh, my God, he thought, following the slim line of her body from her shoulder to her hips. He had no idea Alyssa was made of fire. He never guessed that underneath her beautiful skin ran currents of electricity. But it was there just under the surface—the wild heat of a woman—and the pleasure of it was luscious and shocking. Years of working hard right beside him had made Alyssa strong and firm in places where other women were soft.

The silence stretched and she looked up only to meet Mark's burning eyes.

"Mark?" she asked.

His hands framed her body; his eyes followed her curves.

"You're so pretty," he said on a breath. "Your skin is so smooth." He traced a blue vein with his tongue from her wrist up the inside of her arm to her shoulder, just below her collarbone to her breast. "I've never felt anything so soft. Have you?" He took her hand from his shoulder and placed her palm on the skin of her breast. Their eyes locked and he put his hand over hers and moved it across her body.

He brushed the top of her nipple with his cheek and finally pulled it into his mouth with deep suction. She arched hard into his body and he groaned with the fantastic pleasure.

''Please, Mark. Let me touch you,'' she implored.

''No,'' he said, and took her other nipple into his mouth. He wasn't near done.

Alyssa's eyelids lifted slowly.

''No?'' she asked for clarification.

''Nope,'' he repeated. ''I'm busy.''

Alyssa bent her knee, sliding the smooth skin of her thigh across his denim-clad one. She brought her leg over his hips and in one smooth move pushed at his shoulders and followed him as he rolled to his back.

She smiled at him as her hair fell around her shoulders in a cloud backlit by stars. Her smile had to be the smile Eve wore when she offered Adam the apple because no man on earth could deny a woman anything when she smiled like that.

I'll follow her anywhere, he thought, and he felt something sweep through his body. Something warm and soft and wholly pleasing.

I love her, he thought. It didn't startle him or make him panic. In fact Mark had never felt anything that was so right. He loved her. What he was feeling was warm and cold and pleasure and pain. It was everything worth feeling and this one person brought it all to the surface.

This is mine, he thought, following the curve of her cheek with his finger. *This is mine,* he thought, leaning up to press a hungry kiss to her lips. *This is mine,* he chanted as his hands staked claim to her breasts, the soft skin of her belly. He pulled her legs so she was kneeling across his body and his hands slid across the firm muscles of her thighs.

This is mine, he thought as his fingers found the warmth and heat of her sex. *Mine.*

"More," she whispered against his face. She leaned down across his body and licked his stomach, breathed across his erection. "I want more, Mark," she said, slowly climbing up his body.

He sat up, straddling her across his lap, and eased his fingers into the lush heat between her legs. They both paused for a second, hearts pounding. Mark lifted his head to look in her eyes.

"Please" she whispered, and put her hand over his, leading him where she wanted him to go.

With all the care he had shown her since his seduction began, he set about relieving the pleasure that was becoming agony. She pressed her face to his neck while her body trembled and swayed against his body, his fingers.

"Mark," she gasped. She bit the skin over his collarbone. She moaned, grasping his wrist, her nails sinking into his flesh. She shifted, grinding her hips against his hand, urging it closer.

"Shh," Mark whispered, and he slid his finger deep into her body and when her eyes shut tight he added another.

She was strong and as fiercely aroused as any woman he'd ever known. Her nails sunk into the flesh of his shoulder and her mouth opened with a high clear cry as she came apart in his arms.

Mine, he thought with deep implacable satisfaction.

He laid her on the blanket, his fingers still locked inside her while she arched and shivered. As she relaxed, he eased his fingers from her body and stroked the smooth skin of her stomach.

Mark hitched himself up on an elbow and ran his finger across her nose. Across her lips to her chin, down her neck to her collarbone, back up to where her skin covered her artery and her pulse beat like wings under her skin.

"You're the most beautiful woman I've ever seen," he told her, counting her heartbeats. "The softest thing I've ever touched." Her heartbeat kicked and doubled and Mark pressed his lips to her pulse.

She turned to him, her body lush and pliant. "Make love to me, Mark."

ALYSSA GRABBED the wine bottle and topped off Mark's glass. Mark handed her a Goo Goo Cluster, which she took and ate.

They were lying side by side, wrapped up in the blanket. Her hand reached out of their nest and touched his shoulder, followed his arm down to his hand to the wineglass he held and lifted it so she could take a drink from it. Her wineglass had been broken and tossed aside sometime in the past few hours. While she drank, he pressed kisses to her neck. He couldn't touch her enough, be close enough to her. He wanted to open her up and climb inside.

"White zinfandel goes well with the goo in these things," she told him, trying to dodge his tickling lips.

"Yeah, I read that somewhere," he answered sagely. She giggled and he smiled. He had known that making love to Alyssa would be great, he had known that. What he hadn't guessed was that he would feel so complete.

She took another sip and the wine sloshed over her lips and ran down her chin. Mark used his tongue to clean it up and then leaned forward to take a bite from her Goo Goo Cluster.

"Who needs a napkin?" she said with a smile.

"Who needs food groups?" Mark said, and finished the cluster in one bite.

"Your sweet tooth..."

''I know, it's ridiculous to eat candy first thing in the morning,'' he said and kissed her. ''But I like sweet things.'' He waggled his eyebrows at her and Alyssa groaned with all the cheesiness.

But as complete as he felt he could sense the wariness in her and he knew she could feel it in him.

What does this mean? What happens now?

If Mark had his way he would just see where things went. But she was going to Billings tomorrow for that second interview and if he just waited to see where things went he would be saying goodbye to her and helping her move into some apartment three hours away from him.

At least then we wouldn't have to be making love on the ground, he thought and then quickly pushed the thought away. *I don't want Alyssa three hours away. I want her right here.*

He was suddenly scared out of his mind. With the erotic rush of their lovemaking gone, Mark felt foolish. He had no business staking claim to Alyssa. She's leaving, he thought, if she had any interest in staying here she would just stay. *Wouldn't she?* She has always said her future is back in Billings. For Christ's sake, what was he supposed to do? Ask her to stay the day before she gets a job. Stay on this ranch? Stay in Lincoln when she has a whole life planned in Billings? *Am I that selfish?* he wondered. *Am I that crazy?*

She had told him to forget this. That's what she had said last time, ''Let's just forget this ever happened.''

Mark had the horrible feeling she would say it again.

I've got to try.

''So,'' he said carefully. ''What's this about you not going to the Wild Man rodeo?'' He knew immediately that another mistake had been made. The smile vanished from her face and she pulled the blanket up higher.

Damn, he thought, *how am I supposed to do this?*

"I told you, the animal hospital wants a second interview," she said, picking once at the blanket and then smoothing the edges.

"Is that what you want?" he asked, trying hard not to make it sound as if it was the most important question he had ever asked.

"It's a good opportunity," she said brightly, and Mark felt all of his anticipation wither and die and turn into an agony of unfulfilled hopes realized too damn late.

"Sure is," he said, unable to think of anything else to say.

I love you. I love you and I want you to stay.

"It's what you've always wanted," he agreed, then closed his eyes and hoped breathlessly that this was a beginning and not an end.

"Yes," she told him. "It is. Ever since I pulled Queenie out of that barbed wire I wanted this. And Billings has the best opportunities."

Mark could only nod and after several silent moments Alyssa sighed and said, "I have to get up early tomorrow."

Slowly, carefully, they began to search out their clothes and get dressed. She found his underwear and handed it to him with a small smile. He untangled her shirt while she tried to pull it on and the touch of her skin was more than he could take.

"Don't worry, Mark, this doesn't change things," she said with a half smile. "We're still friends."

"Good," Mark said, and they climbed in the truck to go home.

13

DIRK MASON was a prima donna. He knew it and in certain moments it was something he was proud of. However, as Dirk barged into Mark's room while the man was dressing he could tell it was not something Mark thought much of.

''Mark, this is serious business,'' Dirk said. He held up two different shirts he had swiped from Billy's closet and looked at himself in the mirror on the closet door. Out of the corner of his eye he caught a glimpse of Mark without his shirt and blew out a silent whistle of appreciation.

Nice, Alyssa, he thought. *Very nice.*

''No, it's not,'' Mark replied. ''If there is one thing I'm sure about in this world, it's that it makes no difference whatsoever what you wear to the Wild Man Rodeo.'' As if to make his point, Mark reached into his closet with his eyes closed and picked a shirt to wear. Dirk sniffed in disapproval of Mark's devil-may-care attitude toward rodeo fashion and looked at himself in the mirror from different angles with each of the shirts pressed to his chest.

''What will the other cowboys be wearing?'' Dirk asked. He was beginning to lean more toward the plaid himself.

''Clothes, probably denim in nature.'' Mark tucked in his shirt and tried to get past Dirk and out the door.

''No chance, Mark,'' he said, and shook the shirts for emphasis.

''Wear the plaid,'' Mark finally said.

Dirk threw the denim shirt on Mark's bed and continued

to block the doorway while he put on the plaid shirt. His vote had been for the plaid, as well; it just screamed "wild man." But he wasn't sure if clothes that screamed "wild man" were what were called for. *One just never knew at a rodeo.*

With the clothes issue settled, Dirk felt free to say what was really on his mind. "So—" he began tucking his shirt in "—what happened with Alyssa last night?"

Dirk noticed the blush that creeped up Mark's neck and the way the cowboy couldn't quite meet his eye. Both did not bode well for his behavior the night before.

"So, the wine worked?" Dirk asked, cutting to the chase.

"Look, Dirk, it was never about having sex with Alyssa," Mark hedged, and Dirk crossed his arms over his chest and shook his head.

"But you had sex with her?" Mark remained silent and Dirk had to remind him that he was one nosy man. "We're not going anywhere until you tell me one way or another."

"Look, Dirk, it's complicated..." Mark started, but Dirk interrupted, his patience for the dumb cowboy all gone.

"Mark, it is always complicated. Always. Love isn't easy. And..." *Jesus it was like pulling teeth around here. No wonder Alyssa is leaving.*

"I love her," Mark said in a fierce whisper, filling in the blank. Dirk was taken aback for a moment by Mark's emotion. "But I'm not about to stand in the way of what she wants and she told me last night that she wants to go to Billings."

"Wow." Dirk looked at Mark and could only shake his head. "You are the dumbest cowboy on the planet."

"Oh, for crying out loud, I don't have to..." Mark made his way to the door and Dirk stepped in front of him.

"What she wants—" Dirk began. "What every woman

wants, is for a man to say 'stay.' It's that simple, Mark. You say 'Please, Alyssa, stay here with me,' and she'll stay."

"No she won't," Mark said, his face twisted in disbelief. "She doesn't love me."

"Well, you'll never really know till you ask, will you?"

Mark was silent and still for a moment and Dirk took the opportunity to check out his rodeo ensemble in Mark's full-length mirror.

"Why couldn't you just say all of this before?" Mark finally asked. "Instead of me having to light tea lights and chop wood in the front yard. Why couldn't you just give me this advice first?"

Dirk shrugged in a way he knew was mysterious and aggravating. "I thought maybe I still had a chance," he lied. Maybe jealousy would push Mark in the right direction.

"Well, we're both too late," Mark said, and Dirk realized that Mark was truly heartbroken.

"It's not too late, Mark," Dirk said quietly. "Look, for whatever reason, you are the last person in the world to realize this, but that woman loves you. Is completely devoted to you."

"Well, that would explain why she's leaving," Mark said sarcastically.

"A girl can only take so much, Mark. Think about it, she'll be back tonight after the interview." Dirk met Mark's eyes and willed him to see sense.

"You think she loves me?" Mark asked, clearly skeptical.

"I'm sure of it," Dirk answered firmly.

Mark looked right through him for a few moments, nodding his head and then he turned on his heel and led the way out of the room.

''Do you think this belt buckle is too much?'' Dirk asked Mark's back. Along with the shirt, Dirk had borrowed Billy's Big Sky Country belt buckle.

''Yep,'' Mark said without looking. He was leading Dirk to the kitchen; Dirk could smell the intoxicating aroma of recently fried pig fat.

In the kitchen Mac, Ethan and Billy were standing around the table finishing up their coffee. Each of the men was wearing true testimonies to Western attire. Bolo ties, leather, fancy hats with feathers and beading, the odd bit of rawhide fringe and belt buckles the size of small pizzas.

Dirk Mason, who owned no fewer than twelve Armani suits, caught his breath with the beauty of it all.

Cowboys. Hell, yes.

''Hey, Billy,'' Dirk asked, making his way to the platter of leftover bacon. ''Do you think I could borrow a hat?''

''Well, now, Dirk, there's no need to borrow a hat,'' Mac said with a laugh, looking slyly at his boys.

''Well, I just thought it would add to my whole cowboy image, but if you don't think—'' Dirk had to pull his eyes from Mac's near mesmerizing bolo tie in the shape of the Morning Glory brand.

''Dirk,'' Billy interrupted. ''We're just saying there is no need to borrow a hat when you already have one.''

''Not me, boys—'' Dirk, wondering how Billy was planning to ride anything wearing pants so tight, reached for his third piece of bacon ''—unless you want to count my Dodgers cap, but I don't think that's the kind…''

Ethan opened a box on a chair and pulled out a black cowboy hat. Not one of those work jobs, but a real dress ten-gallon hat with a feather tucked into the snake-skin band.

It was the coolest, most badass cowboy hat Dirk had ever seen.

Ethan reached across the table and put the hat on Dirk's head at the perfect angle. It fit like a dream.

Dirk felt the legacy of Clint Eastwood and John Wayne seep into his body.

Dirk stood straighter, cocked his hips forward, and even squinted his eyes. "Boys," he murmured, and tipped his hat. Cowboy language for "Hey, thanks guys, this really means a lot to me." The Cook men jutted their chins forward in a short, sharp nod. Cowboy language for "You are welcome, friend, and we think you're great."

The cowboys turned and headed out the front door where their trucks, horses and women waited.

Dirk had talked to Guy last night at the motel and had arranged to meet at the ranch and go to the rodeo together. When Dirk stepped out and saw Guy, he felt the same warm rush of happiness he had been feeling for ten years.

Love isn't easy, the movie star thought, looking at the man he loved, *but it's well worth the work.*

Guy, wearing his surgical mask, was leaning against one of the trucks, talking to Missy. When the men came out the door, he slowly pulled the mask off and brought his hand up to his neck in wonder.

"Wow," he said.

Dirk walked up to Guy and shook hands with him. "Glad you could make it, Guy," he said warmly.

"You think I would miss your first rodeo appearance? Where the hell did you get that hat? And that shirt? And that belt buckle? Good God, Dirk, you're perfect."

Dirk pulled his hat down and squinted. "Yes, I am. Let's go to the rodeo." He put an arm around Guy as they headed for his little sports car.

At the last minute Dirk ducked back inside the house for a few more pieces of bacon.

HOURS LATER Dirk was feeling a bit sick. The baked goods competition had been his Waterloo. He had held his own during jams and preserves, had held up admirably during the chili cook-off—it was only the second year and not a popular event, there were only two entries—and even managed to look interested during the pickling event. But the full hour of sampling applesauce cakes, pineapple upside-down cakes, cinnamon rolls, cream cheese muffins, something called a Brown Betty, three pound cakes and five angel food cakes had turned even his ironclad stomach. However, his current queasiness he pinned, along with the blue ribbon, on Mrs. Gensler's Double Dog Dare You Chocolate Mayonnaise Cake.

Dirk Mason had eaten all over the world. Four-star chefs pulled out all the stops when he walked in the doors of their restaurants and he had never in his life felt like weeping over food.

When he bit into that barely baked chocolate goo, his eyes teared and he felt the presence of God. Mrs. Gensler was his hero, and four pieces of her fat and sugar creation had been his downfall. Even Guy, clucking and looking at him as if he had murdered a whole litter of puppies, couldn't stop him from buying the rest of the cake to take home.

But queasy or no, he still had to ride in a rodeo.

STUPID, STUPID, STUPID! Alyssa banged her hand against the steering wheel for emphasis. *Your whole life is waiting for you. Billings. Work. Cute apartment guy. Stop acting like the world is ending.*

But no matter how much she chastised herself she couldn't shake the feeling that she was doing the wrong thing.

It's only because I've chased him for so long. Change is weird. That's all I'm feeling—weirdness.

But she knew, even as she drove the familiar road to Billings that this was more.

Well, having sex with her was certainly not an apology for having kissed her. If it was, Mark was even more backward than she thought. So all of his efforts with the candles and the flowers and the wine had been purely to get her into bed.

Sweetheart, men will have sex with anybody. And you certainly proved yourself more than willing, something in her admonished.

Alyssa was getting very tired of her better sense, which was beginning to sound like a bitter old woman.

"Not Mark," she said into the quiet of her truck. "Mark's not casual about things like that and nobody is casual about having sex with their best friend."

Well, maybe you should have thought of that before driving away this morning.

"Well, maybe if I wasn't so busy listening to you!" she said furiously, and realized she was yelling into thin air at herself. "I'm losing it," she muttered.

She put her elbow on the door and rested her head on her fist. She did not want to go to Billings. She didn't, it was the plain truth of the matter.

It's too late now, she told herself.

Alyssa was quiet and felt sick to her stomach. A mixture of regret and anger was pulling her body into one big knot. When did she start thinking practical was better? That being reasonable and logical would get her what she wanted in life?

Every time she got something that she really wanted, that she really needed, it had been against her better judgment. Making love to Mark, leaving her parents to stay at the

Morning Glory, becoming a vet, returning every summer to cook and to feel just for a few months as though she was part of a real honest-to-god, loving family.

Those were things she wanted, decisions she made with her heart rather than her brain.

"Look at where being practical has gotten you." It was a new voice, a new Alyssa talking into the quiet truck. "You dated all those men that you didn't want to date because they weren't Mark. You went away to a big school that made you nervous and unhappy. It's got you going to Billings *where you don't want to go!*"

An anger bloomed in her chest and made it hard for her to breathe. A righteous fury for all the things she had denied herself over the years. Alyssa pulled the truck over to the side of the road and sat there breathing hard. The Grand Canyon feeling was back: part love, part fear.

"What do you want?" she asked herself, gripping the steering wheel hard. "Alyssa Halloway, what do you really want?"

Answers. I want Mark to tell me why he seduced me. I want Mark to tell me what he wants. And I want it to be me.

"Well, you're certainly not going to get those answers in Billings, are you?"

Alyssa's mouth fell open and her eyes widened as she realized the real truth behind her practical side. She was scared. Being practical was how she rationalized never fighting for Mark, never telling him how she felt.

Not anymore, she thought, filled suddenly with a new purpose.

Alyssa turned the truck around and headed back to the Wild Man Rodeo to find Mark and to get some answers.

14

DESPITE HIS RINGSIDE seat, Mark was oblivious to the rodeo and Dirk's fantastic performance. He was replaying every moment he had spent in Alyssa's company in the past few weeks and he was beginning to see that all of her nonchalance may not have been as nonchalant as he had thought.

Alyssa loves me? he thought in varying degrees of joy and bewilderment.

The public address system crackled to life to announce the start of the bull riding part of the rodeo. The bull riding was mostly just a tradition. Mark craned his neck to see the bull, Marco, who was a hundred years old if he was a day. Dick Raider donated the use of Marco every year and the cowboys, who were mostly on the other side of fifty, were all too happy to ride the complacent, aging bull.

Mark remembered that as a joke a couple of years ago, Dick started riding his bull down to the fairgrounds. He put a saddle and bridle on it and rode it down Main Street, as though it was a horse or a tractor. He got a lot of laughs and proved all over again that staying on top of that animal was no tough feat. The organizers always put the bull riding competition last and all of the riders stayed on for eight seconds. In fact three years ago, Billy and Mark insisted that they put a thirty-second limit on the bull riding, otherwise they'd be there for a week.

It was a given that whomever was in the lead going into the bull riding competition was going to be grand champion.

Looks like it's going to be Billy, Mark thought. *Alyssa loves me?*

"I've been looking for you everywhere!" Mark heard Dirk shouting and he turned to see the movie star stomping furiously toward him. Billy was following on his heels looking as if he was trying not to laugh. Dirk seemed upset about something, but Mark could barely care.

She didn't mean we should just forget everything, did she? And I believed her. He should have pressed harder, gotten more answers from her, Mark realized, cataloging all of his mistakes.

"Never once did anyone at any time say anything about a bull!" Dirk shouted.

"Dirk, look at the bull," Billy said reasonably, pointing to the pen where they kept the bull before the event. The bull was sound asleep and two kids were poking it with sticks. "Trust me on this, there's nothing to worry about."

"I have no idea how to ride a bull!" Dirk shouted.

"You'll be fine." Mark said absently. *Not enough anymore—I get it!*

"Listen to me!" Dirk grabbed the front of Mark's shirt in his fists. "I have no idea how to ride a bull!"

Startled, Mark looked at Dirk for the first time. "Hold on with your knees," he told his pupil. "Put one hand in the air and sit there. Marco hasn't bucked anyone in years," he answered distractedly.

"Hey, Mark, Alyssa was looking for you a little bit ago," Billy said, reaching up to pull Dirk's hands from his brother's shirt.

"What?" Mark asked, suddenly alert. He grabbed onto Billy's shirt. "Alyssa's here?"

"Yes." Billy started pulling his brother's hands off his own shirt. "And she looked very, very pissed off."

There is a God, Mark thought, suddenly seeing this for what it was. A second chance. He wasn't about to blow it.

"Where did you last see her?" he asked, feeling joy and hope collide inside him.

"By the box lunches...but where—?" Billy didn't get a chance to finish, because Mark was already gone.

Mark scanned the crowd frantically. Alyssa was here. She hadn't gone for the second interview. She came back. Maybe—well, those maybes were just going to have to wait until Mark told her how he felt. How he felt and how he would go to Billings with her if she wanted. How he loved her.

Mark headed toward the box lunch booth but didn't see her. He heaved a big sigh and took a few steps closer to the booth. A lunch was up for bid and Matt Groames was bidding on it. Mark stopped walking for a moment. Alyssa had made a lunch. Matt always bid on her lunch.

Is that Alyssa's lunch? Mark wondered desperately, looking at the brightly wrapped package.

Matt upped his bid to fifty dollars and something took over in Mark's brain.

No way was Matt Groames going to be eating Alyssa's ham sandwiches. Those ham sandwiches were his. All of Alyssa's ham sandwiches were his. And that nineteen-year-old wasn't getting his hands on them.

"Sixty dollars!" he shouted, and heads began to turn. Matt looked at him in surprise and Mark met that look with his own of flinty-eyed challenge. Matt turned and faced the auctioneer.

"Seventy dollars."

"Seventy-five," Mark shouted without hesitating. This

was the first step, the first step to claiming Alyssa as his own.

Matt was riffling through his pockets, counting money, and Mark knew he had him on the ropes.

"Seventy-nine dollars and forty-five cents."

"One hundred dollars!" Mark shouted to put the poor kid out of his misery. He fought the urge to punch his fists in the air when Matt hung his head in defeat.

It's a box lunch, man. Get it together.

Mark stomped up to the booth and grabbed his lunch. On his way past Matt, he leaned in close and whispered, "Get your own girl."

"But..."

Mark didn't stop to listen to what Matt had to say. He was on his way to find Alyssa.

Mark turned around and walked backward, hoping to catch sight of her curls among the crowd, and immediately ran into someone.

"Sorry," he said. He turned and realized he had smacked right into Alyssa. "Alyssa!" He didn't give her a chance to talk but quickly hauled her against his chest with one arm. "I'm so glad to see you!"

"Not so fast, Mark." She pulled out of his arms only to poke him in the chest. "You've got some explaining to do!"

"Explaining?" She was so pretty with her flashing green eyes. So pretty and right here and not in Billings. He couldn't quite get over it.

"Yeah! Like what were you doing with wine?" She jabbed him in the chest again and he took a step backward.

"And those candles?" Another poke and another step backward. "And chopping wood in the front yard with your shirt off? You've got something going on here, Mark, and I demand you tell me what it is."

"I—" He started but she wouldn't let him finish.

"I've spent my whole life waiting, Mark. My whole life, waiting and wondering, and it's not fair that you're doing this stuff to me now that I'm leaving town."

"I know. If you—" But she wasn't going to let him talk and the more she talked the more he realized her words were just what he wanted to hear.

"No!" She was shouting and people were beginning to stop and stare.

"But—"

"No buts! I love you, Mark. I love you and I need to know how you feel about me. And I'm not talking about sex." There were snickers in the crowd and Mark felt himself blushing. "Because I'm not sticking around here just so we can meet at dawn in the hayloft."

"Will you keep it down?" he pleaded through clenched teeth.

"No, Mark, I will not keep it down and I will not meet you in the hayloft or fool around in your truck because I love—"

Mark clamped a hand over her mouth.

"Can I say something?" he asked. Over his hand she blinked and then nodded at him. He removed his hand carefully, not quite trusting her.

"Go ahead," she said, crossing her arms over her chest.

He smiled at her and felt warmth fill him up. "I can't let you go," he told her quietly. "If you leave, I'll follow you. And it's not just two friends wanting to have sex. Although, I have to tell you, Lis, I want you. I want you so badly, I'm going a little crazy."

"I know, Mark. I do, too. But it's not enough," she said, holding her own, and Mark loved her even more for it. She wasn't settling and he was proud of her.

"I don't think you understand, Alyssa," he told her. He put one hand to her face and felt the smoothness of her skin.

"I love you," he whispered. "Not like my friend or like my sister. Like my wife."

Alyssa was still in his hands. Slowly, however, the stillness turned to tremors, as a wire pulled too tight. He gripped her shoulders harder, trying to impart the strength of his love and his need and his desire into her body.

"I've loved you forever and just never knew what to call it," he told her simply, and watched her face crumble into a mixture of relief and doubt.

"Really?" she whispered.

"Yes, really."

"This isn't an apology or..."

"For crying out loud, I want you to be my wife. Does that sound like an apology?"

"No, but if that's a proposal it was lousy," she said, but through her tears she was smiling. For just a moment, in the middle of a crowd of people, holding a box lunch in one hand and a crying woman in the other, Mark glimpsed the future and saw that it was perfect.

"I just can't believe this." Tears she didn't try to swallow or to hold back ran down her face.

"If you still want to go to Billings—" Alyssa put her hands to his mouth and looked at him with such joy that Mark felt tears well up in his own eyes.

"You offered to put up the money for me to start a clinic here, in Lincoln."

"Yes," he said, unable to believe that this was going to work out so well.

"Does the offer still stand?" she asked, tilting her head to the side.

"Of course, if that's what you want?"

"That's what I want," she declared, and Mark pulled

her into his arms. "I love you so much," she whispered into his shirt.

"Me, too," he told her, and pulled her tighter and suddenly remembered the box lunch. "In fact," he said into her hair, then pulled back to show her the box. "I love you so much I just broke every box lunch record by paying a hundred bucks for your ham sandwiches."

Alyssa looked at the box and slowly began laughing and Mark began laughing, too. This moment was just as it should be.

"That's not my lunch," she said.

"What?"

"It's not mine. I think you're going to be having lunch with Mary Raines."

"What?" Mark asked again and then turned to see Matt Groames hugging a weepy Mary Raines. "But..." He looked at the box and at the teenaged couple and then up at Alyssa who was laughing and crying. Before he could say anything else, she pulled him down for a long warm kiss that made him forget all about ham sandwiches.

The speaker above their heads crackled and they both jumped, startled by the noise.

"Another great ride by Billy Cook, ladies and gentleman." Mark and Alyssa looked down at the rodeo ring in time to catch Billy sitting on a bull that was standing still, chewing grass in the center of the ring. Billy slid off Marco's back, gave the bull a friendly pat on the rump, and raised his arm to the crowd.

"Our Honorary Rodeo Marshall and screen legend, Dirk Mason, currently in second place, will now take his turn on Marco."

In the center of the ring, a man dressed halfheartedly as a clown was pulling with all his might, trying to get Marco back to the chute. Dirk walked out to the middle of the field and took the reins from the clown. He climbed up on Marco's old back and raised his hand to the crowd.

Word had gotten out about Dirk's appearance at this year's rodeo and attendance was at an all-time high. Nearly everyone in western Montana had shown up and when Dirk raised his hand the crowd went wild and so, surprisingly, did Marco.

The sudden noise startled Marco out of his geriatric daze and sent him bucking like a bull twenty years his junior. Maniacally, Marco leaped and whirled and the crowd got to its feet and screamed louder.

Marco went nuts. And Dirk held on for dear life.

"Oh, my God," Alyssa whispered, and Mark grabbed her hand and together they raced toward the corral. On his way past Matt, Mark pressed the box lunch into his arms.

They elbowed and shoved their way to where Billy was standing at the edge of the fence, his mouth opened in shock.

"I can't believe it!" Billy was saying.

"Look at that boy ride!" someone called out and, indeed, Dirk was riding like a pro. His body was flexible and loose, moving with the bull, his arm up, his head down and most importantly, his butt firmly in the saddle.

Everyone was in such shock that the eight seconds came and went. At twelve seconds the horn finally blew and three aging and clearly nervous clowns rushed to help Dirk off the bull.

Dirk let go of the reins and with the next wild leap of the bull's body he went flying through the air. The clowns distracted the bull and got him into the chute as the Cook family ran out to check on Dirk.

"Dirk!" Guy cried, falling to his knees by the movie star's inert body. The thin man was hyperventilating, his eyes panicked and wide, and Alyssa put a comforting hand to his shoulder.

Slowly, Dirk rolled over onto his back, a slow smile spreading over his face.

"You okay, Dirk?" Alyssa asked, worried.

"I think so," he whispered, and opened his eyes.

"You are one tough bull riding son of a bitch, I tell you," Mac said, laughing and held out a hand to help Dirk to his feet.

"Don't move!" Guy yelled. "We need to get you to a hospital." Guy's face was white and his already thin lips were nearly nonexistent. "Is there a doctor here!" he shrieked.

"I think I'm okay," Dirk said.

"There could be internal bleeding." Guy started running his hands over Dirk's body, checking for broken bones.

"Really, Guy," Dirk said with a smirk. "Now is hardly the time."

Guy sat back and looked around furtively. "He has a head injury," he said loudly. "He doesn't know what he's saying."

"Well, folks, I've never seen anything like it," the announcer was saying. Dirk sat up and finally got to his feet. "By unanimous decision the judges name Dirk Mason the Grand Champion of this year's Wild Man Rodeo."

Dirk raised his hand and the crowd went wild, screaming and stomping its feet against the bleachers. In the distance Marco snorted and kicked his stall door.

"I bet this is the first time a gay man has been the Wild Man Grand Champion," Dirk said with a wicked twinkle in his eye, and promptly turned to throw up what was left of the baked goods competition.

The Cook family was stunned into silence; eyes opened

wide, mouths slack-jawed. Mark turned to Alyssa but saw that she wasn't surprised. Saw in fact that she was laughing.

"You knew?" he whispered in shock.

"Yep," she quipped.

"All those walks and the date and him kissing your hands and..."

"All completely innocent," she said, and brushed a hand over Mark's face. She turned his gaze to where Guy was stroking Dirk's back and fishing a handkerchief out of his back pocket. "He's already in love with someone else. Like me."

"Guy?" Dirk whispered.

"For years apparently. Like me."

"Yeah," Mark said, the information setting in. He wrapped his hands around Alyssa's waist and smiled at her. "I know how that is."

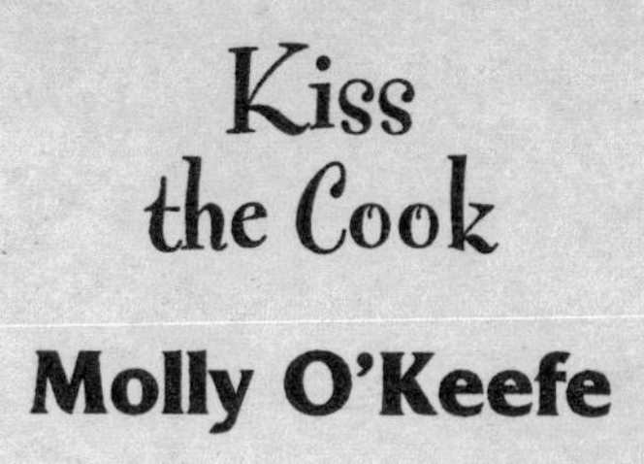

Molly O'Keefe

TORONTO • NEW YORK • LONDON
AMSTERDAM • PARIS • SYDNEY • HAMBURG
STOCKHOLM • ATHENS • TOKYO • MILAN • MADRID
PRAGUE • WARSAW • BUDAPEST • AUCKLAND

Dear Reader,

Billy Cook, the young Casanova of the Cook clan, has left a string of broken hearts across western Montana. But he has only ever met his match in one woman. And now, thirteen years later, Kate's back, she's pregnant and this time she's not going anywhere! Billy's not entirely convinced...not *yet*, anyway!

It has been such a pleasure revisiting the Cook family for two more stories. I hope you have as much fun as I did!

Enjoy!

Molly O'Keefe

Books by Molly O'Keefe

HARLEQUIN DUETS
62—TOO MANY COOKS

1

SNOW IN APRIL. *This night just couldn't get worse.* Billy Cook turned on his windshield wipers to push the gathering snowy slush off his windshield.

Peg Graham started the whole mess. Why in the world she had to turn a nice Saturday night date that was ending in some nice Saturday night sex into a battleground, he would never know. He wondered why she, along with about a dozen other women he had dated over the years, always forgot what he told them from the very beginning.

"Don't pin any hopes on me. I'm not getting married until I'm forty years old."

He made a point of saying this on the third date, because the third date usually involved some kind of nudity. And because he wasn't the marrying kind, he felt he should give the girls the chance to leave before any clothes were shed.

But the girls that stayed, and most of them did, at some point figured that they had changed him. That they had made Billy Cook—lone stallion—into some kind of gelding and Billy would be ready to settle down. So they made "The Declaration."

"Horseshit," Billy mumbled. Distracted and edgy and for some reason a little sad that things had ended the way they had with the lovely and flexible Peg, he wasn't paying a whole lot of attention to the roads that were getting slicker. As he turned up the long winding road leading to the Morning Glory Ranch, the truck fishtailed and went into a skid and Billy had to put both hands on the wheel to fight for control of the vehicle.

He bounced off a tree but managed to stay on the mountain road.

"That's it," he mumbled, out of sorts with the world. "I'm moving someplace with no snow!" He flipped his bright lights on and peered into the darkness past the snow to see the condition of the road. Montana was no place for a snow-hating cowboy like him. The wind had picked up and snow was blowing sideways and tree limbs were thrashing in the shadows. As if someone was playing a cruel joke on Billy, a large limb from one of the pines lining the road snapped and fell across the rough pavement.

"Florida," Billy muttered under his breath. "California." He opened the truck door and hopped out. He was immediately smacked in the face with a million little snow razors ripping at his skin. The wind blew him backward for a second, flattening him against his truck. Of course, since it was April and not January, Billy didn't have his warm coat. His denim jacket with the holes in the sleeves was hardly any help against the bitter wind.

"I'll get myself a nice commitment-phobic lifeguard to date," he told himself. He shoved his hat down on his head, pulled the collar up on his coat and leaned his body into the wind. "I'll live on the beach and sell oranges to tourists." He carefully made his way to the fallen limb. Looking at it through stinging and watery eyes, Billy decided he could lift it. He crouched, furthering his California dreams to include Mexico, and slid his gloved hands under the heaviest part of the limb. He counted to three in Spanish in preparation for his move south and began to straighten his legs, keeping his back straight as his father had taught him. He was nearly upright when another smaller branch ripped from a tree and crashed into his back, knocking him to his stomach on top of the first limb.

Effectively, Billy Cook was a tree sandwich.

Billy practiced all of his Spanish swearwords and made up his own when he ran out of ones he knew.

He growled deep in his throat and stood, heaving the limb off his back and wincing when he was realized that the limb that fell on him was bigger than he thought; and might have done some damage to his ribs. He tried to take a deep breath but the shooting pain in his side stopped him halfway.

Great, he thought, *I can add a couple of bruised ribs to the rest of the evening's successes.* Wincing and swearing, Billy managed to push the limbs to the side just enough so that his truck could get by. He heaved himself back into his truck and put it in gear.

Tenderly, he probed his rib cage with frozen fingers. Yep, he was going to have a nasty bit of bruising come morning.

As he crept forward on the icy road he wondered at what point he might have given Peg a sign that his mind had been changing. In Billy's recollection, at every given moment he reminded her that he simply wasn't a man to hang on to. Which had made it so hard to believe when earlier this evening, as things were certainly going his way, Peg stopped him.

She had put on her shirt, without the bra that was hanging on the lampshade where Billy had flung it in his enthusiasm, and before Billy could even ask what was wrong, she'd turned on the lamp.

Those, of course, had been *his* first clues.

But it was the look in her eyes, soft and sorry and hopeful, that had told him what was going to happen next.

"Billy," she had said. She put her hand to his shoulder and then to his face. "I have to tell you something..."

As soon as she had looked him in the eyes with her soft

pools of feminine assurance, Billy zipped up his pants, pulled on his own shirt and braced himself for the worst.

"I love you," she had said. He'd waited while she'd gathered her courage, taken his hand in hers and let him know just how much she hadn't been listening to him.

"I think you love me, too. You just don't know it yet."

Billy's truck hit another icy patch and his tires spun, sending him weaving across the road.

"Dammit!" Billy muttered, and fought his fishtailing truck, ping-ponging off the trees on the side of the road. With both hands gripping the wheel he managed to stay on the road. Once he was moving in a straight line he put his hat on the passenger seat beside him and turned down the truck heater. Sweat was running in a tickling stream down his back.

He was still thirty miles from home and the storm was getting worse.

Tomorrow, Billy was going to move to his cousin's ranch in Texas. Dry heat and sand. Perfect.

Billy figured that in his twenty-nine years he had learned a few things, one of which, he was sure, was knowing when he was or wasn't in love.

Something, he thought, *Peg Graham is confused about.*

He had watched his two brothers stumble, trip and generally nearly chase away the women they loved. Billy figured he had learned three hard and fast rules about falling in and being in love. Perhaps if Peg had been a little more rational at the end of the evening, Billy might have shared his three rules with her, but even Billy knew that would have been pushing things a bit far.

Billy's Love Rule No. 1: no matter how unlikely, there is someone for everyone. Ethan, his oldest brother, had taught him that one. Ethan went through a messy divorce when he was young and foolish and it had generally turned him into a pretty unlikable guy. Luckily, Cecelia Grady came along.

She initially hated him, then fell in love with him and then married him, saving Ethan and the entire Cook family from a life of his sulking and growling. Billy had a special spot in his heart for his sister-in-law.

Billy's Love Rule No. 2: only idiots don't know when they're in love. Mark, the brother sandwiched between Ethan and Billy, had driven that lesson home. Alyssa Halloway had been Mark's best friend for years and Mark—"the idiot"—had been oblivious not only to her feelings for him, but to his feelings for her. It took a movie star, Alyssa's parents' cold marriage and the reality that Alyssa might not be around forever for Mark to realize that love was standing right in front of him. The way Billy saw it, Alyssa was a saint and more than a little crazy. But, he figured, that's love.

Billy's Love Rule No. 3: affection, respect and lust are no substitutes for love. This was his own little lesson. When Billy was seventeen he had fallen ridiculously in love and it was everything being in love should be, according to Billy. It was the measuring stick for every emotion he had in the presence of any other woman and so far no one had made him dizzy and sick to his stomach. No woman in his adult life had made him feel the same giddy rush of invincibility and pleasure. No other woman had turned him inside out with her laugh; no other woman's touch was as electric.

Granted when he was seventeen, touching *himself* had been pretty electric, but the fact remained for lasting love Billy believed you had to fall headlong into it, and it simply hadn't happened since then.

Which is why he had listened to all of Peg's reasons why he should be in love with her and then, as politely and as kindly as possible, he had told her that he simply wasn't.

She didn't cry—at least while he was still in her apartment. She just watched him with pity and heartbreak in her eyes.

He had seen that look before and, as he had a couple dozen times before, he just wished the woman would cry, scream and throw things at him. That look haunted him. Her parting words seemed to ring in his head, as well.

"You're going to be thirty soon, Billy," Peg had said. "And you're going to be alone."

In the increasingly blinding snowfall, Billy didn't see the second fallen limb. Larger than the first, when the truck collided with it there was a moderately disturbing crunch. Billy quickly put the truck in Park.

"Great. Just great," Billy muttered. He slapped his hat back on his head and opened his truck door. He hopped out of the truck, putting one cowboy boot down on a giant ice patch and before he could get his second boot down, the first skated out from under him. Billy landed flat on his back with one foot still in the truck, wrenched and stuck in the door. His head thudded onto the ice, bounced and landed again, all before Billy could say "Jamaica."

Stars and snow swirled in front of his eyes and for a moment Billy could only concentrate on the pain. His ribs, his head and his ankle all clamored for attention. After a moment he stood and almost fell again because he was so dizzy and disoriented. Bracing himself against the side of the truck, he waited for the world to stop spinning.

When he could finally walk in a straight line he made his way to the fallen tree limb in the middle of the road.

For a second Billy thought there were two trees. He shook his head to clear it and saw three trees—spinning, dancing trees. When the trees finally stopped twirling he saw that there was only one. It was big but not so big that Billy couldn't heave it out of the way. He crouched, slid his hands under the limb and tried to ignore the ragged pain radiating from his bruised ribs. As he began to lift, the pain was considerable and Billy just stopped caring about sleeping in his own bed. He limped back to the truck, climbed in and got his cell phone out of the glove box.

"Hello?" Missy Cook, Billy's mother, answered brightly, as if there wasn't a freakish spring storm raging outside her house.

"I'm moving to Texas," Billy said abruptly.

"The storm's that bad?" Missy asked casually, having heard this a hundred times before.

"Tree's down in front of my truck and the tree I lifted off the road a couple miles back almost killed me," Billy whined. He didn't need to tell his mom that he slipped and fell down getting out of his truck. He was twenty-nine for crying out loud. Concussion or not, he had some pride.

"You need a vacation, honey," his mother said.

"No, Mom, I need to move."

"Well, Uncle Jimmy would love to have you. Texas is nice this time of year."

"Tell me about it," Billy said with a sigh. "Look, Ma, I'm going to backtrack and head up to the line cabin. The road's blocked and I'm mad."

And probably have some kind of brain damage, not to mention a sprained ankle, bruised ribs and shitty attitude, Billy brooded unhappily.

"Be careful. Call if you need anything," Missy said as they hung up.

Billy squinted through the windshield, concentrating on the falling snow and the road, and when nothing outside started dancing and he could tell there was only one road, he turned the truck around. Slowly, his windshield wipers making a soft whir and click as they cleared the snow from the glass, he made his way down the slick road to the line cabin the Cook family kept in working order for just this sort of situation.

Snowstorms in April. Godforsaken country. It amazed

him on an almost daily basis that his family continued to tough out these ridiculous winters. Gluttons for punishment, suckers; the Cook family was both.

It certainly wasn't the ranch or the ranch work that Billy so vehemently disagreed with. And his disagreement didn't last all year. He loved the summer, all four days of it. It was the winter he hated.

As he thought about it, Texas had a couple of things going for it. Within a twenty-mile radius of town almost every girl in the age group Billy considered dateable had declared her love to him or gotten married. Or had kids, which was another big no-no in Billy's Ten Commandments of dating—completely different than the three rules, but equally unbreakable. He didn't have anything against kids. He loved them in fact. He just didn't want to date their mothers. Much the same way as he tried to avoid blondes and old cheerleaders, women who couldn't drive a stick shift or ate too many salads or said they hated the Rolling Stones—they were all hard lessons learned and Billy didn't need to be hit over the head twice.

Everyone has to have rules, Billy thought. Peg and a lot of other women he had dated all somehow believed that his rules were simply a smokescreen to cover the fact that Billy didn't want to be in love, or couldn't fall in love. As if part of him had become so jaded that it would never work right.

"You won't be married when you're forty," Peg had said as Billy opened the door to leave her apartment. He had looked at her over his shoulder, curled up on her couch, clutching her shirt closed, her eyes getting harder by the second. "You don't know how to love!"

As if, Billy snorted. He had loved plenty. He loved his family. He loved Jake and Carl, his two best friends. He didn't even mind hugging them occasionally—if that wasn't the sign of a comfortable, loving man, Billy didn't know what was.

He had loved Kate Jenkins.

Billy scowled at the memory. Sure it was plenty ancient history, but it seemed as though every time one of these girls he dated got it in her head that he should love them, the Kate Jenkins memory came back like heartburn.

It wasn't that it was a bad memory. Even the agonizing heartbreak and consequent heartburn that accompanied her memory could not deflect from the perfection of the summer he had loved Kate Jenkins.

He should, he thought for the hundredth time, write *Penthouse* ''Forum'' about that summer.

He had been seventeen and had just finished his junior year in high school. He had been quarterback on the football team and the star shortstop on the baseball team. He had a pretty girlfriend, whom he had finally persuaded to have sex with him, and it had been great and fun and, while he couldn't exactly remember her name now, he remembered liking her a whole lot. It was promising to be a summer to end all summers.

Then his sister Samantha had arrived home for the summer with her college roommate, Kate Jenkins. Kate was nineteen and the most alluring, luscious, exciting thing Billy had ever seen. After about two weeks of wild flirtation, Billy and Kate began what would be a benchmark relationship and one of the best summers of his life. Kate had had a very educational first year at college and she was up front and honest about sex and how it should be and what Billy should do to make it that way. Billy was an apt and tireless student. They were bold and hot lessons and, as Billy remembered one particular day in the hayloft, athletic.

Kate was smart and sassy and gutsy. Her laugh was magic and just the sight of her had filled him with the lightheadedness of young love. And while those memories were certainly enough to make him smile, it was the moments that hadn't been hormonal that made him grimace; the times they had spent talking and when, in the unguardedness of the moment, Billy had professed all kinds of love to Kate. All kinds of love that a nineteen-year-old girl with dreams of New York and Los Angeles had no interest in sharing.

That had been when the heartbreak had come in. In hindsight, Billy couldn't blame her. But it didn't change the fact that Billy had fallen in love and on the edge of his thirtieth birthday, he had never felt anything like it since.

Ah, well, Billy thought. If he could find a girl that made him feel what Kate Jenkins had made him feel, maybe *he'd* be the one stopping the third date sex, putting on his shirt and turning on the light to declare his love.

Until then he had thoughts of Texas to keep him warm.

Billy peered through the snow into the shadows, hunting for the small red reflector that marked the turnoff up to the line cabin. He could barely see the road much less the reflector that was probably under a fallen tree at this point. He tried to imagine what would await him at the cabin. They kept it stocked with the bare essentials: a few lanterns, a propane stove, some pots, blankets, and enough food and firewood to keep someone warm and fed for a while.

None of the comforts of home, Billy mused sarcastically. The line cabin also held much more than warm memories, as it had been a frequent meeting place for him and Kate during the summer she had spent at the ranch. No doubt his brothers had similar memories of the girls they'd managed to get up there.

For a split second the words of all the girls he had left on beds or on couches with love and hurt in their eyes, rang in his ears and he wondered if part of his heart had become hard and useless over the years. He believed in love—he truly did—he saw it every day with his family. Perhaps his standards were too high. Maybe affection and lust was all there was as an adult. Maybe it was better, safer, to keep a part of yourself separate. Isn't that what he was doing, keeping part of himself… Billy shook his head in disgust.

Women, he thought with a small scowl, *who needs them?*

Out of the corner of his eye he saw the glimmer of the red reflector and, with a little more enthusiasm than was really safe, he swerved the truck onto the icy gravel road. Immediately he saw the error of his ways. There was no controlling the truck this time as it careered sideways through the turn and continued to slide on ice into the ditch, where it came to a jarring stop in a snowdrift, against a tree.

Billy, bracing himself against the steering wheel and the door, tried to protect his ribs to no avail. He slid sideways across the bench seat and smashed into the passenger side door with his bad ribs. Wincing and swearing and kicking his foot against the door, Billy held his breath and waited for the pain to recede.

After the moment passed, he pressed his hand to his side in an effort to keep the pain from spreading across his stomach or back and stumbled out of the truck into a knee-high drift of snow. One look at the wheels of his truck buried to the top lug nuts and he knew his ridiculously bad night had made a sudden almost comical turn for the worse. He put one hand on the open door frame and before he could get his body inside the truck a gust of wind barreled off the mountain, slamming the truck door on his thumb.

Billy swore and danced, the pain in his ribs and ankle forgotten for the moment as the pain in his thumb brought tears to his eyes.

Furious with himself and Montana and snow, Billy pulled open the door again, grabbed his gloves, cell phone and the small flask of whiskey he kept under his seat and began limping the quarter mile uphill to the line cabin.

Never let it be said that things can't always get worse, he thought grimly.

The storm showed no sign of stopping but at least the snow was drifting sideways across the road so Billy could make it straight uphill without the added agony of having to plow through snow. Cradling the flask in his left hand, Billy took a warming drink and thought about counting his blessings, but instead chose to dwell on Kate Jenkins. And the headache blooming behind his eyes. The ground was not so steady under his feet, or perhaps it *was* his feet; whatever it was, Billy was sure it wouldn't happen in Texas.

As was always the case when he thought about Kate Jenkins, after the initial warm memories and nostalgic sexual ruminations, his thoughts lingered on her particular brand of heartbreak. Her brutal honesty carried over into the break-up. Billy cringed again at the memory. It had truly been horrible. After he had told her how he felt she had put on her shirt, without the bra he had thrown into the stream in his excitement. He was too young and stupid to know *that* was the first sign.

But it had been the look of uncomfortable pity on her face when she told him that he was just a kid and she was a woman—horseshit, of course, but what nineteen-year-old girl isn't full of horseshit—that had really turned him cold. Then she continued—as if she hadn't already cut off his balls—and said that he was just in lust, and didn't really know what love was.

The first in what would become a standard refrain.

Billy wasn't so stupid that he didn't see the similarity between what Kate did to him and what he did to every woman since Kate, but the way he saw it, when you're taught by a master why reinvent the wheel?

Billy pushed his hat down harder on his head and winced when he felt the knot that was growing at the back of his skull. With nothing else to console him he took another pull from his flask. He would build a fire, stretch out on the bed and finish the rest of the whiskey. All in all not a bad way to spend the night, although he would have to get off this Kate Jenkins kick. It was depressing the hell out of him. Already the whiskey was doing its job—the pain in the various parts of his body was fading and he felt warm, so warm he unbuttoned his denim jacket. He was getting close to the cabin.

He followed the road as it curved around a granite outcrop and opened up to the small clearing where the line cabin had been built fifteen years ago. Billy stopped and stared in surprise.

Through the swirling snow he could see a light shining in one of the windows.

He blinked and shook his head, seeing two lit windows for a moment, before he truly believed what his fuddled senses were telling him. He wasn't going to be alone.

Excellent, Billy thought with real enthusiasm. One of his brothers or his dad was here, with a fire started and perhaps their own flask of whiskey. The thought of his family was a warming one and he took a second to count that blessing. He continued toward the cabin but stopped again, this time alarmed. He took a step back, and winced at the weight put on his damaged ankle.

In front of the cabin, hidden in the shadows and swirling snow, was a late-model hatchback covered in rust and bumper stickers. He got closer and saw that the license plate was from California.

Samantha. His sister. His steps quickened. Perhaps she was planning a surprise visit home and got waylaid by the storm. It had been months since he had seen his older sister and those months had been too long. He had never seen that car and if being a social worker meant she couldn't afford a decent vehicle, Billy would personally see that she got one.

He got to the door and hoped that when he opened it, covered in snow and coming in out of the dark, that she didn't greet him with a shotgun. Sam had been known to do those kinds of things.

He turned the doorknob slowly and put his shoulder to the door. He pushed it and took a step into the warm and bright room. He could see the fireplace—no, two fireplaces—no, it was only one and what looked like partially ripped-up sheets strewn across the floor of the cabin.

"Sam?" he called, coming fully into the room and shutting the door behind him. The ground beneath him tilted briefly and Billy wondered just how hard he hit his head.

"Sammy, you here somewhere?"

"One more step and I'll blow your brains out." The words seemed to come from several miles away and he could only be sure of two things. It wasn't his sister, but there was a woman in the cabin.

Behind him, Billy heard the unmistakable sound of the old shotgun being awkwardly and improperly cocked.

"What the hell...?" He turned to face the inept gun holder and for a second everything in front of him swam. He peered closer, waiting for his vision to clear. When it did, he couldn't believe what he saw.

"Kate?" he gasped, dumbfounded by the familiar stunning blonde in front of him. His voice to his own ears was slurry and slow. There were two Kates. Three. No, just one. One was all he needed. The whiskey flask slipped from his hands. "Kate *Jenkins?* What are you doing here?"

She was not too steady on her feet and as Billy watched she fell backward against the wall, dropping the gun and putting her hands to her belly.

Her big pregnant belly.

Kate Jenkins was having a baby. Right now.

"Shit," Billy swore before falling to the floor in a dead faint.

2

BILLY WAS VAGUELY AWARE of someone slapping him. He should have cared but having his eyes closed felt so nice that he ignored the slaps. He was warm and Kate Jenkins was visiting him in a dream. She was sitting on his lap and she was laughing. Her blue eyes were soft little pools promising sex and fun.

She was saying something, but Billy couldn't make it out. He strained forward to hear her and she smiled at him and leaned in close. So close he could almost feel her breath against his ear. A soft tickle of warm breath…

"Wake up!" she shouted. Billy's eyes flew open. *She's here.* Kate Jenkins was right in front of him and she looked almost exactly the same. Well, she wasn't exactly laughing and her eyes weren't soft pools of…well anything.

"What's wrong?" Billy asked, not entirely with it yet.

"Billy Cook," Kate Jenkins said as if she was making sure. Her eyes were plenty mad now. He wondered what was making her so mad. The Kate Jenkins he remembered was never mad. Mostly, she was naked.

He put a hand up to her face in an effort to bring her closer. He'd kiss that look right off her face.

"Billy, come on, snap out of it." She slapped his face again and when he dodged her, she lost her balance and had to put her hands against his rib cage to steady herself. All of her weight on his bruised ribs brought him crashing through the clouds into reality.

"Ouch!" he howled, lifting her off of him.

"Good, Billy. I've got enough on my hands without you passing out at my feet," Kate said as Billy watched her try to clamber to her feet. But her belly proved too cumbersome so she crawled over to the fire and the sheets she'd been ripping into shreds.

"Kate?" Fully conscious now, Billy crawled—because the floor was still tilting and diving under his feet—after her. "Are you having a baby?"

"Well I don't think I'm having the dinner special," she said, but Billy ignored her bad joke.

One of them was making some kind of panting-hissing-pain noise and for a moment Billy wasn't sure if it was him or her. Perhaps one of those limbs had hit him in the head and he was hallucinating.

Maybe I'm facedown in a snowdrift bleeding to death while my mind tortures me with visions of a pregnant Kate Jenkins.

That made much more sense than Kate being in his line cabin, pregnant, practicing her Lamaze breathing and tearing up sheets.

Yep, Billy figured, he was dying and Kate was here to welcome him to heaven.

"Oh, my God!" The trauma-induced Kate groaned and reached out with her not-real-blood-loss-induced hand and grabbed onto his arm. Her hand was on his wrist. Under the cuff of his coat, her fingernails dug into his flesh, more effectively than a pinch or razor for that matter.

She was real and Billy was not facedown in a snowdrift; he was here and Kate Jenkins was going to have a baby at any moment.

"*Billy,*" she half groaned, half shouted.

"We have to get you out of here," he said, panic rolling over him and sending him spinning. "You can't have a baby here!" He looked around to make sure there was no doctor waiting in the wings to deliver the baby. There wasn't. Just as he remembered: propane stove, plenty of wood and food and some blankets. Most of which Kate had torn into strips.

They're not going to keep anyone warm, he thought a little hysterically.

"It's too late, Billy. The storm is too bad and the contractions are coming faster," she grunted between thin lips as she grabbed onto his other arm.

"No!" He shouted in full denial. There would be no baby born here. "There will be no baby born here, Kate Jenkins. We'll just pack you and your belly and those sheets in the truck—" He remembered the truck, probably fully under a snowdrift at this point. "In your car," he amended "and get you to a hospital."

At that point Kate fell back, gripping her belly as another contraction seized her.

"No time…ah…Billy…" She stopped, her face drawn tight in pain.

"What?" Billy asked frantically. His blood leaping, his skin crawling, full-blown panic bloomed inside of him. There wasn't anyone on this earth less equipped to deal with this than Billy Cook, he was sure of that. He grabbed Kate's shoulders and gave her a little shake. "'Ah…Billy' *what?* Come on, Kate, we'll just get you standing up and we'll be at a nice doctor-filled hospital in no time."

Billy stood, the earth only dipping slightly beneath his feet, and reached out for the pain-racked Kate. "Up we go, sweetheart."

"Touch me and die." She practically spat the words and Billy jerked his hands back. The contraction was clearly ebbing as her face began to loosen up. "Billy, I'm having this baby and my guess is I'm having it soon. Now, you can leave—" she gestured to the door and freedom "—or you can stay."

Another contraction caused her breath to catch on a sharp

gasp of pain. "Oh, God, that hurts. Please, Billy. Please stay. Help me." She rolled restlessly to her side, away from Billy.

Death, destruction and untold horrors loomed in Billy's imagination. There was no way this was going to turn out okay.

"You sure you don't want me to get you to a hospital?" Billy asked just for clarification. Perhaps he hadn't heard her correctly.

"No, you idiot! How many times do I have to..." Her voice splintered off into a tight cry of pain.

"Do you want me to go get a doctor and bring him back here?" Billy asked hopefully. *Please, please, please...*

"No. Oh, my God! Billy please, I need you..."

Suddenly something stronger than panic exploded in Billy's chest. It was the adrenaline that allowed people to run into burning buildings and lift cars off injured bike riders. It was what allowed people to be heroic when they really wanted to mess their pants and cry.

Kate needed him to stay and help her, to make this impossible situation somehow okay, to be a light in her...

"Move, you jerk!" Kate snarled at him, trying to pull a sheet out from under his feet.

"Sorry," Billy mumbled, and lifted his foot and watched her bite a small rip in the sheet and start tearing.

"All right...okay." Billy clapped his hands together and rubbed them. "We're having a baby. Having a baby in a cabin. Don't know anything about having a baby in a cabin, but that's just what we're going to do. Baby in cabin." Billy looked around the cabin searching for anything that might help. A manual of some kind—*Giving Birth in a Cabin Without a Doctor for Dummies.* Barring a manual, a doctor lurking in the shadows would be very helpful, or even old Mrs. Peuse, who had taught him sex education and health in high school. Hell, Billy would settle for old *Mr.* Peuse, the big animal vet in town.

Oh, where was a big animal vet when you needed one?

"My guess is that cot over there is a bit more comfortable than the floor," he said, proud of himself for his calmness and rational thinking. He looked down at the pregnant woman at his feet and realized she wasn't going to stand and waltz on over there under her own power.

"I'm going to pick you up, okay?" Billy asked hesitantly. After all, just moments ago—in fact, several times in the last few minutes—Kate Jenkins had threatened his life.

"Yeah, Billy, thank you," she whispered, looking so tired Billy felt his heart ache for her.

"How did you get here?" Billy asked, sliding his arms under her body and, ignoring all of the various pains in his own body, lifted her to his chest.

"I drove," she gasped in between pants that were horrifyingly familiar. Both Cecelia and Alyssa, his sister-in-laws, had taken Lamaze. That's where they taught that kind of pant. Birthing school.

"From California? Are you nuts?" he asked, appalled. He was surprised by how light Kate was, despite her giant belly.

"Clearly," Kate said. The brackets of pain around her mouth eased again and Billy realized that another contraction had passed.

She sure is having a lot of those, Billy thought.

"How long have you had contractions?" he asked. He loved the television show *ER* and remembered that was a common question on the show.

And people say you don't learn anything from television, he thought.

"Forever," she whispered, and closed her eyes.

"Oh, no!" Billy jostled her a little bit in his arms on the

way to the cot. "This is no time for sarcasm, kiddo. Stay with me."

"Ten hours," she said, looking at him with murderous eyes. "Stop juggling me or I'll have this baby on your boots."

"Ten hours!" he said, horrified. Horses had babies in a half hour. Kate was becoming less and less horselike as this process went on.

"Are they lots worse now than when they started?" he asked.

"Yesss-sss," she hissed as her body tensed in preparation for the pain of another contraction.

"When did your water break?" Billy asked as he settled her on the bed. Another useful question from the popular television series. Billy was going to write the producers a letter.

"About ten hours ago," she said, and continued with her panting.

He had exhausted his whole human birthing knowledge. He knew that water had to break and that contractions got worse as time went on. On *ER* someone would yell "Stat" and they'd cut to a commercial. When they came back, the baby had already been born.

As far as Billy could tell, she was having contractions every minute if that. He pulled his arms out from under her and stood to leave but she gripped his hands. Hard.

"This wasn't exactly how I planned this," she said. Billy looked down at her red sweaty face. Her short blond hair was plastered to her head and her blue eyes were liquid with more emotion than Billy could handle.

"Giving birth in a freak snowstorm in a line cabin with an old boyfriend, I don't see how you could plan that," Billy agreed, and in the grip of a strange tenderness, he pushed a lock of sweaty hair off her forehead.

"Billy, I—"

"You can tell me all about it after the baby is born. Right now let's try to figure out what we're going to do," Billy interrupted. He stood and looked around at what Kate had been doing before he arrived to really screw things up.

"I'm not sure why you're tearing that sheet in strips, but I suppose that's okay," he said, planting his hands on his hips.

"I read somewhere that strips of clean cloth were good to have around," she said in between pants.

"Well, then I'm glad we've got them." He turned to the counter and pump sink that passed for a kitchen. The propane stove was on and a pot was boiling on top of the flame.

"What's cooking in the pot?" he asked.

"Shoestrings," she told him. "I read somewhere that if you have to, you can use shoestrings to tie off the umbilical cord."

Umbilical cord. Billy started sweating in earnest. At some point in the near future an umbilical cord that wasn't a horse's or a cow's, an umbilical cord that was in fact his former girlfriend's, was going to have to be dealt with.

A baby. Kate Jenkins's baby. He was going to deliver Kate Jenkins's baby.

Never let it be said that things can't always get worse.

"Right...well." Billy looked around, his voice raising an octave as panic threatened to run off with him again. "Looks like you've got everything under control."

Kate started laughing. She was tired and panicked, but her laugh was the same. Music bounced off the walls and he turned toward her.

"You bet," she said, her smile wide and real. "You ever done anything like this?"

"You bet," he answered with her words. "I'm a rancher, remember."

"Right, just pretend I'm a cow or a horse."

"I already am, sweetheart."

"When I'm not pushing this watermelon out of a straw you'll pay for that," she said. Her laughter was cut off as she groaned and arched her back in pain. "Billy..."

He was already at her side.

"Okay." The easy bantering between them vanished as Billy was immersed once more in the realities of giving birth in this cabin. "I'm, uh..." He looked down uncomfortably at his hands and at the woman in front of him. "I'm just going to take a look, uh, okay."

"Wash your freaking hands, Cook," she barked.

Billy went over to the sink and filled the small basin with water from the pump. He soaped up his hands to his elbow and rinsed them, all the time praying that at any moment a doctor would come stumbling in the door. He looked hopefully over at the closed door, but it remained closed. He was just going to have to do it.

He went back to the foot of the bed and began to lift the dress Kate was wearing. She raised her knees and spread them and Billy swallowed hard.

Mommy, he thought, desperately.

He would call his mother, right after he figured out exactly what he was facing. Maybe she could grab the rest of the women on the ranch, hop into a Jeep and just scoot on up here and relieve him of these birthing duties.

Man, he thought, *that would be nice.*

He lifted Kate's dress, his eyes glued to the roof of the cabin, and took a deep breath.

Some of his memories were just never going to be the same.

She's just like a horse, Billy told himself, his eyes squeezed shut. *Or a cow. Nothing you haven't done a million times before.*

"What the hell are you doing down there, Cook? Taking pictures?" she snapped.

Well, he amended, *not quite like a cow.*

Billy turned, his eyes locked on a small crack in the wall above Kate's head.

Maybe, he thought, *I won't even have to look.*

As gently as possible Billy put his hands to Kate's knees. She yelped.

"What?" he asked, jerking his hand back. "What's wrong?"

"Your hands are freezing!" she shouted.

He chuckled wryly. Cold hands, he guessed, were the least of their worries.

He paused for a moment thinking of the last time he had reached into a birthing mother. He had been nineteen and Patty, his mother's mare, had been having trouble with the birth from the get-go. When his father went to call the vet, Billy reached his hand into the horse's uterus, something he did with cows when they were having trouble. With his hand up to the elbow inside Patty she had another fierce contraction and Billy felt something in his wrist snap. Worse than that, he couldn't get his arm out and was in fact stuck inside the horse when his dad came back from the phone. The sounds of his father laughing brought his brothers running and soon everyone was having a good laugh at Billy with a broken wrist and his arm caught up inside a horse. When Patty's contraction passed, Mark helped Billy pull his arm out and Billy promptly fainted.

It had never been the same between him and Patty.

"Did you know you were going to give birth soon?" Billy asked, distracting both of them as he blew on his hands and generally stalled before he examined her. He was trying to hide the fact that he really had no idea what he was looking or feeling for.

"My due date is a week from now," she said between pants and gasps. "Doctor said the baby was big. Billy, I think I'm going to start pushing..."

"Big, huh?" Billy wondered if he was supposed to *feel* a big baby. Perhaps a larger-than-baby-size foot, a huge head.

"Billy?" Kate pushed herself up onto her elbows and looked at him through the vee of her legs. "Do you have any idea what you're doing?"

"None. Absolutely none," he admitted. "If you were a horse, this baby would be out and running around by now. You sure you don't want to stand and walk around, maybe eat some hay?" Billy asked, deadpan and a little frantic.

"Always the comedian, Billy…" She stopped and paused, grimacing. "I'm pushing…"

"Breathe! You have to breathe. Don't hold your breath," Billy said when her face turned an alarming shade of purple.

"Ten centimeters!" she said on a gush of exhaled breath. "My cervix should be ten centimeters."

"Well, now," Billy said, nodding his head definitively. "That's very helpful, Kate. We are getting somewhere with that kind of information."

"Read it somewhere," she said absently, breathing her way through the contractions.

"I'll just bet you did, sweetheart," he said, and hoped with everything in him he could figure out the difference between a cervix and…well anything else that might be down there.

Billy took a deep breath again and when he looked down his head began to swim. He blinked, shook his head, and opened his eyes again. From between her knees, Kate was looking at him with a very panicked face.

"Billy!" she shrieked. "The baby's head!"

Cold sweat. Billy was covered in cold sweat. He looked blankly at the crowning baby. What was he supposed to do? Was he supposed to reach in and yank the baby out?

"I'm going to push!" she shouted.

"Yes, good idea!" he agreed. "You just push all you want." Billy wanted to run. And was in fact considering the validity of racing off into the night when Kate started pushing and Billy felt the world shift.

Kate leaned up and for a moment Billy couldn't believe how red her face was.

"Heeeere iiiiiiit coooomes!" she groaned.

What happened next was a moment Billy would never forget. One second he was wondering where should he put his hands. Should he put them up, baseball catcher style? Should he put them down to catch the baby from underneath? Was the baby going to shoot straight out? Should he get some kind of protective covering for his face? He was still wondering when he heard Kate scream, a wild, crazy, Amazon kind of scream, and suddenly the baby literally slid right into his lap.

"Oh, my God! Oh, my God! Oh, my God!" Billy grabbed the slippery baby before it slid off his lap onto the floor and he promptly started hyperventilating. He looked up at Kate, who was looking at him in panic.

"What?" she asked, frantic. "What's wrong? What's wrong with the baby?"

"This isn't a cervix!" Billy, sad to say, was squealing. "This is a baby!"

"Is everything okay?" Kate asked, trying to push herself up to see.

Billy looked down at the screaming, wiggling baby. Ten fingers. Ten toes. Remarkably healthy lungs. The baby felt heavy and seemed long compared to his nieces and nephews. He looked and realized the baby was actually a girl. Her eyes were squeezed shut and as Billy watched, they popped open. Unfocused and hazy, she seemed to look right at him—and screamed bloody murder.

A baby, blinking and crying and waving angry fists at him, covered in what, he didn't even want to know, was here when moments ago his arms were empty. Billy didn't know whether to cry or throw up.

''It's a girl,'' Billy whispered, and raised his eyes to Kate's. ''You have a baby girl.'' He watched as Kate's eyes filled with tears that spilled down her cheeks in a soft waterfall of joy. Billy, unguarded and awed and probably suffering from a concussion, felt answering tears in his own eyes and let them fall unchecked down his cheeks.

''Shoestrings...'' Kate whispered, her mouth curving in a wobbly smile.

''You can't name a baby Shoestrings,'' Billy said, confused.

''No.'' Kate smiled and rested her head back on the pillow. ''Get the shoestrings for the umbilical cord.''

Right. The umbilical cord. Billy grabbed one of the strips of sheet and realized that the strip was the perfect size for the baby. He wrapped her up, placed her against Kate's belly, and turned away as Kate met her daughter. He could hear her behind him, crying and whispering and laughing, a confusing tangle of emotion, and he kept his back to her. Some things were private.

Oblivious to pain and boiling water and feeling like superman, Billy reached into the boiling water for the shoestrings and fished them out. It hurt and he'd pay for that tomorrow, but he had delivered a baby in a cabin without the help of a big animal vet, much less a health teacher or a doctor.

After all that, what were some third-degree burns?

''Billy?'' Kate's voice was thick and choked and Billy turned to face her, shoestrings in his hands, tears in his eyes and explosions of amazement going off in his chest. ''Thank you, Billy. I couldn't have done this without you... I—''

''Well,'' Billy interrupted, not wanting any kind of uncomfortable acknowledgment to ruin the emotional free fall he was experiencing. ''I couldn't have done it without you, either. Let's call it even.''

Kate Jenkins smiled and chuckled and turned her face back to her daughter's.

Billy walked over to her to deal with the umbilical cord.

What a night, he thought with a smile and a rueful shake of his head.

3

IT WAS THE PAIN that woke her up. The slow, throbbing pulse of pain radiating from her crotch to her jaw hitting all the sensitive parts in between. Slowly, Kate pulled herself from the oblivion she had fallen into after nursing her daughter for the first time.

As she woke she became aware of the small warm weight nestled in the curve of her body. At almost the same time she became aware of the fact that she was being similarly nestled in the curve of a larger body.

Kate opened her eyes and she looked down at her daughter wrapped carefully in the ripped sheets, then at the brown hard hands that were cradling the baby to Kate's body. One of the hands was red and blistered and wrapped in a torn piece of sheet.

Billy.

The sequence of the evening's events was hazy. She remembered Billy coming in the door and her cocking a gun at him and then someone passed out. She was sure it hadn't been her because she'd had all that pain and terror to keep her conscious.

Odd that Billy passed out, she thought idly.

After that, everything was a blur of pain and fear until Billy had placed her perfect daughter onto her stomach. The flood of emotion that had been coming and going came again and tears welled up and spilled. So much amazement.

One of the sets of hands holding on to the baby must have squeezed because the blue hazy eyes opened and tried to focus. A tiny fist came out and waved for a moment. Her face started turning red and then purple. Her rosebud mouth opened and shut and then opened again and the crying began. In force.

Billy stirred behind her and then pushed himself up onto his elbow, coming instantly awake and instantly confused.

"What's wrong?" he gasped. "What's that noise? Someone stop that noise." The three of them were precariously perched on the cot and when he tried to sit all the way up he toppled over the edge and onto the floor.

Billy stayed down there for a few moments and Kate began to worry that he had passed out again.

"You okay?" she asked, looking over the side of the bed as best she could without really moving very much.

"Yeah," he said, his face pressed to the cabin floor. "We had a baby last night, didn't we?"

"Well, one of us just helped," Kate answered. Assured that Billy was okay she arranged herself so she could feed the crying baby. For the second time she realized that those breast-feeding videos, while initially a little creepy and personal, had been a truly wise investment.

"Oh, my God," he said, sitting up. He brought his knee up and rested his arm and then his head on it. Kate chuckled at him, knowing almost exactly how he felt.

"Did I hear the phone ring?" Billy asked.

"No, but I think the snowstorm stopped."

After the baby had been born and all umbilical cord and afterbirth concerns had been taken care of, Billy had made contact with the outside world.

Kate had listened with half an ear as Billy had talked to his mother on the cell phone.

"Yes, Mom, Kate Jenkins...right, she had a baby... Mom, I already told you this...I only passed out for a few seconds...Kate and I both seem okay, but we're not horses so I don't really know...we need a doctor. The baby keeps crying...oh...the storm's worse? Babies are supposed to do that? Yeah, well, I have my cell phone on...have the doctor call.''

Kate had looked down at her baby girl and had felt a heady mixture of love and panic. The baby had seemed okay, healthy and whole. Pink and hungry, and after Billy had cleaned her up a little, Kate was certain she was the cutest newborn in the world.

But that didn't mean that a million things couldn't be wrong. Kate had been reading baby books and *How to Give Birth* books and *What Can Go Wrong With Your Baby* books for nine months and she was plenty aware of the fact that her daughter needed a doctor to confirm what Kate was sure was true.

Her daughter was perfect.

The doctor had called and talked to both of them and promised to get up there as soon as the roads were passable. He made some kind of comment about how women had been doing this without doctors since the world began, which apparently made Billy mad. He told the doctor, with quite an edge to his voice that *he* hadn't been doing this since the world began and the doctor had better get his butt up to the cabin. Kate had smiled as she'd watched Billy try to be fierce while hanging up the cell phone. It was hard to mean business when all you had to do was press a little button.

Then Billy had stressed and paced and gone out into the storm and come back in. He had taken a few bracing gulps from his flask. He'd offered her some and when she'd turned it down, he'd taken her bracing gulps. Tired of watching him and exhausted from the twelve hours of panic and pain, Kate had fallen asleep filled with a general sense of well-being and calm despite the circumstances.

And now she had no idea what time it was. Days might

have passed. But the storm had cleared and soon the cavalry would arrive, no doubt with Missy Cook leading the charge.

Kate thought about seeing Mrs. Cook again in her current condition, covered in dried blood and sweat. It wasn't exactly in her master plan but her master plan had been derailed for six years, so what was one more surprise.

"Storm's over," Billy said from the window. He looked at her and after a long strange moment he smiled. "Are you okay?"

"We're very good." Kate felt an answering smile pull across her lips. There was nothing like having a baby under primitive conditions to bring two people together. She couldn't have written a better story. She looked down and realized that her daughter had stopped feeding and her breast was hanging out in the open.

She wasn't even embarrassed. She wanted to throw off all her clothes and dance around naked with Billy and her baby. She wanted to sit forever in the warm glow that surrounded the three of them. It had been years since she had felt this kind of connection with someone and it was worth every moment of fear and panic leading up to it to have these precious moments of quietude and togetherness.

"Would you like to hold her?" she asked, shifting her baby so Billy could hold her.

Billy looked at the baby for a moment then grinned a false kind of cheesy grin. Kate felt as though he was shutting a door between them.

"You two look plenty comfortable," he said, and turned back to the window.

For some reason it created a small crack in her otherwise blissful scenario.

"Kate?" Billy asked after a moment. It was the tone of his voice that really told her that her little world was coming to an end. Billy had turned from rescuer and friend to someone with uncomfortable questions.

She knew that she couldn't just land on the Cook doorstep after twelve years, give birth and expect there not to be questions. Billy had probably saved her life and the life of her daughter. He deserved an explanation.

She pulled her defenses up tight to her neck, looked up at him and smiled, hoping against hope that this wasn't going to go as badly as she figured it might.

"Billy?" she answered. Carefully she rearranged herself so she could sit and hold her daughter without her boobs hanging out everywhere.

"With the storm over, the doctor and my mom should be here in about an hour if the roads aren't really bad," he told her. He moved from the window to the chair by her bed and put his elbows on his knees. He rubbed his hair with his hands, scratched his neck, rolled his shoulders, and finally looked back up at her.

His grin was both familiar and different and for a moment Kate wondered what had happened to the boy she knew that had turned him into this man. She could still see the charming self-reliant, fun-loving boy, but he was older and it seemed from the look in his eyes, wiser. *But he's still damn sexy.*

Of course, she was suffering from blood loss and post-traumatic stress disorder, so what did she know?

His hair was the same dark brown, and his eyes were the same green. His body had fulfilled the promise it had had when he was seventeen. Some men were just made for women and this man was one of them. His honey-licked voice and casual endearments…the boy she had known had turned into a heartbreaker.

From the look in his eyes she knew he was a heartbreaker with a purpose.

"You want to ask me some questions?" she asked, cutting to the chase.

"Yes. I mean, if you're up for it," he said, even though Kate could actually feel the curiosity pouring out of him.

"I guess as long as the questions don't involve dancing, I'm able to answer some." She smiled, hoping that the questions would be friendly and not turn into an inquisition. She had had enough of inquisitions.

"What...uh, I mean...how—"

"What the hell am I doing here?" she finished for him.

"I guess that's as good a place as any to start," he said, his voice somewhere between laughter and disbelief.

"Well..." Kate looked down at her daughter's head. "Billy, it's not real easy to explain—"

"Give it your best shot," he interjected.

"Well, I'm not sure if you remember, but I can be a...well...some people think I'm a bit irrational and maybe just a tad impulsive..."

"A bit?" Billy hooted. "A tad?"

Kate knew what he was thinking, the things he was remembering. That she had run down Main Street in her underwear on a dare. That she used to climb the tree by his window and throw stones at it so that he would come out to fool around with her at midnight. The Kate Jenkins who had gotten it into her head that her baby had to be born on a mountain in Montana at the only place she had ever really felt accepted: the Morning Glory.

For the millionth time since she had learned that she was pregnant, Kate promised no more selfish, impulsive behavior. She was a mother now and she had someone depending on her. She couldn't simply run around doing whatever her heart told her to do. It was time for her brain to take over. Those crazy days were long gone.

These days, she thought, looking at the soft whorls of hair on her baby's head, *are much better.*

"Yeah, well, this pregnancy made me a bit crazy and a few days ago I got it in my head that I had to give birth at the Morning Glory Ranch. Before I could think twice I was in my car and on my way here,'' she said in a rush, hoping he would just accept her behavior for what it always had been—impulsive. If he started picking it apart, she knew she would fall apart.

''Please don't tell me you drove all the way up here from California in that car out front.'' Billy was clearly judging a book by its cover and imagining all of the million things that could go wrong. ''Your car is a pile of rust…''

''With an entirely rebuilt engine and new tires and brakes. Actually, it's perfectly safe,'' she said smugly. Her skin was beginning to itch at all of the judgment radiating from him. ''I took the trip in four days. I stayed in hotels every night, stopped when I was tired, ate when I was hungry and went to the bathroom almost every five minutes. Billy, it's done and I'm here and my daughter was born and we're both fine. So let's not dwell on what could have happened.''

''Okay,'' he said after a long pause. He scratched his head again. ''But why come up here?''

Kate couldn't answer that question. Her reasons for making the potentially threatening drive up here were far too emotionally based to try to make sense of. There was simply too much she didn't want to dig up. Too much that she simply couldn't admit to Billy.

''Well, it's hard to say, Billy. I only have my mother and she's still in Alabama. She couldn't come until after the baby was born and I guess I wanted my child to be born someplace where love just oozed off the walls. I wanted her to be held by people who were grandparents and uncles and aunts. They didn't have to be hers, but…well…I'm impulsive,'' she finally said with a shrug.

''Why couldn't your mother come?'' Billy asked.

''She…'' Kate looked down at her baby. ''She doesn't exactly approve of what I've done here.'' Her eyes filled up with tears again, remembering all the bitter words between her and her extremely proud mother. Kate could almost understand her mother's abject disapproval but it was an extremely sore spot. Kate's mother had raised her alone after her father had left them. Better than most, Debra knew what Kate was in for and the support she would need, and Debra Jenkins was having none of it. But that wasn't anything Billy needed to know.

Billy was ranting about something and with an effort she turned her attention away from her sleeping child and back to Billy.

"What if you had given birth on the road somewhere? This was completely insane..." he was muttering, and Kate tuned out again. That was a refrain she had heard her entire life and was frankly tired of.

Abby? Abigail? Gayle? Gloria? Ick, she thought. *Jennifer? Josephine? Jackie? Jodi? No, that's not right.*

She looked down at her daughter and tried to see a name in her features. *Hairy?* She smiled and pressed a kiss to her daughter's very hairy head.

"You're not listening, are you?" Billy asked, strangling on his appalled amazement.

"Nope, I'm not, Billy." Kate's head came up along with all of her defenses. They were new, these defenses, and she was simply going to have to work on them. No better time like the present. "One of the reasons I came here was because there is no judgment up here. You and your family accepted me and whatever I did with smiles and hugs and laughter. The world out there is ugly and nasty, ready to find out that you're wrong and wanting and dumb and crazy. I left it behind. So don't talk to me that way," she chastised.

"Maybe," Billy said, his voice a little harder than usual, "the world sees you as dumb and crazy because you really are."

"I'm not dumb and crazy, Billy, but I'm beginning to see that I was wrong to come up here." Sparks flew from their eyes and the air was charged with an impossible tension. She wished she was fully dressed and not sore and tired and that she could get up with her baby and waltz out of here in some kind of grand exit, but it just couldn't be done without showing her bum and possibly bleeding all over the floor.

Billy stood from his chair and walked over to the fireplace. In the silence, the roaring fire that Kate had built in her early labor nesting instinct was popping and snapping its embers. Kate leaned her head down so she could feel her daughter's soft hair against her lips.

Billy turned to her and she looked up.

"I'm sorry," they said at the same time and then smiled.

"I just gave birth..." she said by way of excuse.

"I think I have a concussion..." He smiled. "Kate, no matter what, I'm glad you are here and that I was here to help." He came back to her cot in one long step; his face carved out of contrition and regret for his words and judgment. "This was the most amazing thing I have ever been a part of and I just don't quite know what to do about it. You're safe, your daughter is safe and, after a little more whiskey, I'll be back to normal."

"I know, it's all been so amazing," she said in a rush. "I thought I was going to have to do this alone and I was so scared and then you came in and saved the day. You delivered my baby," she said with thankful reverence and put her lips again to her baby's head while the tears welled up in her eyes and spilled down her cheeks.

"What are you going to name her?" he asked. He brought one hand up carefully and brushed the thick brown hair on the baby's head by Kate's mouth and then put his hand down.

"Billy," she answered deadpan, needing some levity to

save her from throwing herself and her baby into Billy's arms. "After the man who barely caught her as she was born."

"Ah, the Kate Jenkins sense of humor takes a beating and keeps on cracking out the bad jokes. Seriously, what's the little girl's name? We can't keep calling her 'her.'"

"I don't know. Any suggestions?"

"Hell, no!" Billy said immediately. "I mean, I only name horses."

"What was the last horse you named?"

"Lulabelle," Billy answered, fearing the worst,

Kate's eyes opened wide and she smiled. "I love it!"

"No, you don't."

"Yes, yes I do. My daughter's name is Lulu."

"Did I say, Lulu? The last horse I named was Jennifer or Laurie or..."

"Ah, nice try. I think we'll go with Lulu for a while."

"Years of torture and it's going to be all my fault," Billy moaned, and Kate smiled, thinking Lulu was a beautiful funky name for a girl born in a cabin during a freak storm.

"Should we contact your husband?" he tried to ask casually, but the words sounded as if they were stuck in his throat. Oddly, Kate knew how he felt.

"Oh, that was a hard one, wasn't it, Billy?" she said, laughing at his discomfort. "The truth is, there is no husband. Lulu's dad wasn't very excited about being a part of our family."

Billy nodded once and then let the subject go, and Kate was glad for it.

"Isn't there anyone we should call? You're kind of a hotshot in L.A. Someone is going to miss you," Billy speculated.

"Hotshot." Kate smiled ruefully at Billy's words. He was talking about her small but very painful brush with fame. She had written the script for a movie called *Spurs* that had done very well. Last year, Dirk Mason, movie star and good friend to the Cook family, had starred in and ultimately won an Academy Award for his role in her screenplay.

Perhaps in Montana, to the Cook family, she was a hot-shot, but in Hollywood she was food for sharks.

"Nope, I haven't been involved in the hot-shot business since *Spurs,*" she said evenly.

"Then where have you been?" Billy asked.

"Here and there, up and down the coast of California. Mostly in the mountains," she answered, and again Billy backed off from the subject.

"I liked your movie," he said softly. His grin kicked up the corner of his mouth and Kate was flooded again by a million memories and feelings that were more than a decade old.

"I'm glad, Billy Cook. Because it was all about you..." She smiled and the waterworks were on again. Tears in a steady stream fell from her eyes and Billy made a pained noise as he came close to the bed.

"Oh, sweetheart, come on—"

Billy was interrupted by the sound of a car horn. A door slammed in the distance and in the space of a breath Missy Cook was in the doorway. Kate watched sadly as all the warmth and tenderness drained right out of his face. He took steps away from her and tried to fade into the woodwork. She was an emotional mess and she was watching him leave her and it made her want to stop him.

"Billy?" she said, and knew that her voice was filled with all the panic and confusion she felt in these strange new hours of motherhood. Billy shook his head once and shrugged painfully and then the moment was over.

"Oh, my," Missy was saying over and over again. "Look at these children." Missy started crying as she came close to the bed. "Look at these babies. Just look at them."

Kate wasn't sure who Missy was talking to or about, but it was so comforting to be crooned to. Kate didn't protest when Missy brushed her hands over Kate's head and leaned down to enfold Kate and her baby into her giant grandmother arms.

Missy bent her gray head to Kate's and pressed a kiss on the crown and Kate began to sob. Nine months of being strong and scared melted in one hug.

The cavalry had arrived and Kate was saved.

4

"WE CAN'T STAY in the cabin!" Kate looked around the table full of Cooks with horror and disbelief. "There's no running water, or electricity, or phone—"

"You have a cell phone," Missy cut in, clearly missing Kate's point.

"I have a three-week-old baby! What if something went wrong?" Kate asked.

Anything could go wrong. Despite what the doctor said Kate had read *Three Months: Beautiful and Treacherous,* about the first months of life and how anything from a spider bite to croup could spell disaster. Considering Kate had been able to spell disaster on her own for several years, she was sure she didn't need the extra help.

"Where do you want to live, in the hospital?" Mac Cook, put in his two cents' worth. Missy's husband who was an interesting physical cross of John Wayne, Clint Eastwood and Paddington Bear.

"Yes, frankly. If Alice and I could stay at the hospital we would," Kate said stubbornly.

"Alice?" Billy interrupted. "I thought you named her Lulu."

"Well, I decided I liked Alice better," Kate retorted. The only things to read in the cabin had been the childbearing books she had brought and an old copy of *Alice in Wonderland.* After a week of Lulu, Kate opted for Alice. And Alice, who had never shown a real partiality to Lulu, happily complied.

Not that it was any of Billy's business. He walked out of the cabin three weeks ago after Missy had arrived and she hadn't seen him since. *So much for living through the most amazing experience together.* So much for bonding over the umbilical cord. Kate couldn't even look at him without wanting to scream. Kate knew she shouldn't have counted on anything different, but she had hoped Billy would have stayed and she was a little blindsided by what felt like his betrayal.

"Poor kid is going to have some kind of identity problem," Billy muttered. Kate just shot him what she hoped was a dirty look and glanced around the table, trying to find support in Alyssa and Cecelia, the two women who had married Billy's older brothers. They were sitting at the table with children crawling over them, demanding attention.

"Kate," Alyssa, Mark's wife, said as she wiped the nose of her baby Louise. "Where would you go?" Cecelia and Ethan's four-year-old, Sarah, tugged on her shirtsleeve.

"I'd imagine she needs to get back to L.A.," Billy said, and turned to Kate, clearly expecting her to agree.

"Well, no," Kate answered slowly, not looking at Billy and instead finding all the welcome she needed in the eyes of Missy and Mac. "I don't have anything waiting for me in Los Angeles, so I guessed maybe I'd...well...I thought I'd stay here."

She saw the dawning excitement in Missy's eyes and knew she had misunderstood what Kate had meant.

"Well, honey, nothing would make us happier than having you live here. We have lots of empty rooms since Ethan and Mark left," Missy offered.

"That's really nice of you," Kate said, determined to maintain her independence among the long and comforting arms of the Cook family. "But I meant that Alice and I would stay in Lincoln." Kate named the closest town, about a twenty-minute drive away from the ranch. She could tell by the disappointment on the faces of Mac and Missy that even that seemed too far away. She knew it must seem strange, her wanting to stay in this small mountain town, but she did. She could stay for a few months, save some money and wait until Alice was old enough to travel and maybe they could move on to a bigger town. "I think Alice and I need a place of our own. There must be apartments in town," Kate said.

For a girl operating without a real plan, that is not a bad plan at all, she thought.

The Cook's looked at each other blankly.

"Are there?" Mark looked at his wife. Alyssa thought for a moment and shrugged. "I wouldn't know," she said.

Clearly none of these people had ever had to worry about housing.

"Of course there are," Billy said and paused. "Someone has to live above all those stores on Main Street, right?"

"Pete's Place." Ethan named the only bar in town. "I know there's an apartment above Pete's Place."

"Oh, that won't do." Missy turned grandmother eyes to Kate. "Surely a cabin is better than a dirty apartment above a bar."

"Oh, for crying out loud, I'm sure there are other apartments," Kate said, grinning despite herself.

What a bunch of railroaders, she thought fondly.

"Is living in the cabin that bad?" Mac asked, putting his coffee cup down on the table and getting to the root of the matter.

There it was. The real problem. Living in the rustic cabin with no distractions wasn't bad. In fact it was the closest to truly happy she had been in years.

Kate had spent hours looking at Alice, studying her tiny fingernails and eyelashes in that cabin. Kate saw every dream she had ever nurtured in the nine months Alice was growing in her belly in those eyelashes. Days passed with no other thought, with no other activity than feeding Alice and watching her sleep with tears in her eyes.

Desperate to leave California, Kate had only managed to pack her birthing books, every diaper, blanket, stuffed animal and onesie she could get her hands on, two maternity dresses that she hated, and nine pairs of socks.

Luckily, between Alyssa and Cecelia they had been able to wrestle up a relatively functional wardrobe, consisting mostly of sweatpants and denim. Which was fine because except for doctor's appointments and the grocery run, she never left the cabin.

She was absolutely sure new mothers shouldn't behave like this. She should be clean at the very least.

However, what she did have was clean air and trees and her daughter's eyelashes and an entire family of Cooks visiting almost hourly every day.

Missy came in the morning with herbal tea and muffins. Alyssa and Cecelia came with the kids: Sarah, Derek and Alyssa's baby girl, Louise. They brought a newspaper and fruit salads. Mark and Ethan usually dropped by, together or separately, to leave propane and firewood and some kind of dinner, or an invitation to dinner, and in the evening Missy, with Mac, came again in what Kate had dubbed her most favorite visit.

The small-piece-of-chocolate visit.

She tried not to think about it, that Billy didn't come by. She tried to make sure Alice knew that it wasn't her fault that Billy didn't visit, but she knew Alice was hurt. Or maybe it was Kate. Whatever. Someone in that cabin was a little bit hurt by Billy Cook's cold shoulder.

Now as Kate sat across from Billy at the kitchen table, he became one more reason that she *should* leave the cabin. Confusing impulsive behavior was something she was leaving behind. She was resolved to let her head do all the thinking and her heart and hormones were to sit quietly in the back seat. But Billy Cook always did crazy things to her hormones.

For instance, right now even as she sat here confused and angry and sick of him, she kind of wanted to crawl into his lap. *Maybe I'm unstable,* she thought. Wanting to kiss a man who studiously ignored her existence was very unstable. She was beginning to think that maybe Billy was at the root of her impulsive decision to come back to the Morning Glory. It had nothing to do with wanting a big family; it had to do with wanting to get the feeling of that summer back. The last of her innocence, the last of her foolish hope.

Almost the second after she conceived her lovely Alice she had sworn off men. But alone in the cabin with her daughter breathing softly beside her, she couldn't help wishing for a larger shoulder to help carry her fear and the weight of her own head.

Her attraction to Billy and longing for him was mostly nostalgia and some kind of weird gratitude, she was sure, but more distance between her and Billy would do some very soothing things to her nerves and heart.

"I think she's right." Cecelia, Ethan's wife, simultaneously washed her daughter's face at the sink and played peekaboo with baby Derek. "She can't live in the cabin. I'll help her find a place." Cecelia, used to battling the combined will of the Cook family, turned and looked them all in the face. "You can't always be right, you know," she told the family.

"You don't know us very well, do you, sweetheart?" Ethan asked, hooking his arm around her hips and pulling his entire family into his body for a hug and kiss. "We are rarely right."

He leaned away from his family but little Sarah curled

her arms around his neck and kept her lips pressed to his cheek.

"Papa," she said, and blew a giant raspberry against his face.

"Last thing we need around here is more kids anyway," Ethan said, blowing a raspberry against Sarah's face, which made her squeal.

Everyone around the table smiled and sat back in their chairs as Kate choked back the sudden tears.

"We'll help you find a place," Missy said. Kate knew a compromise when she heard it and nodded in thanks, unable to speak past the lump in her throat at the warm family scene.

"Anyone for gin rummy?" Mac asked.

In a blink of an eye the entire mood of the room changed. As the family jostled to find cards and scorecards, Kate stood and took her daughter from where she had been sleeping against Mac's large shoulder.

"I'm going to pass on cards tonight," she told the room. "Thank you so much for having us. This was wonderful to see you all at the same time."

Everyone stood, hugged Kate and Alice, and said their goodbyes.

"It's about time you got down here," Mac chastised.

"I know." Kate smiled and ducked her head. "We'll be back soon."

"Here let me take you back to the cabin," Mark said, as he had been the one to pick her up earlier. He was holding his daughter and turned to give her to Alyssa, who was up to her elbows washing dishes. Mark turned to his mother instead, ready to pass her on when Billy stood. Kate's stomach did a flip.

"I'll take you back," Billy said, unfolding his lean six-foot frame from the chair. Kate felt parts of her body jump and plummet all at the same time.

She gathered up all her stuff and waved goodbye to the crowd that had gathered on the porch to see them off. Then they walked silently to the legion of pickups that waited.

"Probably not what you're used to, but it works," he said approaching his truck. It was just enough of an innuendo about how rich he assumed she was that Kate's back went up.

"You've seen my car. This is quite a step up," she said brusquely. *What's his problem?*

"Why do you drive that heap of rust?" Billy asked, opening the door for her and pushing the front seat up so she could access the car seat that was strapped in the small back seat. Every truck on the ranch was equipped with a back seat and car seat.

Kate put Alice in the chair, took one lingering look at her eyelashes and climbed into the passenger seat.

"Because it was the first car I could buy on my own," she answered, locking in her seat belt. The snow from the freak storm was long gone but the nights were still chilly and Kate watched her breath make small plumes in front of her, measuring her breaths.

"I'd imagine you could buy a lot nicer car with all that money from *Spurs.*" Billy turned the truck out of the small driveway and looked over at her. There was something in his look—the look he had been giving her since the cavalry had come after Alice was born—and Kate finally put her thumb on it.

The expectation of disappointment. He wasn't even going to give her a chance to be a different person than the headstrong kid she used to be.

Well, Billy Cook could screw himself.

"What would you like me to say, Billy? What would really satisfy all that morbid curiosity? Yes, I have tons of money from *Spurs.* Much more than you could probably dream of. And yes, I could buy a really fancy car, but I love my car. Rust and everything. So, how about you drop this casual anger and really let me have it?'' Her heart was pounding in her years.

''I just think it's weird you wanting to stay here,'' he snapped. ''There must be a million places you could go with all your money and Hollywood connections.''

''Sure, Steven Spielberg said I could give birth at *his* cabin in the middle of nowhere, but I turned him down,'' Kate said sarcastically. The awful yawning truth was that she had nowhere to go. All the places she had called home seemed cold. ''I'm actually just sticking around to piss you off. How am I doing?''

''You're not pissing me off,'' Billy answered defensively, shooting a look at her that she couldn't decipher. ''Come. Go. Do what you want.'' He rested his elbow on the door and hitched his hat up higher on his head.

Realization like a bright new day dawned on her. ''This is about what happened ten years ago,'' she said. While she knew it was mean, she couldn't keep a disbelieving laugh from sputtering between her lips. She put a hand up to her mouth.

''Thirteen years,'' Billy said quickly and then cringed.

''You are still burned that I left you at the end of that summer…''

''I am not!'' Billy said defensively.

''You are, too.''

''Am not!''

''Oh, my God, Billy,'' she said, not listening to his heated denials. ''What would you have had me do? I was nineteen…''

''I have completely forgotten that summer!'' he insisted loudly. Kate, unable to help it, threw her head back and laughed.

''No one would be able to forget that summer, Billy Cook. We nearly killed ourselves.'' It had been that day in the hayloft, or maybe the day on the rocks over the river, that had almost caused their deaths. Particularly Billy's, but he was young and flexible and survived. Kate watched while Billy's ears turned red and nearly burst into flame.

"Remember that time we hid behind the church..."

"Of course," he hissed. "Of course I remember. And I didn't expect you to stick around, but I was seventeen and..."

"You were in love," she finished for him.

"I *thought* I was in love," he said, looking at her pointedly. "There's a heck of a difference."

Kate's laughter died in her throat, not liking how that last part stung.

"We were just kids," she said softly.

"Yeah." He shrugged and looked over at her coolly. "We both lived. But it took me a long time to get over some of the things you said when you left."

Kate cringed at the memory. She had been horrible. She remembered the way she had shrugged off his feelings and, in truth, her own. Because she was in such a rush to get out in the world and conquer it, there had been no time to listen to her heart or to Billy's heart. *So many mistakes, so many words she could never take back.*

"I'm sorry, Billy. I was so young and stupid. I had no idea..."

"Ancient history, forget it." The silence between them was so cold and went on for so long that Kate felt tears well up in her eyes.

"I want us to be friends," she finally said. "You have a real special place in my heart and memory and it's dumb to act like we're teenagers again. I'm here because I have nowhere else to go. Money can't buy what's available at the Morning Glory Ranch or what's in your family. It just..." She trailed off, waiting for him to agree, but he didn't stop her or interrupt her or let her know in any way that he felt the same way.

"Look, Kate—" he darted a hard glance at her "—let's not pretend. You're not sticking around here, I bet you'll be gone by the end of the month."

"You don't—" Kate protested, offended. Just because she had never stuck around before didn't mean she *couldn't.*

"Kate," Billy interrupted. "Lincoln is a small town. Small. Like, no fancy restaurants or coffee shops. We don't have a spa or any of the things you're used to." He stopped for a second but Kate stayed silent. "I was hurt when you left last time, I'll admit it. But you've got a daughter now and my family is beginning to fall in love with her, so when you do leave there's going to be enough trouble without you and I being friends." He put a little nasty sneer on the word *friends* that stung.

It occurred to Kate at that moment what she had done to that seventeen-year-old boy with love in his eyes. She had stunted him. She had the reverse of the Midas Touch. She had the Klutz Touch.

Things were going to change. Billy had the right idea; they shouldn't get attached. She and Alice had a long road ahead of them that was better handled without the added complication of men.

That's right, she told herself. *Billy Cook is a man and you have sworn off them, remember?* And having sworn off men, she shouldn't be getting upset by his dismissal. And she wasn't. Well, not really. Okay, she was livid.

"So let me get this straight," Kate said, looking right at him. "I won't call you to baby-sit and you won't be taking Alice to the playground and under no circumstances will you be enjoying slumber parties at my house." Kate watched the tide of red climb Billy's neck. He was never able to handle honesty, he felt better hidden behind the games men and women played with each other.

Well, as my high school phys ed teacher used to say, games have rules so that nobody gets hurt. "In short," she summarized it up, "we are not friends."

"Kate." Billy breathed out slowly. "I don't know what we are, but you, like it or not, are a part of the Cook family. We're going to be around each other a lot and I don't want my family to ask why we can't be in the same room..."

"And why you're being a jerk," she interjected, and Billy slowly nodded.

"And why I'm a jerk," he agreed.

"So, we're friendly but not friends," Kate said, ignoring the stab of regret and longing.

"Exactly," he said.

They both nodded and looked out the window in silence.

KATE COULDN'T BELIEVE IT. There were exactly three apartments in town. Three. One above the grocery store that reeked of the rotting produce out back. One above the Personality Dress Shop, which was tiny with no kitchen. The last apartment was above Pete's Place, the bar in town that seemed to be open twenty-four hours a day.

Surprisingly, for an apartment directly above a dance floor, it was silent. Pete had apparently done quite a job insulating the place to ensure no sound would seep through the floor.

There was a large window and small balcony facing the street and the rooms—a bedroom, bathroom, kitchen and small living area—were large and bright. The apartment came with a small black-and-white TV that received three channels, a couch that seemed almost brand-new and one heavy-duty frying pan. The last tenant had apparently left those meager amenities behind.

Kate stood in the center of the living room. The small

breeze coming in through the open window ruffled her hair and carried with it the sounds of a country song from the bar downstairs. Alice, resting quietly in Kate's arms, smiled and cooed.

"We'll take it," Kate said to Pete.

Despite the vehement Cook response, she moved into the apartment a week after seeing it.

Since there was not much to move—a couple of books, some odds-and-ends clothing, one baby and one mother—Kate didn't make too much of a big deal of her moving day.

She should have known, however, that whenever the Cooks got involved, it's always a big deal. They were like movers and decorators and builders all in one. Ethan put up towel racks in the bathroom, the girls cleaned cupboards as though Kate was going to put Alice down for a nap in them and Missy must have been saving up decades' worth of junk just for this opportunity.

For a girl who had prided herself on her ability to pack all of her possessions into her trusty hatchback, the sudden influx of possessions was daunting.

"What in the world am I going to do with a sewing machine?" she asked Missy as the older woman carried it in and set it up on the kitchen table that had been donated from the farm.

"Every young mother should have a sewing machine," Missy said, testing the old foot pedal and beaming when the machine hummed.

"Maybe every young mother in the 1930s," she said, then whirled to stop Mark and Billy as they brought in a big box of things.

"What's in there?" she asked suspiciously. She looked right at Mark, instead of Billy. So far they were sticking to the game rules. During the move they had both smiled at each other in a friendly but completely unconvincing way.

He laughed when the rest of the family laughed at one of her nervous jokes and she was going out of her way not to accidentally brush against him.

She had however noticed him looking down at Alice in her crib and smiling. He had reached out his hand and covered the top of her head with his palm. He had then whispered something she couldn't hear, and Kate had had to go to the bathroom to hide her tears.

Postpartum depression, she had thought. *It has nothing, absolutely nothing to do with Billy Cook!*

"Ah," both Mark and Billy craned their necks over the sides of the box to see inside, and Kate snapped back to reality.

"Looks like one of those things you toast stuff in," Mark said.

"That would be a toaster," Billy translated.

"And one of those things that mixes stuff up." Mark craned his neck to the side.

"A mixer," Billy supplied. Kate watched in amusement, her head swiveling as though she was watching a tennis match.

"And…oh, a four-quart, programmable, three-temperature Crock-Pot."

Billy looked at Mark as if a big bird had landed on his head.

"I don't need this stuff!" Kate said, laughing at the crazy brothers despite herself.

"I don't know, those Crock-Pots come in real handy," Mark told her.

"When have you ever touched a Crock-Pot?" Billy asked his brother.

"Sometimes Alyssa forgets to turn the thing on before she goes into the vet clinic and she calls me and I turn it on," Mark answered defensively, and turned to Kate. "I would not look a Crock-Pot giver in the mouth."

"Honey, it just breaks our heart to see you raising your little girl without some of the basic amenities a woman needs," Missy said, breezing by Kate with what looked like an old-fashioned ice-cream maker.

"You wanted me to live in a cabin with no running water," Kate reminded them dryly.

"Regardless, the needs are there and we are seeing fit to meet them, aren't we girls?" Missy turned to her daughter-in-laws who were trying to find places in the cupboards for egg poachers and roasting pans.

"Free stuff is free stuff," answered the pragmatic Cecelia, waving a turkey baster.

"And you never know when you might just want to make muffins shaped like hearts," Alyssa added, holding up an odd-shaped muffin tin.

Mac was sliding in past his sons who were blocking the doorway with the giant box of household appliances. He had something behind his back and was looking a little too sneaky for Kate's peace of mind.

"Mac, whatever you have in your hands, you can just forget it."

"Now, don't get smart with me, girl. You're all alone with a baby girl living above a bar. There are bound to be some cowboys who'll get a crazy hair up their nose and try to make themselves at home here," Mac said sternly.

"I don't want a gun," Kate said resolutely, immediately able to read his mind. *As if any guys would ever want to make themselves at home with me and a baby.*

"It's not even loaded," he said. From behind his back he produced the old shotgun from the cabin. The same shotgun she had pointed at Billy when he had surprised her in the midst of her mindless panic.

"Doesn't matter, Dad. I think she already broke it," Billy said, finally getting the box through the door. He and

Mark set it down on the floor and kicked it in the general vicinity of the kitchen.

"So, there's no harm in having it around..." Mac said, and opened the closet door in the entryway and slid the broken relic of a gun high onto the top shelf. The top shelf was already crowded with a large coil of rope, one dumbbell and an old ratchet set. What she was supposed to ratchet, she had no idea.

Kate didn't argue. She couldn't; she knew a brick wall when she ran headfirst into one. Instead, she dug in with the rest of the family that was bound and determined to take care of her and set about making the few rooms into a home.

"HEY, KATE?" Billy shouted, walking out of the bedroom where he had been setting up one of the dozen extra beds his mother had hanging around. She called them "antiques"—the rest of the family called them "in the way"—but in this case, Kate Jenkins was going to have a full bed, completely free of spiders that had been carried over on some relative's covered wagon. Of course the whole thing sagged in the middle and was only about five feet long, but a free bed was a free bed and beat sleeping on the floor.

He wished for the umpteenth time since his mother recruited him for moving duty that he had come up with a suitable lie quick enough to get him out of this. It would be easier to be friendly but not friends with Kate if he never had to see her. If he never had to listen to her jokes and her conversation, if he never had to watch her try to stand up to his family.

If he never had to see Alice.

Kate was still the same gutsy, honest, beautiful girl she had always been and yet part of him wanted to be a million miles away from that apartment. The other part of him wanted his *family* to be a million miles away so he could lay Kate down on that bed and see what else had stayed the same about her.

Friendly, but not friends, he thought derisively. *What crap.*

"What?" Kate answered from underneath the sink, her voice muffled. Billy turned the corner and nearly ran into Kate's waving tush. He closed his eyes and swore silently.

"Where should we put up your computer?" he asked, leaning against the wall and looking anywhere but at Kate's shapely behind. Kate had always been on the skinny side—"all mouth and no meat," he used to call her—but this whole pregnancy thing had certainly put some curves on her and, in Alyssa's old jeans, Billy had a hard time not looking at those curves.

When had life gotten so unfair?

"I don't have a computer," she shouted, and finally crawled backward out of the cupboard and sat on the floor. Her face was red and her blond hair was standing on end.

The entire family stopped what they were doing, looked at Billy and then looked at her.

"Aren't you a writer?" Ethan asked.

"I *was* a writer," Kate answered, looking down at her dirty hands. Billy looked around and saw the amazement on everyone's faces. Kate was a very successful writer. In addition to the *Spurs* script, she had written tons of articles for magazines and newspapers that Missy had clipped out and put in a scrapbook.

"I think I'm going to try my hand at something else for a while," she said into the silence.

"Like what?" Billy asked carefully. *See!* part of him yelled. *Typical Kate. She's completely unstable, completely unreliable. She changes professions and addresses faster than some people change clothes!*

"Well..." It was clear she had not quite worked this out.

"Maybe...I...well I guess I'll just have to see, won't I?" she finally said.

"But honey," Missy said. She put down the sheets she was ironing. "You're such a good writer."

"Well, I was, and now it's time for me to be good at something else." She stood, brushed off the seat of her pants and walked out the door and down the stairs to her car. A tidy and abrupt end to a conversation she clearly did not want to have.

"This is worse than we thought," Missy whispered to Mac.

"What are you talking about?" Billy asked, turning to his parents.

"About the fact that Kate Jenkins is running from something," Alyssa told him. Her green eyes dimmed and she curled her arm around Mark's back.

"I sure would feel better if she would talk about it," Cecelia said, pulling dust bunnies out of her daughter's hair.

"Give it time," Mac said. "She'll talk when she's ready."

"Kate Jenkins doesn't run from anything," Billy told his family. "She's just a flake."

Ethan came over and patted him on the back, the look in his eyes sympathetic. "I remember being as stupid as you," he said.

"Hey!" Billy said, affronted, but then Kate climbed up the steps with the last box of her own possessions and the subject was dropped.

But as Billy put up shelves in Kate's closet he thought about what his family had said and began to wonder what would make her start running. But then he remembered that he didn't care, so he tried to think about something else. It didn't quite work.

BY THE TIME the Cook family left, Kate was exhausted. She looked around at all of her "new" things—a kitchen table, a set of mismatched dishes, a coffeemaker and various other completely useless appliances. She had several pieces of Missy's framed needlepoints hanging on the walls. Home Is Where The Heart Is was outside the bathroom. God Watch Me As I Sleep was over her and Alice's bed and Your Mother Doesn't Want To Clean Up After You Anymore hung over the kitchen sink.

She had blankets and pillows with designs stitched on them. She had glass knickknacks sitting on her windowsills. She even had a wind chime hanging from the eave on her patio. The whole scene made her smile.

Kate had been seventeen when she'd left her mother's home. After that she'd moved from crummy dorm room to crummy apartment to nice houses and back to crummy apartments. She had spent one year in a beach house in Malibu and one summer living in a converted tree house in Mexico. She had lived in a hotel for one year and in a trailer for the summer following. She had carried nothing from anyplace she went so the next place was always as empty as the last. And she had convinced herself that she liked it that way. Why Look Back? had been her motto.

Kate collapsed on the couch that wasn't hers, which someone had covered in a blanket of the variety that could only be described as an afghan. Among all of the things that weren't hers and that she didn't really want, she found oddly that she had a place she could call home.

5

BILLY WAS SITTING on a rock while the sun beat down on him. He stretched out and turned his head to get a better look at Kate as she jumped off the cliff into the clear blue waters of the swimming hole beneath them.

She waved at him and he waved back, entranced by her smile and her tiny red bikini. He watched her make the crazy leap, peddling her legs and screaming the whole way down. She surfaced and started swimming back to where he was lying on the warm rocks. She got out of the water and he realized that she had lost the top of her bikini. Billy swallowed hard. She was beautiful, more than beautiful. She was every dream he had ever had about women. She was sunlight and water and bare skin, and the look in her eyes promised everything.

She stood over him and slowly got on her hands and knees, and he could feel her cool skin, the dripping water. She leaned in close, her mouth a breath away. She began to whisper something and Billy leaned up to hear it.

"It's your birthday."

Billy's eyes flew open and his heart thudded in a heavy rhythm in his crotch. He wasn't on a rock, he was in his bed. The same bed he'd slept in for thirty years.

It was his thirtieth birthday. He groaned, his Kate-dream erection was subsiding, so he flipped over onto his stomach and tried to pretend it wasn't his birthday. That he hadn't just had his millionth almost wet dream about Kate.

Thirty. Could life get worse?

From the hallway outside his bedroom door he heard Ethan's exaggerated whisper, the smothered giggle of his niece Sarah and the wild, excited scream of his nephew Derek, who was no good at playing things cool.

He was a Cook; things could always get worse.

He turned over onto his side and brought one arm up to protect his head and one hand down to protect his genitals just as the door erupted in shouts and singing and laughing. Suddenly it was all knees and elbows, someone was drooling in his ear and someone else was pulling on his nose and his hair was coming out by the roots.

"Billy!" Derek shouted. Of course it came out like "Biwwy" at a triple decimal volume.

Sarah started a very enthusiastic four-year-old rendition of "Happy Birthday" right into Billy's left ear, which Louise was using as a teething ring. Billy felt a slick line of baby drool trickle into his ear canal.

"Call them off!" He laughed, unable to see his brothers or sisters-in-law through the diaper- and pajama-clad bodies. One of the bodies was slipping off the bed so he reached out a hand to grab it. It was Louise. Derek took that unguarded opportunity to make sure Billy would never have children of his own. Sarah continued to sing, getting to her favorite verse about how Billy smelled like a monkey.

If you can't beat them, he figured, the nausea from Derek's bull's-eye dying down, *join them.* Gently, as only a favorite uncle can, he gathered all of the kids and flipped them over onto their backs. And because their bellies were sticking out over the edges of their plastic diapers and pajamas and because he loved them with every breath in him, he tickled them mercilessly.

He was sure Derek, at least, would need a diaper change.

Worn out from the exertions he collapsed on his pillows.

If I were twenty-five, I wouldn't be this tired. Even if I was twenty-nine, I could have done this for hours, he thought. The next generation of Cooks gathered around, curling against his body, holding onto his fingers, tucking their heads under his chin.

"Happy Birthday Uncle Billy," Sarah whispered into his ear. He turned his head and smiled into her eyes.

"Thank you," he whispered back. Feeling the odd lump in his chest that he got when he looked into Sarah's bright green eyes or into Derek's blue ones. A lump he got whenever they ran to him with their arms open or wanted him to read them a good-night story. Him, Uncle Billy and no one else would do.

"Here's where they all went," Alyssa said with a laugh as she came in. "You can blame your brothers for this wake-up call." She leaned down and picked up Louise who cooed prettily and grabbed on to her mother. "Let's go get breakfast, guys," she said to Sarah and Derek and they scrambled off of Billy. Alyssa followed them out the door but turned at the last moment.

"You should get some of your own," she told him, her eyes serious. "You would be a great dad."

"Come on, it's already a crummy day without the Dad talk," he whined, pulling his pillow over his head. He heard Alyssa laugh and leave the room.

Dad. Marriage. Thirty. When would the torture end?

The only good thing about his birthday, as far as he was concerned, was that his mother made him cake for breakfast. It was a tradition that started when he was six and his mother told him he could have whatever he wanted for his birthday breakfast. His brothers had always said it was stupid, but Billy knew it was just because they were jealous that they hadn't thought about chocolate cake when Mom had asked them. It wasn't Billy's fault Ethan chose steak and eggs and Mark chose waffles.

However, even the prospect of triple chocolate fudge

cake waiting for him wasn't enough to light a fire underneath his feet. He flipped over onto his back and studied the crack in his ceiling—the same crack he had been staring at for thirty years.

He sighed and thought about what he really wanted from this birthday. Both of his brothers had married and moved out of the house by the time they were thirty. Moving out was something he was going to do once he got married but until then he worked on the ranch and once a year ate cake for breakfast.

I'll get married when I am good and ready, he told himself. But the empty side of the bed was beginning to feel bigger and bigger. It dawned on him that despite being surrounded by tons of family, tons of girls and two really good friends, he was lonely.

Turning thirty really, really sucks.

From the kitchen, the next generation was chanting "cake," and Billy decided that just because *he* was depressed didn't mean he could deprive kids of chocolate cake. He got dressed, pasted on a grin and went downstairs to blow out the bonfire on his birthday cake.

THE NIGHT didn't get any better. Jake and Carl, his two best friends since preschool picked him up at six o'clock to take him into town for a steak dinner.

"Hey, man, why the long face?" Carl asked.

"Yeah, for a man who's about to eat a free steak and drink all the beer he can drink you sure look mean," Jake agreed.

They were both twenty-nine, they simply had no idea.

Billy didn't answer and his friends decided to ignore him.

"Hey, have you seen the new grocery checker at the A & P?" Jake leaned forward so he could see Carl around

Billy. They were sitting in the cab of Carl's truck with Billy sitting in the middle.

"Yes, I have," Carl said with a grin and telltale twinkle in his eye. Something about that twinkle, although he had seen it a million times over the years, set the hair on Billy's neck on end. *No, oh, no.*

"Beautiful?" Billy asked. He wasn't sure how, but the sinking feeling in his gut told him that the beautiful checker was Kate.

"I'll say," Jake answered.

"Short blond hair?"

"You've seen her?" Carl asked, looking away from the road for a second.

Kate Jenkins was checking groceries at the A & P. The woman was sitting on tons of money and she was checking groceries. Billy couldn't believe it.

The words popped out before Billy could even stop them. Words that would forever damn him. "Leave her alone."

Billy said it and then shut his eyes and leaned his head against the seatback. *What is wrong with me?*

"You holding out on us, Billy?" Carl asked, digging into Billy's ribs with his elbow.

"You sure move fast, man. I just saw her yesterday," Jake said, a little disgruntled.

"Just back off the checkout girl," Billy said sullenly. Billy told himself that he was protecting Kate just as he would his sister Sam, from two of the three biggest players in western Montana.

"You, uh, know her well?" Carl asked, surprised by his friend's surliness.

"You could say that. It's Kate Jenkins," Billy said through his teeth.

"Kate Jenkins?" his friends said at the same time. They recognized her name from the summer Billy had disappeared on them. When he'd reappeared in September he had told them all about Kate Jenkins.

"The one who put—"

"Yes, yes," Billy cut them off, furious and frustrated all at once. "*The* Kate Jenkins. Now let's drop it." He crossed his arms over his chest and tried to look serious, but his two best friends were laughing.

"What's she doing here?" Jake asked.

Billy told them the whole birth story minus the part about him fainting and especially the part about how he had cried.

"Holy shit," Carl mumbled when the story was told. "You're a hero, Billy." He pulled into the small parking lot behind the only steak house in town and turned off the engine.

"Kate Jenkins had a baby?" Jake asked, his face screwed up as though he simply couldn't understand the basic natural fact that she was a woman and had a baby. He wasn't the brightest guy on the block. "You delivered a baby? You're like a dad!"

"I caught the baby, I didn't conceive it."

The three friends sat in the truck for a moment and Billy knew what his friends were dying to ask.

"We're just friends," Billy said. "She's not sticking around here forever and it's better for her not to get attached, you know." He waved his hand in a way that was supposed to sum up the complicated weave of his emotions that had somehow survived the thirteen years since that summer.

"Why is she checking groceries?" Jake asked, turning sideways in the truck. "I mean, isn't she rich?"

"Yep," Billy answered, tired of the subject. It seemed as though his whole world was wrapped up in Kate Jenkins, just like when he was seventeen. If people weren't talking about her he was thinking about her, and there were just so many hours in a day a man could think about a woman before he went nuts, which Billy felt he was precariously close to doing. "Rich and crazy, now let's go eat some steak and drink some beer."

They climbed out of the truck and made their way to the restaurant. They slugged shoulders and tried to trip each other as they always did. Billy leaped up onto Carl's back and Carl trotted to the door while they all laughed.

Kate Jenkins was almost entirely forgotten.

After dinner the boys went over to Pete's Place for all the beer Billy could drink. It was Friday and the place was full and loud. The three found a table and immediately began searching out the night's entertainment. They spied a group of girls who were old college friends visiting Amy McDermott. They were pretty and knew it and were shooting Jake, Carl and Billy plenty of looks from across the room.

"What do you give 'em?" Jake asked his friends over the blaring music. He leaned back in his chair and hooked his elbow around the back. He pushed his ball cap off his head, ruffled his blond curls that girls just adored and put his cap back on.

"Next fast song," Carl answered. He leaned back and crossed his hands behind his head. Casually, he flexed his massive biceps, which girls loved.

"What do you think, Billy?" Carl asked.

"About what?" Billy asked, hunched over his beer. He was suddenly aware he had completely zoned out of the conversation. *Damn that Kate!*

"*The girls,*" he said impatiently. "How long before they get the guts up to come talk to us?"

Billy looked around and saw the group of girls busily tossing their hair and whispering and looking at them out of the corners of their eyes. He looked at his friends in their come-get-me body language positions and wanted to leave.

But he couldn't. He was thirty and somehow he believed

that enough beer and the aimless flirtation with a stranger might turn back the clock—and there was nothing Billy wanted more than to turn back the clock.

And so, Billy turned on his patented charm. He took off his jacket, sat back in his chair and made eye contact with one of the girls; a brunette that looked like a million other girls.

He gave her "the nod" and she immediately split from the group and headed their way. Her friends followed. *She's probably an old cheerleader,* Billy thought glumly, and settled into his night.

"Winner and still champion of the world, Billy Cook," Jake mumbled under his breath. They all grinned, sat back and welcomed the girls to their table.

Billy drank the beer people bought for him and went about getting himself properly drunk. He watched Carl leave with a tall blonde and Jake was making time with another girl from the group. Some girl—*Susan,* Billy thought—kept pressing up against his arm and casting serious looks at his mouth. This was the old routine, he knew exactly how this was going to end up, but somehow instead of bringing him that warm fuzzy, going-to-get-lucky-tonight feeling, he was feeling panicky.

Get a grip, Billy told himself.

After she ran her hand down his arm for the millionth time, Billy stood.

"I need some air," he mumbled to her. She made a pouty face that completely disinterested him and made his way through the bar to get outside.

"Happy Birthday, Billy!" Lou the bartender shouted over the noise and Billy raised a hand and nodded. Other people turned and slapped him on the shoulder shouting things he couldn't understand over the racket. He smiled and nodded and fought his way outside.

He stumbled across the wooden porch and down the

stairs to the sidewalk. He leaned against the streetlight and tilted his head back, taking in big gulps of fresh air.

Happy birthday to me, he thought.

Just above him was the small covered balcony that led into Kate's apartment. The ball of tension and panic disappeared. *Kate.* That's what the girl inside—Susan-what's-her-face-attorney-from-Billings—was missing. She wasn't Kate Jenkins. Some half-sober part of his brain reminded him of the need for distance. But Billy shut that right out.

I want Kate. Had wanted her for what seemed like thirteen years. He could put the distance back tomorrow. It was his birthday and even more than turning back time, Billy suddenly wanted a little Kate to help make the medicine go down.

Searching the ground, he found a bunch of pebbles and scooped them up. Taking one in his right hand, he cocked his arm back and let it fly at the dimly lit window of Kate's living room.

"Ouch!" someone yelped. From out of the shadows on her balcony, Kate leaned forward. In the light Billy could see her rubbing a spot on her face.

"What the hell do you think you're doing?" she snapped.

"Kate!" he yelled, spreading his arms expansively. He was sure the smile on his face was charming and boyish. He had practiced it enough.

"Shhhh!" She leaned forward some more and put her finger to her lips, she looked furtively behind her and then back at him. "Don't wake Laura."

"Who the hell is Laura?" Billy asked.

"My daughter," she replied, as though he should already know.

"I thought she was Alice."

"She was. Now she's Laura."

"Laura?"

"*Little House on the Prairie* reruns. Now, get lost."

Billy started to digest this name change and be upset about it, but something in the way the streetlight fell across Kate's face and hair distracted him.

"You're so pretty," he said, instead.

"And you are so drunk!" she hissed. She wasn't in her normal good humor but Billy wasn't letting that stop him from his one and only birthday wish. Besides, he had enough good humor for both of them.

"Juliet!" he shouted. "Wherefore art thou, Juliet?" He put one hand on his chest and flung the other out while he butchered Shakespeare.

"You've got it wrong, you idiot! Now keep it quite, Billy, I'm serious. You'll wake Laura!"

"Juliet!" he whispered loudly. "You are a rose and I smell sweet and something about the sun!" He put his other hand on his chest and flung out the other one.

"You aren't funny or cute, Billy Cook," she told him, but Billy didn't care what she thought.

He put one foot on the stone and wood column that ran up the front of Pete's and made up part of Kate's balcony.

"Don't do it, Billy!" Kate said, pointing a finger at him.

"I'm gonna do it, Kate," Billy said and pointed a finger back at her.

"I've got that gun in my closet," she warned him.

"You already broke the gun," Billy told her. "I cometh, sweet rosy Juliet," he said, gave her one last look and then began his climb up the column, chanting "Here I cometh" under his breath.

"What a complete idiot," he heard her mutter.

"You know," he said conversationally. "This is a tradition in my family. Many Cook men have climbed walls to get to their women. Not that you're my woman, but..." He smiled as he scaled. "You know what happened to Juliet."

"Yeah, she killed herself!" Kate whispered furiously.

"Well, not until she and Romeo got it on." Billy was having some trouble getting up the wall. Perhaps it was the drink, but it seemed the wall was shifting more than a wall should. Still, he pressed on.

"What a romantic," Kate scorned.

"Hey, I'm risking my life here, that's romantic," he told her.

"You're four feet off the ground."

"Sprains are mighty painful."

Finally, about two feet from Kate's balcony, the stone-and-wood combo that he had found so easy to climb up turned into just stone, smooth stone.

"Kate?" he asked in a small voice.

A rope flopped over the side and dangled in front of him.

"I tied it to the couch." Her disembodied voice drifted over the side to him. "And I put the TV on the couch. It should hold. This is a stupid family tradition."

Tentatively, Billy put his weight on it and when it didn't give, he pulled himself up and over the side. He landed with an "Oomph" on the stone floor of Kate's balcony.

He lay there for a while until Kate leaned over him.

Uh-oh, he thought, *she is not happy.*

"This is the part where we kiss," Billy said hopefully, smiling and ignoring the angry vibes rolling off her in waves. "In high school English class Miss Mayes always fast-forwarded this part of the movie, but I think you take off your shirt."

"Get out of my house," she ordered.

"But I've come so far," he said, still joking. She turned away from him and as she moved her face fell into the light from the street lamps. Even though he was drunk, Billy saw the tears on her face. He sobered immediately.

Things clicked in place. Kate really didn't want him here and she was crying.

''Kate,'' he said, pulling himself up. ''What's wrong? Is it Alice?''

''Laura.''

''Whatever, is she okay?'' he asked, panicked.

''She's fine.''

Kate backed away from him and sat on one of the plastic chairs she had put on her balcony. ''Billy, please just go.'' She looked at him once, the moonlight cutting a bright slice out of the dark night between them, and then put her head in her hands and started crying. Sobbing, really.

''Kate, Kate, Kate,'' Billy whispered. There was no way he could go, as much as he would like to. There was nothing like an openly sobbing woman to make him wish he was somewhere else, but he had climbed the walls to get here. He felt like a hero and she was a damsel in serious distress. He sat in the other plastic chair and awkwardly put his hand on her hair. He patted her head and thought that was a little too pet-like. ''Come on now.'' He looked around for a Kleenex or something—a rag, a hose—anything to clean her up. ''It can't be that bad.'' Finding nothing, he took off his shirt, wadded it up and handed it to her. ''What's wrong? Sweetheart?''

''Oh, Billy. I got fired,'' she wailed. She lifted her blotchy red face and as Billy watched, it turned even redder and screwed up in a way that could only be described as horrifying. Tears squirted out of her eyes and dripped off the edge of her nose. It was like looking at a car wreck and Billy couldn't look away.

''You got fired from the grocery store?'' Billy asked, confused and mesmerized by the tears running off her chin. ''You're crying because you got fired from the grocery store?'' He couldn't quite hide his incredulity.

''And the library.'' She took a shuddering breath and wiped her nose on Billy's shirt. Billy bid his favorite shirt a silent goodbye. ''Did you know that your crazy head librarian doesn't use the Dewey decimal system? She categorizes alphabetically using first names! Have you heard of anything so ridiculous?'' Kate didn't seem to need a real answer, so Billy just nodded and stroked her back. He tried desperately not to smile or worse, to laugh. She was crying like this because she got fired from the grocery store! ''Of course, she's only got about fifty books, so she could categorize them any way she wanted, but when I tried to implement a little universal order she fired me!''

''What happened at the grocery store?'' Billy asked, thinking he had never heard anything quite so funny in his whole life. The multimillionaire writer getting fired from small-town jobs and then crying about it!

''I was giving away food,'' she answered in a small voice. ''Some of the families around here are barely making it. It seems to me that throwing them a free can of chick peas isn't going to break the A & P!'' She was really getting herself worked up and Billy was unable to keep from laughing. ''It's not funny, Billy. I don't have a job!''

''Kate, you've got money. You don't need to work,'' he told her. ''Remember? You're a big shot in Hollywood! You should just relax.''

Kate looked at him and the tears continued to run down her face in a steady stream. Her eyes were filled with something he had never seen in Kate Jenkins, even when she was giving birth in a line cabin without a doctor—*doubt.*

''Oh, shit,'' he whispered. ''You don't have any money, do you?''

''No, Billy I don't have any money! I'm almost broke, I have a baby to support and I can't even hold down a job at the A & P!'' She sat back in her chair and leaned her head back over the top. ''Go ahead and laugh!'' she told him, her voice slightly strangled from her position.

''What happened?'' he asked, his voice hushed. ''Where did all your money go?''

Billy could imagine the noble Kate giving it away to the poor or the impulsive Kate betting it all on a horse race. In the silence that stretched Billy began to imagine the worst about Kate.

"Are you an addict or something?" he asked.

"No! Don't be stupid Billy!"

"Well, you sure didn't spend it on cars or clothes..."

"Sure, go ahead and kick a girl when she's down."

"Come on, Kate..." Billy said in a whisper. His hand reached out and touched her hair, the curve of her shoulder. "Tell me."

Just like that, Kate cracked.

"I never wanted to write movies, Billy. *Spurs* was a short story for *Cosmo Magazine!*" Kate looked at Billy as if she expected him to share the irony, so he nodded. She took several deep breaths, some hitched, and she shut her eyes. Billy watched this struggle for control for several moments while he brushed the hair off her face and tried to mop up her tears. As time passed, he began to think she wasn't going to tell him anything, but finally she took a deep breath and words sort of spilled out of her mouth.

"After I wrote the stupid thing and it was bought by a movie studio, everybody was calling me and trying to represent me and get me to do other projects. But I never wanted to do movies," she said firmly, tears dripping off her chin.

"I know," Billy said comfortingly and moved his hand from under the steady drip off her face.

"Anyway," she continued, "after a year of stumbling around on my own, I got an agent." Kate looked at Billy, her eyes wide and red and deeply wounded. "Joseph. He took over all of my finances. It seemed like the right thing to do, I was thirty and had no idea what I should watch out for. He had been in the business for years." Kate took another deep breath and brought her hand up to cover her eyes. "A year ago we became a couple," she whispered. "He said he loved me and would always take care of me and I..." Her voice cracked and tears leaked out of the corner of her eyes. "I was just tired of having to struggle all the time and he...well, he seemed like Prince Charming."

"Did you love him?"

"I don't know," she answered honestly. "I thought so, but then I found out that the man I thought I knew didn't exist at all. He was so smooth..." She looked at him and smiled, ruefully. "I'm a sucker for smooth guys."

Billy chafed at the idea of being lumped into the same category as a man who was clearly going to turn out to be some kind of jerk.

"What happened to your money?" he asked, knowing the story was going to end badly.

"He tried to start his own movie production company. He put all his money behind a project and it didn't work out, so he used my money and the money of a couple of other people he represented. I had the worst case of writer's block ever, and he, while I didn't know it, was busy losing millions of dollars on an alien movie. An alien movie!" she said, as if that was somehow the worst insult.

"What an idiot," Billy said with scorn.

"I know—alien movie," she snorted. "The next project went worse than the first. He left me with almost nothing. Except Laura."

She stopped for a second; her body was tense with all of the grief and anger she had been repressing. Billy held his breath and tried to pull her closer, sensing the dam was about to break, but she pushed him away.

"Oh, my God," she sobbed, she bent double and locked her arms around her knees. "What have I done?" She sobbed into her legs. "What have I done?"

Ignoring her struggles, he put one arm under Kate's

knees and the other around her back and picked her up as he would his niece and cradled her in his lap. It took a second but Kate soon put her arms around his neck and tears ran warm and hot down his neck and across his bare chest. With one hand he fished by his chair for his discarded shirt and used it to carefully mop up the part of Kate's face he could touch and the part of his chest she was drenching. She cried as if she had never cried before. She clung to his neck and wailed.

"Everything is going to be fine," he murmured over and over again until, finally, it seemed the worst of her crying was over. Her breath was coming in shudders, but the tears weren't running down his chest anymore.

"I'm the worst mother on the face of the planet!" she said into his chest, shaking her head. "Someone is going to come and take Laura away from me and then I'll really have nothing."

"Oh, come on now. You're just talking crazy. Everything is going to work out fine," he told her, and believed it. Kate would always land on her feet.

"No it's not," she said stubbornly, her tears over. Billy chuckled and after a moment he felt her answering smile against his chest. "I don't think it's very funny."

"The situation isn't, but you sure as hell are," Billy told her. He leaned back and looked into her red and blotchy face. She smiled and her swollen eyes nearly disappeared in her face. "Yikes," he said, and smiled again.

"That good, huh?" she said with a smile. Slowly she sat up. "I'm sorry," she whispered, and raised her glittering eyes to Billy's.

Billy suddenly felt very naked and very warm. She had stopped crying and Billy was all too aware of her. Of her weight against his groin, her warmth against his chest. Her body was cool in the moonlight, all shadows and smooth soft skin.

"It's okay, sweetheart," he told her, running his hands up and down her arms. His eyes met hers in the darkness and Billy could see what Kate was thinking, the turn her thoughts had taken. She had that heavy-lidded, come-and-get-me look. The look that promised all the things Billy had ever wanted. He had climbed the damn wall to get up here to see that look, and now that he was here and she was here, soft and warm in his lap, his conscience was screaming to be heard.

Of all the stupid things.

"No one's called me sweetheart in thirteen years," she said, deliberately bringing up the memory of their summer.

"Oh, come on," Billy smiled, not believing her. "A sweetheart like you?" He joked, hoping to lighten the moment, but at the same time wishing the moment wouldn't end.

"No one has ever done to me what you did that summer," she said, looking him straight in the eye.

"Chased you around like a seventeen-year-old boy?" He smiled and stroked her arm, feeling a little bit like a fox in front of the hounds.

"No. No one's ever loved me like you did," she whispered.

"Kate." He tried to sound strong and reasonable, but his voice cracked. He tried again. "Kate." Much better. "I think I should leave." He made efforts—he truly did—to stand and lift her off what was becoming a full-fledged erection. But she sort of slipped through his hands.

"Why?" she asked in a heated whisper. "Why leave?"

"Because," he whispered back, and then realized he whispered and overcompensated with a shout. "Kate. I know that look and it's trouble. You're upset and..."

Kate laughed and Billy couldn't shut it out. He was so turned on, so hot and heavy and achy.

"Stay," she breathed.

Just like that, all the oxygen in the world was gone. The night air was like a furnace and, despite the blotches and swollen eyes, Kate became sex personified. This was something that had been building between them almost since the moment she'd left thirteen years ago. The look she gave him was naked with honesty.

"No attachments." He whispered the reminder of his policy. She nodded and put one finger to his collarbone and followed its length to the curve of his shoulder. They both felt that touch like fire. He sucked in air.

"I'm not seventeen anymore," he told her. "I'm a man." It was a warning and an understanding that this time was different. He was different; he wasn't going to fall in love because she was a gorgeous sexual creature and her laugh made him dizzy.

Kate's lips parted on a breath. The air was infused with attraction and heat and a summer of sexual memories. She leaned down to press her lips to his.

"Yes," she whispered. "Yes, you are."

6

HER LIPS TO HIS were like a match to dry wood. In a moment the almost-innocent kiss turned wicked. Tongues entwined, hands flew across skin, remembering and rediscovering places that made the fire between them hotter.

So much was the same and so much different. Billy's body had grown in all the best places. His shoulders were broad, his hips lean. The stubble on his chin scratched her face and his lips were somehow fuller than in her memory. Kate realized her memories, no matter how many times she went over them, were nothing compared to the real thing. She smiled against Billy's mouth, her tongue darting out to taste the corner of his lips, and she sank into the body that was dwarfing hers.

He was like a glossy underwear model, all smooth skin and rippling lean muscles. He looked like what those underwear models were trying to be. His eyes were heavy and his hair mussed. The moonlight puddled on his abdomen and her fingers traced the muscles there. *Nothing like a six-pack on a handsome man to cheer a woman right up.*

She traced the strong cords in his neck to his ear and into his thick hair. With desperate hands she buried her fingers in his hair and held him still against her mouth.

"Kate..." he gasped into her open mouth.

"Billy..." she answered. She tore her mouth from his and arched into his chest. His hands lifted from her hips to her back and finally around to her breasts.

"Oh, God," she said on a choked breath. Motherhood

and time had changed everything and she felt as though her skin was on fire. She hugged him hard to her and groaned when he buried his face in her shirt between her breasts. Weighing the flesh beneath her T-shirt and breathing on the nipples that hardened with each touch, Billy seemed to read her mind.

Through the thin cotton of her T-shirt and the satin of her bra Billy's teeth closed over her nipple. Her hips jerked at the excruciating pleasure and her head arched back.

It had been so long...so long since anyone had touched her or held her while she cried. Kate let her pride fall away, revealing the hungry woman underneath.

"Please," she whispered blindly into the cool night air.

Billy was good. She had taught him what "please" really meant when it came panting from a woman's mouth, and he turned her roughly in his lap. His hands jerked at the waistband of her shorts and the button flew off into the darkness.

"Is this what you want?" he demanded, his voice rough and low. She felt the coils of heat and hunger inside her turn tighter. Their eyes locked and he buried his hand between her legs. In the hot wet center of her body the entire world sat waiting and Billy, strong and tough and knowing...*so knowing,* set that world spinning.

He took her cry into his mouth, swallowing her scream of pleasure. When she finally tore her mouth away she set her teeth to the soft bare skin where his neck met his shoulder and bit as hard as she could. He grunted once but rode out the pain as she rode out the waves of her orgasm.

Straddling his lap, her head on his shoulder, she sat still for a moment, her body occasionally twitching as though she had been electrified.

A cry and an orgasm, Kate felt as if the weight on her shoulders had sprouted wings and flown away. Carefully, because she couldn't feel certain muscles, she rearranged herself on Billy's lap until she felt the hot hard truth of

Billy's lust pressed against her inner thigh. She smiled, licked the place where she had bit him and luxuriated in the prospect of getting her hands in Billy's pants.

"Uh, Kate?" he said. His voice was so completely unlustful that her smile vanished.

"Yeah?" she asked. She put her chin on his shoulder and refused to sit up and face facts.

"Um...there's something running down my chest and I, uh, think it's from you." Billy looked so uncomfortable, Kate knew Mother Nature had just bridled the night of unbridled lust.

She sat up and looked down at the front of her T-shirt. She and Billy were equally drenched in milk.

"Oh, my God," she groaned, torn between serious embarrassment and laughter. She put her feet down on the ground and stood. Crossing her arms over her chest, she looked at Billy once before embarrassment won out and she ran from the porch into her bedroom.

She had bawled, cried and snotted all over him like a baby, confessed her own stupidity and the true extent of her bad mothering, practically threw herself at him, bit him and then leaked milk all over him. All in all, it was a night of all of her best stunts.

"Way to go, Kate," she murmured to herself. She ripped off her T-shirt and bra, cleaned herself up and put on fresh clothes. She heard the tap go on in the bathroom and knew Billy was cleaning himself up, too. Part of her wanted to stay put until she heard that front door shut after Billy left, but that simply wasn't her style.

So she looked down at her daughter, focusing on her eyelashes for courage, and went into the living room where she intended to be reasonable and adult when Billy came out of the bathroom.

Billy came out, still without his shirt, but now his chest was wet and water dripped from his collarbone through the hair on his chest, down his flat and chiseled abdomen into the waistband of his pants. He was just so damn attractive, with that body and that hair that fell over his eyebrow and those eyes and the hands…

Reasonable adult flew out the window. Stammering idiot took over.

"Ah…um…I don't quite…ha! Funny." She shut herself up and hung her head.

Billy took the three steps between them quickly and put his hand under her chin, forcing her to look at him.

"Do you any idea how exciting and sexy and hot you are?" he said, his voice quiet and soft.

"No," she whispered, lost in the twinkle of his eye. Hours ago she was broke, unemployable, fat, blotchy and grouchy.

"You are, even though your boobs leak." He smiled and Kate couldn't stop from laughing. *Thank God,* she thought. *Thank God, Billy Cook turned into the man he did.*

"Yeah, well, I'm the whole package," she said, and took a step back from his chest and touch. The reasonable adult returned and she took the situation in hand.

"Billy, I can't thank you enough," she said, her eyes warm and sad at the same time. "I was just at the end of my rope and you came along with what I needed."

"Well, I guess I'm glad I climbed up your porch when I did." Billy rubbed his chest and crossed his arms and then put his arms down, only to bring them back up. He put one hand in his pocket, brought it out, ran his hand through his hair.

"Do you want a T-shirt?" she asked, reading his body language. Even though she was dressed, she, too, felt a bit naked. She wished she had an excuse to put on a parka.

"You think you have one that fits me?" he asked, skeptically taking in her T-shirt with the caricature of Mark Twain on it.

"Actually, I have one that's yours," she said with a smile. She went back to her bedroom and after a few minutes came back out with a folded-up gray T-shirt. She shook it out and held it up and Billy recognized his old favorite baseball T-shirt. Lincoln Lords was printed in red across the chest, although most of the letters had flaked off.

"Hey," he said with a laugh. "I wondered where that shirt went." He took it from her and pulled it over his head.

"I took it with me as a kind of souvenir, I guess," Kate said sheepishly. "I'm sorry, I didn't think you would miss it."

"That's okay," he told her. He smoothed the shirt over his chest and looked down at it. He was much bigger than he had been in high school and the shirt hugged his chest and shoulders like a second skin. She sighed inwardly. "Thanks, Kate."

"You're welcome." They smiled warmly at each other, like adults that liked each other and had intimate sexual knowledge of the other. For a second the opportunity was there for Kate to launch herself at him, to tackle him to the floor and to finish what was started on the porch. She could do it. Two steps and she would up against that chest. Those lips against hers, those hands...

"Look, Kate, we should talk," he said, putting his hands in his pockets like an embarrassed cowboy.

"Talk?" Kate asked distractedly, her mind still on the floor with Billy's naked body.

"Yeah, about Joseph and money and..."

It was like a bucket of cold water over her head. She took a second to mentally pick herself up off the floor and regroup.

"Do you want some tea?" she asked brightly, although she felt anything but. She turned her back on Billy and headed into the kitchen to hide her disappointment. Billy followed.

"Exactly how much money do you have?" Billy asked. He leaned against the door frame and watched as Kate opened cupboards and drawers, turned on her stove and set a pot to boil. "And no lying or hedging, Kate. I want to help and I can't if you won't let me."

"That's right, Billy." She turned from the stove and faced him. She put her hands on her hips, her blue eyes flashing. "You can't help me and I don't want you to."

She should have known this was coming. Billy Cook's charity, his pity and duty all rolled into one nice monetary package.

"Man, are you stubborn." Billy crossed the tiny kitchen and got in her face. "You have a daughter, maybe you should think about her and swallow some of that pride!"

"Maybe you should mind your own business!" She leaned into him, her finger up and jabbing.

They squared off, but to Kate's surprise, Billy didn't back down. Thirteen years ago, Billy hadn't shown half of this kind of spine. Thirteen years ago he had been pretty easygoing and, well...to put it bluntly, pliable. This new Billy was bossy and nosy and, as Kate tried to tamp down the slow sizzle in her stomach, oddly exciting. And the slow sizzle and the major explosion on her porch were two more giant reasons she didn't need Billy's money.

"Look, I'm worried about you and Alice," Billy was saying.

"See!" Kate threw her hands in the air. "You don't even know her name!"

"Because you keep changing it every five minutes!" Billy shouted.

"It's Laura!"

"Okay, I get it. Just because I can't keep up with your name games doesn't mean I don't care."

"Oh." Kate put her hands down, smiling sarcastically. "You care. Okay, that's good to know because I couldn't tell."

"Kate..." Billy said, exasperated. Her sarcasm was like a thick wall around her.

"She's two months old, Billy. You've seen her three

times since you helped pull her into this world, you're going to have to excuse me if I don't really believe it when you say you care.''

''I'm sorry, Kate,'' Billy said. ''You're not going to be here forever and saying goodbye will be hard enough without...well...I said no attachments.''

''Look, it's no big deal if you don't come around, but when you do don't start saying that you care when it's obviously not true.'' She pulled down two mugs from the cupboard and they clattered onto the counter. *Get it together,* she thought, feeling edgy and panicked. *See what men do to you? They make you crazy, now relax.*

''Let's forget it,'' she said, leaning against the counter, and they both silently watched the pot, waiting for the water to boil.

''Why don't you just write some more?'' he asked as the first bubbles began to drift from the bottom of the pot to the top and explode. ''That's what you are, a writer.''

Oh, that's a good one, Billy. Her mouth curved into a rueful smile. *That's the million-dollar question.*

''I'm scared,'' she finally said honestly. ''This whole mess with Joseph has ruined it for me. Stage fright or something. Besides, it's not a stable life. I can't support my daughter wondering if the checks are going to keep rolling in.''

''Oh, so bagging groceries at the A & P is stable?''

''It's a job, Billy. An honest, honorable job.''

''Yeah, for high school kids, you're...''

''Back off, Billy.'' She looked at him out of the corner of her eye and was greatly relieved when he backed off.

''Sorry.''

She poured tea in the cups, grabbed milk and sugar, added some to hers and breezed by him on her way to the living room.

''Hey,'' he said, following her, ''what are you doing with Alice while you're working?''

"You mean Laura?" Kate sat on the couch and curled her legs up under her. She smiled at him, just to let him know she wasn't mad, and caught him staring at her breasts. Which, if she did say so herself, were fairly spectacular and were pressed up nicely against Mark Twain's face.

"What are you looking at, Billy?" she asked innocently.

"What?" His eyes snapped back to her face and he had the good grace to blush red to the tips of his hair. "Uh...sorry. Laura, right. What are you doing with her?" Billy sat on the far end of the couch and kept his eyes off her T-shirt.

"I tie her in her crib and leave her a banana," Kate said, watching him over the edge of her cup. He just watched her, refusing to take her bait. She laughed and gave in.

"Well, Alyssa has Louise at work with her so for a few hours Laura goes there, and if Alyssa can't watch her, the receptionist does. It's all very safe and secure and reasonable, Billy. But Laura and I are touched by your concern."

"Is she? I mean, can I see..." He stopped and they looked at each other in the silence. Kate thought about it, she thought about the long road ahead of her and Laura and her vows to keep men at a distance. She thought that sharing the sight of the perfect Laura asleep in her crib would somehow be more intimate than any heavy petting they might do.

She thought about all of it and because she was so proud of her little girl and so wanted to share her with somebody she finally stood and motioned Billy to follow her into her bedroom. In a crib near the far wall, her daughter lay sleeping. Billy carefully put his tea down and approached the crib as though the ground was littered with broken glass.

Poor awkward cowboy, she thought, and felt her heart soften and melt a little in her chest.

Laura slept with her hand over her ear. Brown hair curled around her fingers and, while they watched, her mouth opened and shut on a sigh. The air was infused with warmth and the sweet smell of baby and the soft whir of the fan. Kate felt the whole world shrink to the three of them.

"She's been asking about you," Kate said jokingly over his shoulder. "She wonders where you are."

"I'm avoiding attachments," he whispered, and looked up at her. Kate smiled and tilted her head, watching him.

"I'm afraid two-month-olds don't quite understand such adult fears," she told him. Billy looked at her and then back at the baby sleeping in the bright patch of moonlight. He reached down his hand and touched her fingers where they curled around her ear. Kate watched his face, the sad look in his eyes, and felt that look steal into her body and touch something deep inside her. Something hidden and well protected over the years, something soft and vulnerable, so she flinched and looked away.

"Neither do I," he whispered, and quietly turned and left the room. She followed him and softly closed the door, turning to face him where he stood in the center of the room.

The air was still and silent and Kate sensed that something was going to happen. Perhaps Billy had been as moved as she had been watching Laura sleep. Maybe he realized that their friendly-but-not-friends rule was useless in the face of what had happened this evening. Maybe—

"Kate," he said interrupting her thoughts. "I know what I did tonight was…wrong. I was drunk and you really took me by surprise and…"

Wrong? Kate felt all the soft, vulnerable parts of her retreat at his words.

"Come on, Billy," she said, trying to keep the tremble out of her voice. "We're adults. Save your 'I'm sorry' speech for some other girl," Kate said. As nonchalantly as possible, she leaned against the kitchen door frame and threw out her magnificent new chest.

"I'm trying to explain, Kate," he said firmly, looking at her and then away.

Kate felt a nasty little spike of vindication. "What's there to explain? We both wanted something and one of us got it." She smiled, a flash of teeth. "I'm pretty happy."

"I just want you to remember what I said about attachments." Billy said, looking her in the eye.

"Oh, you can put your hand down my pants but you don't want me to count on it being there tomorrow?" she asked cruelly, deliberately twisting his words.

"You're deliberately twisting my words," he said.

"Yep," she said with a brittle smile. *Enough is enough,* she thought, and walked past him to the door and opened it. "You never were very good at recognizing sex for sex sake, Billy. You keep forgetting I'm the Queen of No Attachments. I won't be falling in love, either, you're not that irresistible."

"Kate, if you need money or anything, you know you can just call me."

"I don't take charity, Billy. I work for my money. I'll get a job and we'll be fine." She held up an arm as if to show Billy the way to walk out the door. "We'll be fine."

She didn't want him here anymore. She didn't want him to see how almost not at all fine she really was. She had erupted in his hands tonight, she was wound so tight the smallest touch, the smallest comfort, had unlocked the floodgates. And she could feel herself winding up even tighter now.

He walked to the door and paused as he brushed past her body. Before she could duck or turn or somehow stop him, he took her chin carefully in his hand and breathed a kiss across her lips.

"Good night," he whispered.

"Goodbye," she whispered back. Billy walked out and Kate slammed the door shut behind him.

THE NEXT MORNING Kate was awake early trying to pretend last night had not happened. She watched the steam rise from her coffee and tried to systematically erase every memory of Billy's touch. She leaned down to kiss her daughter who was far too busy nursing to be much of a distraction from Kate's thoughts.

In fact, as Kate realized just how silent the world was at 6:00 a.m. there was nothing to distract her from replaying every moment of the evening before. She couldn't turn on her TV for fear of seeing another *Little House on the Prairie* rerun. Laura, while gorgeous and brilliant, was just going to fall asleep after eating, and there was no girlfriend to call. While she could sew something, or cook something in the Crock-Pot, none of those things would offer any insight into Billy's...

This is pathetic. You have to stop mistaking comfort for genuine caring. Really, Kate, you're a grown woman, fully capable of fooling around with a man and not hope it was more.

At some point between Billy comforting her and bringing her to orgasm she had allowed herself to be lulled into the relief he was providing. His laughter and understanding, his sense of humor and obvious desire had been a balm to all of her ragged parts and she had been wooed.

She had done it again, she thought angrily. Every damn time she looked to someone for a little comfort and care she ended up getting smashed in the face with a man's excuses and regret and backpedaling.

A man who keeps his distance with one hand while he puts his other hand down your pants is disaster. Add the fact that you broke his heart...

"Really, Kate, you're asking for it," she said out loud. All this silence was making her crazy. "Hear that," she said out loud because she could. "You're going crazy. Forget the underwear model cowboy. You don't need him."

The phone rang as if answering her and Kate jumped, dislodging her single-minded daughter who immediately began to wail. She resettled Laura, apologizing the whole time, and grabbed the phone. Some foolish heart ventricle hoped it might be Billy.

"Hello?"

"Katie?"

Only one person in the world called Kate *Katie.*

"Mom?"

"Hi, sweetie."

"What are you doing?" Kate called her mother every week on Sunday. The conversation last week, ended in a fight as they had been for the last year. But last week's had been a real doozy, and the last person Kate had expected to hear from was her mother. The rules in this mother-daughter relationship were simple. Debra Jenkins would say something mildly offensive, which Kate would take entirely to heart, and they both would hang up. For a week they would stew and simmer and finally Kate would call and apologize for being so sensitive. This process had been working for them for over a decade and Kate was taken aback by this new twist.

"Can't a mother call her daughter on a Saturday morning?" Debra asked with false innocence.

"Well, Mom, last time we talked you said you were never going to speak to me again," Kate reminded her mother; knowing as well as Debra did that she hadn't meant a word of it.

"Did I?" Debra asked, and Kate laughed.

"I'm sorry, too, Mom." Kate looked down at her own daughter and knew that half the blame for the volatile relationship rested with her. Her mother had raised her to be fierce and independent, and somewhere around the age of fifteen it had turned on her. Debra, who had always told her daughter it was "us against them," had suddenly found herself to be one of the *them.* Kate had rebelled, hard. She'd stolen the car, climbed water towers and shaved her head.

She'd dated all the wrong boys and the last straw had been taking off to Los Angeles without so much as an explanation. It amazed Kate that Debra even bothered with her.

"I am sorry, Mom. I really am," Kate said, beginning to realize what she must have put her mother through.

"I know you are, sweetheart."

"So—" Kate readjusted her daughter "—what's up?"

"Well, I just felt horrible about last Sunday," Debra said, and Kate imagined her sitting at her kitchen table wrapping and unwrapping the phone cord around her finger.

"Me, too, Mom. We just have the same horrible temper. We should realize that by now."

"I know, I know, but last week was so ugly," Debra said, and Kate bit back a sigh. Her mother was the best dead-horse beater in the world.

"Well, you did call me an ungrateful wretch," Kate said, her temper warming.

"Honey, I know I did, but you called me an overpowering cow."

"Really? I said cow?" Kate asked, a little horrified. No woman should call her mother a cow.

"You did," Debra answered.

"Mom..." *How many times does a woman have to apologize? Has Mom even apologized once? No. This is why I moved away. Why I call once a week...*

"I know you're sorry, sweetie. That's why I've done the only possible logical thing," Debra said, sounding as though she had resolved the world hunger issues.

"What?" Kate asked, suddenly worried what "logical" might mean to her mother.

"I bought a plane ticket. I'm coming to Montana."

That's what Kate was afraid of.

ON MONDAY Kate was pounding the pavement with new enthusiasm. Her mother was coming. If she didn't have something to get her out of the house every day, one of them would probably end up in the hospital. While there wasn't much pavement in the town of Lincoln to pound, she did her best.

Kate couldn't help but make comparisons between Lincoln and Los Angeles. The little town of Lincoln could really use a Starbucks, that was for sure. If the loyal citizens had any idea what they were missing out on by drinking the barely warm water that Josie's Café served up as coffee, there would be riots in the streets.

And bagels would be nice, she thought. *And smoothies. Oh, I'd give my life for a soy milk, carob and coffee smoothie.* The cottage cheese plate at Josie's, while good in a completely geriatric kind of way, was nothing compared to a cinnamon-raisin bagel and honey-walnut cream cheese.

But other than the lack of certain breakfast necessities, she was surprised at how many times Lincoln came out on top in the comparisons. Kate could just leave her house and walk to all the places she needed to get to, as downtown Lincoln consisted of one street about five blocks long.

I'm going to save a fortune on gas, she thought as she left Josie's with a takeout cup of the bad coffee. As she made her way down the street someone across the street started waving at her. Kate looked around, wondering who the person was waving at, but she was the only one around. She raised her hand and waved back and the stranger across the street kept walking.

Everyone she encountered on the street waved at her and some, people she had met in her brief stints at the library and grocery store, stopped and talked to her.

Mrs. Davis stopped to tell her how sorry she wasn't at the library anymore. "I loved those novels you recommended," she said in her high whispery voice, and so Kate wrote her a list of other books to try.

There is no one in L.A. even noticing I'm gone right now, Kate thought as she watched Mrs. Davis walk away.

She went into all of the stores looking for work—the pharmacy and the hardware store and even a place called the feed store—and if they didn't have an opening they pointed out a place that might. At the end of the day Kate had several new leads on jobs and had finagled interviews for next day. She could be a receptionist at the hair salon, a ticket taker at the movie theater or a used car salesman.

She tried to work up any kind of enthusiasm about her prospects, but there was little to be had. Billy's words about how she was a writer and she should just write rang in her ears. But her inner demons had plenty to say about the subject.

Kate Jenkins, for the sake of her daughter, was going to have to become a working stiff just like everyone else in the miniscule town of Lincoln, Montana, and if that meant selling used cars, then so be it.

Kate walked into Alyssa's veterinary clinic and smiled to see her daughter, sitting in her carrier, blinking and blowing spit bubbles. Maria, Alyssa's receptionist and assistant, was working at her desk. Most of the vet business in the area was on-call jobs, so Alyssa was often traveling to far-off ranches, leaving Maria to hold down the fort and keep an eye on the kids.

Maria looked up at the sound of the tinkling doorbell.

"Hi, Kate. How did the job search go?" the twenty-year-old asked. She reached over and turned down the radio.

"Great," Kate said with enthusiasm she didn't feel.

Kate walked over to her daughter and her heart thrilled at the recognition she saw in Laura's eyes. Laura squirmed and wiggled, clapping her hands, and remarkably the bottoms of her feet. Spit spilled from her mouth like a fountain and Kate had never seen a more clever child.

"Hey, sweet pea," Kate cooed, and kissed her daughter.

Maria smiled and looked back at her computer screen.

"I heard your mom was coming to town," Maria said, her eyes lifting from the screen for a moment.

"Yep," Kate said through clenched teeth. "Mom's coming next Friday."

Something in Kate's tone alerted Maria, who looked up quizzically at Kate. "Is that a good thing?"

"Probably not," Kate answered. "But, she's my mom and Laura is her granddaughter and you won't have to baby-sit while she's here," Kate said, looking for that silver lining.

"Well, I don't like the sound of that," Maria said. "You tell your mom to bring this little girl over for visits."

"I will," Kate said with a smile, although no one really told Debra to do anything, least of all her daughter. "Anyway, Maria, thanks again for watching Laura."

"Wait a second!" Maria said, looking up, a bright astonished smile on her face. While Kate watched, the girl actually lifted her hand and knocked her own head. "I can't believe I almost forgot," she said. "Bob Green came by today to get his dogs their heartworm pill and we got to talking and guess whose name came up?"

"Well," Kate said, picking Laura up and curling her against her shoulder. She swayed a little bit and her heart leaped when her daughter turned her head against her neck. "Having no idea who Bob Green is, I can only imagine that he would want to talk about...me?"

"Right!" Maria said. She put one elbow on the desk and beamed at Kate. "He's the editor at the paper..."

"Paper?" Kate asked, stilling. "As in newspaper?"

"Right."

"You guys have one?" she asked, surprised. Lincoln seemed to consist of about four people.

"Well, the three counties share one and it keeps Bob pretty busy traveling around and writing, editing, printing and distributing."

"I can imagine," Kate said sympathetically. *What in the*

world could fill up a newspaper about the three surrounding counties?

"Anyways, we got to chatting..."

"So, you said," Kate said encouragingly. She loved this girl's enthusiasm and lack of sarcasm. What a change from the people she used to have conversations with.

"And he asked about Laura and I told him about you and when he found out we had a real honest-to-God writer in town he about fell over."

"I can imagine," Kate said, not really able to imagine it at all.

"So I told him where you lived and I think he wants to offer you a job," Maria said, finishing her tale with a small squeal. "Isn't that great?"

"It is," Kate agreed, seeing her life as a used car salesman fall off into the distance. She didn't think that writing about the latest in barbed-wire technology and church circle groups was at all like writing blockbuster movies, or even greeting cards.

Kate put Laura back in the carrier, thanked Maria sincerely for her news and for looking after her daughter and went off to find Mr. Green to offer him her services.

Kate Jenkins—Reporter to the Cows. Her smile kicked up and she decided it had a nice ring to it.

7

"DELIVER?" Kate squeaked. "You want me to *deliver* newspapers?"

"Right." Bob Green scooted his chair in closer to his desk and put his hands on the top, which caused a waterfall of paper, Styrofoam cups, pencils and about a dozen squishy stress balls to fall from the left side of his desk onto the linoleum floor.

Both of them dove to grab the stuff that had fallen off and reached up their hands to stem the next wave of junk that teetered on the edge of Bob's desk. Kate clasped a couple of yellow notebooks, a brown paper bag that smelled bad and some back issues of the *Tri-counties NewsLeader* to her chest and sat back in her folding chair across from Bob's desk.

Bob threw the stuff in his arms onto the floor behind his chair where another pile was growing and turned back to Kate with a grin.

"All of our employees begin by delivering papers and if they prove reliable then they move up," he told her enthusiastically.

"To what?" Kate asked incredulously, "Secretary?"

"Exactly." Bob smiled at Kate with all kinds of approval and pushed his glasses up a little further on his nose. "Now I'd imagine a person with your talents would move up rather quickly..."

"I wrote a blockbuster Hollywood movie!" Kate told him just so he knew what kind of fool he was being.

"Like I said, I can't imagine you'd be delivering papers for very long." Bob sat back, the very picture of confidence, and Kate thought she might either rip her hair out or what was left of Bob's.

"What are you going to pay me?" she asked. So help her if it wasn't more than what she'd earn at the hairdresser's she would walk out of here, give up her Reporter to the Cows fantasy and learn how to trim bangs.

"Well, considering your past experience and your talent, I think I can offer you a very competitive rate of ten dollars an hour." Bob crossed his fingers over his small middle-aged pot belly and smiled at her.

It was a testament to how far Kate had fallen that she was floored by the offer of ten dollars an hour. At one time in her life she had spent two thousand dollars on a dress to wear to the Oscars. Just one dress.

"You've got a delivery girl, Mr. Green."

"Call me Bob," he said. She filled out the appropriate paperwork, met the other staff, which consisted of a secretary who wrote the gossip column and a high school kid who also delivered the paper.

"Make sure he gives you gas money," the kid whispered as Kate walked by. She turned to look at him and he hissed, "He'll stiff you."

Kate nodded and hurried to catch up with Bob Green who hadn't noticed she lagged behind.

"We come out once a week. Tuesdays," Bob explained as they walked through the miniscule office, his sensible brown shoes squeaking on the linoleum. "So Tuesday mornings you start at about 4:00 a.m."

"You're kidding?" Kate asked.

"Nope," Bob answered without breaking stride. "The rest of the week we will expect you at eight-thirty."

They were at the front door; Bob shook Kate's hand and opened the door for her.

"I'll see you tomorrow," Kate said, not entirely sure what she had gotten herself into. Tomorrow was Tuesday and she thought maybe she should go home and go to bed at once.

"Excellent," Bob said, and Kate turned to walk away.

"Oh, Kate," Bob said, and she turned. "I loved *Spurs,*" he said with a big smile.

"I'm glad, Bob," she said with a laugh. "I really am." She'd probably be mopping the floors if he didn't.

BILLY WALKED into Alyssa's vet clinic on Friday and Maria looked up at the tinkling of the bell.

"Hi again, Billy," she said, smiling. "You're getting to be a real regular around here. Four days in a row."

"Yeah, well, lots of veterinary needs up at the farm," Billy said, not quite able to look Maria in the eyes.

"I'm sure," Maria said innocently. "What do you need today? You about bought us out of cat food yesterday."

"Right." Billy looked around the store. "I need a dog collar. Where's Laura?" he asked, unable to see the little girl and feeling for some reason a sharp jab of panic. He knew leaving her at the clinic was a mistake. *Someone came in and grabbed her while Maria was giving flea baths…*

"Kate already came and got her, you just missed them." Billy's heart flip-flopped and finally fell a little bit, but he grabbed a dog collar as though it was what he really came in to find and took it up to the counter.

"Have you got a poodle or something up at the Morning Glory?" Maria asked, holding up the tiny dog collar he had grabbed.

"Oops, wrong one." Billy smiled sheepishly and grabbed a bigger collar and got out of the store as fast as he could.

This is getting ridiculous. He was creating every excuse

in the book to get himself into town, and worse, he was trying to get himself to believe them. Yesterday it was cat food. Two days before that he brought in one of the barn cats for a checkup, which was ridiculous in two ways: Alyssa was at the farm almost every other day and barn cats never got checkups—not even the ones he liked. Billy rubbed the scratches on his hands that the ornery one-eyed fighter had given him. He really didn't like that cat.

He had been running to town for groceries, meeting his buddies for lunch, he even made a dentist appointment—all so he could drop by the vet clinic to see Laura. Billy just wanted to see her, to make sure she was okay and to watch the bright light of recognition in her giant blue eyes. He wanted to make sure she was healthy and being cared for. No matter how much he tried to get himself to believe otherwise, he also hoped to see Kate.

He told himself that he just needed to make sure she was okay, that she had a job and wasn't starving to death. But the way his breath shortened every time he saw a blond head out of the corner of his eye told him he was lying. And he was.

He just wanted to see Kate. Period.

He felt seventeen again, walking past his sister's room five thousand times a day. Sneaking peeks at Sam and Kate while they sat giggling in their pajamas at the kitchen table. At seventeen she had been the brightest thing he had ever seen and thirteen years later he was still trying to get a glimpse of her. He felt like a fool, but every day he thought about Kate and Laura and every day he made some flimsy excuse to go to town.

He walked out of the clinic and into the street, trying in vain to talk some sense into himself.

You're a grown man, he told himself. *You can have any woman, any single, young non-mother you want. Time to remember who you are—Billy Cook, Champion of the World.*

Out of the corner of his eye he saw two blond heads making their way across the street and immediately recognized both of them. Kate and his buddy, the blond Adonis, Jake. His breath shortened and his blood began to simmer.

What did Jake think he was doing?

Billy ducked behind a car as they crossed the street away from him. He followed their progress down the street by running and crouching behind a series of parked cars. At the stop sign at the end of the block, Jake leaned his head close to Kate's and said something to make her laugh. She put her hand on his forearm as she laughed and as they took the step up to the curb Jake put his hand on the small of her back and let it linger there.

Billy rose from his crouch, ready to tear Jake apart, but Kate looked his way and he ducked back behind the car. He sat there for a moment praying he had been fast enough and Kate hadn't caught him following…

"Billy?"

Damn.

"Billy?" Kate repeated. "What are you doing behind this car?"

Quickly, Billy picked up a dirty penny, something that looked like a nail and a hard piece of chewed gum from the ground and stood with a smile on his face.

"I dropped something," he answered, putting everything in his pocket. "How are you, Kate? Hey, Jake." Jake stood behind Kate and looked at Billy with a smirk. Billy put as much dangerous threat into his eyes as he could, but Jake just put one hand on Kate's shoulder in response.

"You sure have been in town a lot, Billy," Jake said, the smirk growing smirkier. Kate looked up quizzically at Billy's blond friend and shook his hand off. Billy reminded himself that she hadn't been so quick to shake *his* hand off the other night and he began to feel a little bit better.

"Well, errands...you know how it is." He smiled at the two, burning the image of Kate in a pair of shorts and a short-sleeved plaid shirt in his brain and turned to walk away.

"Billy," Kate said, stopping him. "Maria said you came in the other day looking for me. Did you need something?"

Blabbermouth Maria!

"Yeah, uh..." Billy turned to face Kate and the soon-to-be broken-nosed Jake and thought fast. "Mom and Dad want you to come up for dinner."

Perfect, Billy thought, *I'll be able to see Kate and Laura without having to think up another excuse to search them out. Nice thinking, champ. I hope she wears those shorts.*

"I just saw your folks." Kate was beginning to smirk, too, as she unraveled his plan. "They didn't say anything about dinner."

"Yeah, old people, you know how they are." He lifted a finger and twirled it around his ear, the kindergarten symbol for crazy. Billy felt the slippery slope of stupidity beneath his feet.

"When?" Kate asked, smiling brightly.

"When what?" Billy asked, dazed for a moment by her smile.

"When do you want us to come to dinner?" she asked slowly. She turned to Jake and lifted her hand and twirled it around her ear.

Too much smirking for Billy's taste.

"Forget it, Kate." He turned and walked away.

"Grace misses you," Kate called quickly.

"Grace?" Billy turned confused. "Who is Grace?"

"My daughter." Kate smiled at him.

"I thought you settled on Laura." He didn't know what

to do with all of this jealousy and desire and it was making him testy.

"She didn't like it." Kate shrugged. She was so nonchalant, so unconcerned and it was making him crazy!

"Where the hell did you come up with Grace?" Billy almost shouted. The crazy woman couldn't even settle on a name for her daughter. What was he doing chasing her around town and spying on her from behind cars?

"The United Methodist Church on Third Street. I went in with Laura and one hour later I came out with Grace."

"You know only crazy people do this kind of thing," Billy told her, not caring that he sounded a little mean.

"Hey, Billy. Back off." Jake stepped up, having never seen Billy act so rude to a woman.

"This is the last name change, I promise," Kate said with a smile completely unruffled by Billy's temper. "Grace likes seeing you every day at the clinic but wants to see you for dinner." Kate told him and he cringed knowing that she had heard about his visits. "It's a small town, Billy. Someone was bound to tell me you were checking in on her every day sooner or later."

Billy shook his head; Kate Jenkins had his number. She always had.

"Sunday night," he said. "Come to dinner Sunday night."

He nodded at both of them and left before he could be any more foolish.

THAT EVENING Mark and Billy left the stables and headed across the yard to the house.

"Mom says we're having some people for dinner on Sunday and wants Alyssa and me to come up," Mark said. "She says she wants to do something festive."

"Festive?" Billy asked, suddenly concerned. Festive to

Missy Cook could mean any number of things and almost all of them would make anyone worry.

"Yeah, she said you're bringing Kate and her baby up here for dinner," Mark said.

Billy wanted to groan. Of course his family was not going to see this as something casual, which is what it was. Totally casual. One hundred percent not at all serious. He just wanted to make sure that the Jenkins girls were okay. And if Kate happened to wear those shorts and some kind of tight shirt, well then that would be just fine.

"It's not like I'm *bringing her* bringing her," Billy said reasonably. "She's all by herself and I thought she might like to have dinner with the family."

"I wouldn't say she's all by herself," Mark said.

"Well, sure, she has Laura—I mean, Grace, but you can hardly…"

"Are you telling me you don't know what's going on?" Mark asked, surprised. He stopped and put out a hand to stop Billy. "The way you keep tabs on those girls, I would have thought you would know…"

"I'm not keeping tabs on them," Billy said defensively.

"You're at the clinic every day," Mark pointed out.

"We have a lot of veterinary needs," Billy said defensively, and then shook his head. "What are you talking about, them not being alone?" Billy asked, and suddenly the image of Jake and Kate walking down the street flashed through his mind. "Did Jake—"

"Her mom's here," Mark interrupted, saving Billy from flipping out.

"Her mom?" Billy repeated, relieved.

"Yeah, flew in from Alabama on Friday." Mark started smiling, and put a hand on his brother's shoulder. "That might put a crimp in your plans."

"I don't have any *plans,* Mark," Billy said firmly, but certain parts of him were howling with disappointment.

"Yeah, you do. Billy, I know it's tough falling for a girl you don't think you should fall for..."

"I'm not falling for Kate Jenkins," Billy said firmly, refusing to give on his position of friendly interest. "I am interested in Kate Jenkins's well-being and the well-being of her daughter. That's all."

"Billy, I was here thirteen years ago. I saw the way you guys lit everything on fire. And now you're spending so much time in town, you're becoming a regular. You've got to face the facts here, Billy," Mark told him, arching a knowing eyebrow. "You can't tell me you're not interested..."

"Of course I'm interested," Billy said quickly, his temper flaring. "But, if you remember the sequence of events thirteen years ago, Kate left. And my bet is once she gets tired of small-town life she's going to leave again. And I don't need that kind of hassle."

Remember that, Billy told himself. *Remember your own words. She's bound to leave and you don't need that again.*

"You're right, Billy." Mark took a step back, and kept walking toward the house. "I'm just an old married man, what do I know?"

"That's right," Billy said mulishly, and walked after him.

DEBRA JENKINS was a force to be reckoned with. Billy saw that in the first ten minutes she was in the house on Sunday night. Initially, Billy's breath caught at his first glimpse of Kate's mother. It was like looking into Kate's future, the resemblance was so strong. Debra's silver-blond hair was cut short and they were both dressed in loose pants and tennis shoes. They had the same skinny build and take-charge attitude. Their combined energy nearly blew Billy back in his chair.

Debra's eyes were the same blue as Kate's, clear and

bright. But Debra's glittered with something far harder than what made Kate's eyes glow. They made Billy nervous for Kate; he felt the urge to protect her from whatever might make her eyes that cold one day.

"Thank you for your invitation," Debra said to Missy, her soft Southern accent completely at odds with her tough demeanor. She was carrying Grace against one shoulder and shook hands with her free hand. Her grip was firm and cold.

"Do you have a quiet place my granddaughter can sleep?" she asked.

"Sure, I can take her into the den..." Missy, said reaching for the child.

"Just show me where," Debra said, holding on to the baby just a little tighter. Billy immediately saw exactly how it was. She was going to protect her own against all strangers. And according to Debra, the Cooks were strangers.

I cut that baby's umbilical cord! he wanted to shout after her. *While you were disapproving of Kate, your granddaughter was sliding into my hands!*

Missy led Debra into the den where they put Grace down to finish her nap. Billy turned his attention to Kate, searching for any signs of harm due to having the Ice Queen in town.

She stepped up to Billy and he automatically slid his arms around her. His hand spanned the small of her back and he could feel the warm tense pleasure of her skin beneath her cotton blouse. "Everything okay?" he whispered into her hair, and fought the sudden urge to close his eyes and sniff her hair in front of his whole family. As if things weren't weird enough.

"Don't worry about us Billy, we're fine." She leaned back and smiled at him. "Mom's here now." With his hand on her spine and her stomach pressed to his, they both felt her deep breath. Everyone began to sit down for dinner.

Billy let Kate go and deliberately sat as far away from her as he could. He needed space to keep a clear mind.

One thing became clear right away—Debra didn't feel good about anything. Billy couldn't be sure if Kate's mom was a blessing or a giant pain in the neck.

"Remember, honey, everything you eat goes right into Grace," she warned when Kate lifted a bite of food to her mouth.

"Grace happens to love Alyssa's spicy baked beans," Kate answered with an edgy smile.

"Kate, rumor around town is you're delivering the newspaper," Mac said, smiling, deftly changing the subject as he had every time Debra found fault with her daughter.

"I sure am," Kate said with a giant smile, and Billy's stomach flip-flopped and he found himself smiling back at her.

"My daughter delivering newspapers. Have you ever heard anything so ridiculous?" Debra muttered just loud enough for everyone to hear.

"How are you fitting into small-town life?" Missy asked quickly. "It must be an adjustment."

"It is." Kate laughed graciously and Billy braced himself. *Here it comes...* "I won't say that I don't miss some things. It would be nice to have an ATM..."

"I've heard of those," Mac said, joking.

"A decent cup of coffee wouldn't be bad, either."

"Now just a second here, I made this coffee," Missy said, teasing Kate.

"And it's perfect, you should give Josie some lessons." Everybody laughed and Kate kept going. "It would be nice to see a movie that wasn't a year old."

"I'll agree with that one," Cecelia said, wiping her daughter's face. "It would be nice to actually rent a new movie."

"It'd be nice to see something that didn't have John Wayne in it," Alyssa added.

"Well, when you're renting movies from the hardware store I think you have to take what you can get," Kate said, laughing with his family.

The family kept talking about the things they would like to see in town and Billy realized two things: his plan was backfiring. What had he been thinking believing that this was going to be easier? Watching Kate blend in with his family was a strange kind of torture and knowing Grace was sleeping on the leather couch in the den made him restless.

He had just wanted to keep an eye on them, he hadn't asked to feel good about it.

He also was beginning to feel vindicated. He knew that Kate would hate it here, he knew that it wouldn't take long for her to draw the comparisons and find Lincoln coming up short.

"Well, the good news is my first story comes out next week," Kate said.

"What's it about?" Alyssa asked.

"They're building a new room on to the library and they're getting two computers," Kate told the table.

"Really?" Missy asked, kind of gasping with joy. "Well, will you look at that. Mac, I believe we just got the scoop. I can't wait to tell Mary Gensler, she usually gets all the good stuff first."

"You want to know what else?" Kate dropped her voice to a whisper and, like a fish rising to the bait, Missy leaned in closer, her eyes wide.

"What?" she whispered.

Kate paused, looked around the table and finally leaned back, playing Missy like a fiddle. "I can't," she said, and everyone except Missy howled with laughter.

"That's not funny, teasing a woman like that," Missy said, affronted.

"Oh, now look, honey." Mac draped his arm around his wife's back. "It's your own fault wanting to out-gossip everyone in town."

"That's not true, I just think it's a citizen's right to be informed."

Everyone started laughing and telling stories about Missy Cook's far-reaching ring of gossip. With all the laughter and with Kate sitting next to Mac, who was laughing the loudest, no one heard Grace's first few cries. Except Debra.

When she came back into the room with Grace, her face was pinched with displeasure and Billy felt a sense of impending doom. But before she could say anything Mac stood and took Grace from Debra's arms.

"What a baby," Mac said, clearly entranced by Grace's few tricks. She blew bubbles and blinked her giant blue eyes. She reached up a tiny fist and grabbed Mac's hair. He laughed and she smiled and the whole family scooted in closer to admire the baby. Billy resisted as best he could, leaning back in his chair and drinking his coffee.

They're leaving...no attachments, he told himself, repeating it over and over.

"She going to be trouble," Mark said, smiling at Kate. "Get ready for marriage proposals in kindergarten."

"I think she'll be able to handle it," Kate said with a smile. Billy could see that she was all but bursting with love and pride for the gorgeous creature in Mac's arms and Billy wanted to share in the joy of the little girl, but he didn't.

This is what he had wanted to avoid. This closeness, this general feeling of happiness and rightness. He felt frozen cold and stuck between his desire to grab onto that baby and the desire to stand and tell Kate and Grace to leave, before everyone's hearts were broken. *Before my heart is broken. Again.*

"She's awfully alert for a three-month-old," Alyssa said. "She's going to be a bright one."

"Two and a half," Kate corrected, clearly proud to be the mother of a child genius. Billy watched everyone nod. He took a quick gulp of his coffee but didn't taste it. Didn't notice that it was hot and had burned the roof of his mouth.

The family began to talk about bright babies and child geniuses and nobody noticed the storm cloud that was building on Debra's face, except Billy. He thought for a moment that Debra would insist they leave. Perhaps in all of this Debra was an ally.

"You have no idea what my daughter's in for," Debra interjected with an edge to her voice that cut through the happy atmosphere like a knife.

"Mom," Kate said in warning.

"Well, we're all sitting here talking about what a beautiful little girl Grace is and isn't wonderful that she's here and I think someone needs to tell the truth." Debra sat back in her chair. Her eyes, so much like Kate's, were narrowed and angry. "Kate has put herself behind the eight ball. She has no one to help..."

"We're here," Missy said calmly, and the Cook family nodded and murmured in agreement. Except Billy, sensing change in the air.

"You sure are, and that's wonderful, but you're not a husband or a father. And that's what those two girls need. A husband and a father," Debra insisted.

"Mom, this is not 1954. I am fully able to take care of my daughter without a man," Kate said, and from her tone this had become an old argument. "This isn't the place for this..."

"Yes, I think it is. These people—" Debra looked around at the Cooks, who were sitting around the table in various stages of disbelief and anger "—are telling you it's all going to be okay and I bet they haven't been lonely one day in their lives. Not one of these women with babies has wondered if they could provide everything that child needed while at the same time wondering who was going to provide what *they* needed."

"Mom!" Kate stood, her face flushed in anger, and Billy felt a similar blush travel from his toes to his hair. He was holding on to his coffee cup so hard that his hand was going numb.

"These are good people," Debra was saying. "I am not saying they're not, but they don't know what you're up against." Debra stood. "If you'll excuse me." She left the room and walked out of the house onto the front porch.

"I apologize for my mother," Kate said wearily into the stunned silence. "She's never gotten over my father leaving and I guess this is all somehow stirring it back up." Kate smiled, but it wobbled at the corners.

This, Billy thought in a strange moment of selfless insight, *is heartbreak.*

Something long simmering in Billy's chest erupted.

"Kate," Billy said, not caring if his whole family was watching and wondering. "We're here. We're always here. You are a part of our family and any one of us would do anything for your girl and for you." Billy took a deep breath. "Especially me."

What are you doing? his better sense howled.

Kate looked at Billy with eyes that were surprised and skeptical. He felt the same way, but he knew that someone had to stick up for this woman and her baby. Someone had to say "It's going to be okay" and "I'll help you as best I can," and that someone had to be him.

"We know—I know you're leaving, but for as long as you're here, and Grace is here you can count on me. Do you understand that?" he asked. "I'm in this with you."

"Billy, really we're okay..." Kate said.

"Yep, you are," Billy said and meant it. "But it doesn't change the fact that you can count on me, okay?" Billy's eyes were strong and steadfast and gave Kate no room to move under that gaze.

"Okay, Billy," she said slowly. "We can count on you."

It seemed somehow like a vow, a promise. And for a guy who never ever promised anything, it felt somehow better to have done it.

8

KATE WASN'T EXACTLY SURE how Billy's promise would materialize. But on Monday night, when Billy showed up on Kate's doorstep with an ancient game of Scrabble under his arm and resolve in his eye, he could have knocked Kate over with a feather.

"What are you doing here, Billy?" Kate asked. His unexpected and passionate declaration the night before had kept her up until three in the morning. She wanted to believe, but she had learned comfort was never what it seemed and help always had strings attached. And help that looked like Billy Cook, well, that was whole different kind of trouble.

"I'm here to play Scrabble," Billy said, and charged in like Patton storming the shores. He brushed past her into the kitchen where Debra sat openmouthed with Grace on her lap. Kate turned to watch him approach her mom and Grace and for a moment with the look on his face she thought he was going to say something horrible. And Kate could only gape.

They were all stuck in some kind of surreal tableau of doubt and distrust until Grace lifted her arms up to Billy. He took a deep breath, reached down and pulled her into his arms where she curled into his shoulder and sighed.

"Billy?" Kate asked, still standing at the open door.

"Don't you like Scrabble?" he asked with mock horror.

After a moment Kate shut the door and walked back into the kitchen, feeling suddenly much better than she had since picking her mother up at the airport four days ago. She crossed her bare feet at the ankle, threw her dish towel over her shoulder and decided that instead of trying to figure out Billy's angle she would take this diversion as a gift. The endless battles she had been having with her mother were wearing her down. The never-ending discussions about the future were tiring, but Scrabble with Billy sounded like the perfect pick-me-up.

"We love Scrabble, don't we, Mom?" Kate said, and turned to Debra just in time to see the gleam in her eye. A gleam that Kate would have to dispel after Billy left.

"We sure do," Debra said with a sly Southern belle smile, and Kate almost groaned.

Kate knew, sitting at the old kitchen table that they both meant well, but only one of them could win. Kate, as usual, put all her money on herself.

FOR THE NEXT two weeks Kate's life fell into a strange rhythm. She was no longer delivering newspapers; she had been promoted to secretary and to what seemed to be assistant editor. Whatever the job title, it meant she didn't have to get up at 4:00 a.m. anymore and for that she would be plenty grateful to Bob Green. Debra watched Grace during the day and when Kate got home she would fight with her mom, play with her baby and a couple times a week, Billy would come by with ice cream or movies or card games.

Everyone in the Jenkins house was happy to see him at the door. Especially Kate, although it was not an easy thing to admit. And she would drop dead before admitting it to her mother. Debra had given up on Kate's job and had moved on to harassing her about Billy.

"You aren't going to wear that, are you?" Debra had whispered as they heard Billy's boots on the steps outside the door one evening.

"What's wrong with this?" Kate had asked, looking down at her cutoffs and *Spurs* T-shirt.

"At least go put on some lipstick..."

"Mom!" Kate shrieked.

"And brush your hair!"

Kate ran her hands through her short blond hair, deliberately making it all stand on end and stuck out her tongue just as Billy walked in the back door.

"Billy seems like a nice man." Tonight Debra started in while putting out chicken salad for dinner. Kate rolled her eyes and braced herself for round twelve with her mother over the Billy issue.

"He is, Mom. A very nice man," Kate agreed. It wasn't hard—she'd watched him closely over the past two weeks when all of his defenses were down, and she realized he was a truly nice man. But things were finally beginning to work out for her—she had a job she liked, her daughter was thriving and Kate could even feel herself thriving a little bit. Some part of her was growing toward the sunlight and she wasn't about to get involved with a man. Even Billy.

It was Kate's experience that the second she got involved with a man it ruined everything, so Billy came around but she kept the distance there. He kept his own distance, she could feel it in him and that was fine. It was easier that way, no matter what her heart, body or mother wanted.

And if the sight of him barefoot in her apartment holding Grace sometimes made her feel light-headed, or if she woke up from dreams about Billy feeling as if she were on fire, then it was just too bad. She blamed it on out-of-control hormones if she sometimes wished she could meet him at the door in something slinky and sexy and he would be unable to keep his hands off her. Because *he* was able to keep his hands off her, even when she wore tight shirts and flaunted her new boobs, so she was determined to be just as strong.

Not that she cared, most of the time anyway.

But the combination of her hormones and Billy's underwear-model looks were making it hard for her to keep her hands to herself.

"A LIFESTYLE FEATURE?" Kate repeated Bob Green's words, making sure she had heard correctly. "We don't even have a lifestyle *section.*"

"Well, now that's not exactly true," Bob said. He put his hands on his desk and Kate just barely caught the bagel that slid off the side. "We just don't have a *complete* section."

"We don't have a complete page," Kate said.

"Exactly," Bob said as if Kate had proven his point. After three weeks of talking to Bob, Kate guessed maybe she had. There was just no way of knowing. "We have a gossip column and a couple of recipes, but I think the good people of the tri-county area are hungry for more." Bob leaned in toward Kate with an excited gleam in his eye.

"And that's where I come in?" Kate guessed warily. "You want me to write some features about how to decorate the bunkhouse, or how to put together a spring roundup with pizzazz."

"Exactly!" Bob simply had no grasp of sarcasm. Kate shook her head in disbelief. Maybe it wasn't too late to get that job at the hair salon.

"But first I have a series I want you to do to help us grab some younger readers." Bob fished through the piles of paper on his desk, sending avalanches of junk to the floor that Kate didn't even try to pick up. *Crazy small-town newspaper editors can pick up their own moldy lunches and broken pencils.*

"Thirty-five percent of the tri-county population is between the ages of sixteen and thirty and according to our latest circulation figures, almost none of them read the paper.'' Bob looked at Kate over the edge of it. ''That's a whole lot of audience we're not reaching.''

''I don't think they care about decorating bunkhouses,'' Kate said slowly, wondering just where Bob's plan was going.

''Exactly!''

Kate buried her head in her hands.

''What they care about is dating and getting married and having fun. And that's where you come in.'' Bob put down the report. ''I want you to find the five best places to go on a date in the tri-county area. Places that cover a whole range of prices and activities and interests.''

Kate sat silently waiting for the punch line, but Bob continued to look at her as if he had actually discovered gold.

''Well?'' he finally said when Kate continued to sit in silence.

''I'm a single mom,'' Kate said slowly. ''I'm not dating anyone.''

''Well, I'm sure you can figure something out,'' he said, and began searching for something on his garbage-laden desk.

''Bob, I'm not from around here. I wouldn't know where to start.'' Kate was beginning to feel a sense of inevitability. Bob Green was a dense object who had come to rest on this idea and wasn't moving.

''You're a very resourceful girl. I'm confident you'll find great places to date.'' He swiveled in his chair and shifted his search to the pile of papers behind his desk.

''Do you have any ideas?'' she asked, watching the patch of hairy skin on his back visible between his brown pants and equally brown shirt.

''Well, now I'm a happily married man. I don't date, either,'' Bob said, swiveling back around, his comb-over hopelessly mussed with an envelope in his hand. "The good news is, I have a small stipend for your expenses." He pushed the envelope over to her. "Good luck, and I think if you could have the first installment on my desk on Monday, that would be in plenty of time for the next week's paper." Bob stood and put out his hand. Kate picked up the envelope of money, stood, put her hand numbly in his and walked out the door.

"PEOPLE AROUND HERE date?" Debra asked over their meager dinner that night.

"I guess. I wouldn't really know," Kate answered, still frazzled from the meeting with Bob. A cool breeze floated in the open door and brushed her face. "They must. Right? I mean, they can't all just fall in love in kindergarten and get married after high school." She took a bite of her chicken and filled up a spoon of mashed bananas for Grace. She absently put the spoon in her daughter's mouth, scooped up the stuff that squirted out the sides and filled up the spoon again.

"What do you say, Mom? Want to go on a few dates with me?" Kate smiled slyly at Debra and Debra tipped her head back and laughed, a sound that had reverberated through Kate's childhood. The sound made her nostalgic for the good old days when her mother was a phone call away and couldn't harrass her unless Kate dialed the phone.

Sweet, peaceful, guilt-free days.

"I'd rather go on a date with Grace. Why don't you find yourself a nice man to take you?" Debra said, beating what was a very dead horse. "Why not Billy? He's here almost every night anyway."

"Oh, come on, Mom." Kate sat back, a spoonful of bananas in her hands, pretending the idea hadn't occurred to her. "I thought you were done with this stuff."

"What stuff?" Debra asked a little too innocently.

"Mom, all I need is someone to go do some investigating with me, that's all. I don't see why you take this—"

"Am I interrupting something?" Billy stood in the open doorway, leaning against the door frame as if he had been standing there for a while. Kate's mouth suddenly went dry.

Oh, my God, look at him, she thought, feeling the deep tremble in her stomach. *He's too handsome.*

He pushed his cowboy hat back on his head and grinned. It was the grin that said he knew a secret, a secret about her, and it made him happy to know it. That grin made Kate crazy.

"My daughter needs a date," Debra said, and she sailed out of the room with Grace and the bowl of mashed bananas. "I'll leave you two alone." Debra shut the bedroom door behind her.

Kate let out a long sigh and put her head on the table and vowed that she would never embarrass Grace the way her mother seemed to relish embarrassing her. She was hoplessly aware of the fact that she was a thirty-two-year-old mother, with mashed bananas in her hair and baby drool on her T-shirt. She wasn't even wearing shoes.

"What's wrong, Kate?" Billy sauntered into the room and pulled out a chair at the old scarred table.

"Before you start splitting your sides, I don't need a date." She sat up; the crease from the table where she had been resting her head lined her forehead.

"Your mom says you do."

"I don't need a date!" she said, and to her utter disbelief she found herself starting to tear up. "So, just get yourself out of my house, Billy Cook!" Kate put her head back down on the table and tried to pretend Billy wasn't there.

Before her mom had come to visit Kate had thought all of her postpartum depression was over. She had read the book—*You're Not a Bad Mother You're Just Depressed*—and laughed at all the stories in it about women who were so depressed they couldn't get out of bed or get dressed, or walked around in their robes eating ice cream out of the container.

Kate had read it and thought, *Thank God!* But now that the panic had worn off and her mother was here to remind her at every passing moment what a mistake she had made, she sometimes found it harder to get out of the bed in the morning. She occasionally locked the bathroom door so she could sit on the toilet and bawl her eyes out. She found herself every once in a while thinking that just maybe she had made a mistake.

"Ah, sweetheart, we've done this before..." Billy reached for her and Kate sat back away from him.

"Well you just keep your hands to yourself because I don't need a date." *And I don't need you shirtless on my balcony kissing me senseless,* she thought and then immediately changed her mind. *Yes I do. Yes I do. Please let's drop this casual friend thing and get naked.*

Kate felt herself sliding into an unwelcome place. She felt desperate and edgy and she knew the best thing to do was to get away from Billy Cook. Really, it was the best thing.

BILLY SAT BACK with his hands in the air at Kate's rebuff. He was determined to be her friend, to help. Not to throw her to the ground and put his hands all over her. It was, however, getting harder to do. Or not do. Whatever it was, something was getting harder.

Since the strange Sunday family dinner with Debra and Kate, Billy had taken his vow to heart and had been much more present in Kate's life. Since that Sunday he had come over every time he had had a free night.

He brought Kate's favorite chocolate ice cream, played cards with Kate and her mom and held Grace who was more firmly wedged into his heart than ever. He had done the impossible and charmed Debra into thinking he was one of the good guys.

He thought about staying away or coming over less often, but there was no point. Evenings in the Jenkins House of Estrogen were fun. He got to watch Kate bend over in blue jeans and to listen to her laugh and to argue with her and to beat her at cards all while having the warm perfect weight of Grace in his arms. It was like heaven, except no sex.

"You want to tell me what's going on here?" he asked idly. He picked up a barbecued chicken leg off the platter in the middle of the table and began to eat it, trying to mask his interest in these "dates."

"I'm supposed to write a feature for the newspaper—five of them—on the best places to date in the tri-county area. Can you believe it?" She sat back in disgust. Having had two occasions to witness Kate Jenkins in tears, Billy realized that Kate, while a beautiful woman, was really an ugly crier.

"Well, I think it's a real good idea," Billy said, and helped himself to a piece of corn on the cob. "I can think of several just sitting here." He rolled the corn in butter and began to eat it. "I've been known to show a girl a good time, you know."

"I can't write a five piece feature on the back of your truck," Kate snarled, reaching for a piece of corn at the same time.

"Ah, honey, not all the girls get to go on *that* date." He winked at her and watched Kate eat her buttered corn with tears in her eyes. It was a wrenching combination.

"You want to tell me about all these great places?" Kate asked, narrowing her eyes.

"What?" he asked, distracted in a purely adolescent way by her glistening lips.

My God, look at her, he thought. *She's so beautiful.*

"Date places, Casanova, stay with me."

"Well, now I figure I can do one better." He poked his corn at her. It was the tears that made him do this, he wouldn't be this kind of glutton for punishment unless she had been crying.

Or it was the glistening lips...whatever it was, he opened his mouth and let himself make a mistake. "I, for the sake of journalistic integrity, will take you on five of the best dates you've ever been on all within the tri-county area."

"I've never been on a date in the tri-county area," Kate told him and blinked.

"Neither have most of the residents of western Montana. We all fall in love in kindergarten and get married after high school." He threw her words back at her and bit back into his chicken.

"Except you," Kate said softly.

"Not the point we're discussing here, Kate. We're talking about you and I taking advantage of your expense account and writing some articles for the newspaper."

"What can there possibly be around here that's worth writing about?" Kate asked darkly, and Billy felt some of his enthusiasm dry up.

"Well, it's not L.A., but we manage to get along okay," he said sarcastically, disappointed she was still so critical of his small town.

"Billy, that's not—"

"Hey, we've been over this," he said, interrupting, not wanting to hear about how she was comparing his hometown with the city, not wanting to hear about all the ways it was coming up short. "I'm just offering to help you as *a friend* to write your articles," he said, suddenly wishing that he hadn't opened his mouth.

"Just two friends," she said softly, and Billy nodded, reaching for some salad. He watched her wrestle with the idea and part of him wanted to say forget it.

"Okay, Billy. Thank you," she said, and the dye was cast.

"Now, where's the girl I really came to see?" he said to change the subject and as Kate stood to go get Grace Billy sighed. *How am I going to get through five dates with Kate? Me and my big mouth.*

TWO DAYS LATER, Billy arrived all polished and shiny at Kate's door. Kate, who had been seduced and charmed by some of the most attractive men in Hollywood, found it hard to look directly at him. The past two weeks had been so G-rated and her X-rated dreams crowded her brain so that all she wanted was to get naked on the kitchen floor with him. Despite the fact that she was trying to keep all the boundaries right where they were. Despite the fact that she knew he was only doing this out of love for Grace and maybe a little pity for Kate. Not romantic stuff to say the least.

Depressing really, she thought, trying to push all thoughts of kissing out of her head. *Have some pride, Kate.*

"You ready?" he asked, his mouth kicked up in his familiar grin.

"Ready as I'll ever be," she said, smoothing an uncharacteristically shaky hand down the front of her short denim skirt. She grabbed her purse and called goodbye to her mother and started toward the door.

"Where's Grace?" Billy asked, still blocking the doorway.

"Mom's watching her."

"No way, Kate. This date is a threesome and I'm not going anywhere without Grace." He crossed his arms over his chest. Kate smiled and with mixed emotions went to collect her daughter from her mother. Billy really couldn't be sending his point home any better; who planned a seduction with a baby around? It was a hard pill to swallow that Billy didn't want her at all.

It took Kate a while to guess what a baby might need on a date. It would have helped to know where they were going, but Billy only said, "It's a surprise." So Kate put sunscreen on Grace and a hat and stuffed her diaper bags with the appropriate blankets, a jacket for inclement weather, two changes of clothing and a small baseball cap.

"So where are we headed?" Kate asked again once they were settled in the truck and bouncing down the road.

"Well, it just so happens that this weekend is a very special weekend around these parts." Billy drove with one hand and stretched his arm across the back of the seat. Every other bounce his hand brushed her hair or her neck or the collar of her shirt and for Kate it was like a small electrical shock.

Friends, just friends, she reminded herself, trying to keep her heart under control.

"Every weekend in western Montana is special," Kate said with a little sarcasm that she really didn't feel. This place was becoming more special every day. It was becoming fun and welcoming and home, and that was very special.

"That's true, very true." Billy moved his hand from the back of the seat. "But every summer, once a month for three months, they hold auditions for rodeo clowns and this weekend it just happens to coincide with the Home Brew Competition."

"Home Brew?" Kate asked, her eyebrow arching.

"Beer, some wine, if we're lucky we'll sample some of the best moonshine ever made."

"You're joking."

"Hell no, this is a great date." He grinned and Kate wished for a blinding second that this was a true date. She wished that this wasn't just a favor and that they weren't just friends, that maybe they were lovers, interested in each other in a million different ways.

THE FAIRGROUNDS were filled to capacity, which Billy guessed was about a hundred people, and almost all of them were there for the Home Brew Competition. The clown auditions were in full swing; men in homemade clown costumes with painted faces were all gathered around the arena, looking seriously at the action. He watched Kate's face carefully for the disdain he expected to see, but instead she started laughing, looking around with an incredulous wonder that made Billy want to smile with relief.

"This is the real thing," she said almost to herself. "Those men really want to be rodeo clowns."

"What were you expecting?" Billy asked a little guardedly.

"I have no idea, Billy." She looked at him with a smile on her face and her eyes wide with laughter. "But this is great. Nothing like this in L.A."

"Yep," Billy answered, trying not to feel glad or proud. "You want some moonshine?" he asked, looking out at the booths set up beside the arena.

"Of course," she said, and they set off to find the best of what western Montana home brewers had to offer.

An hour later after Billy did most of the moonshine and beer sampling, Kate, Grace and Billy sat in the stands watching the amateur rodeo clowns compete for their chance at glory.

"That guy's drunk!" Kate said aghast as a poor man in badly applied makeup stumbled into the ring with a bull.

"I think that's his act," Billy said, leaning forward and squinting. "Yeah he's just pretending to be a drunk rodeo clown." They watched with held breath while the clown, in slouchy pants and drooping suspenders, barely avoided the dulled horns of the bull. Billy had told Kate earlier that the bulls were all past their prime but still moderately dangerous. *Particularly if you were a drunken rodeo clown with a red target painted on your butt,* Billy thought.

The drunken clown seemed unaware of the threat the bull was posing; he actually seemed altogether unaware of the bull. The crowd loved his act and cheered him on and the clown turned and blew kisses to the adoring dozen in the stands. As he bent over in a deep bow, the bull took aim at his target and started to charge. At the last possible minute before being gored—or at least badly bruised—the clown turned to bow to the other side of the stadium, stepping gracefully out of the path of the bull.

"Good one," Kate said firmly. "That is *very* clever."

Billy winced as the bull winged the clown and put his hands over his eyes.

"It wasn't an act," he said from behind his fingers. "He *was* drunk."

"I think the Home Brew Competition and rodeo clown auditions is a bad combo," Kate said vehemently, and Billy had to agree, though not quite so passionately. All day long they had been watching clowns in various stages of inebriation enter into the ring only to be taken out on stretchers, or slung over people's backs.

He turned to Kate and saw her sway a little bit in her seat and decided Kate and the Home Brew Competition had been a bad combo. The poor girl was drunkenly cheerful after one small drink of moonshine.

"Did you eat?" he asked.

"Eat?" She looked at him with such a prim, very un-Kate expression that Billy had to laugh. "No, not yet. This is supposed to be a *date.* Dates usually include eating." She arched her brow at him and Billy craned his neck, looking around for something that might be considered dinner.

"I hope you like corn dogs," he said, and picked up

Grace in her carrier and grabbed Kate's hand and together they slid off the bleachers. Billy stopped at the truck, put the carrier into the cab, rested Grace against his shoulder and began walking toward the hills and the concession area.

"So, the newspaper job seems to be going well," Billy said after they had gotten their corn dogs and found a seat at a picnic table.

"Love the newspaper," Kate said. "Hate Bob Green, but I love that job."

"Does he know you won't be around long?" Billy asked, then wanted to kick himself when Kate's smile left her face. Studiously he balanced Grace against his chest and put ketchup on his corn dog.

"It hasn't come up," she said, and looked at him. "Anxious to get rid of me?" she asked with a wry smile.

"No, I'm just wondering…"

"I'm joking, Billy," she said quietly and bit into her corn dog.

"Fancy food, huh?" Billy asked sarcastically, reading the look on Kate's face.

"What is this?" Appalled and fascinated, which was, Billy thought, the proper response to cornbread around a hot dog.

"I'll bet you weren't served such classy food on your last date." Billy watched the smile fall off her face again. *That's what I call showing a girl a good time, bringing up another man who happens to be the father of her child,* Billy thought, and immediately chafed at the idea. If he hadn't earned some kind of parental rights bringing the baby into this world then he certainly had earned some in the last two weeks. He and Grace were, for lack of a better word, bonded. *Far more than that stupid Joseph character,* Billy thought.

"Joseph would not be caught dead eating this," she said and took another bite.

"Have you told him about Grace or even where you are?" Billy asked carefully, unsure where the boundaries were here. He wanted to know where the other man stood with Grace, if he stood anywhere near her at all. And especially where he stood with Kate.

"I called and left a message with his secretary," Kate said. She stopped eating for a second.

"His secretary?" Billy asked, aghast. He threw his corn dog stick on the table in disgust and then pushed it further out of the way when Grace reached for it.

"Wasn't my idea. He wanted it that way," Kate told him.

Billy was floored, amazed that a man who knew his child was being born somewhere in the world, would want to hear about it through his secretary.

"He was always kind of a cold man," Kate said with a shrug that in its nonchalance spoke volumes.

"I'm sorry," Billy said, at a loss for words. Apparently they were the wrong ones and Kate turned suddenly angry eyes on him.

"Don't feel sorry for me, Billy. Don't ever feel sorry for me."

"Hey," Billy said, a little tired of being blasted by her every time he tried to apologize or to offer comfort. "I don't feel sorry for you. I just think the circumstances you've had to deal with suck. That's all. Some rotten things have happened and as usual you've fought back and are standing here on what's turning into a horrible date with an ex-lover and your daughter. Sometimes things are just bad, it doesn't mean I pity you."

"It's not a bad date," she said after a moment. "The moonshine was really good."

"Well, what a relief," Billy said, not ready to be swayed into laughing with her yet.

"The drunk rodeo clowns were pretty funny."

"Glad you thought so." He shifted Grace to his other shoulder and waited for a better apology.

"My date's a hunk."

Billy couldn't help it; he threw back his head and laughed. "Yeah, well mine is quite a looker, too," he said, and together they looked at Grace sleeping against his shoulder.

"Yes, she is," Kate said, and smiled.

They watched the last of the competition and in turn laughed and groaned. But when drunken rodeo clowns began to drink moonshine from the cups of their trophies, Billy and Kate decided to call it quits.

Warm and sober and happy they climbed back into the truck and headed home.

Kate rolled down her window and put her hand out into the air that rushed by. Billy watched her as she got up on her knees and stuck her head out the window and then her arms. Billy grabbed onto the tail of her shirt, not pulling her in but just holding on to her. It was these odd moments when she did things that adults just don't do anymore that somehow made him sad. Kate was her own woman and sometimes it felt as if he would never understand her. Wanting her the way he did was a booby trap, that's all there was to it and he didn't know how much longer he could resist her.

When she ducked back in, her face was flushed and her hair everywhere and she had that special smile that she seemed to pull out for him during his weakest moments on her face. She slid across the seat and put her arms around Billy's neck and Billy felt the warm press of her all through his body.

He could feel her studying his profile and Billy fought the powerful urge to stop the truck and pull Kate into his lap. She put her finger in his dimple and traced the laugh lines at the side of his eye. She touched him as if she had the right, and Billy could barely breathe. *What is she doing?*

"You're handsome," she said, her voice a quiet whisper. Billy smiled but kept his eyes on the road. "You're the handsomest man I've ever known."

"I doubt that," he said, and cleared his throat.

"It's true," she said, tucking a piece of hair behind his ear. "Thank you, Billy, for this date."

"My pleasure," he said easily. He darted a look at her and then turned back to the road. Kate kissed his cheek again and slid back over to her side of the truck.

Billy slowly exhaled and wondered painfully if he was a fool for thinking that Kate would ever want him again or that he wouldn't fall apart when she left him again.

9

"HEY KATE, I loved your date piece in the paper," Maria told her as Kate walked into the vet clinic. "Greg and I are going to go to the clown auditions next month with a group of friends."

"Really?" Kate asked. She felt a warm little glow in her stomach and fought the ridiculous urge to reach up a hand and pat herself on her back. "You read the paper every week, don't you?" Kate asked, unable to believe Bob Green had his finger anywhere near the pulse of twenty-year-olds.

"Heck no," Maria said quickly. "My mom showed your story to me. What are you going to do next week?"

"I have no idea," Kate said honestly, and hoped Billy had something else up his sleeve.

Kate couldn't help but smile at thoughts of Billy. He had completely surprised her, completely caught her off guard on their date. He had been sweet and charming and sexy as hell. Now Kate was caught, sandwiched between what she knew was right, staying friends and ignoring all of the sexual undercurrents that had nearly flipped the truck over the previous night or going with the flow to see what might happen next.

Really, what might happen? she thought as she left the clinic with Grace and headed toward Josie's. She was in need of coffee and Josie's was the only option. An option she was sadly resigned to. She found that if she drank the coffee fast, all in one shot she got a little zip from it. She had to take what she could get in this strange Starbucks-less town.

The world would hardly end, she thought as she waved at Mrs. Davis across the street and Mandy Eiker who was the new ticket taker at the movie theater. *It's just sex. I'm not asking him to raise my daughter with me. I am not relying on him for anything more than what I am willing to provide.*

She knew she wasn't alone in those feelings, either. Billy had been right there with her in the truck. She knew he wanted her, too. She saw it in his eyes, on his flushed face. *The stupid man had an erection and had calmly waved goodbye to me!* Kate shook her head.

"Hey, Joe," Kate said as she walked into Josie's. "Fellas, how are you today?" She greeted the table of old men who sat at Josie's every morning. They sat in the same place, ate the same breakfast and as far as Kate could tell, they talked about the same things every day.

"Right as rain, Kate."

"Can't complain."

"Coffee?" Claire, the owner of Josie's, asked and Kate nodded. Josie, the original owner, had died several years ago and Claire had never bothered to change the name of the diner.

Kate continued to weigh the problem with Billy as she waited for her coffee. The issue was clearly how they would have sex and keep things in perspective. *She* had it in perspective, she thought confidently. It was Billy she was worried about. Kate was not about to let him pity her or to use her so he could get close to her daughter.

Just my luck Billy has a Jerry Maguire complex. Kate paid for her coffee, waved to Joe and the boys and started home.

She stopped at the nearest garbage can, took off the lid

of her coffee and on the count of three drank as much of the tasteless brew as she could.

"Heeyah!" she said and dumped the rest of the coffee out. With a burned tongue, Kate decided what Billy needed was to have his world rocked. He needed to be seduced. Fireworks and spinning ears, the whole nine yards. He needed to forget about what was best and ground rules and keeping his distance.

And I am just the girl to do it, Kate mused with a wicked little smile.

BILLY PULLED a frilly dress out of the paper bag he had brought to Kate's apartment. A red gingham dress with white petticoats.

"You've got to wear this," he said without preamble.

"What's wrong with what I've got on?" Kate asked, looking down at her khaki shorts and T-shirt. Granted it wasn't a frilly dress but she thought she looked pretty good for their second date.

"Because I have to wear this." Billy dropped the bag and opened the jacket he was wearing despite the seventy-five-degree temperature. He was sporting a red gingham Western shirt with pearl buttons and some kind of red-and-white scarf around his neck. "It's all part of our date."

"You're kidding?" she asked deadpan.

"Sorry, but no."

"Where are we going?" Kate asked, slowly holding the dress up to her.

"Why, we're going dancing, sweetheart."

"BILLY," Kate protested out of the corner of her mouth, "I don't know how to do-si-do!" She hauled up the neckline of the dress that was sliding down her body. The dress was almost four sizes too big and she couldn't move without risking flashing everyone in the building.

"Just watch the other couples. I'm sure you can figure it out." Billy eyes were glued on the brightly clothed couples whirling and dipping and promenading home on the dance floor around him.

The weekly meeting of the Tri-county Square Dancing Association was in full swing. The sign in front of the community center had read Newcomers Welcome. But Kate was pretty sure that the newcomers should at least know how to star right and star left or some such thing.

She took another look at Billy who was still following the movements of the dancers and shuffling his feet and shifting his body to mimic their bodies.

"I think I've got this, Kate," he said confidently without looking at her. "Let's go!" Billy grabbed Kate's hand and pulled her into a forming group of dancers. They shook hands all around with the older couples who were even more extravagantly dressed than they were.

"I have no idea what I'm doing." Kate said apologetically to the group, pulling up the neckline of the dress.

"Well, honey, I imagine we can help you out," an older man with no hair and wearing a shirt in screaming yellow with a blue scarf around his neck told her.

His partner, Kate could tell by the matching screaming-yellow dress, patted her hand comfortingly. "It's so nice to see young couples here."

"We haven't had fresh blood 'round here since Jimmy and Enid joined." A freakishly tall man wearing unfortunate vertical stripes in purple and red jerked his thumb at a couple behind him, who were sixty-five if they were a day.

"That's us," Billy said straightening his red scarf. "Fresh blood. You ready, sweetheart?" Kate read "I dare you" in the twinkle in Billy's eye and if there was one thing Kate couldn't refuse it was a dare.

"You bet, *sweetheart,*" she said with a saccharine grin

as she grabbed his hand and hoped she would come out alive.

"OOPS! SORRY," she said for the millionth time as she promenaded the wrong way and ran into the tall man. She caught her sleeve as it slid past her elbow and pulled it up.

"Right," he rumbled. "Promenade right."

Billy found her hand and twirled her in the right direction. "What's the caller saying?" Kate asked frantically, hurrying to keep up with Billy's long steps, only to be cut short when he stopped, twirled her and began walking backward. "What's he saying now?" Instead of answering, Billy twirled her and then left her to grab onto one of the other women in the circle and twirl her. The tall man grabbed Kate, twirled her and then shoved her in the general direction of the next man coming down the pike.

"Now, honey, you're doing just fine," placated the man in screaming yellow. "Just listen to what the caller is saying."

"I can't *understand* what the caller is saying," Kate protested, but the man had already moved on. She stopped fighting her dress and just kept her fist knotted in the extra fabric at her neck. She fought a blur of bright shirts and pearl buttons until Billy's smiling face came into view.

"Having a good time?" Billy asked as he promenaded her home and the caller took a deep breath, said one more thing at a non-human speed and everyone bowed and finally clapped. Billy grabbed her arm and began to escort her from the dance floor. "Kate?" he asked again when she didn't answer. "You having a good time?"

Kate looked at all of the folks laughing and smiling in their ridiculous outfits. She thought about her sore feet and her general inherent confusion. She pulled up her dress and smiled. "I'm having a ball," she told him.

They chatted with the other dancers and neither one of

them corrected anyone when they assumed Billy and Kate were a couple. Kate slipped her arm through Billy's and he didn't protest, which Kate took as a good sign. She pressed up against him in small ways, found a million reasons to touch him and back off. It was a game and a dance and Kate was very, very good at it.

In fact, as they walked, Billy sometimes put his hand on Kate's shoulder, or the small of her back. Which Kate took as an invitation to lean in close and whisper things in his ear, her breath fanning his face.

Kate felt as if she was nineteen again. She was electrified by every "accidental" brush of their skin. Kate couldn't help but remember the ease of his seduction thirteen years ago. Careful nonchalance, the surprise flash of leg and a kiss on the cheek at just the right time had been all the push he had needed. Kate wondered, feeling flushed and womanly, if it would work as well on the man as it had on the boy.

"Let's sit this one out," Kate suggested when the next set started up.

"Sure, I'll get some snacks," Billy agreed, and headed over to the table of refreshments. When he came back with small paper cups of lemonade and cookies they hoisted themselves up onto the small stage and sat with their feet swinging. Kate could barely see over the heavily starched skirt of her dress, but Billy crushed it down for her.

"Where did you get these clothes?" Kate asked after they subdued her dress.

"Well, believe it or not, Missy and Mac used to be champion square dancers in their day," Billy told her. "I borrowed Mom's dress for you." He spread out a napkin and three cookies between them. He chose an oatmeal raisin and took a big bite. "Apparently that's how they met, some big square dance."

"That's sweet," Kate said, and grabbed a cookie of her own. "Why don't they do it anymore?"

"They're getting older." He shoved the cookie into his mouth and grinned at her.

"Happens to everyone, Billy. Even you," Kate reminded him. "I didn't realize that heavy petting session on my porch was your birthday. Happy belated birthday, you old man."

"Thank you, and in case you forgot, you're a couple of years older than me."

"How could I forget," she said with a groan. She laughed and nudged his shoulder with hers and she thought, for a few moments, that all was right with the world. Her sleeve slipped off her shoulder again and before she could lift her hand to put it back in the right spot, Billy did it for her.

His fingers grazed her skin, lingered a moment too long. His heat seeped into her and she felt her skin flush. He leaned back and smiled. Their eyes met and Kate knew he was right there with her. He was just as unnerved and just as wildly turned on.

Billy Cook, you are in a world of trouble, Kate thought, looking forward to the long ride home.

TROUBLE, Billy told himself firmly in the silence of the ride home. *She's a friend and a mother and…trouble. Don't do what you're thinking about doing, buddy, knock it off.*

Kate was sitting on her side of the truck, seemingly unaffected by the tension that was killing Billy. She gazed out the window, and while he watched her out of the corner of his eye, she curled her feet up onto the seat. Billy memorized the smooth lean line of her thigh disappearing into the white petticoats of her dress.

She's leaving. His better sense changed tactics. *Remember that, cowboy, she's not sticking around…*

But she's not leaving tonight, something in him answered, and his body—parts of it, anyway—stood up and cheered.

When they arrived at Kate's apartment Billy walked her up the stairs to the door. Electricity and tension and the sweet smell of the lilacs growing in the back of the building clouded Billy's head. He couldn't think past the curve of Kate's bared shoulder and that long lean thigh he had seen. They climbed the steps in sync and their hands brushed, each of them entirely aware of the other.

They got to the front door and Kate dug through her purse for her keys. She turned to Billy and smiled.

"That was a lot of fun, Billy," Kate said, her voice coming out of the half darkness. "Who would have guessed?"

"Yeah," Billy said. Sweat was beading under his hat and he found it impossible to lift his eyes above the breasts that pressed against the red gingham fabric. He was better than this, he told himself and tore his eyes away from her body.

Oh, God, he thought, *her eyes...*

Like a dream, Billy watched her lean in, closing the electric distance between them to press a kiss against his cheek.

"Thank you, Billy," she whispered against his skin, and his self-control snapped.

Billy growled deep in his throat and pushed Kate up against the side of the house. Her purse and keys fell to the ground as she wrapped her arms around his shoulders.

He was taking huge biting kisses from her mouth and she was letting him. She pressed her body against his, a taut bow of willing Kate Jenkins, and Billy lost his head.

"Yes," he hissed, plowing his fingers through her hair. Sweeping his hands down her back.

"Come on," she urged. She knocked his hat off and took his earlobe between her teeth. The short sharp jab of pain edged him on and roughly he filled his palms with as much of Kate as he could. He reached into the bodice of her dress while her fingers made quick work of the buttons on his shirt. The warm trembling curves of her breasts filled his hands, her nipples, hard with the need he was feeding, stabbed his palms and Billy wanted to take her on the ground.

Kate forgot his shirt and snaked her hand between their bodies to find the ridge of flesh behind the zipper of his pants. With another groan, Billy's hands slid out of her dress and went to the wall beside Kate's head to brace himself. Kate put her teeth to the sensitive skin on his neck and quickly undid his pants until she could touch him with nothing between their skin.

It was heaven and hell, torture and the best kind of bliss. Their eyes caught as she lifted her fingers to her lips. She put her thumb in her mouth and brought her hand back to the open vee of his pants. Her thumb, shiny and wet and hot, circled the head of his penis.

"Kate," he sighed. "Oh, my God..." Trembling and clumsy, Billy moved his hands up her legs, under her skirt, but she stopped him.

"It's okay, Billy," she whispered into his ear. "I owe you one."

THE MONDAY AFTER their Friday date, Kate tried not to think about whether Billy was going to come over as he had been for the past few weeks. Of course, the harder she tried the more she thought about it.

At work she sat in front of her computer screen unable to write anything. She misplaced messages and deleted a file. She realized as she caught herself doodling Billy's name on a message pad that she was in danger of becoming obsessed.

Perspective. You said you had this all in perspective, she told herself. *Don't get all girly on me now.*

She went home and tried to focus on anything but Billy, but her mother made it impossible.

"What's wrong with you?" she asked as Kate washed a dish for the third time.

"Nothing." Kate jumped and put her dish in the drying rack. She turned toward the living room where Grace was lying on a blanket. Debra followed.

"You're acting weird," Debra said. She sat on the couch while Kate sat on the floor.

"I'm just tired," Kate lied, pulling Grace into her lap.

"Tired from your *date.*" Debra hummed.

"Don't want to talk about it." Kate made faces at Grace and she laughed. *Damn Billy for not showing up!*

"Okay, I'm just saying you're acting weird."

After Kate had put Grace to bed and Debra had retired to the bedroom, Kate collapsed on the couch she was using as her bed and wondered why she felt as if an elephant was sitting on her chest. It wasn't as though Billy had broken a promise. He had never *said* he was going to come by. He just usually did. And tonight, two days after breaking all their commitments to just being friends, he hadn't shown.

You don't care, she thought, and tried to believe it.

At ten o'clock the phone rang.

"There he is," Debra shouted from the bedroom, and Kate ran to the phone. She took a deep breath before answering.

"Hello?"

"Kate?" *It's not Billy,* was her first thought. *Oh, no, please not this.* She reached behind her for a kitchen chair and sat heavily.

"Hello, Joseph."

"SQUARE DANCING?" Bob Green asked the next day when Kate submitted her article a day late. He pushed his glasses further up onto his nose and put down Kate's article. "You went square dancing?"

"Very popular activity around these parts," Kate said with false conviction. *Very popular with the senior citizens,* she amended mentally. But from the response Kate had gotten from Maria and a couple of her friends when she told them about the second article, it sounded as though it might become a more popular activity with the younger crowd.

"Well, Kate, from the number of letters we received about your first article I'm confident in your abilities." Bob was saying. "The people around here are thirsty for some fresh air. That's just what you have provided."

"Well, thanks, Bob, that's quite a compliment." And much to Kate's amazement she thought maybe it was the nicest compliment she had ever been given. She had been complimented plenty in Hollywood, but not a single one of them had felt sincere. Or entirely deserving. She was filled with a kind of unfamiliar pleasure and she walked out of the office with a bounce in her step.

BILLY SAT in his pickup outside Kate's apartment giving himself a little pep talk before date number three.

Perspective, man, just keep it all in perspective. You fooled around, so what? This doesn't have to be a repeat of thirteen years ago. You are not in love, and you're not going to be in love, so just relax.

He had wanted to come over to Kate's house every night, which is exactly why he had stayed away. It was time to put the boundaries back because the feelings were creeping in and that just wouldn't work.

Two friends, that's all. Two friends. He got out of the truck and took the steps up to Kate's two at a time.

He insisted on Grace being there on their third date as a preventive measure, but as soon as they got settled in the truck, it didn't appear as if a preventive measure was going to be needed.

Kate was giving him the cold shoulder as he had never gotten before and it didn't take long for it to drive him crazy.

"Want to know where we're going?" he asked, trying to lighten the mood. He put his hand along the back of the seat and hit all the potholes he could.

"Not really," she said, looking out the window.

They drove out past the parking lot in front of the grocery store where a sign had been put up announcing the Fourth of July carnival that was going to take place all next week.

"That's going to be our grand finale of dates," Billy told her, jerking his thumb at the sign.

"The carnival?" Kate asked, looking behind her as they drove past, but not really paying attention.

"Complete with pie-eating contest. Grace will love it," Billy said, hoping to get some kind of reaction.

"I'm sure she will," she agreed, although she was distracted.

"What's wrong?" Billy finally asked. "Is this because I didn't come by? Because I—"

"Believe it or not, Billy, my life does not revolve around you," she said, looking at him levelly. *See,* he told himself, *she's kept it in perspective.*

"I've been busy," he said, and he felt all the old boundaries just slide right back into place.

"Me, too, really, Billy." She put a hand on his arm and looked over at him. "No attachments."

Billy nodded and looked back out the window. *What the hell is wrong with you?* he silently seethed, *this is what you want!*

"So, what's on your mind?" he asked past the heaviness in his chest.

''Joseph called,'' she said, darting a look at him. ''He wants to come visit.''

''What did you say to him?'' Billy asked, and everything he felt exploded into jealousy, which was much better than the regret he felt earlier.

''That I didn't think it was a good idea,'' Kate said. ''He wants to see Grace.''

''He has no right!'' Billy exploded. ''He can't just come waltzing up here after four months and expect to see a baby he never wanted.''

''That's what I told him,'' Kate said, watching him with a small smile that didn't reach her eyes.

''Good!'' he said. ''He needs to know he's not welcome.''

''Billy.'' Kate reached up her hand and put it on his arm. ''He knows. Relax. It's my problem.''

Billy turned to face her. ''No, it's not, Kate. That girl was born into *my* hands, and that makes any kind of problem relating to Grace my problem.''

''She's a four-month-old, Billy. She doesn't have a lot of problems,'' she said wryly.

Don't do it! Don't...

''I am a part of your life around here and that makes your problems my problems,'' Billy told her.

''Thank you, Billy,'' she said and smiled, obviously not believing him. ''If I need you to meet him for a shoot-out at sundown or anything I'll let you know.''

She was making fun of him and he felt the anger slowly drain away. She started laughing and before long he couldn't help but smile. He couldn't take this too seriously; they were just having a good time.

''So we can go back to being friends?'' he asked.

''We've always been friends,'' Kate told him.

''HERE WE ARE,'' Billy said with a flourish as he parked his truck. They had made the rest of the twenty-minute drive in silence and Kate had used her time wisely. This was exactly what she had wanted, sex with no attachments or commitments. She was happy with this and she was absolutely not getting attached. Not at all.

"Now, Kate." Billy looked at Kate from the driver's seat. "You and your darling daughter are about to witness one of the great landmarks in western Montana. One year *Life Magazine* came out here and did a photo shoot. 'Course it was 1957, but still, they were here."

"Mini putt?" Kate asked, looking at miniaturized mountains and what appeared to be a small-scale White House.

"This is not just *any* mini-putt course," Billy said, indignant. "This is the United States of America East to West Miniature Golf *Challenge.*"

"Challenge?" Kate arched an eyebrow at Billy. He hopped out of the car, came around to her side and opened the door for her, helped her out and lifted the seat forward to get at Grace who was secured in her car seat in the back.

"That's right, Ms. Skeptic, Miss Rain on the Parade. Challenge." Billy took Grace's baby sling out of Kate's hands, quickly made sense of it and slipped it onto his back. He handed Grace to Kate and turned around, so she could put Grace inside the sling. Kate, without thinking twice, did.

"I will have you know," Billy was saying as Kate figured out all the loops and straps that secured Grace in place, "that at one time this was considered by experts as the toughest miniature golf course in the world."

"Let me guess. In 1957?" Kate teased. Billy turned and, without skipping a beat, grabbed Kate's hand and together they walked toward the entrance. Kate tried to remember she was a thirty-two-year-old woman. She tried to remember that she and Billy were not really dating much less really a family, but her heart wasn't listening.

"It might have been 1957, but I'm willing to bet you've never mini-putted on Abraham Lincoln's nose." Billy pointed to hole five where Lincoln might have at one time been standing to give the Gettysburg Address—hole six was Gettysburg—but at some point since 1957, Honest Abe had fallen down and no one had bothered to pick him up.

"This is probably the most popular dating spot in western Montana." Billy snapped her attention back to mini putt by putting a small putter in her hands and handing her a green ball.

Kate looked around and noticed how packed the place was. Families waited in lines to play and congregated at the snack bar. Couples held hands and walked from the White House to the Riverboat to…

"Billy?" Kate squinted and took a few steps forward to get a closer look at the monuments and landmarks on the golf course. "Mount Rushmore only has two heads."

"Well, it's kind of fallen apart over the years," Billy agreed, and for a moment they looked over the decrepit golf course. The White House was covered in graffiti. The Riverboat had no paddles on its wheel and was listing a little bit to the side. What Kate assumed was a Southern belle and not Venus di Milo was missing her arms and head. Only her giant plaster hoop skirt remained.

"I guess," Kate said with a laugh, and together they walked to the first hole.

In the distance a series of sparks flew into the air and a mother shrieked and grabbed her children while the father beat the fire out of the grass near what was once a fake buffalo that charged over the grass on a small electric track. However, now it was reduced to random shakes and rattles and resulting small electrical fires.

The teenage golf course attendant came out with a fire extinguisher and covered the whole thing in white foam. He then turned and gave the kids suckers.

"Don't worry," Billy said, watching the scene by hole sixteen. "We'll skip that hole."

"All right," Kate said absently, looking around the course for any other near-death experience that might be awaiting them. Seeing only broken-down riverboats and other American landmarks in various states of disrepair, Kate took faith in Billy and headed toward the first tee.

"Prepare yourself, Billy," she said, lining up a shot to go straight through the front door of the White House. "I'm planning on schooling you on the niceties of—"

A blaring of horns cut off Kate's words. She dropped her putter, clapped her hands over her ears and looked around for the brass band that had snuck up on her.

"It's hole eighteen!" Billy shouted. He took off the baby sling and pulled Grace to his chest, covering her ears. "If you get a hole in one it plays 'Yankee Doodle Dandy.'"

"*That's* 'Yankee Doodle Dandy'?" she shouted, unable to pick out a recognizable tune in all of the noise.

"Sometimes, though, it just goes off," Billy shouted. The noise stopped and he dropped his voice. "The loop was broken years ago and no one has bothered to fix it." He put Grace back in her sling and lifted her across his back as if nothing had happened. Grace squealed with laughter and clapped her hands. "You were saying how you were going to school me in something?" he taunted, smiling.

"Yeah," Kate said after her ears stopped ringing. "I happen to be a heck of a mini putter." She reached back down for her putter, and got back into position. She took her first swing and sent the ball right through the front door of the White House and it came out through the *o* in Tim Loves Leslie that someone had scrawled on the backside of the monument and right into the cup.

"Hole in one," she chirped. She took the scorecard out of Billy's front pocket, wrote down her score and put it back in his pocket with a pat. The muscle under his shirt felt good so she gave it another little pat, just for herself. Memories of their passion on the porch and on her balcony buzzed in her head, as they had since it happened. ''Good luck.''

Billy slid past her and waved to a small group of girls that seemed to be watching him. They waved back and Billy turned to get down to business. The girls were still watching so Kate waved and they scattered like birds. She felt a small twinge of pride being the girl with the handsomest man on the golf course.

Billy made a big show of lining up his shot. He took several dramatic practice swings. He did a little light stretching, making Grace laugh and Kate smile at his theatrics.

''Let's go, hotshot,'' she said. Although as he leaned over the ball and wiggled his butt at her, parts of her wished he would take his time.

Finally, he pulled back his putter, too far in Kate's estimation, and smacked the ball.

Much, much too hard, Kate thought with a grimace. The ball sailed through the front door of the White House, through the *o* in the back, smashed into the wooden barrier and came rolling right back through the *o,* through the front door and right back to Billy's feet.

''Stupid game,'' Kate thought she heard him mutter.

Billy, of course, said that the extra weight of Grace on his back threw him off, but as the game progressed he refused Kate's offer to hold her and continued to lose.

''You're hitting the ball too hard,'' Kate told him after he nearly took a kid's eye out three holes away.

''Kate.'' He turned to her with barely constrained patience. ''If I wanted mini-putt tips, I would ask.''

''Okay, but...''

''Kate?'' he warned. ''Zip it.''

"Okay," Kate conceded, hiding her smile.

Kate was celebrating two under a par five on the Battle of Gettysburg when an angry-looking cowboy charged through her shot. He told Billy to stay away from his girlfriend, his fist waving in Billy's face. Billy calmed the guy down, convinced him that he had no interest in the guy's girlfriend and sent him on his way, muttering under his breath.

Kate looked at Billy cryptically and he put his hands up innocently.

"I don't even know who he's dating!" he insisted. Kate believed him but the burning jealousy remained in her belly. *Not that you have any rights,* something in her whispered, *these are only pretend dates between friends.*

On hole seven she split the skirts wide open on the Southern belle for a hole in one. She looked back at Billy triumphantly and saw him talking to a woman who seemed to have more than two arms and Billy was trying to avoid all of them.

Kate tried not to be jealous and took comfort in the fact that Billy was being polite but distant to all the women that came up to him, but there were a lot of them. Kate was beginning to feel embarrassed. She was clearly only the last in a long line of women taken in by Billy Cook's heady brand of charm.

Slowly, despite the sound beating she was giving Billy, the fun seeped out of her night and nagging suspicion was taking root in the back of her mind.

While Billy was still trying to stay under one hundred on the grasslands of hole ten, Kate had already moved on to Mount St. Helens.

"Hey, Kate..." Billy called when he got up from digging around on his knees looking for his ball in the tall weeds that were supposed to be the golden grasses of the plains. He was bleeding from a tiny cut on his cheek where he had run into some thorns. Kate got up from placing her ball on the starting point and turned to look at him.

"Yes, loser?" she said with a smirk, but Billy only beamed back at her, immediately making her suspicious.

"Bet you can't get a hole in one on Mount St. Helens. It's the hardest hole on the whole course," he challenged.

"Billy." She leaned on her putter and crossed her feet at the ankles. "I've gotten four holes in one, you don't think I can do this?"

"It's been years, Kate. *Years* since someone got a hole in one on Mount St. Helens." He looked dubious and Kate stood straight.

"Watch me," she said, and lined up her shot. A hole in one required her to bank her ball left and up a small hill past the false hole on top of the volcano and into the proper mouth where red paint that represented lava was chipping off. She took one small practice swing, stepped up and smashed her ball. She banked it left, up the hill past the first hole and into the hole.

"Ha!" she laughed, and turned to gloat. "Told you I could do it." Billy was looking at her expectantly and then he frowned. "What's wrong?" She laughed. "Is it getting too painful for you?"

"Go get your ball," he muttered. As she walked away she thought he heard him mutter, "Stupid mini putt."

She walked up the side of the volcano and reached into the hole to retrieve her ball. It was unusually deep so she had to get on her hands and knees and reach her arm in, almost to her elbow. She fished around, peering into the hole until she finally felt the dimpled ball. As she pulled it out a hissing noise came from the hole. Instinctively, she peered closer, just as a blast of talcum powder exploded in her face.

She couldn't stand, she couldn't see, she was actually having a hard time breathing.

''Kate! Are you okay?'' Billy asked, and although she couldn't see him she could hear the laughter in his voice. Still on her hands and knees she hacked and coughed, trying to get enough of the powder out of her mouth so she could scream at Billy. But there was just so much talcum and it was in her eyes, falling out of her hair and covering her clothes.

''Kate? Kate talk to me…'' he said, not laughing anymore.

''Jerk!'' She finally managed to yell.

''It's supposed to be ash, volcanic ash.'' He put his hands on her shoulders and tried to help her out, but started to laugh again. ''Oh,'' he was shrieking, ''that was great! I didn't expect you to get on your hands and knees. You looked right into the hole, I can't believe it!''

Billy, still weak and wiping his eyes, helped her up and led her to the bathroom. She went in while Billy waited for her outside with Grace. She wet her hair and dusted off her face and clothes, but there was still talcum powder in her eyebrows and on the ends of her hair that wouldn't come out. Her shirt was just a lost cause.

She looked at her reflection and decided she looked like a Halloween costume gone wrong. She couldn't even really blame Billy for doubling over and pointing a finger at her when she reemerged.

''Shut up!'' she shouted, not really angry, and started to cruise right on past him. But he snagged her arm and hauled her against his chest.

''You were being such a show-off, can you blame me?'' he asked breathlessly.

''Of course,'' she said. She wiped the edge of her hair against his neck and smiled at the streak of powder she left on him. But, after a moment, her arms stole around his back and she hugged him hard. ''It was a good one,'' she conceded in a whisper against his cheek.

"Maybe the best one ever," he whispered against her cheek.

"Maybe." She smiled and they held each other hard for a few moments longer.

I'm not going anywhere, she almost said. *I'm here and this is home. I've been lying since the beginning, I am attached.*

Finally, Kate pulled away and side by side they headed back to the course. Billy couldn't stop laughing and Kate couldn't keep her lips from curling. He put his arm around her waist and pressed a kiss to her neck and Kate wanted to melt, right there.

"Hi, Billy," purred a woman as they passed by. She looked Billy up and down and all but licked her lips.

"Hi, Peg," Billy said to the woman, and turned to the man she was with. "Howdy, Jim." The man nodded in greeting and as Kate and Billy passed, the look Peg shot Kate's way was frigid and angry. Kate remembered her suspicions and embarrassment. She pulled away from him.

"You seem to have a few admirers," Kate said to Billy as they approached the last hole. Billy only grunted and lined up his shot. "Your admirers hate my guts, Billy."

"It's because you're not from around here," Billy said. He smacked the ball too hard and it bounced off the wood dividers and rolled back to him.

"I don't think so, Billy. I think it's because I'm here with you." Deciding to let him have it with her suspicions.

"That could be," Billy answered as if it wasn't a big deal, not even looking up from his shot. Kate turned to stand in front of him, directly in the way of his ball. Finally he looked up and the embarrassed look on his face seemed to say it all.

"Do you have a girlfriend?" she asked him, feeling hollow and bottomless.

"Kate." Billy turned and put a hand on her arm, which she shook away. "Calm down, I don't—"

"It's one thing to go on a bunch of fake dates with a girl when you have a girlfriend but I'm not sure any girl would forgive what we did on my balcony." Kate couldn't even find the words for how despicable Billy was.

"I don't have a girlfriend," Billy told her in a firm whisper.

"Then why are all these girls staring daggers at me, particularly Peg?" Kate snapped.

"I broke up with Peg the night you gave birth to Grace in the cabin."

"You *broke up?*" Kate's eyes narrowed. "That's convenient."

"Yeah, she wanted more and I wanted less and so we broke up." Kate looked doubtful, so Billy crossed his heart and took off his hat. "I swear on my mother, Kate Jenkins. I have no other girlfriend."

Other.

The word hung between them like dancing red flags. Other. Kate wanted to smile and laugh. She wanted to waltz around all the other admirers and tell them about how there was no one for Billy except her and Grace…

"That came out wrong," Billy said suddenly. His neck was red and his eyes uncomfortable. "Kate…"

Kate felt her body burn up in a flush and suddenly needed some distance between herself and Billy's calm denunciation. "I'm going to get a drink, you want one?" she asked, and walked away before he could answer.

Stupid. You're being so stupid, Kate! she told herself.

At the snack bar she felt as if wolves surrounded her. Billy's old girlfriend, Peg, stood at the counter and watched Kate approach.

"You must be Kate Jenkins." Peg observed with barely concealed malice.

"That's me," Kate said, looking up at the menu.

Of course, she thought. *Of course I have to get into some catfight covered in talcum powder. I don't have the energy for this.*

"You having fun?" Peg asked, playing with the straw to her soft drink.

"Great time. Billy's a great date." She turned to Peg. "I'm sure you remember."

The barb visibly hit home and Kate saw Peg all but rear up and arch her back, bearing claws.

"He'll dump you," she quipped. "Just like he dumped almost every girl here. You know why?"

"Please, Peg, please tell me why!" Kate said with dripping sarcasm.

"Because he is a cold bastard," she stated.

Kate only smiled at Peg, the satisfied smile of a woman with a secret that warmed her from the inside. "Billy Cook, cold?" she asked, pretending to be confused. "Not with me."

"He's not getting married until he's forty!" Peg told her, strangling in her jealousy.

"So who wants to get married?" Kate asked, shrugging delicately. She was every bit the picture of a sophisticated worldly woman, whose heart wasn't turning cold as she spoke.

Peg leaned in, her drink forgotten. Her eyes glittered and Kate fought the urge to end this ridiculous conversation by punching the nasty woman in the face.

"We all know he's not really dating you," she said in a whisper, "because Billy Cook doesn't date mothers." Peg filled the last word with as much scorn as humanly possible and Kate suddenly felt as if there was a scarlet M on her chest.

There was nothing Kate could say and Peg knew it.

When she walked away Kate could almost imagine a black tail sweeping the ground behind her.

Kate ordered her Coke and turned around, fuming. The whole damn situation was ridiculous. She had no business ever caring about Billy Cook. She should be concentrating on getting her life back together and getting out of Lincoln, Montana. She didn't have time to worry about Peg Graham and whether or not Billy dated mothers. For crying out loud, she was a— Kate's thought ground to a halt.

Billy was sitting on Abe Lincoln's leg. He had pulled the baby sling carrier around to his chest and he seemed to be having some kind of earnest conversation with Grace. And it hit her then, just like a face full of talcum powder.

She had no other life but this, nothing to get back to or to find or to sort out. This was her life and it was the only one she wanted. She loved Billy, and it wasn't just nostalgia or the mountain of desire she had for him. It was right there in his eyes as he nodded seriously at something her four-month-old daughter gurgled at him. It was in his laugh lines and the touch of his hands. It was the way he called her bluffs and saw through her bravado. It was the way he said her name.

It was...hopeless.

She walked back to where he was sitting and stopped in front of him.

"Why isn't this real?" she asked point-blank. "You and I dating?"

"What?" Billy asked, baffled by her sudden inquisition.

"Why are you thirty years old and all alone?"

"I'm not alone!" he said, standing.

"Right, you are surrounded by old girlfriends. Very healthy, Billy," she said derisively.

"What is all of this about?"

"It's about..." Kate's never-there-when-you-need-it self-preservation kicked in at long last and stopped her from spilling her guts. "You don't date mothers," she finally said.

"Kate." Billy looked Kate in the eye and broke her heart. "We're not dating."

"Exactly," Kate said through the agony in her chest and took Grace away from Billy. "Let's go home."

10

KATE PICKED UP Grace and paced the small kitchen with her. She sang lullabies in the little girl's ear and pressed a cool washcloth against her face and still Grace cried and her fever still burned.

"Shhhh," Kate crooned, near tears herself. She swayed and patted and jiggled Grace and prayed that her mother would return quickly with the prescription. Kate had the feeling the end of her rope was incredibly close and was fraying fast.

She heard footsteps on the stairs and hurried to the door and swung it open, ready to kiss her mother for her speed. But instead of her mother it was Billy—the womanizer—and she wouldn't be kissing him for anything.

"What's wrong?" he asked, clearly concerned at Grace's wailing.

Kate was in no mood to be comforting to anybody else and turned her back on him and walked back into the kitchen to continue her pacing.

"Kate!" Billy followed, shrugging off his denim jacket and throwing it over a kitchen chair as he continued toward her. "What happened to Grace?"

"She has a fever," Kate replied over Grace's cries. "An ear infection."

"Oh, no," Billy murmured. He came up close to them and swept a hand over Grace's head and pressed a kiss to her red and warm forehead. "Did you call the doctor?"

''Of course,'' Kate snapped. ''Mom went to get the prescription filled.'' Kate spun around and walked to the sink.

''How long has she been crying?''

''Forever,'' Kate answered.

''Let me take her,'' Billy said when she paced by him. He reached out for Grace but Kate didn't stop moving.

''Forget it,'' she told him. ''What are you doing here, Billy?'' Kate asked.

''It's Wednesday. We're supposed to be going on a date,'' he answered. This time as Kate neared him he gave her no opportunity to walk away. His big sure hands just swept between her body and Grace's tense hot form and pulled the baby into his arms.

''Sit down before you fall down,'' he told her, and took over the pacing duties.

Kate wanted to be outraged and to demand that Billy give her back her daughter and get out of her house, but the relief was so immense that she melted into a chair feeling like a wet rag.

''We're not dating,'' Kate said wearily. She leaned forward and propped her elbows on the table and rested her heavy head in her hands. This is what her mother was talking about when she said it was so hard to raise a baby all alone.

Is it ever, she thought wearily. *And I'm not even alone.*

''Come on, Kate,'' Billy pleaded.

''Hey, they're your words, not mine.'' Kate didn't even have the energy left to stay mad at the man. There he was pacing up and down her tiny kitchen with her daughter screaming in his ear and she didn't care that he had dated every woman in Montana. She didn't care that he had smashed all of her budding girly dreams of raising a family with him. She didn't even care that he was tracking mud all over her kitchen. She just wanted to curl up on his other shoulder and wail her heart out like Grace.

"Oh, good, you're here." Debra rushed in the front door, smiling warmly at Billy and Grace.

Traitor, Kate thought.

"Poor little thing," Debra crooned, ripping open the bag from the pharmacy.

Kate stood and walked over and helped her mother and Billy as they administered one set of drops down Grace's throat and the other drops in her ears. Grace screamed and writhed, and Kate felt herself falling apart it was so awful and painful to witness.

"Billy..." she moaned, wanting him to make it stop.

"It's okay, Kate," he said pressing a quick kiss to her forehead, "it's almost over."

The three of them stood close and murmured comforting sweet nonsense to Grace. Soon, under the influence of the medicine, she quieted and finally with a small hiccup let her eyes close and her body rest still against Billy's shoulder.

"Oh, thank God," Kate whispered, and fell back into her chair. Debra sat in the chair opposite hers and Billy took Grace into the bedroom to put her down.

THE BEDROOM WAS COOL and filled with moonlight and the perfect stillness that comes with unoccupied rooms at night. Billy stopped, taking in all the changes Kate had made to the space in the weeks since he had last been in the bedroom. Kate had painted the wall next to Grace's crib light blue with fluffy white clouds. There was a mobile above Grace's crib with stars and moons made out of shimmery fabric. The mobile reflected the moonbeams coming in the window and scattered small rainbows across the walls. There was a rocking chair by the window, with a blanket across the seat. Billy imagined Kate feeding her daughter in that chair, surrounded by moonbeams and scattered rainbows and he suddenly was filled with an unfamiliar pain.

Billy had a strong desire to see Kate in that chair with Grace pressed to her body. He wanted the right to see that. He wanted the right to put this baby to bed every night and to fall asleep with Kate in his arms and wake up in hers every morning.

He knew he had said the wrong thing at the mini putt. He knew that on the course they were on he would never see Kate nurse Grace, he would never wake up in this bed with Kate. He knew this because he had done everything in his power to make sure it wouldn't happen.

Grace stretched out her arm and her fist came up to rest on his chin and Billy turned his head to kiss it. He put her in her crib and pulled her blanket over her shoulders. His hand lingering on her back, feeling her small breaths. Billy took a step back, colliding with the silvery mobile, and rainbows careened across the room and reflected onto his face while he watched the sleeping baby, wishing on impossible things.

Before he reached the kitchen he heard Debra talking fiercely to Kate who sounded as though she was barely managing to keep her own head up.

"Now, do you see what I mean?" Debra was saying. "I wanted better for you, Katie. That's the only reason I'm saying this. My little girl shouldn't have to raise another little girl all on her own."

Kate numbly nodded her head and Billy could almost see the end of her rope slide right through her hands. Kate's big blue eyes were filled with weary pain and suddenly Billy couldn't take any more, either.

"Debra, I'm going to take Kate for a drive. You don't mind, do you?"

"Go right ahead. I'll look after Gracie."

"No, Mom, Billy. I just want to stay..." She looked up at her mother helplessly and it broke his heart. Billy took matters into his own hands and hauled her up by her shoulders and all but carried her out of the house.

He expected her to fight; he was kind of hoping she would. She let him put her in his truck with no struggle. She sat up straight, her eyes focused on the light in her apartment window.

"Where are you taking me?" she asked quietly.

"On our date."

He made a few quick turns and put the truck into four-wheel drive as they drove along a narrow dirt road up the steepest part of the mountain.

"Why are you doing this?" Kate asked, as she put her hand on the roof to keep herself from bouncing into it.

Billy turned to look at her, wrestling with the truck to keep it on the road. "You have an article to write, remember?"

"Are we going cliff diving?" she asked as he swerved back into his own lane.

"No, but that's not a bad idea." He smiled wickedly at her and gunned the engine. He was gratified to see her answering smile.

"No, there's supposed to be a meteor shower," he said. He had been planning a serious seduction—wine, meteor shower and a Grace-and-Debra-free evening. An attempt to get back into her good graces and her pants, but looking at her haunted eyes seemed to echo how he had felt earlier in Grace's room.

When was the last time someone did something just for her? he wondered. *I haven't done a single thing for her without some ulterior motive.*

Kate squealed as Billy accelerated over the last hump and finally spun the truck around and stopped. He turned off the ignition and reached around to grab some of the things behind his seat. He slid out of the driver door with his arms full, happy to see Kate follow.

He spread a blanket on the ground, carefully laying it out while he reformulated his plan.

"Billy?" He looked up. She was so small against the vast black sky. She was so small and there were tears in her eyes and suddenly for the first time, Billy didn't need a plan.

He stood and took the one step that separated them and hauled her into his arms.

"Billy," she said, trying to push away from him. He sensed her hysteria, the million little cracks in the dam.

"No, shh." He put his hands in her hair, trying to hold her still. Trying to hold her against him. "Let me just take care of you," he whispered against her mouth and cheeks. "Let me make you feel good, that's all. Just feel good."

Slowly he felt the careful easing in her body, the graceful willingness where she had been tense. Her muscles relaxed and she curled her arms around his neck and he felt his heart swell. He felt proud and humbled all at the same time and for the former Champion of the World, it was not an easy thing. But he was going to do the best he could. For Kate.

He held her for a little while, pressing kisses to her face and neck, swaying slightly and wondering why he felt so nervous. As if he had never done this before.

"You're beautiful," he whispered, pulling her face from his neck. "The most beautiful woman ever."

She smiled and ducked her head again. "Knock it off and get to the good stuff," she muttered.

"This is the good stuff. The best stuff." He found himself a little chagrined that he meant it. He had uttered hundreds of smooth lines over the years and not meant a single one. "Lie down with me."

"Okay," she whispered and, hand in hand, they walked over to the blanket, lying carefully on their sides.

"I want...you," he whispered, wondering why the

words were so hard. He had said these words a million times and it shouldn't have mattered that it was Kate. That he meant it this time just because it was her. "I'm on fire, Kate."

"Me, too," she whispered.

"It's always been this way..." he said, feeling wonder that he was telling her this. Telling her just how much he needed her. As a rule he never let the woman in on his end of the proceedings, he kept that careful distance there. But the distance was gone, burned up in Kate's need and his own strange desire to care for her. To give her something that was just for her. So he told her the truth and found parts of himself breaking open in the process.

"I've thought about you—" He stopped the words clogged in his throat. "You were everything."

"I know," she said, and he felt her words brush his skin. "I know exactly what you mean." He felt the pulse of the desire in her eyes in his own heartbeat and in an explosion in his chest.

One hand that had been lying against his side snaked down to her throat, across her chest and down to the waistband of her shorts. One finger slid beneath the cloth and Kate bit her lip.

"You make me crazy," he murmured. He felt the soft skin of her stomach and the deep breath she took. The anticipation and memory coiling in his gut was almost painful.

"Billy..." she said, and that was all, and he knew that she was right there with him.

He leaned close, breathed a kiss across her mouth and ran a hand down her trim stomach past the waistband of her jeans to the lush heat waiting. She rolled her head back, letting him do what he wanted.

Ah, Billy thought, *there is nothing more beautiful than this woman in surrender.*

"You know me, Kate," he whispered. This felt new, he felt naked even though he was fully dressed. "I know you," he said, his voice thick.

Her eyelids fluttered and started to open and Billy brought his hand up to cover them. "Shh, keep them closed."

His hand floated over her face just enough that she knew it was there. His finger settled to trace her lips and Kate parted her lips and took his finger inside her mouth. She bit the tip and ran her tongue across the edge and Billy truly thought that he would lose it then and there.

He chuckled low and deep and felt all the screws tighten.

Using one hand he reached out to the buttons on her shirt. He teased the first one open, revealing her fluted collarbones. He bent to trace the skin stretched over bone with his lips. The next button revealed the flesh of her breasts as they rose against the edge of lace that was barely visible. He leaned close, breathing softly on her skin and he watched in the moonlight as she shivered. He brought his hand to the boundaries of that lace and slid his finger just under the edge and ran the length of it to the warm scented valley between her breasts. Reverently he pressed a kiss to that place and smiled as she caught her breath.

The next button opened under his fingers and it was his turn to catch his breath.

"Ah, honey, you're beautiful," he said, running the back of his hand over the cotton and lace that covered her breasts and returning to press against her nipples.

"Billy," Kate whispered with her eyes still closed. He brushed his cheek across the lace-clad curves and found her nipple, hard as a testament to her need, and took it between his teeth with just enough force to let her know he was just as aroused as she was.

"Oh, Billy," she gasped, and he raised his head to meet her smiling mouth. "You're so good at this."

"Well," he whispered against her skin, "when I was seventeen I had a good teacher."

"You sure did," she breathed, and he laughed.

Billy slid his hand around her waist to roll her body against his. Arching into him, she wrapped her arms around his neck and met him more than halfway. His hands slid down to her hips and as her tongue did something particularly heady with his lower lip his fingers bit into her flesh and she laughed softly into his open and gasping mouth.

She leaned back and opened her eyes. Watching him, she pressed her hips slowly and surely forward against the hard edge of his erection. She pressed and retreated and pressed again until Billy could not stop his eyes from rolling back in his head or stop his hips from meeting hers.

He moaned. She put her leg over his hips and turned her teasing into something far more erotic.

This is for her, something in him whispered and he pulled her into his lap as he sat up.

"This one's yours," he whispered against her lips, ignoring the throb and pulse of his own body.

"Come on, Billy." She leaned back, her green eyes dark with promise and sex. "Let's do this one together." Her hands pressed and flexed into his chest, her fingernails found the sharp bead of his nipples and squeezed. Billy moaned again and bit his lip.

"Kiss me," he whispered and, as though she were dying, Kate lifted herself up and rolled on top of him. He fell onto his back and Kate devoured him.

They were a tangle of arms and lips, desire and need.

"More…"

"Yes…"

Fingers bit into muscle and smooth flesh. Sensitive skin was found and teased. They were old lovers, but the years between them melted and they became new again.

Kate welcomed him, her body warm and pliant. Her legs

and arms wrapped around him and he searched for all the things he had only known with her.

''Kate,'' he groaned into her neck, feeling as if the world were moving too fast. He had nothing to hold on to, nothing familiar except her. *Please,* he wanted to shout. *Help me get over you. Help me survive this.*

11

THE BREEZE was turning cool and Kate's flesh, once fevered, rose in goose bumps. She sat up, searching for her clothes.

"Have you seen my shirt?" she asked. Her voice cracked and she laughed. "I think I screamed myself hoarse." She looked down at Billy and pressed a hand to his abdomen, hard and white in the moonlight. Billy immediately sat up, brushing her hand off his body and looked around the ground.

"There it is." He grabbed it and handed it to her. Kate took it with suddenly numb fingers. She watched him shove his body into his clothes, search for his boots and his hat. He found her clothes and dropped them into her lap, careful not to touch her.

He didn't look her in the eyes.

Kate's breath caught and her heart squeezed into her throat, choking her. She looked up at the sky, blinking rapidly. Suddenly panicked, suddenly hurt and wounded and vulnerable beyond words.

"We should get back," Billy said. He reached out a hand and barely touched her shoulder. Kate felt it all the way to her stomach. She dressed quickly and got into the truck where Billy was already waiting with the engine running.

Kate's mind was seething with a million I-told-you-sos. Billy pulled down Main Street and finally made his way to Pete's Place and Kate's apartment. He pulled into the small parking lot, stopped the truck, put it in Park and, it seemed, reluctantly turned towards her.

"What the hell is this?" Kate demanded before she could stop the words, before she had even known she was going to speak. The rope she felt slipping from her grasp earlier in the evening was long gone and every defense was breached. She was a woman and she was in love.

And she was pissed off.

"What do you mean?" Billy asked carefully.

"Why can't this be real? You and me? Grace. All of us." Her voice cracked with anger. All of the crap he had laid on her tonight, how he had thought of her and how she made him feel. Men don't get to say those things and then pretend they didn't say them. *Nope, not with Kate Jenkins they don't.* "Why can't these dates be real? And tonight, why do we have to be so sorry that we had sex?"

"Kate, I'm not sorry." Billy rushed to assure her. "We had an agreement going into this that we weren't going to form attachments."

Kate laughed harshly.

"I think we both broke that agreement at one time or another," she said fiercely. He didn't look at her and Kate went cold. "I told myself that I knew what I was getting into here," she said under her breath. "I have got to get on with my life," she said bitterly.

Billy jerked and turned his eyes away.

"What a plot twist," she said, searching for her shoes and self-control, now desperate to get out of the truck. She found her shoes, dropped one and left it. It didn't matter, she would walk barefoot over coals to be away from him. She jerked open the door and began to slide out. "I couldn't have written this any better. It's some kind of revenge for thirteen years ago."

"Kate, it's not revenge," Billy said fiercely, grabbing her arm.

"Sure feels like it," she said, and jerked her arm free.

"I know, Kate. But I don't know what you want from me." He exploded. And there it was suddenly, the chance to tell him everything, to drop the game and the pretense and to tell him how she felt. *You know better,* she told herself, *you know where this kind of vulnerability leads. Last time it left you pregnant, alone and broke. Get out of the truck before you say anything stupid.*

"I don't want anything from you," she said. She slammed the door and walked up the stairs to her apartment with only one shoe, and forced herself to not look back.

IN ALL OF HIS EXPERIENCE of being miserable, Billy had never been as miserable as he was now. He was angry and frustrated and sorry and confused. He knew he should have avoided Kate, never gotten attached to Grace, never taken them on those ridiculous dates. He never should have gotten used to Kate's laughter and wit again, or her eyes and body. *He shouldn't have made love to her.* In the two days that had passed since that night he had been tortured with the memory of her skin against his, her body against his, her heartbeat against his.

He was tortured by the way she had made him feel.

"You look like a man with something on his mind." Missy came out of the front door and sat on the steps with her son.

"Women," Billy muttered, and hung his head in his hands.

"Seems to me you've always had women on your mind. Never made you act like this." She looked at her son's hangdog expression. "You hardly eat. You don't talk to any of us. And you've been working harder in the last week than I've ever seen you work."

"Is it a crime to get some stuff done around here?" Billy asked hotly.

''No,'' Missy answered. ''It's just strange when you're doing *all* the work.''

''Hey, I usually do plenty of work around here!''

''Honey, I'm not fighting with you,'' she told him, and rubbed his back with the palm of her hand, as she had when he was a kid. Billy felt a little stab of guilt. The last person he should take his bad mood out on was his mother. ''Does this have something to do with Kate Jenkins?'' she asked.

''It always has something to do with Kate Jenkins,'' Billy answered, taking a deep breath. ''Mom, I think I love her.''

''Well, honey, that's wonderful.''

''It doesn't feel wonderful.'' He kicked the dirt in front of his boot and fought the urge to put his head in his mother's lap. ''Mom, she broke my heart and she'll do it again if I let her.''

''How do you figure?'' Missy asked, surprised.

''She'll leave. She said it herself. She's the Queen of No Attachments.''

Missy shook her head in disbelief. ''She's got a job and a baby and an apartment. Those are roots, Billy. They're cleaning up the mini putt because of her article. She's a part of this town.'' Missy looked at her son's woebegone expression and softened her tone. ''The only thing that's going to chase her away is you.''

''But, Mom, what if...''

''Oh, for crying out loud, it's always a risk, honey. You've just got to make the leap and trust that she'll catch you on the other side. I'd say she's waiting for you to get your act together.''

''Mom, I really don't think she's waiting for me—''

''Honey,'' Missy interrupted. ''You've got to trust me on this one, even when they aren't, women in love are always waiting.''

''I don't know, Mom. I don't think she loves me.''

Why can't this be real? You, Grace and me, why can't this all be real? Kate's words echoed through his head and things suddenly shifted into place and he saw then what he had done. He had made a million mistakes.

"Oh, no," he groaned. "I've got to go, Mom." Billy stood, ran to his truck and before Missy could say goodbye Billy was heading down the mountain.

WHEN BILLY PULLED INTO the small parking lot behind Kate's apartment he was alarmed that her car wasn't there. Instead, a dusty, midsize SUV stood in its place. Somehow it made Billy sad that Kate had gotten a new car without telling him. Without letting him help her. *It's your own fault, idiot, you and your distance.* He got out of his truck and ran up the stairs to the apartment, two at a time.

He pounded on the door and shouted Kate's name but finally had to concede that no one was home.

He drove by the newspaper office but no one had seen her there. Same at the vet clinic.

"You going to the carnival tonight?" Maria asked Billy cheerfully. "Kate said she and Grace were going to be there. You'll probably find them there." Still a few hours away, he thought. Time to get my act together.

KATE STOOD at the bathroom sink of the grocery store that was open late for the carnival. She ran her hands under the cool water and pressed them to her burning eyes. Looking at her reflection in the mirror she wondered briefly who the hollow-eyed stranger was looking back. She touched her face, the black circles under her eyes and the pinched corners of her mouth and wondered what had happened to her.

Someone else came into the bathroom, snapping her out of her reverie, and she shook the water off her hands and pulled open the door to walk outside. There was a group of people gathered outside the door watching something that was happening a few feet away. A feeling of dread passed over her as she pushed through the crowd and immediately recognized Billy's voice.

"Let go of her," he was saying.

"I don't know who the hell you think you are, but I am Grace's father." Joseph Calhoon's voice was a high-pitched squeal. Kate pushed aside the last two people in her way and burst into the small circle surrounding Billy and Joseph.

Billy had Grace's baby sling in his hands and he was trying to remove it from Joseph's back without waking up Grace. Joseph's glasses were askew and his hands clutched at the sling straps.

"Billy, let go of him," Kate demanded sharply, stepping up to the two men. "Right now!"

"Kate!" Billy said, his hands unmoving. "Who is this guy?"

"Joseph Calhoon. Grace's father. Now let go of him." Kate reached up to pry Billy's hand from the sling and gathered Grace into her arms.

"What are you doing?" Billy asked. His voice was low and his eyes questioning and to Kate it seemed for a moment as if the whole world disappeared except the two of them. Joseph, the crowd, even Grace, faded for a moment as she looked into Billy's eyes.

She wished more than anything that the pain she saw there was a reflection of her own, but it wasn't. *It isn't even close,* she thought sadly. She pulled herself together and managed to speak calmly.

"Joseph arrived today," Kate said, shaking off Billy's hands. "He's just visiting." She shot a meaningful look at Joseph and then put her attention back on Billy.

"Kate," Billy said, "how can you let this guy back into your life? How can you let him even touch Grace?"

"My problems aren't yours anymore, Billy," she told

him, grabbing Grace's sling from him and arranging the baby on her back. "Please leave us alone." She looked into his eyes for a moment and then turned and walked away, past Joseph, clearly expecting him to follow.

BILLY WATCHED Kate's blond head as she pressed through the crowd and felt as though his only opportunity for something good was walking away and he had no idea how to get it back. He couldn't just yell out that he loved her, that he wanted more. In her unpredictable mood there was no telling what she would do and he didn't want to be made a fool of in front of all these people.

Joseph took two steps toward Billy and leaned in, and Billy's attention focused in on this roadblock.

"She's my daughter," he said to Billy. "Not yours. Just like Kate."

Joseph walked away and a rage took over Billy's body. Not the rage of a grown man, but the thwarted rage of a school kid. Billy followed.

"Come on, Billy, you can take him!" Jim Manning shouted from the crowd.

"I know all about you, Calhoun," he said, catching up with the man.

Kate stopped and turned around to glare daggers at him. "Billy..."

"This does not concern you, Kate. This is between us." Billy held up a hand and looked Joseph in the eyes. "Isn't it?"

"No," Joseph said bluntly, and turned to walk away.

"Kate said you were always a cold man," Billy taunted.

"Billy!" Kate shouted.

Maybe this isn't the best idea you've ever had, he told himself, but then the crowd oohed in appreciation of the dirty slander.

"No wonder she left." Billy crossed his arms over his

chest and grinned like a playground bully. He looked around at the crowd and people nodded their agreement. Joseph's back went rigid and Kate put her head in her hands.

Joseph slowly and carefully removed the baby sling and handed it to Kate.

"Joseph..." Kate said miserably.

"The stupid cowboy is right. It's between us," he said, and turned to face Billy.

"Well," he said when he turned, "if I have Kate's history straight, she left you crying in your boots."

The crowd made a small gasp.

"It's not like I was really crying," Billy scoffed childishly.

Joseph stepped toward him again, smoothing the front of his cashmere sweater.

"Do you understand that Grace is mine?" Joseph said. His words hit Billy like razors. "*Mine.* It doesn't matter what kind of history Kate had with you."

Billy took a step toward the older man. Suddenly his anger was very real and very focused. Joseph had no claim on Grace. None. "Where were you when she was born, huh? Where were you the last four months?"

"Show him, Billy!" Little Joey Meyers, shouted from where he sat on his father's shoulders.

"I'm here now," Joseph whispered. "You can beat your chest like a Neanderthal but it won't change the fact that I am Grace's father." The smug smile on Joseph's face ignited Billy's temper.

"I delivered that little girl. Me."

"If you do this, Grace and I are leaving and neither one of you will ever see us again," Kate said, her tone brooking no argument. "Do you understand me, Billy? I will walk right out of here and take Grace with me."

"You go, girl!" a woman in the crowd shouted.

Billy stopped and Joseph's grin got wider. "Must be nice to have a woman fight your battles for you," Billy taunted.

"We're gone," Kate said, and whirled away, the crowd splitting apart to let her through. Billy turned and ran after her, Joseph on his heels.

"I'm sorry," Joseph said to Kate. "I'm sorry. You know I'd never do this."

"Kate." Billy's skin was turning red and blotchy. "Let me explain. Please."

"Billy, leave," Kate demanded.

"Yes, Billy, leave," Joseph echoed snidely from over Kate's shoulder. Billy reached for him at the same time Joseph reached out and their hands got tangled in each other's collars.

"Joseph!" Kate put her hands on their chests and pushed them apart. "Billy! Knock it off."

The crowd began shouting encouragement to Billy, the hometown hero, and it seemed to make Kate even more anxious to get rid of him.

Billy ignored her, he ignored everything but the gut-wrenching panic he was feeling that Kate might leave with this yahoo and Billy would never get to punch him in the face for what he did to Kate and Grace.

This was of course not to mention all the things he had to say to Kate. All the love he felt that he might never be able to give her. He was desperate and angry and didn't know what he could do to get rid of Joseph that wouldn't burn bridges between him and Kate.

"Please, Billy," Kate pleaded.

"You're at a standstill gentlemen." A barker in one of the booths suddenly began speaking over his microphone and the crowd hushed into silence. Billy and Joseph slowly turned to face the man. "Damned if you do and damned if you don't, that's quite a tight spot." Both men continued to stare at the barker, their fists knotted in the collars of each other's shirts.

"A test of will, gentlemen," the tall, skinny barker said, "is what you need."

Joseph didn't look as if he was going to back down and Billy sure as hell wasn't. Without taking their eyes off each other they began rolling up their sleeves and headed to the booth where the barker stood.

"Gentlemen," he said, and swung down from the small rafters of his tent, where he had been watching the scene. "One ball each, to knock down the target. The man who knocks down the target is the winner. Agreed?"

Both men threw down money and picked up their balls.

"I was the star shortstop for my high school team," Billy bragged.

"I pitched for U.C.L.A.," Joseph countered, and Billy's heart fell to his feet.

Billy wound up, eyed the target and let it fly. The target bent backward but stayed upright. He swore and turned away. Joseph grinned, wound up, cocked back his arm and let his ball fly. He hit the target and it went flat. A gasp spread through the crowd.

"You idiots!" Kate hissed. Her mouth white with anger. "You're acting like children! You haven't proved anything but the fact that you are the two biggest mistakes I've ever made!"

Billy's eyes swung from Kate to Joseph. "Two out of three?" he asked.

"You're on," Joseph agreed.

They swung back to the barker who was grinning with satisfaction. They threw down money, grabbed the balls and neither one of them noticed that Kate had left.

Billy won the two out of three.

"Well, you know what they say about the best man..."

Billy let the sentence hang and he looked over at Joseph who was scanning the booths.

"Ringtoss," Joseph said.

"I don't know why you want to delay the inevitable..."

"Fifty dollars."

Hey, this is supposed to be about Kate and Grace, the rational part of his brain reminded him. But the rest of him just wanted to win.

"Okay," Billy said, and followed Joseph to the ringtoss.

"Double or nothing on Skee-Ball," Billy challenged, having lost miserably at the ring toss.

Now, Skee-Ball that's my game.

It was apparently Joseph's game, too, because they tied after two games.

Billy broke the tie at the duck hunting tent and the stakes were up to two hundred dollars when they wound up at the Fishing for Bottles tent. Billy grabbed the miniature fishing pole and carefully tried to aim the lure into the mouth of the bottle, onto the small magnet in the bottom and lift the bottle out and into a pile in front of him.

"Might as well give up, Calhoon," Billy taunted, watching the older man's progress with his own fishing pole. "Kate is never going to forgive you."

"What do you know, cowboy?" Joseph snickered. "Kate's meant for a hell of a lot more than some town in the middle of nowhere and she's meant for a hell of a lot more than you."

"Show's how much you know..." Billy said, and began to panic when he saw that Joseph was pulling ahead. When all the bottles were out and only ten had been broken, Joseph had one more bottle than Billy.

Billy looked around frantically for some other contest they had not tried.

"Seems to me that I just might be the better man," Joseph said, his face ringed in sweat, his linen sport jacket left somewhere. "So stay out of my way."

"Never, Calhoon," Billy said. His cowboy hat was gone and he had no idea what had happened to his watch. At the duck hunt booth it had gotten in the way of his shooting and so he had ripped it off. He scanned the booths and buildings and finally settled on the only contest they had yet to try.

"One more," Billy said with menace.

"One more chance to prove that I'm the better man." Joseph planted his hands on his hips. "Bring it on."

Billy led the way to the pie-eating contest.

JOSEPH THREW UP on his sixth pie. He just stopped eating and leaned over to hurl up the Ladies Auxiliary's best-baked goods. Billy, his mouth full of blueberry pie, punched his arm in the air and stood. *Victorious in the pie eating contest!* He had won the girl, all he had to do now was collect.

"I win!" he shouted, spraying the surrounding crowd with crust and spit.

Joseph groaned, clutching his stomach as he heaved again.

Without looking back, Billy charged off the small stage and looked around for Kate. He only found his brothers standing side by side with identical expressions of disbelief and disapproval.

"Way to go, Billy," Ethan said sarcastically. He dug into his back pocket and pulled out a bandanna. "You have whipped cream all over your face."

"Where's Kate?" Billy asked, spraying his brothers with pie.

"She went home before the ringtoss," Mark said, brushing crust spit out of his eye.

"Home? She wasn't here?" Billy asked in disbelief as he grabbed Ethan's bandanna and tried to clean up his face.

"You mean for your heroic show of love and devotion?" Ethan asked as if there was some question. "Nope, she skipped out. You know you're just smearing cherry filling all over your face?" he pointed out.

"You've got one seriously mad woman avoiding you," Mark said. He reached up and pulled piecrust out of Billy's hair. "And when they're mad, they can be tricky."

"Look, Billy, this isn't going to be easy," Ethan said, his eyes serious. He grabbed the bandanna out of Billy's hand and took over the cleanup efforts.

"What isn't?" Billy was beginning to panic from the looks on his brothers's faces. He had never seen them look this way.

"Finding Kate," Ethan said. He went to put a brotherly arm around his brother but stopped when he saw the amount of pie filling on his shirt.

"It's going to be even tougher getting her to listen," Mark added, more to Ethan than Billy. They had been in the same position as their baby brother, only without the pie up the nose.

"They're unpredictable when they're this mad," Ethan said, wiping his hands on Billy's shirt. "You've got to be careful."

Mark took Billy's shoulders, turning him to face him. "You've got say you love her right away."

Ethan grabbed Billy and yanked him his way. "Don't try and touch her until she's crying *and* laughing."

"If she's only crying or not crying at all, she's probably still pretty mad," Mark added.

"Whatever you do, don't try and make a joke," Mark warned.

Ethan nodded. "Jokes will only get you smacked in the face."

''Is there anything else?'' Billy asked, the pie in his stomach getting restless from all the jerking around.

''Don't let her go until she agrees to marry you,'' Ethan said.

''Keep your eye on her,'' Mark said. ''Good luck.'' He clapped Billy on the shoulder and whipped cream flew up in a small plume.

''I gotta go,'' Billy said. He ran between the booths where he had made a fool of himself, toward his truck.

Behind him, two barkers, one in a linen sport coat and the other wearing a new watch and a beat-up cowboy hat, smiled at each other and counted fistfuls of dollars.

12

BILLY RAN UP THE STEPS to Kate's apartment and hammered on the door. When the door swung open, Billy was ready to fall on his knees in front of Kate, but it was Debra.

Debra looked very, very unhappy with him. Of course, the rifle she was cradling like some kind of frontier woman wasn't helping, either. Billy was glad it was broken or, from the look in Debra's eyes, he could have been in serious trouble.

"I know that gun is broken, Debra," Billy said, gasping for air.

"Looks good enough to beat you over the head with," she told him fiercely.

"Debra," Billy panted. "Where's..."

"She's not here." Debra's eyes were mean and Billy guessed Kate had at least been by to tell her mother the story.

"Do you know where she is?" Inside the apartment behind Debra someone was violently throwing up.

"Is Joseph here?"

"Not for long. As soon as he stops throwing up, he's leaving. And if you know what's good for you you'll do the same and leave my little girls alone."

"Debra, I am sorry..."

"I'm very disappointed in you," Debra said. "It's one thing to play around with a woman's heart, but she's got a baby."

And a mean mother with a gun, Billy silently added.

"I know, Debra." Billy took a deep breath and tried to salvage his future with the woman he hoped would be his mother-in-law. It would make for unpleasant Thanksgivings if she met him across the turkey with that gun. "I love your daughter, and if I can find her I'll tell her that and ask her to marry me."

Debra sniffed. Billy wasn't too sure what it meant, so he pressed on.

"I love Grace. I love her like she was my own."

"That's good. She's the only one who likes you right now," Debra said. She looked him up and down and closed the door in his face. Billy stared at the door, wondering if he had been accepted into the family or marked for death at a later time.

Thwarted but far from defeated, Billy ran back to his truck and sat trying to guess where Kate might go. After a moment of consideration he drove out of the small parking lot and headed out of town up the mountain toward the Morning Glory Ranch.

He made the turn to the line cabin and was gratified to see the fire in the fireplace reflected in the windows. Kate's small, rusted hatchback that he thought she had gotten rid of sat in front of the cabin.

He put the truck in Park, climbed out and carefully shut the door. He didn't want her to know he was here yet; he didn't want to give her warning so she might have a chance to find a weapon.

He got to the door, thought about knocking, but slowly pushed it open instead. As soon as he opened the door and stepped inside he saw them, sitting in front of the fire. His breath hitched, burning and needful.

Kate was nursing Grace. Billy wanted to fall to his knees in front of them.

He was so entranced that he didn't see Kate reach behind her and grab a cup, but she did and she sent the missile flying at his head. It erupted against the wall behind his left ear. If she wasn't sitting and nursing an infant she would have gotten him square between the eyes.

"Get out!" she stormed.

"Now, Kate," he said, approaching carefully with his hands up.

"Don't you dare," she said clearly and coldly. "Don't you dare try to come in this cabin, Billy."

But Billy took another step forward and this time Kate launched a plate at his head. He ducked and the stoneware clattered against the wall.

"Billy, I am warning you!" She stood and turned, untangling her daughter from her arms to lie her down in her car seat. With her back to Billy, she buttoned up her shirt. Billy longed to touch the stubborn bend of her neck.

When she was decent she turned to him, nothing but frigid anger radiating from her. "So who won?" she asked bitingly.

"I ate nine pies," Billy said with more than a little shame. It had seemed like such a good idea at the time. "Joseph threw up at six."

"Congratulations, Billy. You must be very proud of yourself," she said with narrowed eyes.

"I'm not. I'm very sorry, Kate." He smiled his best charming smile. "And a little sick to my stomach."

Kate's mouth opened and closed in what appeared to be shock. "Do you think that's going to work?" she asked. "Do you think I am going to be suckered by your stupid cowboy grin?"

"No..." He had, but confession did not seem appropriate. His brothers were so dead-on with that joke advice.

"I know you," she said quietly. Before his eyes Kate seemed to grow taller, her shoulders were thrown back and her chin was high and Billy thought briefly of queens and saints. "I let myself believe you were what I wanted even though I knew you. You're smooth, Billy. You were in and out before I even knew what hit me. You're just like Joseph."

"Don't you dare say that!" Billy's gentle persuasion tactics and every bit of brotherly advice he had been given flew out the window and he covered the three steps between them to grab her arms and haul her against his body. "I am nothing like that man. I would never ask you to give up a baby! I would never take your money and leave you."

Kate did not struggle in his firm grip. She lifted clear eyes to his and they did not waver. Billy saw his reflection in her irises, the burning fire was reflected there, too.

"Let me go," she said, her voice so unaffected that something tense and trembling in Billy snapped and he lifted her against his straining body and kissed her. He kissed her forcefully with every ounce of desire and pain and love inside him. He licked and stroked, trying to seduce her into kissing him back, but she didn't. Her hands were still at her sides. Her eyes open, her mouth open, waiting for the kiss to end.

He tried to demand a response from her: anything. Anger, lust, disdain, hatred—he would take anything from her that he could battle against. But she was like a rag doll in his arms, lax and malleable. He wasn't going to get a response.

Billy carefully set her down on her feet. He took one look at her swollen, bruised lips and liquid eyes. She took a breath and Billy felt her chest quake against his. At that moment, Billy hated himself.

"I'm sorry, Kate," he whispered roughly. It was over; he had lost just as he'd found out how badly he wanted to win. She took a step backward, away from him, and Billy let her, one arm up, a hand ready to catch her if she was unsteady. But she was steady. Kate had always been steady.

The heartbreak when he was seventeen was nothing to the pain that filled him now.

He turned, ready to walk away—ready to open the door and walk into the night and away from Kate for good—but something stopped him. With his back to her, his hand on the door, Billy told her what he couldn't hold in anymore. He knew it was too late but she had taught him that the heart was unpredictable at best.

"I love you," he said. "I've loved you my whole life and probably will always love you." He didn't wait for a response but opened the door and walked out of the cabin.

Numb and broken, he was halfway to the truck before Kate stopped him.

"Billy!" she shouted from the door.

Billy turned, hope not yet an option amid his pain.

"I'm staying in Lincoln," she said, backlit by the light in the cabin. "I'm not going anywhere."

Billy didn't know what she wanted him to say so he said nothing.

"Do you love Grace?" she asked.

"Yes," Billy answered. The moon passed behind a cloud and came out again.

"I thought you didn't date mothers?" she asked. She looked down and then back up and Billy felt for the first time the clear perfection of hope.

"I don't date other mothers. Only Grace's," he answered. A smile tugged at her lips and Billy felt an answering pull on his own.

"I could raise her on my own, you know," she said, as if he doubted her.

"You can do anything," he said and meant it. Kate Jenkins could move mountains and split the sea and make Billy quake like a schoolboy and love like a man.

"But I want to raise her with you, as a family."

"Me, too," he said firmly, and took the steps back to

her in quick strides. A foot away from her he stopped. "I wouldn't mind having a couple more. I'll let you change their names however many times you want."

"I thought you weren't getting married until you were forty?" she asked.

"Did I say forty?" he asked. He ached, positively hurt to grab her, but he was only too aware of her bruised lips and heart and would wait for her to say it was okay. "I meant thirty."

Billy's breath was knocked out of him as she threw herself against him. Pie filling squished and dripped down his chest, but he ignored it. She wrapped her arms around his shoulders, burying her face in his neck. He lifted her off the ground, supporting her with arms that trembled, and carried her into the cabin.

"I'm so sorry," he whispered into her hair. "I've been such an idiot."

"Yes, you have," she mumbled, her voice muffled by his neck.

"I love you," he said, and pulled her face from his neck so he could look into her eyes. "I love you so much I ate three more pies than Joseph. If that's not a declaration of love and devotion, I don't know what is."

"I love you, too," she said and smiled, tears trembling on the edges of her lashes. Her finger reached up and touched him behind his ear and she pulled it back covered in cherry pie filling. "You taste like pie," she said and laughed as the tears spilled down her face.

They were right about that, too, Billy thought.

She put the finger in her mouth, her eyes dancing with delight, and Billy groaned and pulled her back to his chest. Her face in his neck, her tongue searching out pie filling and whipped cream he had not wiped off.

"You've got some on you, too," he said, pulling crust off her cheek and out of her hair.

"Jeez, Billy, it's everywhere." Kate stopped hugging him and took a handful of pie from beneath his collar. Slowly she unbuttoned his shirt and found what was left of a whole pie smashed onto his chest.

"No one can eat nine pies," he said defensively. "Joseph wasn't cheating. That's why he's barfing and I won the girl. Both girls actually."

"You shoved a pie down your shirt?" Kate asked, laughing and happy.

Billy only smiled and walked her backward toward the bed, his eyes warm and his touch familiar.

"Not only my shirt," Billy said, his voice a rough caress, which was ludicrous considering what he was telling her. Kate couldn't help but laugh at him. "I've got another pie stuck down my pants."

"Really?" Kate asked.

"Honey, I wouldn't lie about a thing like lemon meringue in my underwear." He smiled and laughed and felt as if the whole world was in this cabin. "In case you were wondering, it's not comfortable."

"Show me." She pushed him onto the bed and followed him down.

"Why don't you find out for yourself," he whispered, and Kate set about doing just that.